D1230550

THE TAU CETI AGENDA

Travis S. Taylor

Baen Books by Travis S. Taylor

One Day on Mars
The Tau Ceti Agenda

Warp Speed
The Quantum Connection

with John Ringo:
Vorpal Blade
Manxome Foe
Von Neumamn's War
Claws That Catch (forthcoming)

THE TAU CETI AGENDA

Travis S. Taylor

THE TAU CETI AGENDA

This is a work of fiction. All the characters and events portrayed in this book are fictional, and any resemblance to real people or incidents is purely coincidental.

Copyright © 2008 by Travis S. Taylor

A Baen Books Original

Baen Publishing Enterprises
P.O. Box 1403
Riverdale, NY 10471
www.baen.com

ISBN 10: 1-4165-5539-0
ISBN 13: 978-1-4165-5539-1

Cover art by Kurt Miller

First printing, May 2008

Distributed by Simon & Schuster
1230 Avenue of the Americas
New York, NY 10020

Library of Congress Cataloging-in-Publication Data: t/k

Taylor, Travis S.
  The Tau Ceti agenda / Travis S. Taylor.
      p. cm.
  "A Baen Books original"—T.p. verso.
  ISBN 1-4165-5539-0
  1. Presidents—Election—Fiction. 2. Space
warfare—Fiction. 3. United States. Central Intelligence
Agency—Fiction. I. Title.

  PS3620.A98T38 2008
  813'.6—dc22

                                    2008002988

Printed in the United States of America

10 9 8 7 6 5 4 3 2 1

*This book is dedicated to all of
freedom's veterans—past, present, and future.*

PROLOGUE

"With just three days until the election, it's anybody's guess as to who will take the White House. The polls are solid in most precincts, and the election is likely to hinge on central Florida and Luna City. At this point, the Indies can't take the election, and the race has come down to two parties this time. Will the Dems' nominee, Senator Rita Webb from Queensland, knock down the incumbent, Republican candidate President Alexander Moore? Stay with Earth News Network for up-to-the-second election coverage. . . ."

CHAPTER 1

October 31, 2388 AD
Tau Ceti Planet Four, Moon Alpha, aka Ares
Madira Valley Beach Spaceport
Saturday, 5:00 AM, Earth Eastern Standard Time
Saturday, 1:00 AM, Madira Valley Standard Time

Kira, behind you! The artificial intelligence voice rang loudly in her mind.

Kira watched the glare in the computer monitor as it suddenly darkened, and the reflection of a soldier filled the screen. She clicked off the direct-to-mind link to the Separatist ship's computer manifest that was displayed virtually around her head and prepared herself for action. She had successfully managed to board the ship, stow away long enough to hack into the Separatist control database, and download what she felt would be extremely important intelligence data on the Seppy regime plans. The plans might enable the United States to counter them—if she managed to escape the ship with them. The Separatist soldier sneaking up on her from behind probably intended to prevent that.

Quickly, Kira ducked and then back-kicked the man in the shin. With a swift and fluid clockwise turn, she slammed an elbow into his rib cage, forceful enough to crack bone, and followed with a backfist to the face.

"Uh!" the man grunted, but he somehow managed to stay on his feet and lunged toward her with blood starting to trickle from his lower lip.

He was a fairly large man. Kira surmised that he was most likely of full-blooded Martian lineage because of his pale skin and dark hair. From the size of his midsection, she also guessed that he had never missed a meal.

The bigger they are . . . , Allison started.

The harder they hit, Kira finished, as she attempted to sidestep his advance, unsuccessfully.

The force of his lumbering weight was enough to push Kira off balance and to the ground underneath him. The man probably assumed that he was going to use his size to overpower Kira easily—a mistake often made by large men when it came to women—because he tried to grapple with her and force her into a bear hug on the deck. But Kira knew better than to let that happen and forced herself up from the floor onto all fours and threw her head backward into the man's nose twice.

"Goddamn bitch!" he screamed. He grabbed at his broken nose with both hands while sending an alert via his direct-to-mind, com-net connection.

Security detail to maintenance office 13B on hangar deck C. Alarm klaxons sounded and filled the ship with flashing yellow lights.

The backward head-butt had stunned the man slightly and enabled Kira to work one of her legs free enough to direct a sweeping kick to his crotch with the heel of her foot. The blow to the man's private parts made him let go of her completely and clutch himself in pain instead.

Kira crawled like a bear from underneath him to avoid several telegraphed punches in her general direction as he recovered. She jumped to her feet only to find that a security guard was coming through the doorway and was raising the bad end of a stunner toward her. The young security guard hesitated too long before pulling the trigger, allowing Kira to slip under his line of fire. The blue electric bolt whizzed past her head, causing her hair to stand on end. The bolt made contact with the clumsy man behind her and incapacitated him. He convulsed from the stunning electricity dancing down his body and collapsed.

Kira spun around, placing her back to the security guard, while at the same time grabbing his wrist—the one with the stunner in it—

with both hands. She then turned his hand, palm upward, and yanked his arm down, forcing her body upward and pushing her right shoulder against his elbow. The elbow snapped through at the joint with a clean break, causing the guard to drop the gun with a wail of agony and surprise.

Before he had time to complain a second time, Kira rammed her left elbow through his nose twice, rendering the young man bloody and unconscious.

Get his gun, Kira! Allison said into Kira's mind. *I can hack the ID code.*

Got it!

Kira hefted the stunner in her left hand, feeling the weight of it. The small red light on the safety lock flashed yellow twice and then turned green.

The ID code has been overridden, Allison assured her.

Good.

Kira poked her head around the doorway. The hallway was dimly lit with the flashing yellow security lights but was otherwise typical of any Separatist battle cruiser, except for the fact that there were three men and two women in uniform rushing toward her with firearms at the ready. And Kira was pretty certain that they weren't holding stunners. If only there had been a way to sneak on board through the ship's security with her handgun, she wouldn't have felt as vulnerable as she did with that damned range-limited stunner.

Shit! Kira thought to her artificial intelligence counterpart implant. *We're cut off.*

Yes, we are, Allison agreed.

The computer terminal that she had been hacking into was in a small storage clerk's office, which was two decks up from the lower and aftmost hangar deck of the ship. It was probably the maintenance clerk that first stumbled upon her and triggered the alarm. That was unfortunate for him. Unfortunate for Kira was the fact that her presence had been compromised, and there were guards coming for her. The data she had just stolen needed further study to understand what it really meant, but she was certain that it meant trouble for Earth. She had to analyze it in greater detail and find a way to get it back to the Sol System. First, however, she had to escape from the Separatist battle cruiser, get her hair dyed back to her normal color, change her costume, and blend back into her cover story without being exposed, all without getting captured or killed—piece of cake.

This is a lot like that time in New Africa when we got stuck in that meat truck for an hour during a firefight, Kira said through the mindlink.

Yes. We were outnumbered then and trapped. But then we had more ordnance with us, the AI reminded her.

And a rifle!

That would be handy now, Allison agreed.

Any suggestions? Kira checked the charge of the stunner. It was nearly full, a good thing.

What do we do when we are only slightly outnumbered? Allison asked rhetorically, fully knowing the answer. *Just like in New Africa?*

We attack! Kira leaped head first through the doorway into the hall, blasting blue electric stun bolts and dropping the larger of the men in a convulsive reaction to the eltrocution of the nervous system. She continued to fire as she rolled through a forward handspring to her feet, dropping another of the men—the second-largest. The element of surprise was working in her favor, for the moment.

The members of the security detail were clearly young and inexperienced with real combat situations and had been hesitant in firing their weapons as they approached. This slight hesitation was long enough for her to close the gap between them, making it more likely for them to shoot one of their own while trying to get her. Only one of them managed to take a shot at her, which passed through the outer fleshy part of her left biceps. Kira ignored the pain and pushed forward. Her rushing tactic forced them to go hand-to-hand, which was just what she had wanted.

With a headlong attack into them, she was able to target their weapons and even managed a couple of shots from her stunner, which went wide and sizzled into the bulkhead. At first there was a flurry of arm grabs, punches, kicks, knees, and head-butts. The end result was that each of their weapons was knocked free to the deck, and all of them were rubbing new bruises while they postured away from each other, readying like lions circling prey.

Get me access to their guns, Allison. Lock them out if you can, but get me access.

I'm on it.

Kira quickly assessed her attackers and used the "snowball" rule. She would start with the easiest opponent first and then snowball her way through them one by one, progressively, to the hardest. Hopefully by then she would figure out a better means of escape and wouldn't have to face the toughest opponent.

She chose the smallest one and attacked her first. It quickly became clear to Kira that the guard wasn't an amateur and was flexible as hell. The woman managed to hook-kick Kira in the back of the head, forcing her to loosen her grip and bite her tongue. The smaller woman pulled free and jumped out of the way so that the other two could step in with more clear lines of attack.

Kira swallowed the salty blood from her tongue and forced the attack, trying to keep the security detail from picking up one of the handguns on the floor. The man and woman in front of her began testing her with front-kicks and punches that Kira either sidestepped or countered with blocks and punches of her own.

Somehow, and she wasn't quite sure how, she had managed to get herself between the two, while letting the smaller woman whom she had first attacked work around behind her. The tactic was probably part of the security team's training—flank and attack from behind when there were superior numbers. Trained tactic or not, it wasn't a situation that she liked being in.

She's getting the drop on you, Kira! Watch your flanks!

I know!

Then do something about it, damnit!

Okay!

Kira had trained most of her life, from adolescence on, in combat encounters. She had nearly two decades of intense hand-to-hand training and years in actual covert ops and combat, and her reflexes were honed like the edge of a Damascus steel blade. But she barely managed to drop her right forearm in time to weaken the blow from a roundhouse kick to the gut. Kira heaved out and backpedaled, while at the same time she took a punch to the side of the head from the man on her right. The room blurred slightly, and Kira saw stars briefly.

Green light, Kira! The guns are open access! Allison exclaimed.

About time.

Kira shook the stars out of her eyes and counterattacked. She dropped her center of gravity, lunging with all her strength backward into the smaller woman behind her. The force of the lunge slammed the woman into the ship's bulkhead, cracking her head against it with a *thwack.* Kira reached both hands over her right shoulder, grabbing the woman by the neck, ears, and hair, tossing her over her shoulder as she dropped onto her right knee. This put the stunned woman between her and the other two that were pressing the attack and gave her time to scramble across the floor to one of the handguns.

There was a moment where the smaller woman that Kira had just thrown to the floor cleared her mind long enough to see what Kira was doing. And the two of them struggled for control of the weapon briefly. With a knee to the woman's sternum, Kira pulled the gun free.

Unlike the security detail, Kira wasn't concerned with friendly fire at all. She rolled over onto her back, gripped the weapon with both hands, and put a round into each of the guards still standing. Her first shot was dead-on the forehead of the man to her right, blowing out the back of his head and spreading bloody gray matter against the bulkhead. The second shot caught the woman on her left in the neck, stunning her and spraying blood profusely from the wound. Kira put another round in her chest and one each into the other guards on the floor before she turned back to the storage room to finish off the two incapacitated men in there.

No witnesses, she thought.

Too bad for them.

The younger guard in the storage clerk's office was beginning to come around but still couldn't move. Kira looked into his eyes as she raised the weapon and dispatched him. The other man was still out cold, and now he would never wake up.

No witnesses, she thought again.

Kira slinked back to the doorway to check for more soldiers. They *would* be coming soon, but they weren't yet. The storage clerk's office was pretty deep inside the belly of the battle cruiser, and the hangar was two decks down and more than a hundred meters out from there. That was a long way to go on a military ship without running into soldiers, especially soldiers that were going to be looking for you.

We'd better get out of here, Allison warned.

You think?

CHAPTER 2

October 31, 2388 AD
Sol System, Earth
Orlando, Florida
Satuday, 5:25 AM, Earth Eastern Standard Time

"Kudaf, what have you got out there?" Thomas Washington subvocalized over the Secret Service wide-area quantum membrane transmission tactical network. The day was just any other day at the park—literally at the park since the Secret Service had managed to convince Disney World to let the president and the First Family visit the Magic Kingdom hours before it opened to the public. The Secret Service didn't like the idea at all, but President Alexander Moore had been absolutely insistent that he was taking his daughter, Deanna, to see Mickey Mouse while she was still a child, and there wasn't anybody, and that included the Secret Service, who was going to keep him from doing so. Finally, the director of the Department of Homeland Security had put pressure on the amusement park to cooperate with the Secret Service on the issue. Thomas Washington had direct charge of the First Family's security at all times, and from that point of view, the day would be no different than any other day. It truly was a walk in the park, but Thomas had been trained to believe that there was no such thing.

He had been on Mars for many "typical days," and that one day when the Separatists decided to perform an all-out attack on Mons City, he just happened to be on the aforementioned planet. That day was, for an armored environment-suit marine, just any other day. So, Thomas had learned from the school of hard knocks that there was no such thing as a "typical day."

"We're clean out here, so far. Teams are on post, snipers own the high ground, and I'm doing a walk-around," Secret Service agent Vincent Kudaf replied to his team commander. "Are you and the sarge holding up in there?"

Thomas looked at the hovercoaster behind him and could see the smile on the president's twelve-year-old daughter as she shouted excitedly. The president white-knuckled the roll bar of the rocket-ship-shaped amusement park ride as he ducked the virtual meteor that whizzed by his head. The expression on his face was nothing but teeth from his wide smile, and it was clear that there was no place else the president would rather be than on vacation with his wife and daughter.

"Ain't this great, Dee?" President Moore asked his daughter in his long, slow Mississippi accent.

"This is more fun than base jumping, Daddy!" Deanna answered. The cape of her animé superhero MegaWoman costume flapped behind her making a clapping sound.

However, the very big black man sitting beside the tall, slender, pale-skinned, dark-haired woman in the coaster car behind the president and his daughter was not having as much fun. Clay Jackson might have been a U.S. Marine, might have seen some serious action in his day, but the hovercoaster at Space Mountain was getting the better of him. Thomas tried not to chuckle at his longtime friend and colleague.

"*Semper fi*, marine," Thomas chuckled on a private channel to his former NCO.

"Oorah," Jackson replied with little enthusiasm. Sehera Moore, the First Lady, seemed about as enthusiastic as her bodyguard. Other than the occasional muffled squeal, she had mostly remained quiet, as was her nature.

The hovercoaster cars streamed through the meteor storm and banked with more than two gravities of acceleration through the virtual asteroid field surrounding Belt Station. The alien invaders from the Andromeda galaxy were hot on their tails. Thomas didn't have time to pay close attention, but he could tell that the president's daughter was fearless, like a Marine mechajock. Who knew? Her old man had been one hell of a marine, and maybe it was in her blood.

She pulled the joystick to the right to bank the hovercoaster formation, and then she swiveled the wheel with her left, yawing the middle car—the one she was in—on its axis so that they were looking orthogonally to their direction of travel. The three coaster cars were connected as if they were flying in formation with each other, and the next set of cars was more than five meters behind them and empty. The car in front held Thomas. Thomas continually swiveled it from side to side, scanning for anything out of the ordinary. His artificial intelligence counterpart (AIC) also scanned with multiple sensors attached to his personal armor system. *So far, so good,* he thought.

Occasionally, Thomas would make eye contact with the president and his daughter. Moore would sometimes nod in return, and Deanna always smiled at him. The car attached behind them holding the First Lady and Jackson seldom pitched or yawed. The First Lady apparently didn't enjoy the adrenaline-filled ride. But Deanna and President Moore were at the central controls of the three-car spaceship, and they continuously piloted the cars around and over each other like fighter planes in combat formations. The occupants of the front and rear cars were to be mainly gunners and shoot at the alien invaders.

"Shoot the alien, Daddy!" Deanna cried.

"I got him!" Moore fired the plastic multicolored cannon, sending blue and red bolts of lightning across the virtual asteroid field and destroying the alien spacecraft with a mixture of computer-generated holography and real-to-life pyrotechnics. It was a good coaster.

Moore looked over his shoulder at his wife behind them. Then he smiled at her with a sincerely affectionate grin. Thomas had always admired that about President Moore. Unlike many politicians throughout history, Moore was *really* married to his wife. And he revered his daughter as the epitome of love for their family. Thomas was certain that Moore would lay down his life in a heartbeat for either of the women in his life. In fact, he had seen him attempt to do just that.

Back when the man was just a senator from Mississippi and had gotten himself and his family caught up in events of the Separatist Exodus of 2383, he stood tall and faced a fierce enemy because of the love he had for his wife and daughter. Moore had single-handedly faced down several enemy mecha with nothing more than a rifle, attempting to lure the enemy mecha away from his family. And he had come out on top.

Thomas Washington had been there and had fought right beside him on that violent Martian day. Alexander Moore was a man he respected. Moore had been Major Moore of the U.S. Marine Corps once upon a time. And there was no such thing as a *former* marine. Thomas knew that it would be no problem for him to lay down his life to protect the President or any member of his family.

Knowing what he did of the then-senator Moore, it had been a no-brainer when Thomas' company commander had told him that he was being offered a detail with the Department of Homeland Security to be President Moore's personal security team leader. Then U.S. Marine Captain Washington went inactive and trained at the James J. Rowlings Training Center just outside Washington, D.C., for a year in order to take the position. To Washington, it was the biggest honor he'd ever received in his life. The president of the United States of America had specifically requested *him*. The president had also asked for the other two surviving marines who fought with him in the Martian desert that day. Gunnery Sergeant Clay Jackson and Corporal "Kootie" Kudaf had been nothing less than gung-ho for their new assignments.

Thomas, I'm getting an urgent relay from HQ, Tammie, his AIC, informed him.

Patch it through.

Be advised of unusual bandwidth usage on the local area wireless networks. Disney World authorities don't understand the increase. Recommend protect and return protocols.

Tammie, you heard them. Shut this thing down and get Marine One in here. Thomas thought through the procedures that had been trained into him like instinct. His first thoughts were that there was a simple and harmless technical glitch going on at Disney World, but he couldn't take any chances with the people's lives that he had been charged with. *Nothing is typical,* he thought.

Tammie, you better tell Abigail to pass the information along to the president. We'll get off the ride and out quickly and smoothly.

I have already, relayed the info to the president's AIC, Thomas, Tammie replied.

Good. Now get this ride stopped. Thomas opened the channel to Kudaf and Jackson. "Boys, we have a glitch. Let's roll 'em up and get 'em out of here. Kootie, do you have Marine One yet?"

"It's inbound from MCO Airport, and Air Force One is waiting hot," Kootie answered. "Snipers show nothing on sensors or eyeball."

"Clay, I hate to end all the fun you were having on the ride," Washington commented with a hint of dry humor, but continuously scanned across the dome of the amusement park ride for danger. "We may have trouble coming."

"What seems to be the problem, Thomas?" the president asked subvocally over the net. His AIC was clever and had a tendency to be able to hack into most networks, so they had quit trying to keep her out. Not that the president couldn't order them to give him access, but he never did, as if he were continually testing his AIC. It was rumored that his AIC was one of the smartest ever born. "Abigail is detecting some sort of wireless noise level increase that is delaying our long-range coms. Could be that there is a rogue command signal in here somewhere."

"Yes, Mr. President. That's why we're rolling you out of here."

"If we are rolling out, then why hasn't this ride stopped?" Moore asked nonchalantly. The man was cool, collected, and methodical—a true U.S. marine. Thomas knew the president's history. He had read all about how Moore had seen serious action during the Martian Desert Campaigns as well as being a prisoner of war for years. Moore's years of tribulation had made him a force to be reckoned with and a man with a resolve of the hardest metals known to man.

Tammie, what gives? Thomas inquired.

I don't know, Thomas. I've relayed the stop-ride command to the system several times, but nothing seems to be happening, Tammie said.

What does Abigail say?

She doesn't know either, but we are working it. So is HQ.

"We have a situation! The President is at risk, and we need a convergence at this location and immediate extraction!" Thomas announced over the tac-net to the team.

The hovercar path led downward to the bottom of the mountain and continued to pick up speed. The three cars aligned themselves one behind the other and all of them pointed forward. The virtual spacescape didn't seem to change from the standard amusement ride scene, and the cars continued to the drop-off point for passengers but were traveling far too fast to stop.

At first, Thomas thought it would be the end of the line for them, literally, if he couldn't either veer the cars upward from the floor or somehow get the safety restraints off of them and get them out of the cars before they hit. The problem with the latter was that they were moving at least seventy kilometers per hour. The president and First Lady might be able handle the fall at that speed, but for certain, their daughter couldn't.

Open channel, he told Tammie.

"All right, everybody hang on and try to keep your heads down. These cars are out of control, and we have to slow them down." Thomas pulled his M-blaster from inside his black, armored dress coat and placed the barrel on the safety bar interlock for his car. He squeezed the trigger, frying away the five-centimeter steel restraint with a brilliant white and blue flash. Some of the chromium-molybdenum steel splattered molten hot against the side of his face, searing deep into the flesh of his jaw muscles. He braced for the pain and then repeated the process on the other side of his car. The bar pulled loose as he turned and tossed it over the side of the car.

Tammie, where is the power system for these cars?

Here and here. A three-dimensional map of the hovercoaster cars filled his mind's eye, and two points on the underbelly flashed on and off in red highlight.

Make sure Clay is getting this.

I am relaying this to Susan now. Tammie sent the information to Clay's AIC. Unfortunately, the First Lady was sitting with Clay, and he was hesitant to blow the restraint bar free as Thomas had.

"Clay, can you get a shot on the power system for your car?"

"Not without getting free. But I've got a clear bead on Hovercar One's."

"Take the shot," Thomas ordered. Jackson took aim and began firing white and blue bolts of directed energy into the back of the president's car.

"Done!" Jackson responded as the two front cars dipped forward from the abrupt power loss but then corrected themselves to normal flight. The three-car amusement ride was being propelled through the air by the propulsion system of the front and aft cars. The Disney imagineers had overengineered the ride with triple redundancy. "Thomas, we have to take the propulsion out!"

"I know, Clay! I'm working on it!" he shouted.

Thomas stood in the front car trying to maintain his balance as it sped faster and faster toward the deck of Space Mountain. He aimed his blaster at the first highlighted spot in his mind's eye and pulled the trigger twice, searing holes through the plastic in the bottom of the amusement park ride. The power system vaporized with a shower of pungent burning plastic and sparking vapors. Then the car lurched, tossing him upward more than a meter over the middle car.

As he passed over the president and his daughter, Thomas could see the panic in the twelve-year-old girl's eyes. She covered her face with her arms and screamed. Thomas continued to fly upside down through the air as the rear car approached. Clay instinctively rotated the axis of the rear car and stretched his hand upward as far as he could. Thomas reached down with his left hand just in time to be grabbed by Clay's right. He could see the First Lady's face contorted with fear as he passed over them.

His trajectory arched over the car, slamming him into the back side of the only car still powered. The force of his body colliding with the car stretched Clay's arm to its limit. The impact of Thomas's torso and head against the vividly colored plastic knocked the wind from him and bruised his already burned face. Clay clutched at his right arm with his left hand but didn't let go until he saw that Thomas had a handhold on the hovercar.

As Thomas came to his senses, he searched frantically for a handhold with his right hand, which still held the blaster, until he managed to get the grip of his weapon wedged over a faux instrument panel that could support his weight. He let go of Clay's hand and quickly found a better handhold for his left hand, freeing his blaster hand. Thomas held on tight and scrambled for a foothold on the plastic rocket nozzles jutting out from the back of the hovercoaster car. Finally gaining his balance, he trained his blaster on the power system and fired once. Sparks flew in his face, forcing him to lose his grip and balance, and he was flung free from the hovercar. As Thomas watched the car pull away from him, he maintained his focus and aimed his weapon at the remaining power unit of the ride. He held his aim tight and pulled the trigger.

The directed energy bolt danced across the darkened virtual space room toward its target, passing through a holographic asteroid and hitting home on the remaining power plant. The explosion of the supply threw the same cloud of vapors when it hit. "Yes!" Thomas thought. Then something pounded into his back and his head cracked against it too—the floor.

Thomas tucked as best he could and rolled with the impact. At seventy kilometers per hour, he continued to tumble wildly until he smashed into a wall of chain-link fencing that was surrounding several racks of the ride's special-effects computer equipment. The final impact against the fence knocked him unconscious briefly.

He came to looking upward into the darkness with his feet above him resting on the fence. There was a serious pounding in his head, and the moist feeling he had on his face was probably blood from the broken nose he was certain that he had.

Thomas! Thomas Washington! Get up! Snap out of it, marine! Tammie yelled into his mind.

Without hesitation or complaint, Thomas reached into his breast pocket with his left hand—his right was now broken—and pulled out the immunobooster injector and jabbed it into his neck. He then followed the booster with a painkiller and an adrenaline injection. A few seconds later, the pain was gone, and he managed to get to his feet.

Where are they, Tammie? Thomas inquired.

The cars came down seventy meters west of here, she replied.

"This is Washington; somebody talk to me!" he announced over the net. Thomas ran as best he could in the direction of the crashed cars. His AIC told him that his M-blaster was more than fifty meters behind them, but his railpistol was still in his rear holster. He pulled the railpistol free with his left hand and the safety interlock recognized his biometric signature and went green, ready to fire.

"Everybody is fine, sir," Jackson reassured them. "It was a bumpy landing, but we came to a stop with no injuries. I'm removing the restraints now. We need backup in here."

"Kootie! Backup converge on the sarge's signal," Thomas ordered. "I want Marine One, now!"

"Yes, sir!"

Thomas found a large hole that the falling hovercars had apparently made in the wall of the virtual-effects dome and into a "backlot" area. Drywall, sparking electrical conduits, and broken aluminum studs protruded like jagged teeth on the gaping hole. Being careful not to touch the electrical wires, Thomas quickly weaved his way through the jumbled mess of rubble and debris until he stepped into a larger cavernous room filled with amusement ride vehicles in need of repair. The three crashed hovercars rested sideways against a large metal I beam on the other side of the room. The car that Thomas had been in was cracked in half and was wrapped around the beam, while the beam was basically unscathed. Had he stayed in that seat, he would have been a slimy spot on the metal beam and would be dead for certain.

"Mr. President! Are you okay, sir?" He rushed up to the middle car scanning the president and his daughter for injuries. His AIC assured him that they were alive and in stable condition.

Thomas! Deanna has a broken right ulna, Tammie exclaimed.

Tell Abigail.

"I'd say we are in at least as good of shape as you, Thomas," President Moore replied. Neither he nor his daughter realized that the latter was injured yet. "What the hell is going on?"

"Uh, not sure yet, Mr. President," Thomas replied. From the look on the president's face, he could tell that his AIC had just informed him that his daughter was injured.

"Deanna?" President Moore turned to his daughter and helped her down from the car.

"I'm okay, but my arm hurts, Daddy."

"Don't worry, baby," Moore said unwaveringly, and kissed her forehead.

"Mrs. Moore?" Thomas turned to the third car, where Clay was dropping the First Lady to the floor carefully.

"I'm fine, thank you, Thomas." Sehera straightened her blouse and dusted herself off. Thomas pulled another immunobooster injector from his coat pocket and handed it to the First Lady.

"Ma'am, Deanna has a fractured right ulna. This is immunobooster."

"Understood." Sehera took the injector from him and calmly hugged her daughter to her as she administered the medication.

"I have no detailed information about what has just happened. The most important thing is your safety right now. We need to move along the wall to the exterior of this building, and from there we'll make our way to Marine One." Thomas scanned the room and caught a glimpse of motion. He quickly raised his pistol to the ready and made certain that his body was between the motion and the president.

"Clay!" He nodded in the direction of the motion.

"See it, sir," he said. Clay squared up his shoulders and stood slightly to the left of Thomas. The two men held their weapons at the ready and began running scenarios in their minds for escape routes to Marine One.

"Sniper Three to Boss. I've got your motion in sight. Do you want me to take action, sir?"

"Negative, Sniper Three. Hold for further instruction," Thomas ordered subvocally. He didn't want to kill any innocent civilians by accident.

Disney World emergency teams began to flood through the hole in the virtual-effects dome and move toward them. Thomas waved the pistol up in front of him so they all could see it and stepped cautiously toward them. The emergency teams were shocked by the sight of the weapon and froze in their tracks.

"Nobody moves!" Thomas said. "There are snipers with a bead on you right now. Any false moves and you will not get a second chance to explain it. Back through the opening slowly, and wait there until you are given further instructions."

Michael and a squad of other agents pushed through the crowd from behind and then turned and forced them back with weapons at the ready. Once it looked like the Disney crew was under control, Kootie moved to his commander's side; he didn't seem to react to what a bloody mess he was.

"Marine One is on the ground and ready to go, sir."

"Mr. President, let's get you and your family out of here," Thomas said.

CHAPTER 3

October 31, 2388 AD
Sol System, Oort Cloud
Satuday, 5:25 AM, Earth Eastern Standard Time

"Happy Halloween, Lieutenant, and welcome aboard," Executive Officer USMC Colonel Larry "EndRun" Chekov welcomed Buckley to the flagship of the United States Navy, the U.S.S. *Sienna Madira*. The *Madira* was *the* pride and joy of the U.S. military might and was named for the most revered, popular, and heroic president in history. Every seaman in the service would give their right nut or ovary, whichever the case might be, to serve on her. The marine mecha pilot turned XO saluted the new main propulsion assistant as he stepped from the transport onto the deck.

"Thank you, sir," Lieutenant Joseph Buckley II said, returning the salute. The new crew members filed out of the rapid transport behind them. They had been in hyperspace for nearly eleven and a half weeks on the small crowded ship, and Joe was looking forward to the wide-open spaces of the two-kilometers-long supercarrier flagship.

"The commanding officer wants to talk with you." Chekov led Joe from the hangar deck up to the captain's office.

"Any reason why, sir?" Joe hesitated. "I mean, we just off-loaded fifty new sailors and marines. Why me, uh, sir?"

"Son, that is for the Old Man to tell you, not me." The XO nodded in the direction of the elevator and waited for the new crewman to join him. He tapped thirty-six, the doors closed, and it felt to Joe like they began moving backward. Finally, the backward motion stopped and the elevator moved upward for a few seconds.

"Have you managed to acquaint yourself with the blueprints of the ship yet?" the XO said, making small talk with the young officer.

"Yes, sir, Colonel," Joe replied nervously. Buckley wasn't sure, but he didn't think that he had done anything to warrant the CO's attention in a bad way. Hell, he had been on board the transport, cramped in with fifty other sailors so close that he could smell what kind of toothpaste they each used—and when they didn't. Those damned marines could learn a thing or two about hygiene. There was one Army tankhead that was kind of easy on the eyes, and Buckley had tried on more than one occasion to make time with her only to be shot down.

Since he hadn't been able to implement his favorite pastime with the hot tankhead, he spent his time with his other love—supercarrier propulsion. He had been able to read and reread the *Naval Ship's Technical Manual* and the *Ship Information Book* several times. He even used his direct-to-mind (DTM) link with the transport's database to do some further reading on the *Sienna Madira*'s history and design. Occasionally he would eat and sometimes sleep, and never did he get into any mischief or even slack any duties. So he was certain that he was clean. But being singled out by the CO on the first day of duty couldn't be good. He decided that the best approach would be to just keep his mouth shut and listen.

The two men exited the elevator and then wound through the large corridors of the supercarrier's upper decks. The dull gray metal bulkheads were lit by dim red exit signs and white fluorescent lighting overhead. Several times they would go up a ladder, walk a few meters across another corridor, and then go back down a ladder, only to travel a few meters more to go back up another ladder. Eventually they reached the elevator for the command tower and made it to the CO's office.

The XO tapped on the office door and waited for the captain to look up from his papers. "Captain, Lieutenant Joseph Buckley, sir."

"Yes. Come in, Lieutenant. Thank you, Larry. The rest of the crew is being taken care of, I take it?" Captain Wallace Jefferson asked his trusted XO.

"Yes, sir. Looks like a good bunch, sir."

"Good, Larry. Carry on." Jefferson nodded at his XO and longtime friend.

"Aye, sir," Chekov answered. He nodded and winked at the captain and left Buckley standing at full attention. "Good luck, Lieutenant," he whispered with a chuckle on his way out of the CO's office.

"At ease, son." Jefferson grinned and stood from his desk, offering Joe his hand. "I just wanted to shake your hand."

"Sir?" Joe took the captain's hand and shook it firmly, more confused than anything. The captain seemed sincere, and when he began speaking, Joe immediately understood what this was all about.

"Your father was a hull tech under my command on the day the damned Seppies did their mass exodus," the captain said.

"Yes, sir. You wrote his letter, sir. I've read it many times, sir." Joe choked down a lump that was starting to well up in his throat.

"If it hadn't been for Hull Technician Third Class Joe Buckley, we might have lost the ship and the fight. He gave the ultimate sacrifice so that we could stop those bloodthirsty heathens from destroying an entire city and the millions of people in it. Your father was a hero, and I'm proud to have had him serve under my command. We would have never known of his sacrifice had his AIC not downloaded a record of his actions just before they were both incinerated. I tried to capture the feel of what he had done in the letter, but I can let you hear the final report from his AIC if you would like."

"Yes, sir. That would be nice." Buckley thought it would be nice for his grandma to hear, but more than five years had gone by, and he wasn't sure that it would really do anybody any good to bring up those memories.

"I'll have my AIC, Uncle Timmy, pass it along to your AIC. And I hope to see you do your father's memory proud."

"Thank you, sir. I'm proud to serve under your command, and I will do my best, sir."

"Well, I'm afraid there's little time to get acquainted. We're about to start an operation in a little more than an hour from now, and I'm sure we'll need you down in the Engine Room. Good luck, Lieutenant."

"Aye, sir." Joe saluted the CO and thought of his father for the next several minutes as he wandered around the ship—absently trying to find his duty post.

✧　✧　✧

"So the *Madira* will drop out of hyperspace just Solward of the Seppy outpost. We think there are frigates and battle cruisers in the area with the possibility of a hauler. Intelligence does show the area very active with Gomers. The last count showed more than a hundred Gnats and probably as many Stingers." Commander Jack "DeathRay" Boland continued with the recon portion of his premission brief to the pilots. As commander of the air group, or CAG, the pilots, all thirteen hundred or so of them, were his responsibility.

"There we will do rapid deploy and cover. I'll take the Gods of War out first in the initial ingress to the Seppy target and fly support to the *Madira*. Following the deploy phase, we *will* take this base. Poser and the rest of the Demon Dawgs will fly cover for the ground forces on the first pass deployment. I want you Dawgs sticking to your wingmen but nobody else. No, and I mean no, groups. The sky should be full of VTF-32s in random two-by-two locations covering the drop tubes so the tankheads make it down safe. There shouldn't be an arcminute of angle that I can't see an Ares-T fighter in." DeathRay paused and scanned the ready room to make certain that his orders were sinking in.

For the last four days he had wargamed this attack over and over in the advanced virtual Battle Operations and Scenarios Simulation Room at the center of the ship, which was officially known as the BOSS but more affectionately called the "Looney Bin." He had every intention that the mission should go off flawlessly. "Any enemy Gnats or Stingers you see out there, bring them down. If any other ships pop out of hyperspace on you, keep them busy. We must take this base at *all* costs."

"At the same time as the Dawgs are getting spaceborne, Colonel Warboys and the Warlords M3A17 drop tanks—"

"Hooah!" was interjected by one of the tank drivers. Bolan ignored it.

"—along with fifty armored environment-suit marines will be deployed on the enemy facility. The AEMs —"

"Oorah!"

"—and the tankheads will set up lines and hold them here and here. Note for you groundpounders and tankheads: space-time fluctuations around the facility show artificial gravity on the surface of about one-half Earth gravity, and there is no detectable atmosphere." At that point, two locations on the map of the Oort Cloud Separatist facility lit up in the three-dimensional display at the podium as Jack tapped them with the laser pointer.

"At the same time the lines are being formed, Deuce will have the Utopian Saviors in the FM-12 strike mecha crawling around that facility like stink on shit. Remember, we are not to destroy this construct here." Boland shined the green laser beam on a very large octagon shape with multiple towers at the limb of the planetoid facility.

The entire facility consisted of four irregular shaped Oort Cloud objects, each roughly twenty kilometers in diameter. The four icy objects were moored in the center via a large Seppy hauler starship that was about three kilometers long and one kilometer wide. The misshapen objects were stuck together with massive grids and metallic structures. The ships were moored between the four planetoids, and there were metal and composite structures crossing and zigzagging the base in a very makeshift and almost random fashion. Looking at the facility images conjured up thoughts of spliced wiring and miles of duct tape, all of it having gone horribly wrong.

Like an afterthought, or perhaps because the base was unfinished, there was a fifth, much larger, asteroid-sized planetoid about one hundred and fifty kilometers across, looming over the base on the same thousand-year orbit track around Sol. The object was only ten thousand kilometers or so from the main facility. From the surface of the facility, the asteroid would appear twice the size as the Moon does from the Earth.

It would have taken the Seppies generations to tug the asteroids together and build such a construct. Jack couldn't imagine how they had managed to conduct such a massive construction effort right under the noses of the American people. The combining structures and catwalks looked as if they were converted from Separatist battle cruisers and cargo ships.

A large octagonal structure more than ten kilometers in diameter stretched across the entire surface of the icy facility. Jack had his AIC highlight the odd construction in bright red on the image and then zoom in on it. At each vertex of the octagon, there was a tower. There were concentric octagons within it that diminished to a solid tower structure in the middle. The central tower stood more than three times taller than the ones at the periphery and stood from the middle of the hauler, extending in both directions into and out of the surface plane by about a kilometer in height.

"We believe this is the facility that enabled the Seppies to teleport from the system following the Martian Exodus. Also, recall that the existence of this facility is Top Secret and compartmentalized to this operation only. We must capture this facility intact because we need it to determine where the Seppies went and how they did it. And, since they are still guarding it, find out what they plan to do with it."

"DeathRay, you gonna give us some more substantial info on this thing, or do we just assume that it was based on Stonehenge and tin-foil hats?" one of the Army tankheads asked.

"The intel we have on this facility is that it is some sort of teleportation facility. How and why it works is above the classification of this briefing. We were cleared to show the following video." Jack gave a thought command to his AIC and a new three-dimensional movie started playing. The narration of the video first warned of the classified nature of the movie and then filled in some historical background on the Exodus.

"During the Separatist Exodus of 2383, more than thirty million people from the Sol System literally vanished into hyperspace. The majority of them left from the Separatist Reservation in the Martian desert of the Elysium Planitia and the Phlegra Montes and other less-populated regions of Mars. Some Separatist vessels that were equipped for hyperspace travel also left from Earth, the Belt mines, Kuiper Station, Triton, and Luna City. Intelligence reports from a deep-cover CIA operative, which were delivered to the Reservation in the Top Secret project code-named Bachelor Party, uncovered the only information available about the Exodus. The operative has since disappeared."

Jack thought about the last statement. He had delivered that agent himself deep into the Martian Reservation just as the Exodus was beginning. He liked what little he knew about the agent and hoped that she was still alive and well. The acknowledgment that she hadn't been heard from since the Exodus wasn't a particularly good sign.

"The information relayed to the CIA via this operative has led the Joint Chiefs, the secretary of defense, and the director of National Intelligence to the conclusion that the Separatists teleported from the Sol System to Tau Ceti nearly twelve light-years away, which is a capability that nobody had thought possible for mankind. Further analysis of the hyperspace capabilities of the Exodus fleet led to the theory that the Separatists must have escaped by known means of transport to somewhere no farther than the Oort Cloud and from there made their miraculous teleportation. Interrogations of the Separatist terrorists captured from the battles on Mars that day have corroborated the Oort Cloud theory," the narrator explained.

"After four years of searching in the deep space of the Oort Cloud nearly a light-year from Earth, reconnaissance teams have finally found a base that was heavily guarded. On several occasions, the recon teams have even monitored space traffic that literally appeared and disappeared out of nowhere over the large octagonal platform, which was built into the facility's surface structure. The vessel appearances are similar to a vessel entering through a hyperspace conduit, but there are far more gravitational and electromagnetic distortions created. This is not a typical hyperspace activity. Observe."

The video image of the facility zoomed in on the octagonal structure, and a large green and blue sphere of light began to grow, centered directly over the central tower. The sphere grew to several kilometers in diameter and looked like a giant plasma ball resting atop the tallest spire. Then the giant ball of plasma instantaneously collapsed to a flat disk of light with blue and white lightning shooting across the surface. A ripple, like waves on a pond, traveled in a circular wavefront from the center of the disk, and then a Separatist hauler and two support frigates emerged from the event horizon of the disk. As soon as the ships appeared in local space, the disk collapsed inward on itself and vanished with a final flash of white light from the center. The scene almost appeared to be a ship jaunting out of a normal hyperspace conduit—almost. Jack noticed that there were a few *oohs* and *ahs* and nodding heads around the room. He saw this as an opportunity to start back into the battle plan.

"Once we've all been deployed and are making our way toward taking this facility," Boland continued as the simulation holo started up again, "the *Madira* will make a second pass, deploying in mass all active battle-shift pilots. And the entire complement of Army Armored Infantry and the rest of the AEMs will be deployed. We will be putting thousands of troops on the ground. The Looney Bin sims show that at this point of the battle, we would likely be grinding down into a stalemate with the enemy force protecting the facility by digging in deep and holding a line."

"This is when Captain Walker will jaunt from hyperspace on the deep space side of the battle with the brand-new U.S.S. *Anthony Blair*.

They are already moving into prehyperspace position, and if how Captain Walker performed at the Exodus with the *Thatcher* is any sign of how her new ship and crew will function, we can expect her to bring all kinds of hell out of hyperspace with her. That hell will include Colonel Masterson's Cardiff's Killers in their FM-12s, along with two full squadrons of VTF-32s. There will also be a drop contingent of seventy-five AEMs from the *Blair*. If we need more, they will be in reserve on the *Blair*. Your AICs have further details and blue force tracking codes. There will be a shitload of mecha in the air, so watch the blue-on-blue.

"And one final thing," Jack started. He paused briefly, not certain of how he wanted to handle this next piece of business. "It has been nearly four years since there has been any real combat in this system. I know most of you are hardened with combat from before the Exodus and from that day itself, but we have all had a long time to soften up. Wargames are good but nothing like the real thing. For you rookies, pay attention to your seniors because that's why they are here. Let's keep our heads and kick some Seppy ass!"

Jack told his AIC to stop the virtual display, and the room lights illuminated to an almost annoyingly bright level. He squinted and then asked, "Army, any questions?"

"Hooah!" resounded through the room. Boland nodded in affirmation.

"Marines?"

"Oorah!"

"Navy?"

"Hooyah!"

"All right! Let's mount up then."

"All right, XO, let's mount up," Captain Sharon "Fullback" Walker ordered. She settled into her command chair and scanned the bridge crew for last-minute questions. There were none. It was a good crew. It was a good ship.

Her ship, the U.S.S. *Anthony Blair*, was the newest supercarrier in the U.S. space fleet and was given to the South England contingent of the Navy to replace the loss of the U.S.S. *Margaret Thatcher*. Captain Walker had been sitting in the command seat of the *Thatcher* during the Separatists' Exodus and used the ship as a battering ram to stop an enemy hauler from plummeting into the central part of Mons City on Mars. She managed to break the enemy hauler's structural integrity, causing it to fall apart on reentry into the atmosphere, while at the same time crash-landing her supercarrier onto the side of Olympus Mons. The *Thatcher* was rendered irreparable, but the city and its millions of occupants were saved. That was how the state of South England had lost one of its two supercarriers.

It lost the other the same day. The start of the attack on Mons City had begun by the U.S.S. *Winston Churchill* being sabotaged and subsequently crashing into one of the outer domes of Mons City. The *Churchill* had been totally destroyed with all hands, and to the present date, nobody had been able to figure out how it had been sabotaged.

The politicians in Washington, D.C., had decided that since there was little threat from the Separatist terrorists (now that they had left the system), there was no need to spend the money on new battleships. President Moore had literally threatened Congress with an executive order of police action if they didn't at least approve the appropriations to add one starship to each state that had lost one or more during the Exodus. Nobody was one hundred percent certain where the Separatists had gone, and most certainly nobody knew if they were planning to come back to the Sol System with force. President Moore had warned the public that there could be a war coming and that America had better not be caught with her pants down. In the end, he had convinced the public to put enough pressure on Congress to approve over twelve new supercarriers. Captain Walker was glad that he had because the *Blair* was an awesome ship and a great command.

"Flight crews and sorties are packed in and stacked up for deployment, ma'am," the XO reported to the captain. Commander Auburn Brasher tapped a few keys on her console and relayed several command thoughts to her AIC and then looked back up and nodded to Fullback. "The AEMs are sardines waiting for the drop."

"COB, how's my boat?" Fullback asked her chief of the boat.

"Good to go, ma'am. The boat is in top order, and there are no complaints from the crew other than the long hours, the shitty pay, and a goddamned slave-driving SOB of a CO." Command Master Chief Petty Officer William H. Edwards had been the COB of the *Thatcher,* serving under Captain Walker, and he had ridden the supercarrier all the way to the surface of Mars with her. His last-second heroic efforts to bring the power back online to several key systems of the crashing starship enabled them to save Mons City. The COB had gotten a medal for his actions: a metal crowbar that he had been attempting to use as a circuit fuse was explosively thrown through him, impaling his shoulder. After hearing of the story, several members of the bridge crew had found the same crowbar and had it bent into a heart shape and painted it purple. Captain Sharon Walker presented it to the command master chief at the decommissioning ceremony of the *Thatcher*. The two had a bond from that battle and were nearly inseparable. There were even rumors of a budding romance between the two of them, but nobody could substantiate them or really imagine it. The captain at just under two meters tall with her bodybuilder's frame—hence the callsign Fullback—towered over Edwards by a full head, and the COB looked like he could use some serious PT. Romance or not, that the two most certainly shared something was obvious. But the crew respected them and minded their own business.

Besides, the CMC had earned the unique relationship with the captain in combat. Sharon would allow him to speak frankly to her on most issues at most times when she might be less approachable to other members of the command crew. This relationship had actually led other officers to approach the COB when they were unsure of approaching the captain with "touchy" situations. Edwards had become Sharon's buffer zone and moat dragon.

"As it should be, Bill. Make a note to increase the beatings until morale improves. You should put yourself in for a few lashes as well." Fullback smiled, flashing her brilliant white teeth, which contrasted with her dark ebony skin.

"Aye, ma'am." The COB nodded.

Fullback took a deep breath and concentrated on the ship. Around her head was a virtual display of information about the flight and battle plans, the health of the supercarrier, and millions of other pieces of information continuously moving around her head in multicolored, three-dimensional overlays. The data came from the ship's diagnostics and battle management center and was transmitted to her by DTM link. The virtual information reached out in a sphere around her about a meter in diameter that only she could see.

Marley? she thought to her AIC.

Aye, Captain?

Are the hyperspace calculations set and ready for jaunt?

Aye, Captain.

Okay then, make the announcement.

Aye, Captain.

✧　✧　✧

"General quarters! General quarters. All hands, prepare for hyper-space jaunt in one minute. Prepare for battle stations call," Marley said over the 1MC intercom.

"Boulder, you've got the second deployment group." Colonel John "Burner" Masterson, commander of the U.S. Marine Corps FM-12 strike mecha squadron Cardiff's Killers, went through last-minute strategies with his second-in-command, Marine Captain Jason "Boulder" Cordova. "Once you get thrown out of the cat field, I want you and the other twenty Killers in your group to go to bot mode and get on the ground to find cover. The rest of us will be mixing up to cover you from above and behind. Your only thoughts should be to move forward and take that damned teleporter facility as quickly as you can. Got it?"

"Maximum velocity with maximum ferocity, Burner! Got it, sir."

"Take the hill, marine. And happy Halloween," Burner added.

"Oorah, sir."

"We are gung-fucking-ho, Gunny!" Lance Corporal Tommy Suez shouted as he strapped on the shoulder harness for the ammo can on his armored e-suit. The AEMs of the *Sienna Madira* filled the deploy-ment hangar and loaded the Starhawk SH-102s with gear. More than a dozen boxy armored troop carriers sat scattered about the hangar bay. Their pilots and gunners ran through systems checks and pre-flight planning. The marines scurried about the SH-102s with their personal armor, gear and mission-essential supplies. The gray deck plating was covered with armored crates and deployment tubes, which were filled with high-end explosives and ammo for the mission.

Suez locked his jumper boots into safe mode and attached the tether to his helmet, letting it dangle on his back next to the hyper-velocity automatic railgun (HVAR) that was strapped on there. The Seppy teleporter facility was only a few minutes away on the other side of a hyperspace conduit.

"Marines," Gunnery Sergeant Tamara McCandless shouted over the noise of the bustle for their attention. "We've got less than a half hour to get this gear strapped on and good to go. When we get the sig-nal from our goddamned heroic flying angels that we can board these

Starhawks, I want to see it done in record fucking time! Is that understood?"

"Oorah, Gunny!" The hangar echoed with excitement and anxiety that could only be generated by the knowledge that the 3rd Armored E-suit Marines were about to be dropped into a grinder. Intel had uncovered the base and that there was Seppy activity, but there was little more than that. Nobody was quite certain how many Separatist armored troops were actually manning the facility. Some imagery had shown some Seppy mecha—Stinger transfigurable mecha like the U.S. Marine's FM-102s—and Orcus drop tanks like the U.S. Army's M3A17-Ts. The reconnaissance had also shown several squadrons of Gnat fighters and a couple of battle cruisers. So, there was nobody doubting that the base was protected. The question remained, however, as to just how protected.

Lance Corporal Suez had never seen battle before, and the pre-mission preparation was causing sweat to bead on his forehead. He didn't know if the sweat was from nerves or the fact that his e-suit temp was set too high, and he hadn't taken the premission meds. The marine ignored the salty streams for the most part unless they got in his eyes—but even then, he could only blink or shake his head. Rookie or no, the thousands of hours of training he had in the armored e-suits had removed the instinct of trying to wipe away the sweat with his hands. The armored gloves could rip his nose off if he was not careful. But Tommy was good. So good, in fact, that he'd demonstrated earlier to his fellow marines how, with the proper control of mind and body, you could unwrap a piece of Halloween candy and put it in your mouth without crushing the candy or ripping your lips off.

Tommy squinted his eyes a few times and then shook his head, flinging sweat droplets asunder.

"Goddamnit, Suez, watch where you're flinging your slimy funk!" PFC Sandy Cross cursed at him. A droplet of Suez's sweat slowly dribbled down her cheek. "That shit is just fucking nasty."

"Sorry, *Private*," Suez smirked, emphasizing the word "Private" with disdain. Tapping a few keys on his forearm, he adjusted the temperature of the suit to cool him down. But that would only help a little. The intimate contacting membrane in the seal layer in the suits tended to make the human body's thermal regulation go nuts if the wearer didn't have a helmet on. In some of the earliest suits, perfectly healthy soldiers had actually had heat strokes, while others had developed hypothermia. The problem had been corrected several decades prior, but the effect of not wearing the helmet while wearing the rest of the armored e-suit was still noticeable. Medication had been developed to help the body adapt to the suit, but it was used by only about fifty percent of the marines. Some didn't like the side effects of the meds, while others just accepted the profuse sweating as a badge of honor of being an AEM.

Besides, Suez knew that when he was ready to don his helmet, the suit would pressurize, and the closed thermal environment of the system would function flawlessly and quickly to correct the imbalance. The sweat would be evaporated almost instantly, but another facet of the culture for AEMs was to breathe "real" air until the last minute and then "twist your head on." Part of the reason was that when a marine was finally deployed, there was no certainty as to when they would be able to take the helmet off. Salty sweat in the eyes was a common hazard for AEMs and was a badge of honor that even rookies understood.

"Hey, Suez, give me a hand with this." Sergeant Karen Nicks grabbed one end of a two-ton ammo crate with her armored hands and heaved it off the deck plating.

"Oorah," Suez replied. He fumbled for a handhold on the crate for a second and then managed to get his gloves into the slots designed for the suits.

"Take it easy, Tommy. You need a fucking chill pill?" They hefted the two-thousand-kilogram ammo box and walked it up the ramp of one of the SH-102s. The ramp resounded with a heavy clanking sound from each step of the heavy armored suits. The large troop-mover vehicle had racks on the floor that were designed for the deployment boxes. Tommy and Karen dropped the box into the tracks with a *kachunk,* and the rails clicked in place. Once they were in flight and ready to jump, a cat field would toss the box out at nearly one hundred kilometers per hour, careening to the surface below. The AEMs would be jumping out right beside the supplies, and hopefully AEMs and supplies would make it to ground unharmed.

"I'm good, Sergeant. I don't like the way the meds make me have to pee."

"They don't do that to me, but I've heard horror stories of marines pissing their suits full." Karen laughed, and then scanned her DTM virtual planning screen for the next box that needed to be loaded. The sergeant pointed at another set of crates and said, "Those two next."

"No shit. It pretty much happened to me at the suit quals. I mean, hell, I know the suit can handle it, but I had to keep drinking nonstop to keep from getting dehydrated. I've never pissed so much in my life. I thought it was gonna make my equipment raw on the inside. I'd rather just sweat." Suez grinned at the sergeant, showing his white, perfect smile. Tommy's smile and stocky build could have opened doors for him as a model if he were a few inches taller, but he was a second-generation AEM. His mother had been an AEM at the end of the Desert Campaigns on Mars and was one of the few survivors. Tommy was her fourth and youngest child, but he was the only one who had followed his mother's footsteps and become a marine.

"You ever do a complete vac drop before, Nicks?" Suez inquired.

"Yeah. I was with the recon team that dropped on Kuiper Station back before the Exodus. Vacuum or not, low atmosphere is low atmosphere, and it will kill you just as quick. You did training drops on Luna, didn't you?" Staff Sergeant Nicks asked, though Suez was certain that she knew what the answer would be. No AEMs were combat-qualified without doing four full vac drops, and the training grounds were just outside the Navy base near Luna City.

"Affirmative," Suez said.

"Then you got nothing to worry about, marine, except for maybe getting your ass shot off." Nicks gave the lance corporal a quick smile. "Come on, we better get the rest of this shit loaded and battened down before Gunny rips us a new one."

Gunnery Sergeant Tamara McCandless filed her way through the sea of helmetless AEMs, Navy aviators, and gunners, and mountains of mission-essential equipment. She nodded at the smooth efficiency and preparedness of her marines. Major Roberts had a good team in the 3rd Armored E-suit Marines Forward Recon Unit, and Tamara was proud to be a part of it. She had been with Roberts' Robots since before Triton when the major was just a lieutenant. She was with him at Mons City during the Seppy Exodus, when he was a captain, and had fought hard beside him on the northwest exterior wall of the main dome against an overwhelming force of Seppy drop tanks and support troops.

She and Roberts were the first soldiers to push past the enemy and into the dome, where they found the mass murder of the civilians taking place by the few Seppy motherfuckers that had stayed behind to fight to the death. The Separatists had gone through the Martian city, herding all of the civilians into central open court locations using force fields. There had been many tens of thousands crowded into the main dome Central Park. Once it was clear to the Seppies that the Exodus was over and that they were the only ones from the Reservation left behind, they started executing the civilians with automatic railgun fire. Men, women, and children were slaughtered. Tamara saw firsthand how horrendously bloodthirsty the Seppy fuckers were, and she had every intent to stay in the AEMs and do as much to stop them as she could. She knew that the major felt the same. That *one* day on Mars had molded them into hardcore, Seppy-hating, life-taking, motherfucking U.S. Armored ESMs. And Tamara was proud of it.

Tamara, the major wants to see you, her AIC informed the gunnery sergeant.

Where is he, Jolly?

He's in the aft section of the hangar nearest the launch line, AI Sergeant Juliet Oscar One One Yankee Seven Mike, or Jolly, replied.

Roger that. Tamara picked up her pace and turned aft toward the end of the hangar. The red and yellow stripes painted on the deck of the catapult field launch line led her to the end of the Starhawk hangar into the launch bay. Just around the corner was a line of M3A17-T tanks in drop tubes, lined up and ready to be jettisoned. Major Ramy Roberts stood beside the lead tank, talking to a tankhead. Emblazoned on the side of the mecha was "Warlord One," and a full-bird colonel tankhead dressed in his mecha hardpoint armored g-suit leaned against it. The colonel's helmet rested on top of the tank that he was leaning against.

Who's the full bull? she asked Jolly.

That is Colonel Mason Warboys of the tank squadron known as Warboys' Warlords.

Yeah, I figured that's who it was. Heard of him. Tamara thought about it.

Hell, everybody had heard of Warboys' stand against the Seppy line outside Mons City during the Exodus. He alone had been credited with over thirty kills that day! When the tankheads and AEMs had been overrun in the desert outside Mons City, instead of running, Warboys led the charge of his Warlords headfirst into the Seppy line, where he fought them almost to a standstill, until the numbers game finally had caught up with the tankheads. Then, as any good marine knew the story, a group of FM-12 Marines—Cardiff's Killers—had to come in and save their Army asses in the nick of time.

"Tamara, are we clicking along all right?" Major Roberts asked her as she approached them. She half saluted the major who, likewise, half returned it.

"The Robots are a well-oiled, heart-breaking, life-taking machine, sir. They are gung-ho and good to fucking go," Tamara replied with a salute.

"Just what I wanted to hear, Gunny." The major turned and motioned his armored hand toward Warboys. "Gunnery Sergeant Tamara McCandless, I'd like you to meet Colonel Mason Warboys. Mason and I played football at Ohio State together." Major Roberts grinned at Tamara, and she was sure that he knew what her response would be.

"Well, sir, I'll try not to hold that against either of you." Tamara grinned and saluted Warboys, saying, "It is an honor to meet you, Colonel Warboys. You know what the only sign of near sentient life in Columbus is, uh, sir?"

"What's that, Gunny?" Warboys returned her salute and asked with a raised left eyebrow.

"It's just off Highway 33. There's a sign that says Ann Arbor three hundred kilometers."

"You got something against my Buckeyes, Gunny?"

"You see, Mason," Major Roberts interjected, "Tamara here played basketball in college."

"Is that right? Let me guess. . . ."

"Wolverine, sir!" Tamara stuck out her armored chest rigidly and laughed proudly, as any self-respecting student from Michigan would have at least some loathing and seething hatred for Ohio State grads. The two senior officers chuckled for a moment, and then Tamara quickly realized they were ready to talk business. "What can I do for you two, sirs?"

"Well, Tamara, as you know, we are to disperse on the ground with the tank squadron. What I'd like to do is for you to pick a team of recon AEMs to ride down with them." The major had a blank stare for a second as if he were reading something DTM, and then he continued. "The Warlords are likely to burst through to the target first, but they probably will not be able to sustain the location. But a small recon team could get past the enemy lines of defense and wreak havoc from the other side."

"I see, sir," she replied. "Do you have any particular team in mind to do this recon?"

"Your discretion, Sergeant, minus one. I'm going with you. But coordinate with the colonel here and get it done."

"Yes, sir." Tamara had gone to ground in a drop tube before but never one filled with a tank. Her thoughts were that it was going to be a hell of a ride. "Colonel Warboys, I hope your tankheads don't mind getting awfully cozy with a bunch of marines, sir."

"They shouldn't, Gunny, as long as you don't put anybody from Auburn in the tube with Warlord Four. We'd likely not be able to put up with the continuous shouts of 'War Eagle' and 'Roll Tide'!"

"Damn, sir, I don't think we've got anybody in the whole company from the SEC," Tamara responded with disappointment in her voice. "That might've been fun."

"Skinny, once we drop through, you six of the Saviors shag ass to the southwest apex of the octagon," Major Caroline "Deuce" Leeland explained to her second-in-command while she slipped into the organogel layer of her armored g-suit. She slid the cool pseudo-liquid garment up over her naked body, causing her to shiver slightly. But just as soon as the gel layer *schurrped* into place, the topical drugs and chemicals embedded in it immediately adjusted to Deuce's body temperature. A faint fluorescent hue shimmered down the length of the bodysuit. "I'll take Hawk, Beanhead, and PayDirt through the middle, and then let's work toward each other."

"Roger that, Major," Captain Connie "Skinny" Munk acknowledged, likewise pulling up her organogel bodysuit. Connie and Deuce were veterans of the Exodus and had fought hard alongside their previous top pilot, "Bigguns," who had given her life in the battle to save Mons City. Skinny had actually been holding her commander and best friend in her mecha's hand when she had died. Something like that stuck in a pilot's craw, and it didn't increase her love for the Seppies.

Over the years, Deuce had moved into that top spot with the Saviors, and Skinny had moved into the number two. Both of them were very accomplished mecha pilots.

"That suit you, Captain?"

"Yes, ma'am. HoundDog, Goat and Volleyball, and Popstar and Romeo are on me. Since we ain't supposed to damage the target, I guess we just recon for things to kill?"

"They'll be flying their support out of somewhere. Find where it comes from and take it out." She snapped on the thin armor over the organogel and the compression layers and then stood straight to work the suit into place.

"Oo-fuckin'-rah, ma'am!" The marine pilot pulled the zip cord of her armored g-suit up her back and fastened it over her right shoulder. The armor healed over the zip seam and hardened, hiding any evidence of the seam. Skinny picked up her brain bucket, snapped to the tether, and let it hang over her shoulder like a backpack.

"Gung-fucking-ho, marine."

CHAPTER 4

October 31, 2388 AD
Sol System; Orlando, Florida
Saturday, 5:35 AM, Earth Eastern Standard Time

"Marine One is across the bridge from Tomorrowland in the open area in front of Cinderella's castle, sir," Kootie informed his boss. "About two hundred meters that way." Kootie pointed along the walkway that wound around the castle that had for centuries been an icon of American family entertainment.

"Let's move and stay on your toes," Thomas ordered. He stood directly in front of President Moore while Clay sandwiched in behind him. The president held his daughter's right hand, while Sehera held her left. The immunobooster was doing its job and Deanna's arm was mostly healed now.

Kootie took the right flank, and several other agents took up post around them. The group walked at such a fast pace that Deanna had to take several running steps every few walking steps to keep up. She never complained.

Thomas, Abigail has notified me that the bandwidth in the local area has just filled. HQ is still trying to understand what that means. Abigail also says that the signal-to-noise ratio has just gone through the roof, Tammie warned him.

What does that mean, Tammie?

If the SNR has increased within the bandwidth of the LAN, that could only mean that there is an increase in encrypted communication signals within it. Abigail says that the same thing happened when the ride was taken over, Tammie explained.

"Okay, everybody, let's pick up the pace," Thomas said. "Dee, if we're going too fast for you, Clay will carry you."

"I can run faster than Clay, Thomas!" Deanna challenged.

"That's the spirit, honey." Sehera smiled.

The walkway began to wind through some ornamental shrubbery and trees. One of the shrubs had a particular likeness to a certain famous little wooden boy while another looked like a flying elephant. Thomas noticed that the trees directly across from them near Frontierland were beginning to sway as if a breeze were picking up, and then suddenly a hovercar shaped like a magic carpet whirred through the vegetation, scattering leaves and flowering blossoms asunder. The magic-carpet-ride car was large enough to hold two adults in front and in back and most likely used the same type of hovercar propulsion that the Andromeda Invasion ride had used. The large plastic hovercar accelerated way beyond the safety protocol speed it had been designed for, and like a guided missile, it collided with Marine One.

"Everybody down!" Thomas turned and pushed the president to the ground and crawled on top of him, using himself as a shield. Clay and several others did the same for Deanna and Sehera.

The magic carpet crunched like an accordion against the armor of the president's aircraft. The plastic fuselage of the amusement park ride didn't make a dent in the armor, but it managed to push the hovercraft up on one skid from the force of the impact. Marine One fell back on all three skids just as the power pack of the magic carpet ride exploded, sending multicolored shrapnel in all directions. A jagged composite material piece of the carpet's tassel penetrated the neck of one of the men standing guard around the vehicle. The shrapnel entered his neck from the side, ripping through his esophagus and the major arteries. He died almost instantly as a spray of bright red blood glinted in a ray of the rising Florida sun.

The rest of the guards around the vehicle had little time to react. A second carpet zoomed overhead and hit the president's hovercraft again. This time the trajectory of the carpet seemed more calculated, and it swooped down low enough just before impact to sandwich several of the other guards, killing them rather efficiently. The few that survived were hammered by third, fourth, and fifth carpets. Finally, a squadron of slightly larger hovercars shaped like flying elephants with gigantic ears swarmed in from Fantasyland behind them and collided with the vehicle, at once inflicting enough damage to topple Marine One up and over, landing completely upside down on a nearby sidewalk. A final car hit the underbelly, tearing through several power conduits of the vehicle. Sparks and hydraulic fluids spilled out from multiple torn junctions in an array of electric colors and goopy liquids. The electrical system flashed bright white with just enough heat in the right direction to trigger the volatile liquids to flame. The lift began to smolder and then slowly burn. Pieces of the plastic from the hovercars began to flicker from the heat and distort as the surface charred and melted.

"Marine One, do you copy?" Thomas called over the tac-net.

"Roger that. Pilot and copilot are okay but I don't think we'll be able to roll over or to pull out from under this pile of debris," the pilot replied. "We're dead in the water here."

"Hang in there, Marine One. You are on fire and you need to get out!" Thomas replied.

"Negative. We're trapped unless somebody can roll this thing over."

"Damnit!" Thomas wanted to help them, but his priority was the president. He needed his detail for that mission.

"We should try to help them, Thomas," President Moore told him.

"I'm sorry, sir, but that isn't our protocol. We have to protect you first and foremost, and moving out there could be a trap."

At that point the discussion was moot, as a third wave of flying vehicles crashed into the flaming underbelly of Marine One. The impact sent even more fluid spurting from the hydraulic systems, which in turn fueled the already growing flames. Soon, the hovercraft reached a critical flashpoint and burst into roiling orange flames. Finally, it exploded as the ordnance on board must have reached some critical temperature. The explosion flung debris high into the air across the central fountain on Main Street. There was little left of the president's vehicle or the crumpled amusement park hovercars.

"HQ! HQ! This is a full-scale attack alert. The president is under attack and Marine One is down! I repeat Marine One is down! We need immediate backup and extraction. President is in jeopardy!" Thomas called over the net. He pulled one of the other agents from the periphery over the pile to cover the president. Then Thomas crawled forward to make a better assessment of the situation.

Tammie, give me the virtual map of the Magic Kingdom, he thought. A virtual three-dimensional map appeared around his head.

Done.

Now, overlay any free-flying coaster rides and their locations. Can you track them by any means? Thomas longed for his armored e-suit and all the sensors and instruments that had been available to him as a marine. The lidar or the quantum membrane (QM) sensor alone would be enough to track the flying fantasy cars.

I'm not sure how, Thomas. I'll ask Abigail to think about it.

Okay.

Thomas got his bearings straight from the virtual map and from simply looking around the park. They were on the path between Tomorrowland and Fantasyland, between Storytime with Belle and the Cosmic Starlight Café. A quick zoom in on the virtual map showed that Storytime with Belle was in a small amphitheater surrounded by a rock wall. It would be pretty good cover, and they were only about twenty meters or so from it.

Okay, we are moving here! Thomas ordered via the DTM com-net. He had the map highlight the path to all the agents and to the First Family—all but Sehera, that is. The First Lady had refused to have an AIC as long as he had ever known her, but she was good at taking visual and verbal cues. She also wore a dermal ear transceiver. Although she didn't have an AI inside her head, she did have a communication device there.

Move! Thomas ordered, leading the way around the rock wall to the small outdoor theater.

"Groundcrew One, be advised that backup has been deployed. ETA is four minutes."

"Roger that, HQ!"

Mr. President, I think I've figured out a way to track the flying vehicles, Abigail alerted her human counterpart.

How? the president thought to his AIC. She was one of the smartest AICs anyone had ever heard of and had helped him through scrapes that dated back nearly four decades. Moore had learned that when Abigail had advice, he needed to listen to it.

There are several Internet hubs scattered across the park. I'm connected to each of them. Any motion within the park creates multi-path reflections between us and those hubs. I've generated some algorithms that have allowed me to track the motion based on the connection speeds I have with the Internet at each of these hubs. In essence, I'm using the wireless routers of the park like multi-path radars, Abigail informed.

So, you are tracking them now? the president asked.

Yes, his AIC replied.

Relay that info to the security detail, Abigail.

Already did, Mr. President.

Good girl. Give me a DTM view of the park with overlays of the enemy movement.

Yes, sir.

A transparent three-dimensional view of the Magic Kingdom filled his mind with red dots moving in the distance and a cluster of blue dots on top of his location in the map. Moore noticed that the red tracks were more or less setting up a perimeter on the edge of the park's boundaries. Rather than attacking, they were circling like a pack of wolves trapping an injured cow.

Abigail, is Thomas seeing this map?

Yes, Mr. President. They have the multi-path track live now, she said.

"Thomas, give me a gun," Moore ordered his bodyguard.

"Mr. President, we can handle this," Thomas replied, although Moore was certain that the marine knew better than to argue. Moore had a way of getting things done the way he wanted them done. Moore had been in combat with Thomas and didn't expect that there was apprehension on Thomas' part about handing a civilian a gun. It was probably more of an insult to the marine that the president feared that they couldn't protect him and his family.

"Thomas, I understand that you are looking at the same virtual map that I am now. We are outnumbered, and I think there is some-body putting up a no-fly zone around the park. Give me a gun."

"Alexander, are you sure you want to make yourself a target?" the First Lady asked. Some of the times when the president wouldn't listen to his bodyguard service, he would listen to his wife. Some of the times he did, but it was clear that today wasn't going to be one of those times.

"Better me than you," he commented with a very political smile. Then Moore reached out a hand toward his guard.

"Oh hell." Thomas shrugged. "Agent Browning, give me your railpistol."

"Sir?" the short muscular female agent kneeling behind the brick lamppost at the edge of the amphitheater replied.

"Now." Thomas held eye contact with the president.

"Yes, sir." The agent reached behind her and pulled a pistol from her waistband holster and tossed it over to Thomas. "Good thing I carry a spare," she said, and reached inside her skirt and patted the railpistol in her garter for comfort. Instinctively, she also checked the extra M-blasters strapped under her cleavage armor.

"Here you go, Mr. President. With all due respect, sir, don't use it unless you have to. No need to make a target out of yourself." Thomas handed the pistol to President Moore.

"Thanks, Thomas. What's your plan for getting us out of here?" Moore asked.

"I say we take cover here and wait for the backup. Three minutes away by now." Thomas checked his watch.

"This is good immediate cover, but I'd prefer someplace less exposed," the president added.

"Thomas, we could make a dash for the Starlight Café," Clay replied.

"Very well, let's make a move down the street to the restaura—" Thomas started but flinched as he was interrupted by railgun fire *spitapping* into the brick wall above their heads. He reflexively pushed the president back down and covered him.

"Thomas, where the hell did that come from?" Moore scanned the map in his head for red dots, but all the red dots were in the air and not in the direction of the railgun fire.

Abigail, what the hell is going on?

One moment, sir. I didn't think about ground movement. Let me adjust the algorithm . . . there.

"Holy shit!" Moore gasped as the map flashed red dots all around them. Whatever was controlling the flying vehicles of Disney World had also commandeered the robot theme park creatures. Moore pushed Thomas up enough so that he could see over the pile of bodyguards. About one hundred meters across the river and farther down Main Street were railgun-toting cowboys and cowgirls, several aquatic creatures, and two aliens from Andromeda. "Thomas, we're being flanked! Get the hell off of me."

"Sir." Thomas reluctantly rolled off the president and took a knee very close to him. If things got bad, Moore suspected that the marine would probably try to tackle him and forcefully cover him. The thought sort of tickled Alexander, since he was far bigger than the marine, and following that long, horrific day on Mars, the president had made it a point to keep in really good fighting shape. Of course, Thomas knew this since he had been the one the president had been sparring with on a regular basis.

"Look over there, toward Mickey's Toontown Fair and also back toward Tomorrowland. The robots are hemming us in here." Moore crawled toward the wall of the amphitheater entrance to get a better vantage point. The theme park creatures were surrounding them. "How the hell did they get armed?" the president pondered.

"This is like a nightmare gone nuts," Sehera added as more railgun fire pitted the brick wall above them. "At least they're not very good shots."

"Good shots or not, it only takes one lucky one to ruin your day," Clay warned—a lesson he'd learned several times over from his combat experience on Triton and Mars.

"Thomas, I don't know about you, but I don't like getting shot at, even if they can't seem to hit a bull in the butt with a base fiddle." Moore raised his pistol and released several hypervelocity rounds over the wall at the robots to emphasize his Southern euphemism, which he topped off with a few choice nonpresidential phrases. One of the rounds separated a toy soldier's right arm from the torso with a shower of sparks, and the red and white robot subsequently shut down, standing in place. The other robot theme creatures continued their advance. An advancing line of Halloween monsters, godmothers, sprites, pixies, animals, aliens, cartoon characters, and even dead presidents pressed toward them, firing automated HVARs as they plodded along.

"Well, what are y'all waiting for?" Moore asked the agents. "Shoot the damned things."

"You heard the president, fire!" Thomas ordered.

The security detail spread out along the perimeter of the Storytime with Belle amphitheater and started to pick targets. As hypervelocity rounds penetrated the robots, they typically would shut down. The theme park robots had been designed for lifelike realism, not for combat, and so the redundancy systems were not designed to withstand having major parts of their circuitry gutted by railgun bullets.

What the robots lacked in toughness, they made up for in numbers. More than seventy strange Disney characters marched toward them from all different directions, one after the other, and there seemed to be no end to the supply of them. The president and his guards would take an advancing line of them down, only for it to be followed by several more. The scene was as abstract as anything out of the old zombie movies from centuries past where the undead just kept coming in wave after wave.

Abigail, where is the evac team?

Less than a minute away, sir.

Just in case, Abigail, you might alert our backup plan.

I've already done that, Mr. President.

"Thomas, I'm running low on ammo, and there has to be more than a thousand red dots on the map!" Alexander checked the clip readout. The little green light displayed the number seventeen. Judging by the many fairy-tale creatures directly in his line of fire and across the river in front of them, the president knew that there were many times that.

"Here, sir," one of the other agents replied, handing him a clip.

"Thanks." Moore nodded at the young woman and then went back to firing his weapon. With each shot, he carefully chose a target from the virtual projection in his mind, and then he raised and fired, more often than not dropping an attacker. So far there had been no casualties in their group, other than those at the Marine One site. The robots seemed to have a problem aiming their weapons at range, and Moore and the bodyguards were keeping them at bay for the time being.

Somehow, whoever was controlling the theme park rides and robots had good intel, because the red dots of the flying vehicles began shifting formations and scattering into less of a sentry pattern and more into an attack pattern. The red flying forces in the virtual map in Moore's head scattered across the Disney World footprint, and in every single case they stayed in groups of two.

They're flying with wingmen, Moore thought to his AIC.

Amazing. It does appear that way, sir.

They must have detected our evac team. Abigail relayed the information to the agents in order to protect them and then continued to monitor the local wireless traffic for further leads.

"Thomas," Moore called to his bodyguard over the M-blaster and railgun noise.

"Yes, sir?"

"Do you have a plan if our backup can't stabilize the situation?"

"I'm working on it, Mr. President, but I don't think it will come to that." Thomas looked upward and nodded toward a squadron of Marine FM-12 strike mecha zooming in from overhead. "I doubt there are enough flying elephants in the world to overpower a squadron of marines in fighting mecha!"

"*Semper fi*, sir," Clay added.

"Oorah," the *once* Major Moore replied. But then again, all marines knew that there was no such thing as a former marine.

"Keep your head down, Dee," Sehera scolded her preteen. The girl was so much like her father that it was all Sehera could do to keep her from trying to run out and kick one of the advancing robots in the crotch. Sehera kept her body on top of her daughter and wedged between the rock wall and the sidewalk on the back side of the amphitheater as far out of the action as they could get—which amounted to about three meters behind the others. One of the bodyguards stretched over the two of them with her weapons drawn but not firing. The president had ordered them not to draw attention to themselves.

"Listen to your mother, *Miss Alexander*. Now is not the time for you to be thinking of any action movie heroics," the agent reinforced the First Lady's scolding and emphasized the similarities between Dee and her father. "It would only take one hit from one of those railgun rounds to do a little girl in."

"That's not stopping Daddy! I want to help. I hate just hiding here like a coward."

"You're not hiding like a coward, Dee," Sehera said. "You're taking cover like a wise person should."

"I can shoot. Give me a gun. I wanna help like Dad. Why does he get to help and we don't?" Deanna squirmed against her bodyguard and her mother's grip. The twelve-year-old was most definitely her father made over. Sehera could hear the railgun rounds ionizing the rock wall all around them. There were strange-looking robots marching toward them and flying overhead shooting at them. Most twelve-year-olds would have been frightened out of their minds beyond reason. But Sehera frowned and kissed her daughter on the forehead, knowing that Dee was pissed off and not scared—just as Alexander had been so many years ago as a POW when they first met.

Moore had been tortured nearly to death and beyond what any human being should have had to endure. The only thing he had been afraid of then was dying before he could get up and impose vengeance upon the bastards who had been inflicting the pain upon him. Once Sehera had managed to help him escape, he didn't leave the Martian desert to return home; instead, he gathered his wits and a whole lot of ordnance and returned in a wake of Hell and damnation. The Separatist soldiers at the encampment far outnumbered him, but they didn't stand a snowball's chance in Hell of stopping him.

Sehera could see that same look on her daughter's face. Dee would have her vengeance for ruining her one and only trip to Disney World. And Heaven help the poor bastards if she ever got loose on them.

"If Dad can do it, so can I!" she resounded defiantly.

"Sweetheart, you will stay put and do what we tell you, and that is enough of that for now. The Secret Service is here to protect us."

"Then why is Daddy fighting?" The tone in Deanna's voice rang true. The three of them looked across the theater benches to see the president rising to fire a handgun several rounds and then duck down for cover behind the rock wall.

"Because, Dee, he is Alexander Moore." Sehera hung her head. There was just no other explanation that would suffice.

CHAPTER 5

October 31, 2388 AD
Tau Ceti Planet Four, Moon Alpha (aka Ares)
New Tharsis Peninsula
Saturday, 5:36 AM, Earth Eastern Standard Time
Saturday, 1:36 AM, Madira Valley Standard Time

Elle Ahmi stood at one of the tall arched windows at the penthouse of the capitol building, looking to the north across Madira Valley at the spaceport several tens of kilometers away. The dome at the vertex of the Separatist leader's home allowed for three hundred and sixty degrees of view through the transparent armored walls. The giant arched windows sat side by side, completely around the office. The lack of opaque materials of the office would frighten sufferers of ago-raphobia beyond their wits. But Elle was paying little attention to it, since her DTM links were buzzing at full bandwidth with battle-plan simulations, planetwide logistics data, food-distribution issues, and a million other things that the Separatist general-turned-leader had to deal with.

The room was reminiscent of the Oval Office in the White House on Earth in that it was a room with a circular floor plan, and it was the room the leader of the nation called his or her office. Where it dif-fered was that Elle actually lived in the room. Her four-poster bed made of Martian oak sat near the east window, so she could watch the Jovian rise several times a day and Tau Ceti rise in the mornings. She also could look out in any direction and see across several states of the Separatist Nation. So maybe it really wasn't like the Oval Office at all—Elle thought of it as better.

The Ares Capitol Building was atop the highest peak of the capitol city of New Tharsis. The peak was an eons-dormant volcano at the center of a broad peninsula that had stretched as high as six kilometers above the Tharsis Sea. To the south, the mountain base stretched all the way to the ocean and then again several kilometers below sea level. That side of the mountain had kilometers of black sandy beaches covered with ancient lava stones. Even before Ares had become the new Separatist Nation, the Earth colonists had chosen the area as an ideal resort location. That side of the mountain was as much like Mauna Kea in Hawaii as any volcano mankind had discovered. At the shore were condominiums and resorts that spread across the beaches. The south-side beaches were the most relaxed culture in the entire nation, and clothing—along with most morals—was definitely optional.

To the north, the mountain stretched down into a plush green valley that wound its way to the northern side of the peninsula and to the ocean. The mountain was covered with tall vegetation and large trees resembling the hybrid Martian oak trees of the Sol System and some that resembled the giant conifers of the western parts of North America on Earth. As the valley twisted toward the ocean, the giant trees stopped, and there flourished canopy trees that resembled those in Costa Rica and Belize. The New Tharsis Peninsula environment encompassed everything from extremely high mountains to tropical rain forests, all within the confines of one Virginia-size peninsula. The area had been a haven for planetary ecologists and biologists when it had first been discovered over a century before.

The northern face Madira Valley was named for one of the greatest and most widely loved presidents in U.S. history, Sienna Madira. Elle always got a smile from that as only a handful of humans alive knew the truth about Sienna Madira. Madira had indeed led the American forces to squash the Martian secession movements and forced them into the Reservation. She had indeed led the Sol System firmly and passionately and fostered a great era for the American people. She had been a great president.

But Sienna Madira hadn't died when the Separatist terrorist cell managed to shoot down Air Force One while on a routine campaign tour of Kuiper Station, as most of humanity thought. Instead, it had been an inside job from the beginning that had been planned for years, even before Madira's unprecedented third term in office. It had taken a system-wide grassroots effort, but enough congressional support was drummed up to overturn the Twenty-Second Amendment of the United States Constitution that had limited presidential terms to two. With the advent of the rejuvenation procedures and medications, people pretty much could live forever or until they were hit by a truck or shot through the head by an HVAR or had a Separatist hauler crash on them. The oldest human to date had been recorded as over three centuries old. This new technology, and the fact that Madira was so loved by the public, made spreading the seed to amend the Constitution easy. There were no longer any term limits for the office of president.

The system was shocked and filled with sorrow when only a year into her third term, President Sienna Madira was killed. Following, there were candlelight vigils for months, and the flag flew at half-mast for nearly a year.

Elle, of course, knew the truth of the matter was that Madira and several of her aides had transformed themselves into a movement to change the government of the Sol System in a manner that, in their minds, would be more natural and beneficial for mankind. Madira and her close followers had long begun to fear that America had become a stagnant welfare state that was being ruled by majority vote. Her inner circle had come to the conclusion that a truly successful nation could not be run by majority, as the majority was not necessarily the smartest group for making tough decisions. Of course, Madira and her followers hadn't bothered to ask the general populace their opinions before making the decision to set events into motion that would change humanity's history forever if they were successful.

To the knowledge of the general public, Air Force One had gone down somewhere in the Kuiper Belt. There were no survivors, and only traces of the spacecraft were found. Madira had her body rejuvenated to that of a woman in her early twenties and let her hair grow long and jet black, which was typical of Martian women and of her heritage. The gray hair and wrinkles gone, Madira was no longer the elder stateswoman. She had become Elle Ahmi, a persona that took credit for the assassination of the greatest president since Lincoln,

Roosevelt, or Reagan. This gave Ahmi immediate credibility as a terrorist organization leader.

After several more years of struggle and terrorist actions, Elle's organization grew and absorbed other cells and factions, making her the undisputed leading terrorist within the Sol System. Ahmi was at the top of every Most Wanted list that the Americans had. Although her name was known throughout the system, she had been extremely cunning in keeping her true appearance and identity unknown. Her body and face had been rejuved; therefore, Ahmi was a young woman who was only videotaped or seen wearing a red, white, and blue ski mask. Only a select few had ever been allowed to see her face. Her true identity being unknown to the general public made it easier for her to operate and to move from location to location without being spotted. It also helped that Elle had been a software engineer most of her life as Madira, and she had spent years preparing and stealing new classified technologies for her movement.

She used her technical savvy to enable productivity within the Separatists that rivaled the economic machine of the United States. She used her carisma to become the catalyst of the Separatist movement, which had taken the Martian Reservation and the Separatist Laborers Guild by emotional storm. After several labor disputes, strikes, walkouts, and some very bloody and devastating battles with the U.S. military, she had risen to the top of the Separatist Reservation and become what could only be described as the supreme ruler of, as she called them, the "Free People."

Even now that she was free from the Sol System and effectively the leader of the Tau Ceti System, she maintained her secret identity. There would always be spies and assassins. And she still had plans to complete. Elle didn't want to rule *just* the Tau Ceti System. Besides, she doubted that America would let one of its colonies fall to the Separatists' rule for long. So rather than wait for the military might of the Sol System to come to her, she planned on taking the fight back across the stars to Earth—and soon. Everything was going according to plans that she had made and followed for decades and decades. There were plans in motion even at the present, on Ares and on Earth.

Elle turned from the windows and sauntered across the cavernous circular penthouse—her bare feet that squeaked against the hardwood flooring echoed in the mostly empty room with each step. Straightening her blouse and unsnapping one of the fasteners at the top, she sat down at her Queen Anne style desk, not sure whether she should keep on working or take a break. For a brief moment, she closed her eyes and rested her head against the back of the chair. The DTM information came into her mind fast and furious and continuous even though she made an attempt to relax.

Copernicus?

Ma'am?

Shut off the mindlink for a moment, will you?

Yes, ma'am. The DTM virtual sphere went blank in her mind.

Elle sat quietly and tried to relax her shoulders and her thoughts, but even without the DTM pouring images into her brain at high bandwidth, her mind still raced with anxiety and what-ifs. But exhaustion was slowly taking its toll on her, and after a couple of minutes, she nearly dozed off. Her head slumped forward and startled her awake.

She opened her dark eyes wide and blinked a few times, then rubbed the bridge of her nose with her thumb and forefinger. Elle exhaled between her lips, making a soft motorboat sound. She gazed out the window across the valley at her dominion, at the results of her decades of planning and action, and took the brief moment to smile triumphantly. Once she had taken in all she could from that viewpoint, she ordered her AIC to increase the magnification of the northern portrait window. The scene zoomed all the way to the northern coastline of the New Tharsis Peninsula, which was sixty kilometers or more away. Separatist haulers, frigates, battle cruisers, and mecha were coming and going like a flurry of insects in a very busy colony—like a colony preparing for a full-scale war.

The colony at Ares had already consisted of nearly seven million people before the Separatist Exodus from the Sol System. More than thirty million had teleported from Sol's Oort Cloud to Tau Ceti nearly five years prior. Since that time, the population of the Tau Ceti System had grown to approximately fifty million. All who were old enough were working hard on the war machine.

For the most part, the fifty million Separatist citizens were free to do whatever they wanted as long as it did not interfere with the overall plans that Ahmi had laid out for them. The society was almost completely capitalist and very open although it was predominantly run by networks of businesswomen.

From the beginning, Elle had singled out strong women that she could trust and put them in charge of upper echelon terrorist cells. The main goal of those cells was to usurp as much power from the legitimate Reservation businesses as they could. After several decades, there were no businesses within the Martian Reservation that weren't controlled by the Separatist movement. The women managed to maintain their power positions by following Elle's example and by putting other women they trusted in cells as their lieutenants or as leaders of cells adjacent or beneath them. Sometimes men were put in those positions, but most of the women tended to "be like Elle."

After some time, it became clear that the business leaders of the Separatists were women, and a matriarchal culture of multiple wife families arose as the norm around the business society. Men were still equal, but there were just more women who had made it to the top and managed to stay there.

Purposefully, again from the beginning, Elle had placed men in charge of the actual "boots on the ground" terrorist cells. The outcome of that approach had been to generate a military arm that was led mostly by men. Elle had come to believe from her personal experience with men that it was easier to manipulate them into hostile and dangerous action than it was women. Machismo and bravado were emotions that she could readily manipulate. Men were better at war, and women were better at business, she thought. It was her personal preference, whether there was actual truth to her beliefs or not. Her being the head terrorist-in-charge was enough to make the belief embedded in the culture for good.

As the Separatist Laborers Guild grew and became an extremely powerful economic engine, fiscal classes began to emerge. Effectively, within the Separatist society, there was an upper class of business-women and an upper class of warrior men. There were likewise many others in classes from poor to wealthy. The culture mimicked the cellular leadership structure from top to bottom. It was common in most families that the dominant wife led the household and ran it with the help of several other wives, while the men were in some form or other connected to military matters. There were, of course, men in business and women in the military, but the average was the other way around.

Copernicus, normal zoom on all windows, please, she told her AIC.

Yes, ma'am.

The window decreased to normal zoom. The sky was filled with stars, and the limb of the gaseous, giant planet that Ares orbited was beginning to peek over the horizon, bringing a faint violet hue to the night sky that Elle had grown to love. The view from the Capitol Building was nothing less than breathtaking.

Make the dome transparent, Copernicus. And you can turn the DTM desktop back on.

Yes, ma'am. Ah, Sol is rising just above the horizon now. Her AIC switched the polarity of the electromagnetic field on the armor, changing the ceiling of the dome from opaque to clear. Sol was just rising above the Jovian's rings in the constellation Boötes. The star of her birth world, Mars, was nearly twelve light-years away and appeared as a bright, second-magnitude star in the constellation. It was a wonderful view of the heavens but was mostly lost on Elle, as most of her attention reverted back to the datastreams coming in through the direct-to-mind link, describing the macroscopic details of the Separatist Nation.

Ma'am?

Yes?

Scotty would like to see you now if you are available. Your calendar is free for the next few hours. You have a sleep cycle scheduled.

Send him in.

Yes, ma'am. He is bug-free as best we can tell. When Copernicus assured Elle that someone was bug-free, the odds were high that that was indeed the case. Elle had seen to it decades earlier that Copernicus was the smartest AI she could find, and her penthouse had all the latest scanners known to humanity.

Elle sat back in her desk chair and looked at a picture frame sitting next to her redwood pen and pencil set. The frame held a picture in it that Scotty had given her at the end of the Exodus day. Elle examined the picture fondly and picked it up with both hands while tracing the outline of the picture with her thumbs. It was in a nice Mars cherry tree wood frame and covered with an anti-glare pane of glass. The photograph it held was of the newly elected Democratic President Sienna Madira with the freshly congressionally approved Supreme Court Chief Justice Scotty P. Mueller. The chief justice had just sworn in the new president, and they were shaking hands. There was handwriting on the picture that amused Elle to no end. She laughed at it as the memory of autographing the photo flooded her mind. It was a quote that she had often used in her term as president—one that she had stolen from a centuries-past president, Ronald Reagan:

"*The best minds are not in government; if they were, business would hire them away.* Thanks, Sienna Madira, President of the United States of America."

Elle sat the photo back on her desk at the southwest window, which was slightly open. Scotty casually strolled toward her with a blank stare on his face. Elle was pretty certain from the look that he was reading something DTM. She didn't interrupt but instead watched him as he stood in thought for a few more seconds.

"General, thanks for seeing me," Scotty said as the stare melted to a smile. The two had known each other for decades. They had died together and had also been resurrected together. They had planned the Exodus and the movements of historical events in at least three star systems together, and there was more to come. Much more to come.

"We're alone, Scotty," she said. "Well, other than Socks over there." Elle nodded to the kitty at the foot of her bed.

"Meow," the artificial intelligence kitty replied.

"Aww, Socks. Now come here, kitty," Elle called to her AIK. The artificial cat jumped up from its comfy bed and ran across the hardwood floor with a pitter-pat of tabby feet and then nuzzled up to Elle's shins and purred. Unless the AIK was analyzed with quantum-membrane technology sensors or it was torn apart and examined, it was indiscernible from a real orange tabby cat. Elle picked up the AIK and gently stroked the robotic pet's fur. It continued to purr softly, which soothed Elle's nerves. She relaxed in her desk chair and continued to scratch behind the cat's ears.

"Oh, well then, if we are alone, it is good to see you, Madam President," Scotty said earnestly.

"Oh, knock that shit off will you, Scotty?" Elle said with a dismissing wave of her hand. "What can I do for you at such a late hour?"

What time is it anyway, Copernicus?

1:36 AM, ma'am.

"Well, Elle, I've been running some more simulations of the election, and I think today could be too early to make the assassination attempt. It won't impact the large group of voters at Luna City anyway, and that is where this election is going to be lost or won. The values we used for the GROWTH-star and the WAR-sub-t coefficients seem to be low when you consider the economic fuel that Moore has created in his military buildup. And the DURATION-sub-t and the a7 coefficients just seem to me to be pulled out of thin goddamned air. If you ask me—"

"Scotty." Ahmi held up her hand to stop the former chief justice. Scotty paused midsentence. "Listen, Copernicus and I have hashed through the dynamic models of the general elections and economics and behavior of the Sol System over and over, and every simulation we have run curve-fits to those values. Granted, Luna City could prove to be a problem in this election, but we'll just have to overcome that with the press. You've been in on the sims from the beginning. You know good and damned well that we've even used the weather-control data, sunspot activity, and literally more than a million other factors in this model. It is probably the most complicated scientific model of human culture ever generated. If we weren't using it to over-throw a government or two, we'd probably get a Nobel Prize for it. Granted, there are a lot of moving parts, but the model is good. So don't go getting cold feet on me now."

"I realize all the work we've put into the model, Elle, but it still almost seems like magic rather than mathematics." Scotty rubbed the one o'clock shadow growing on his chin and then threw his hands up. "I'm not going to get you to change your mind on this, am I? Something could happen at the last minute on Tuesday morning that could shift the election. Whether we want that damned bullheaded Mississippi redneck marine in office or the Ivy League brat, we might not be able to alter the outcome of the election if we impact events too early or too late."

"Sorry, the plan is already in place, and it is too late to stop it. And we sure as hell don't need to go monkeying around with things at the last minute without having simmed the outcome. Now, is that all you had on your mind?" Elle leaned back in her chair and propped her feet up on her desk. Her skirt slid to knee level, revealing her athletic legs and the fact that she wasn't wearing hose—they were curled up on the floor next to her boots and had been there for hours. Elle stretched her arms wide over her long black ponytail with a yawn. "It's getting late."

"I'm not certain what else to say about it then. I guess you *have* been right, pretty much, for about fifty years now. Or you've been really goddamned lucky," Scotty joked. "You know, you should try to take a break, Elle. You look tired."

"I've been tired for about forty years, Scotty. Knowing that I'm gonna burn in Hell for all eternity will do that to a person." She added the last comment as an old joke the two of them had shared for years. When they first had the plan of developing a Separatist organization, Scotty had warned her of the potential carnage that could result. Ahmi—President Madira at the time—had assured her chief justice that burning in Hell to create a truly functional world for all people was worth it. Scotty had commented to her that she almost sounded nuts. President Madira laughed and again explained that that would be another good reason for burning.

Elle raised her left eyebrow to her old friend in an invitingly flirtatious way. "But we're all gonna burn for something. Besides, I'm thinking about taking a break, though I could think of better things to do than sleep."

"Why, Madam President, whatever would you have in mind?" Scotty closed the distance to her slowly, yet deliberately, and took Elle's hand, helping her to her feet. Elle stepped towrd him as Scotty wrapped his arms around her. Lost in the moment, a flurry of action between them and toward the bedroom side of the penthouse ensued. Scotty slid his hand down the small of Elle's back to her firm buttocks and then grasped them solidly as he kissed her. In return, Elle tightened the muscles there with a slight quiver of her thighs and pulled Scotty tightly into her lips. After exploring his mouth vigorously with her tongue, she pushed him back with both hands, planting them on his chest—her fingertips massaging into his pectoral muscles. She then slid them down his stomach to his waist, fingering at his waistband. Elle continued to push him backward until they both nearly tripped as they stepped on the AIK's tail.

"Meeoow!" Socks wailed as he made like a rocket across the room to hide underneath the desk.

"Oh, shit, sorry kitty," Elle managed to say, muffled between kisses and fumbling with Scotty's belt buckle. She backed him up against the Martian oak bed and pushed him backward onto it while at the same time untying her ponytail. Scotty rose up and pulled the fasteners loose on her blouse and then slid it over her milky white Martian shoulders to the floor. The leader of the Separatist Army and Nation stood topless in front of her most trusted male companion and eyed him like a tiger about to devour its prey. The two of them had decided years before that they were going to get lonely at the top unless they added some extracurricular activities to their friendship. Sex had turned out to be the best one they could think of.

With a swish of her head, left-to-right, her long black hair fell softly over her naked shoulders, hanging just over her firm breasts, her erect nipples peeking out between strands of her glistening hair. Scotty grasped both breastly gently but firmly in his hands and eyed her hungrily.

Dim the lights, Copernicus, she thought. Her AIC dimmed the room lights and left the windows and dome transparent. He didn't reply, as he surely would regret interrupting unless he had to. *Yeah, that's good.*

Elle grabbed Scotty's dress shirt and ripped it apart and then pushed him backward again. He lost his balance and plunged down onto the bed. This time she crawled on top of him, fondling his chest and biting at his neck and torso. She paused and looked into his eyes and then bit his lower lip, tugging it just hard enough to stimulate and not leave a mark. Her tongue again searched into his mouth eagerly, as eagerly as a teenager kissing for the first time. Scotty's tongue returned the exploration genuinely. Their most recent rejuves had left both of them with very early twenty-something bodies, and they definitely reacted that way sexually—a well documented side effect of the rejuve process.

Elle shivered with chill bumps and writhed ecstatically to the feel of Scotty's hand squeezing her left breast. She leaned her head back, shaking the hair out of his way, and again he grasped her firmly with both hands, a hand to each breast. Her enthusiasm only increased, like pouring pure rum on a red hot flame, as Scotty tugged eagerly at her aroused nipples. She raised and jostled her hair over her face again before she slithered off the bed and back to his belt. The zipper and snaps went easily aside and she knelt to the floor in order to slide his trousers and underwear off, dragging her long, free hair across his naked crotch and legs, teasing him with the tickling sensation.

Somehow in the passionate throes, Scotty had already managed to kick off his shoes and was toeing at his socks frantically. Elle helped him finish removing them with a gentle caress of his toes and then a slight nibble at his left foot. She eased upward, kissing and nibbling at his legs, with her hands exploring his body as she rose. She kneaded his thigh muscles as she kissed his calf, and then she kissed his thighs.

Elle grasped Scotty's penis gently at first between her right thumb and forefinger and fondled it carefully before her. Then she firmly and more aggressively gripped it with her entire hand, while unzipping her skirt the rest of the way with her left hand. All gentleness finally thrown aside, she took him into her mouth with the same unwavering concentration that she would any task or battle plan. Goose bumps rushed in a wave over her skin as her skirt hit the floor. With a rhythmic motion, Elle worked over Scotty for a few moments longer. The motion of each of her down strokes was emphasized with his blissful moans. The pale violet hues of the gas planet filled the room, casting strange flickering shadows of their undulating motion across the hardwood floor. The strangeness of the lighting and shadows added a sharp edge to the mood and titillated their visual sense.

The taste of him in her mouth and the feel of his strong hands running through her hair and down her back fueled her desire for Scotty to the boiling point. Elle looked up and caught his eye and kissed her way up his stomach, stopping to bite his right nipple. Scotty flinched slightly at the bite but didn't protest. His flinch triggered Elle to bite him again and again in soft, slow, nibbles across his chest and up the side of his neck. She bit into him and lingered there, feeling his pulse rush through his carotid artery with her tongue before she continued up to his mouth. Elle tugged with his lower lip between her teeth and then playfully kissed him.

Finally, she wriggled like a cat on top of him and pushed him into her. Elle exhaled with each rhythmic thrust and rocked her hips forward then back. Her body and his bounced against the mattress of the old bed, producing a faint squeaking of the Martian oak posts against the floor. Then and there, that moment, the few rare moments like that that Elle and Scotty had managed over the past few decades, those moments were the most real to each of them and the moments where they felt truly alive. The two would-be, most-wanted terrorists in the known galaxy forgot all about plans to destroy America and revolutions and wars for a fleeting, frolicking moment. They weren't in love, but it was the closest thing either of them could manage under the circumstances.

Elle moaned softly as her breathing quickened and her back tensed. The faint squeaking of the bedposts against the floor grew louder and faster, and the strange lighting from the Jovian, now nearly half-risen, caused their motion to be overemphasized from shadows dancing hysterically across the room. She could sense that Scotty was getting close to climax as well.

"That's it, Scotty," she sighed. And then she sighed again as her toes curled into the comforter of her bed and she gripped Scotty harder and bit down on his left earlobe.

Ma'am, I've got an urgent alert from the spaceport at Madira Valley Beach, her AIC interrupted just as Scotty let go. His body shook, and he exhaled forcefully three times. With each exhale, he dug his fingernails down Elle's back, leaving light pink scratches in her pale epidermis. Then he relaxed his neck muscles and let his head fall back onto the bed, followed by a final grunt of ecstasy. Elle's DTM virtual sphere kicked alive with alerts and other *distracting* data.

"Unhh," she moaned and shivered a final time, and then as if someone had thrown a switch, immediately snapped out of the mood and into Elle Ahmi, Separatist Leader mode. It was as if someone had screamed "Incoming!" and she had jerked to scrambling for cover and her weapon. *Nobody'd better be fucking with my plans!*

"Elle . . ."

"Goddamnit!" she cursed, startling Scotty out of the moment and completely destroying the mood for each of them. There was work to be done, but Elle didn't have to like it. *Turn the damn lights on. Fuck.*

"What the . . . Elle?" Scotty looked at her, bewildered and squinting from the light in his eyes.

"What kind of alert?" she said verbally.

There has been a security incident, and several soldiers and guards have been killed, the AIC reported.

What do you mean security incident?

Vital information to the battle plans has been downloaded: some background information on you, the Oort Cloud facility, and knowledge of the QMT-4 prototype, the AIC replied.

"Shit!" As if the encounter had never happened, Elle was in General Ahmi mode and was standing at her bedside, pulling her uniform out of a drawer near her bed and getting dressed. "Who, and how, Copernicus? Go speakers for Scotty."

"Yes, ma'am," the AIC's voice filled the room. "There may be more data that she copied, but nobody is certain of that yet. Also, there is no identification on her, but it appears to be a young red-haired woman of average build. My guess is that her physical appearance is under disguise if this is a professional attempt. Somehow the security cameras were overridden, and there is no image of her available. She managed to infiltrate a battle cruiser and hack into the secure network. All of this does suggest a pro. CIA perhaps?"

"Too early to guess. Damn. All right, find her. Alive! We need to know what she knows." Elle looked at Scotty, who was still lying naked and spent on her bed with a tired and very angry expression. Her sleep cycle would have to wait. "It's always something.

"We have to go, Scotty," Elle said as she stormed to the edge of the penthouse toward the door and donned the forever-present red, white, and blue ski mask. She pulled her long black hair into a ponytail through the hole in the back of the mask and slapped the door open, never bothering to look back at her lover. "Copernicus, have my Lorda troop lifter ready. Come on, Scotty."

CHAPTER 6

October 31, 2388 AD
Tau Ceti Planet Four, Moon Alpha (aka Ares)
Madira Valley Beach Spaceport
Saturday, 5:40 AM, Earth Eastern Standard Time
Saturday, 1:40 AM, Madira Valley Standard Time

Any luck, Allison? Kira thought to her AIC. After the altercation in the stockroom, she had been having a hard time avoiding interaction with the Seppy battle cruiser's security detachments. The entire ship knew that she was there now, and she had been lying low for the better part of half an hour, trying to come up with a new escape plan. She had heard several announcements over the ship's 1MC intercom for all hands to watch for the intruder. And *that* wasn't good.

No. The structural integrity fields of the ship's outer hull have all been activated, and I haven't been able to find a way through them yet. Kira knew that Allison was a smart AIC and had trained all her life—ever since her AI family had activated her—to hack codes. It was fun to her, which was part of why she had followed the path to becoming an AIC for an intelligence operative. It was just a matter of time before she would figure a way out of the ship's structural integrity fields (SIFs).

Well, the longer we stay, the less chance we have for getting the hell out of here, Kira urged her. *Can we blow a SIF generator somewhere?*

I've looked at that, Allison responded. *The generators are really deep in the ship. And I'd suspect that is the one direction we should avoid since I'm certain the Seppies have thought of that approach too.*

Shit. We can't just wait around. Sooner or later, somebody is gonna find us.

I understand, Allison replied. The two of them had been together a long time, and there was no real need for Kira to tell her such obvious things—of course they couldn't just keep waiting around, and Allison understood that. The AIC had always found it interesting how humans had a habit of trying to add stress to a situation with hopes of making it better. It neither helped nor hindered the AI. It was more data, however. And Kira liked to nudge her AI partner-in-crime a little every now and then just to keep her motivated.

What if I steal a ship and blast out? Kira squirmed a bit against the coolant pipe that she had been becoming one with for about the past thirty-five minutes. She had gotten used to the periodic yellow flash of the warning lights flickering off the dull gray interior walls of the battle cruiser.

She had almost grown comfortable on her perch. There had been several close calls when troops had hurriedly marched underneath her down the hallway to the hatch at the aft end of the hangar. The hangar had been her original plan, but now she wasn't sure that it was really much of a plan more than just a general idea or a natural instinct to run for the door. All would have worked fine had she not slipped up and let that damned stock clerk sneak up behind her the way she did. After more than four years of working undercover as a second wife in a rich household, Kira was afraid that she was getting soft and sloppy. The immunobooster she had given herself as soon as she had the opportunity to hide and recover was doing its job. The injection had almost completely healed the railgun wound in her arm. The adrenaline and pain meds in it had also reduced the throbbing to a point that she didn't remember the wound being there—well, at least she no longer paid attention to it.

Maybe. Let me run some numbers real quick, Allison replied.

Well, do it quick. I'm getting tired of just sitting around. Kira was skeptical that just a shuttle ramming the SIF-protected hull from the inside would be enough to get out. On the other hand, the SIFs were designed to protect ships from external threats, not internal ones.

Do you still remember how to fly mecha? Allison asked.

Man, I was hoping you weren't gonna say that. It had been years since the skirmish in New Africa, where Kira had been undercover in the resistance as a mecha pilot. Years. And that mecha was *way* different than modern-day mecha. If push came to shove, Allison could always walk her through it, provided there would be time enough to do so.

I think I have a plan, Kira. First you have to get aboard one of those shuttles at the starboard side of the bay. Then we can hack it to fly the profile we need.

Okay. Sounds easy enough. Then what?

Then you have to steal an Orcus drop tank or a Stinger and follow in behind it at the precise moment the shuttle crashes into the SIF, Allison instructed. *The field will weaken enough for a few tens of milliseconds so that the mecha can pass through it and survive. At that point, I would recommend ejecting from the mecha, as it will likely be in rough shape.*

Oh, is that all? I just have to steal a troop shuttle, which I might add is waaay the fuck over there. Then we hack it. Then I steal a mecha. Then I fly the mecha through a fireball, where the troop shuttle smashes into the hull with millisecond timing before the SIF snaps back into place crushing me. Oh yes, and then ejecting from the now blown-to-hell-and-gone mecha. All without getting caught, shot, or killed. Does that sound about right? Kira replied. The sarcastic overtone in her mindlink voice resounded like a heavy-metal bass guitar.

Yes, that about covers it. Allison was unphased by Kira's wit.

Piece of cake! Well, at least it was a plan, and it would be a damned sight better than staying hugged up against the cold metal coolant pipe she was on. Condensation was gathering on the pipe where her body was touching it, causing droplets of moisture to collect and run down her skin. It didn't help her grip on the thing at all.

Just one thing more, Allison.

What's that?

Let's try to steal me a Stinger, Kira said. *They are waay cooler than those damned drop tanks.*

Allison ignored the comment, saying, *From what I can tell, the mecha are stored on drop hooks above the shuttles in the high-bay part of the hangar. If we get close enough to them, I might be able to hack in on the QM wireless channels.*

Kira searched the corridor forward and aft for any hint of motion and could see nothing. She strained her hearing to its limit to listen for bootsteps against the deck plating. Nothing. After assuring herself that the coast was indeed clear, she dropped herself down from the overhanging conduit. Her boots clanked to the floor and made a faint echo down the hallway.

Goddamnit, that was clumsy, Kira thought.

Perhaps if you'll bang the stunner against the bulkhead, you'll get better results? Allison had been counterpart to Kira for so long that her sour wit had rubbed off on the AIC.

Nobody likes a smartass, Allison.

I like you. Allison played a comedic drum roll to follow her zinger.

Touché, Kira grinned. She made a quick scan in both directions and then quickly began to slink toward the open hatchway into the hangar bay.

Across the bay on the starboard side were several troop shuttles similar to the U.S. Starhawk SH-102s. Most of the Seppy vehicles tended to resemble the U.S. countersystems but in cheaper, more rugged, and less tech-savvy versions. The Seppy troop shuttles were no exception.

Kira had flown the troop shuttles before and with Allison's help could fairly easily hotwire one. It was getting across the bay that was going to be the hard part. The ship was locked down, but it was a big ship—nearly a half kilometer long and a quarter of that wide—and just waltzing across the hangar would be risky, but probably the least suspicious approach. Even though there were guards scattered about, there were also crew chiefs and enlisted men and women going about their daily grind of keeping the battle cruiser operational. The daily grind was her best shot. *Fit in and look like you belong,* she thought to herself.

Kira noticed a tool rack about ten meters to her right. She casually entered the hatch and pulled a pair of welding goggles and a handheld directed energy cutter from the rack. She flipped the safety and toggled the welder beam a few times, flashing the bright white-pink plasma on and off, and then smiled approvingly.

To complete her disguise, she also strapped on a set of knee and elbow pads and a reflective vest that was hanging from a hook near the tools. She pushed the cutting visor up on her forehead and started in a straight line across the bay to the nearest unattended shuttle. The forty meters or more to the troop carrier seemed more like an astronomical unit, but after a little less than a minute, she had closed the gap to it.

So far so good, Kira thought.

Nobody seems to have noticed us. Allison began handshaking with the vehicle as soon as she was in wireless QM range. The ship asked for a password. Allison ignored it and set about hacking other wireless weak points in its security system. The exterior sensors on the vehicle had both active and passive capabilities and were perfect entrances to the ship's control systems. Of course, there were firewalls, but the sensors were harder to protect from subtle electronic attack.

Kira, on the other hand, was less subtle. The troop hatch was wide open, and the ramp sat against the deck. Kira sauntered up the ramp, still unnoticed, and applied the directed energy cutter to the hardwire cables between the command console and the low-level controller AI. The AI was instantly cut off from the rest of the ship other than through wireless, but Allison was jamming that by raising the QM wireless carrier-to-noise level within the shuttle with her own broadband transmissions. Kira pulled the small black AI chassis from the computer rack and tossed it into the copilot's seat. She then set about cutting the box itself open and kept digging into it with the cutter until she found the small sunflower-seed-shaped, plastic-coated casing of the AI. Kira held the beam of the cutter to the small device, vaporizing the artificial life with a quick foul smell of burned plastic followed with a short white flash of light. Kira kept her mind focused on the job and kept only a cold background awareness of the life she'd just extinguished.

Can you program the shuttle controller?

Already on it, Allison informed her.

Can you do it from a distance? Kira asked.

Why?

Because, here comes somebody! Shit, too late. We'll have to sit tight. Kira ducked down behind the pilot's chair as best she could manage, trying to stay out of sight. The chair swiveled with a faint squeak as she twisted her body around the flight control panel and into a decent hiding place.

A man in orange overalls entered the vehicle from the ramp and sat what could only be described as a "big fucking wrench" or "BFW" against the bulkhead with a *kachunk* beside the heavy-caliber HVAR mounted at the gunner's seat. He pulled a cordless ratchet from a tool apron and went about removing several bolts at the base of the gun. Kira sat quietly and watched cautiously as the tech continued about his work. He grunted a few times as he dug his fingers underneath the panel and pulled. The panel screeched metal against metal and came free. The tech almost lost his balance and he cursed briefly. Once he had taken the front panel off of the gun's ammo housing, he slipped the ratchet back into the proper slot on his toolbelt and reached over for the BFW. All the while between grunts and curses, the man whistled to himself off-key versions of current pop songs. Kira almost recognized one of them.

Got it. The ship is under my control now, Allison told her.

What about a mecha?

I'm handshaking with one in the drop-down rack above us. There are access codes for some of the Stingers in the shuttle's database. Long story short, I hack, therefore I am.

Good job! How do I get there?

We'll fly up to it. But we should wait until I've finished hacking it and got it warmed up and ready to go.

You think we should wait on our friend in there? Kira added, pointing to the tech fiddling with the gunner's station. He dropped something that rattled across the floor of the shuttle. A large bolt bounced on the dull gray metal and continued to roll down the walkway into the cockpit and up underneath the pilot's chair. *Shit,* Kira thought.

"Shit," the tech mumbled to himself, only absentmindedly interrupting his whistling. He sat the BFW down and turned to chase after the bolt. Dropping to his hands and knees, the tech tracked the bolt to the pilot's chair. The bolt wasn't there, but a black boot was. To his surprise, and quite unfortunately, he found the bolt in the worst way. Kira twisted upright in front of him holding it up at face level.

"Lose something?" she asked, and startled the tech by jamming the bolt through his right eye. Quick, quiet, and very deadly, Kira raked the directed energy beam cutter across the man's throat, toggling the white-pink, hot plasma beam on and severing his head completely from his body. Both of which fell to the deck plate with a thud. The beam cauterized the cuts and there was very little blood. A low gurgling sound came from the man's esophagus, and some red murky fluids oozed slowly from it with each failing heartbeat. Kira looked away. "Sorry, dude. Wrong place, wrong time."

You know, you could have used the stunner, Allision thought.

No witnesses and too noisy. Dead men can't testify or be probed.

Understood.

Are you jamming his AIC? Kira asked.

He didn't have one, Allison assured her. It was not uncommon for Seppies not to carry AIs because of the aftermath of the "mind police." A few decades before, Elle Ahmi had used AIC implants to reprogram Separatist cell leaders and to interrogate her people to expunge any who had sympathetic views toward the United States. The effectiveness of Ahmi's brainwashing and cleansing efforts was widely debated by the intelligence community, but it had created enough fear within the Seppies that many of them wouldn't even consider carrying AIs. Many others (the intel community had also learned) thought it was just a silly myth and depended on AICs as much as people in the U.S. did. But the latter were the younger crowd that hadn't lived through the cleansing. But for troops, tankheads, and mecha pilots, AICs were a necessity, and they typically had the implants. Some of them did wear external AICs so that they could discard them if they felt the need. Elle had managed to keep most of them out of command positions. If a Separatist commander wasn't willing to have an AIC implant, he wasn't worthy and loyal enough to serve Ahmi from a leading position of any relevance. And Elle couldn't keep tabs on them as well, otherwise.

Okay then, he was a nobody. You got me a mecha ready yet?

Patience, Allison replied. Just as she did, the engines of the shuttle spun up and lifted the vehicle off of the staging platform. The deck plating of the little spaceship rumbled and reverberated from the engine's hum. *I'm quite certain that we are attracting attention at this point.*

What makes you say that? Kira felt the ship list sideways and then heard the sound of HVAR rounds pinging against the exterior armor. *Shit! Those idiots are firing railguns in the hangar. No telling what they'll hit.*

Yeah, like us. I'd suggest you keep your head down.

Good advice! Kira ducked reflexively as a hypervelocity round spalled against the forward screen of the cockpit with a brilliant flash of purple and blue ionization. Several rounds followed it, spalling with a thumping sound and leaving a long growing crack in the transparent armor. The rounds ionizing against the armor continued to flash. The armor wouldn't last much longer. Apparently, it wasn't as well made as the U.S. ship's.

One Seppy Stinger mecha, just as you ordered. Allison yawed the shuttle about and an eagle-mode Stinger pulled up beside the open troop hatch of the shuttle. The mecha's right hand reached out toward the side door of the shuttle and kept formation perfectly. The fighter looked like a hybrid between a bird of prey, with clawed feet and wings swept back ready to pounce, and a large metal beast, with humanlike hands.

Railgun fire continued to ping and slap against the ship. Several rounds came through the open door just past Kira's head. The rounds sizzled through equipment on the other side of the vehicle, throwing sparks and metal splinters about. Kira flinched and covered her face to avoid being blinded.

The cockpit of the Stinger cycled open and tilted slightly toward them, giving Kira her cue. Kira took two running steps from the shuttle and leaped across the gap between the door and the mecha's outstretched hand. Her right boot touched the mecha just long enough for her to make another jump like a track and field star doing the triple jump. She dove headfirst, tumbling clumsily into the pilot's couch of the mecha and slamming her healing arm against the control console.

"Ouch, shit!" she cried out. As she impacted the seat, the cockpit cycled shut, and the mecha pulled upward in evasive maneuvers, bouncing her around violently.

Squirming into the controls of the mecha while trying to ignore new bumps and bruises, she pulled the fighter away and above the shuttle to use it as cover. The high bay was only about twenty-five meters to the ceiling, and there were mecha and other equipment hanging down that made flying too far off the deck like flying through a maze. Dodging and maneuvering around the maze while being shot at and trying to strap in just added a more exciting level of difficulty to her task. Hell, it was almost fun—except for the small fact that people all around her were trying to kill her.

Kira pulled the six-point harness straps around her and fumbled to close the buckles. The mag-seal buckles pulled together and sealed her in place in the pilot's seat. The helmet that had been sitting on the dashboard was jostled free and flew into her nose as the plane pitched and rolled upward to keep its cover position behind the shuttle. Kira tried to ignore the wet trickle of blood running down her left nostril onto her upper lip and squinted away the tears forming in the corners of her eyes.

I suggest you put that on, Allison warned her.

Right, Kira replied, and rubbed at her nose and eyes with a thumb and forefinger. *Okay! Let's go.*

Kira's hands uncomfortably fit over the hands-on throttle and stick (HOTAS) and searched for fire controls. It had been a long time since she had flown mecha. Allison guided her as best she could and in some cases took control for milliseconds. But each time she had to take control of the mecha, she had to put the shuttle on autopilot, which Kira had torn out and torched to death so that the shuttle would fly uncontrolled with a locked-in vector for those instances. After a few seconds of bumping and crashing and thrashing around, Kira finally got the hang of the mecha. Sort of.

"Like riding a bicycle!"

Yeah, one that has a shitload of bells and whistles, buttons, levers, controls, and foot pedals on it, Allison said. *We're taking some serious fire.*

"Warning, incoming hypervelocity fire. Warning, evasive maneuvers required," the Bitchin' Betty—the mecha's automated warning system—alerted her.

No shit!

"Guns, guns, guns," Kira said, spraying the directed energy gun's blue-green bolt across the hangar. The large directed energy gun in the left hand of the eagle-mode mecha swept left to right, firing bolt after bolt at the Seppy troops and techs below. Impact and secondary explosions erupted with each new energy bolt. "Let's get the hell out of here!"

This way. Allison illuminated a flight trajectory in the DTM virtual display. The spherical map around her head showed a path for her to follow. The trajectory led them downward and across the hangar toward the aft end of the compartment. *See if you can soften the wall right there!* A red X appeared in her virtual view on the aft hangar wall.

Got it. Kira toggled the fighter left and scrolled the weapons list to missiles with her pinky finger on the HOTAS. "Fox three! Fox three!" she shouted, loosening two mecha-to-mecha missiles careening and spiraling wildly through the hangar. The two missiles tracked a purple ion trail across the room and vanished with an orange and white fireball on the hangar blast doors. The percussion wave tossed equipment, vehicles, and Seppies in all different directions, resulting in a reduction of incoming railgun fire.

More!

"Guns, guns, guns! Fox three!" She poured more energy into the same spot. "Railgun auto, fire!" The big forty-millimeter railgun cannon on the belly of the mecha began chunking armored rounds at large fractions of the speed of light into the bulkhead SIF marked in the DTM with a big red X. Cannon rounds, directed energy bolts, and missiles exploded against the force field with ripples of blue evanescence across the surface and with the orange and white flames of vaporizing bulkhead.

Full throttle, now!

The shuttle zoomed out from underneath the Stinger at max thrust and slammed into the already weakened blast wall. The craft's velocity generated whirlwinds in the growing fireball as it slammed through. The impact of the armored troop carrier against the molten metal flung red-hot composite and alloy materials in a violent, deadly splash backward, washing the hangar and setting most of the room ablaze. Large chunks of armor plating ejected like magma from an exploding volcano, pinging against the mecha.

Kira was right behind the shuttle and could see, and feel, the shrapnel and secondary blasts pounding against the forward armor plating of the fighter mecha, leaving smoldering flames on the nose and wingtips. She rolled and pitched the mecha wildly to avoid the larger pieces of flying debris as best she could manage. The last bit of the shuttle poked through the structural integrity field and vaporized into a violent fiery finale. The SIF separated in a cascade of rippling circles radially across the hull of the ship, putting undesirable torques and squeezes in the alloy surface of the battle cruiser. Armor plates buckled, and weld joints popped free from the stresses and strains of the extremely high electromagnetic fields generated by the oscillating SIF. Smaller explosions erupted, and smoke and gases poured from damage across the exterior hull of the Separatist ship. The SIFs were designed to protect the ship from exterior threats, not interior ones. Fortunate for Kira and Allison, the ship's force field designers had never considered an attack from within.

The breach in the SIF continued to ripple like waves on a pond, expanding outward from a pebble that had been dropped into it, phosphorescing at each crest and valley. Kira held the HOTAS full forward and plowed through at maximum velocity. If the field collapsed back together, she wanted it to be over with as quickly as possible. The fireball consumed the fighter for a brief instant, and Kira ground her teeth and prayed that the SIF didn't regain strength at the wrong microsecond. She was lucky. Allison was good.

The mecha burst through the other side of the fireball in a tornado of shear forces, and the battle cruiser's exterior-mounted automated-defense systems started firing anti-aircraft weapons at her immediately.

Out of the frying pan!

Indeed.

Kira yanked and banked the HOTAS with her right hand and continued to push full-throttle forward on the stick. The g-forces pressed her body into the seat with the weight of a small hovercar on her chest, nearly knocking her unconscious since she was not wearing a g-suit. Kira realized all too quickly that she couldn't take the forces of combat without the proper gear and would have to get out of this vehicle as soon as possible.

Bursting out of the side of a battle cruiser in dock was hard enough, but Kira quickly realized that she was flying directly inland toward the spaceport city's skyline, where further high-g maneuvers might be required. On the other hand, flying toward the city actually worked to her advantage. She altered her vector slightly away from the beachfront and more inland, directly at the city skyline.

In order to avoid unwanted civilian casualties, the battle cruiser's automated defense system ceased fire. The AI controller would no longer continue to fire when civilian casualties became part of the firing solution. Unfortunately for Kira, the battle cruiser hadn't stopped firing until after it had managed to pepper the engine section of the fighter pretty well with the anti-aircraft guns. Smoke and flames consumed the rear of the fighter.

"Warning, power module rupture in starboard engine. Warning, engine failure eminent." The Bitchin' Betty of the mecha repeated her message of doom several times before Kira yelled at Allison to shut it off.

"Well, we couldn't fly this thing out of here anyway, and the gees are killing me," Kira commented. Already soaked from head to toe with sweat, her body ached from the extreme g-force pressuring against her. She just couldn't take much more maneuvering. Kira pulled the visor of the helmet down and banked the fighter onto a collision course with one of the fast-approaching skyscrapers. The visor sealed against the chinbar with a sticking sound, but the hiss was vacant as there was no g-suit sealed to the helmet.

"God, I hate doing this. Eject, eject, eject," she shouted out of trained habit and jerked down on the red-and-white-striped, do-not-ever-fucking-touch-this-under-any-circumstances-unless-all-has-gone-to-hell handle.

The cockpit blasted away, and then the pilot's seat launched with more than four gravities upward. Kira struggled to maintain consciousness and not to throw up. The fighter mecha continued forward with black smoke pouring from its tail. The ejection seat thrusters shut off, leaving Kira tumbling head over heels in the night sky. The spinning weightlessness was almost a welcome change from the harsh g-forces.

For a brief moment, her mind could only focus on the wondrous spectacle of the large purple, red, and violet Jovian planet spinning overhead, coming into view and going out of view, then the beach, then the Jovian, there were some stars, then the city skyline and a flaming mecha, then the Jovian, and so on. Then her spinning was abruptly disrupted with a mind-jarring snap.

A primary gliderchute had popped free from the rear of the seat's harness, stopping the roll with a good solid yank, throwing Kira hard against the restraints. As the motion slowed to within the design limits of the safety system—a second later—the larger secondary chute popped open too.

Finally in an upright position, Kira shook her head to clear it just in time to see the flaming mecha explode against a high-rise building just ahead of her about a kilometer or so from the beach. Kira could barely make out the breakers crashing from the violet lighting reflected across the night from the gas giant. The early-morning winds were very cold and blowing between the skyline buildings and out to sea. Chillbumps raced down Kira's arms and back from the sudden temperature change.

The spaces between the buildings acted like rocket nozzles funneling and accelerating the night winds, and they formed wild, eddy currents in the airflow that whipped her gliderchute around violently. Kira fought against the shrouds of the chute, struggling to keep the glider wings in a stable flight mode. She knew that if she drifted too close to the wrong building, there could be even worse turbulence and probably even severe downdrafts, which would mean serious problems. Serious problems.

So, Kira tried to guide the chute to the surface as fast as she possibly could by pulling the guide handles to bleed off her altitude. A ripstop section of the chute opened up, flapping against the wind and reducing the drag. Doing so doubled her drop speed, but it couldn't be helped. Besides that, she was a sitting duck in the air. There was no doubt in her mind that she was currently lighting up multiple radars, lidars, and QM sensors at the spaceport. Her presence was being tracked. Sooner or later, somebody might start shooting at her or at the least chase her down and apprehend her.

She had to get down and lose herself in the populace quickly. She circled rapidly in a downward spiral over the smaller buildings at the outside of the city. There were several major highways leading into the city and away form the beach with stores, shops, and apartment complexes lining them. Kira turned the chute beachward as best she could, hoping not to get caught in a swift air current that either slammed her into a condo or dragged her out into the ocean. The high-speed gusts blowing through the tall buildings persisted and several times turned the chute almost parallel to the ground. The main streets below her ran north and south, parallel with the shoreline a kilometer or so from what was the major part of the city. That street was the main strip along the beach and would be the easiest place to get lost in a crowd of late-night partiers. But there were plenty of obstacles to avoid on the way, like buildings, light poles, communications towers, holoboards, and the occasional local version of a palm tree.

I sure would like to know my vertical speed, she thought. *I'm gonna go for that condo's parking lot over there.* Kira focused on what appeared to be a fairly lush condo that had a large parking lot and was farthest from other tall buildings. There was a lighted patch of Sol System grass—probably Bermuda, as that stuff would grow just about anywhere in the known universe—large enough for a putting green and surrounded by several local trees just in the center of the parking lot. The lot was filled with cars and had two lanes for traffic between each row. If Kira was lucky, or good, or a little bit of both, she just might be able to land between the putting green and the condo front-to-back and within the traffic lane between rows of cars in the parking lot side-to-side. It was a damned tight squeeze all around, but she had done as tough before. Hell, once she'd even bailed out of a fighter plane at high speeds, under fire, while a nuclear bomb was exploding a few tens of kilometers away and then landed on a jumperball field between giant Martian fir trees in extremely high, nuclear-blast high, winds. This would be a piece of cake. Of course, that was years ago.

I've got an idea about your speed, Allison said, and paused for a brief instant that seemed like forever as the ground continued to loom ever closer and faster. *Way too fast, Kira! Flare now! Flare now!*

Kira let up on the control handles, flaring the chute to its full size. The wind filled it almost instantly and threw her back against the seat restraints. Seconds later, the seat collided with the surface at nearly fifty kilometers per hour and rolled forward, tossing Kira helmet-first into pavement. The chute caught another gust of wind and pulled the seat back upright after dragging her upside down for a few meters. Dazed from her head being pounded into the asphalt, Kira saw stars briefly.

Release the chute, Kira!

"Uhn . . . right." She struggled to regain her wits about her and then pulled the yellow-and-black-striped release pin. The camouflage gliderchute pulled free of the ejection chair and was whisked away by the seaward breeze. The last glimpse Kira caught of it was it dragging across the top of the several-story condominium looming above her and then flapping out toward the ocean.

Move, Kira! Allison shouted in her mind. As if someone had slapped her across the face, Kira regained her focus and began unstrapping herself from the ejection seat as rapidly as she could. She was several kilometers from the battle cruiser at the spaceport now, but it wouldn't be long before the beach would be crawling with troops.

The ejection seat? Kira kicked at the monstrosity sitting in the middle of the parking lot traffic lane.

Leave it; you were probably tracked all the way to the ground anyway, Allison suggested.

Right. Spysats overhead? Kira looked up for any bright spots in the sky moving against the star field or in front of the gas giant. She saw none.

It would have been damned lucky for the Seppies if the orbit just happened to match when you landed. Now forget about it and get the fuck out of here.

When you're right, you're right. Kira scanned around her to get a full three-hundred-sixty-degree view of her surroundings. The bird's-eye view she'd just been privy to had been filled with far too many rapid decisions at once for her to conduct proper recon. Hell, she was lucky she'd survived that far. Kira tossed the helmet and other gear off. The helmet skittered across the pavement and then rolled up underneath a multi-passenger hovervan.

Fortunately, it was the middle of the night, and there was nobody on the beach as far as she could see. Kira got her bearing about her and then started moving. She ran underneath the condo parking garage and onto the beach. She followed the footpath from the condo to the beach. She walked until the breakers crashed around the soles of her boots and then looked up the mostly deserted beach. There were a few couples lying on loungers here and there and the occasional drunken partygoer wandering his or her way back to one of the many condos lining the ocean. None of them were concerned with her, so she wasn't concerned with them.

About three kilometers northward up the beach was the hottest nightclub in town. She'd been there once a year or so before with Elise Tangier, her first wife. That is where she needed to be. Kira rolled her head stretching her neck and then flapped her arms to loosen them.

I guess I could use the exercise, she thought, and then began to run along the beach, letting the crashing waves wash her footprints away.

You said it; I didn't, Allison added with a laugh. Kira ignored the comment and focused her mind on her footsteps. The crashing breakers made running all the more difficult.

Okay, Allison, we've got a few minutes while I run. Tell me how you knew my drop speed. A moment of just running had allowed her mind to focus, and she realized that Allison had pulled off something short of a miracle a few minutes earlier. It had been a miracle that had saved them both. Now she wanted to know the trick. She wiped at the sweat beading on her forehead and continued splashing one foot after the other. Occasionally, the sea spray would mist her and chill her slightly. It was a welcome, refreshing stimulus each time.

It occurred to me that we were near a whole bunch of condos. I did a quick check, and all of them had wireless network hot spots. Allison paused briefly.

And? Kira kept focus on one foot after the other.

And, I connected to several of them and watched how the data rates changed as we fell. It only took a few clock cycles to estimate our velocity to within a ten-percent error margin.

Why'd you need to access more than one hub? Kira asked.

Triangulation.

Duh.

The run had taken less than ten minutes, but the evening was beginning to take its toll on her. Kira was tired and looked a mess. Sweat and seawater poured off her forehead and down her back. If her pants hadn't been baggy battle dress, she was certain there'd be sweat-soaked spots running down her legs. She rinsed her face off with a handful of seawater and ran her wet fingers through her red hair. That reminded her.

Kira reached into her back pocket and pulled out a small tube, then squirted all the contents of it into her hand. She rubbed her hands together and then massaged the gel quickly into her hair and scalp. The gel reacted with the red hair chemicals and returned it to a more natural Martian black. Once she was certain the gel had been worked in thoroughly, she tossed the tube into the ocean.

"Let's see, this won't do." She pulled at her sweat-soaked top and flapped it to cool her off. The black T-shirt had to go. She removed it and used the only dry corner of it left to wipe off her face. Then she tossed it out into the water, leaving her in nothing but her synthskin black jogbra. The material was microfiber and thinner than paper but did wonders for support and wicking sweat from the body. It left very little to the imagination, however. She was on the beach, so it would do. Kira looked at the camouflage pants she was wearing and the black combat boots and thought they would have to do too. Even though she had been dragged across a parking lot by a runaway gliderchute, the pants had only minor frays and merely looked worn.

The wonders of modern materials, she thought. After all, the club was only a few kilometers from the spaceport, and there were soldiers in and out all the time in worn BDUs. Besides, from the sound of the heavy thrashing music coming from the deck of the place, her attire was likely to fit right in.

Kira walked casually up the steps leading from the beach to the club's deck. There was a hybrid hardcore rock and thrashfunk band playing on stage that was all the rage with the Seppy youth. There were literally hundreds of people there partying and paying no attention to the fact that a flaming fighter mecha had just whizzed overhead and crashed into the city. Kira doubted that they'd have cared if they knew. And that was exactly the crowd that she needed to be within.

Kira paid a bouncer at the top of the stairs the cover charge and paid little attention to the way he ogled at her nipples protruding through the thin material of her jogbra. She managed her way into the lake of people jumping and thrusting their fingers in the air to the music. Once she stopped to dance with a purple-haired thrashfunker, who was wearing nothing but pink and green cotton boxer shorts and flip-flops. Kira let her buy her a drink and finally managed to tear away from her with the excuse that she needed to go to the restroom.

She managed to force her way through the crowd to the restroom, where she freshened up a little more. Then she returned to the bar on the other side of the deck opposite the band and ordered another drink. And then she ordered another one. Allison used a fake account to pay the tab. After a couple drinks more, she stumbled to the front door and bought a bright green T-shirt that read "Beat it. Grab it. Suck it. Swallow it." The shirt had something to do with a new cocktail specialty of the club that was mixed and drunk from within the peeling of a local citrus fruit. Kira hoped to come back and see what that was about someday.

She took a cab to the Madira Beach Spaceport. At the spaceport, she changed her hair color again, this time to blond, and then took another cab farther out of town to a local rural airfield and tipped the cabbie an extra fifty bucks to forget he ever saw her, saying something about her husband not needing to know where she had been.

When she had slipped out of the mansion at New Tharsis to "go for a drink" several hours earlier, she had rented a single-engine plane under an alias and flown it to the rural airport several kilometers outside of Madira Beach City. The plane was still there, and nobody seemed concerned one way or the other that she was getting in her plane and heading out at that time of night. Small airports had been that way for centuries. Pilots could come and go any time of day or night with no need to get clearance from any tower or airport authority.

Allison, I'm tired. You take the stick, okay?

I've got it. The little single-engine craft lifted off the pad and vanished silently into the evening sky.

DTM me some of that download we just stole. And you might want to scan the news boards to see if there is anything about the crash of a stolen mecha fighter into downtown Madira Beach.

Roger that.

CHAPTER 7

October 31, 2388 AD
Sol System; Orlando, Florida
Saturday, 5:55 AM, Earth Eastern Standard Time

". . . thank you for joining us for this Earth News Network Breaking News Alert. I'm Gail Fehrer coming to you live from the anchor desk in Washington, D.C. Sources tell us that a detachment of U.S. Marines have been deployed to Walt Disney World in Orlando, Florida. We have no information as to why this has occurred this morning, but we do have reports of gunfire and several explosions taking place at the Magic Kingdom. There is also a report that there are several troop carriers loaded with U.S. Army Airborne Armored E-suit Soldiers headed in that direction. Again, we are not certain why. Another note here is that my inside sources at the White House tell me that the president was taking an unannounced vacation with his wife and daughter, and it is believed that they were spending the evening at the amusement park after hours. If this is true, we can only speculate as to what this means. Is there an attack on the president? Are President Moore and his family in any danger?" Gail Fehrer tapped the desk with her fingers repetitively and then looked into another view angle.

"We're going to go now to Orlando to field correspondent Calvin Dean. Good morning, Calvin," the anchorwoman said into the screen.

"Good morning, Gail." The screen split, showing Gail's once-cameraman turned famous action correspondent. He nodded at her as if he were looking right at her. Of course, he could see her in his DTM link as if she were right there in front of him.

"Calvin, what can you tell us?"

"Well, Gail, as you can see in the distance, there is Cinderella's castle at the Magic Kingdom. Seconds ago, there were several serious explosions and what we think sounded like gunfire. We tried to get an aerial view, but for some reason, the airspace from here all the way to Orlando International has been completely restricted and has been all night according to my sources. We did get this shot earlier." The screen switched to an image of Air Force One sitting on a runway.

"Ah, Air Force One is what we are looking at, I assume."

"Yes, Gail. That is Air Force One sitting on the runway at Orlando. President Moore is here, somewhere. Now, if he is actually at the Magic Kingdom, we can't say for sure."

"I see. What else can you tell us, Calvin?"

"Well, we got this video seconds ago. Twenty or thirty U.S. Marine strike mecha zoomed over us at high speed toward the park." The screen again switched, showing a group of fighters passing into the night sky. The image zoomed in as several of the planes converted to bot mode and dropped near the place where the explosion had occurred previously. There were multiple missiles fired and what appeared to be a serious dogfight taking place above the park.

"That is incredible, Calvin. Thank you, and keep us posted."

"We're gonna try to get closer."

"Good luck and stay safe. Wow, we can only hope that the president and his family are okay. Could this be a new terrorist attack? And what does it mean with the looming election in a couple of days? We have with us Colonel Timothy Vann, U.S. Army Intelligence, retired. Colonel . . ."

"All right, we've got multiple targets and some of them are armed with railguns. The extraction includes all of the First Family and its bodyguard contingent," Captain Adam "Heehaw" Elliot briefed the rest of his marines on the secure tac-net. The FM-12s approached the centuries-old theme park at full velocity and had tied in to the data passed along to them from the president's AIC. "The second group is on me. We will go maximum velocity with maximum ferocity straight to the VIP. There we go to bot mode and drop in to surround and protect the extraction. Just before that, Jawbone, you and first group take out anything flying that ain't one of us. Got it?"

"Roger that, boss," Lieutenant Delilah "Jawbone" Strong responded. The rumor was that Delilah had gotten her callsign as a cadet when she promised a larger male cadet named Sampson—last name—that if he didn't get off her back, she was going to beat him to death. She likely would have, had several others not stepped in and pulled her off of the young and stupid, bleeding cadet. The story had spread later that she had taken Sampson's jawbone of an ass and pummeled the living shit out of him with it. "Jawbone of an ass" was a bit too long, but "Jawbone" had stuck to her like Acme coyote glue, forever.

"Oorah, Heehaw!" the rest of the squad replied over the tac-net.

"We'll have this thing cleared out before the Army pukes drop in. Approaching attack zone. Commence, commence, commence!" Heehaw ordered. He toggled the Transfigure button on the HOTAS and stomped the right, lower foot pedal to give him more slip as the Marine FM-12 strike mecha transformed from a fighter plane into a giant armed and armored robot. He gripped the throttle and pushed it full-force forward with his left hand, while controlling the flight path with the stick in his right. The standard HOTAS controls mimicked most fighter control systems that had been developed for centuries. The exception, of course, was the direct-to-mind control links between the plane and the pilot and the AIC. The DTM connections enabled modern fighter mecha to do things that no others in history could have done, even if that did happen to include attacking the Magic Kingdom and an army of flying elephants, magic carpets, and pixies. The rest of second group followed. Nearly a dozen mecha slowed and transfigured to bot mode while another dozen screamed past in fighter mode, yanking and banking into randomized approach patterns.

"Holy shit, Heehaw! We've got incoming. There is a literal fucking no-fly zone of red paint on the lidar." Jawbone accelerated ahead and split her group off the main squad and started flying interference patterns against several flying elephants, hoping to create enough of a distraction that Heehaw's group could get down and cover the extraction without drawing much unfriendly attention on the way. The virtual sphere around her head was filled with vectors and red blips. She looked through the sphere with her eyes, lidar, and QMs for real-scale views. Almost immediately she caught a reflection from the moonlight off of an inbound vehicle. Make that several inbound vehicles, at once. Her biggest concern was trying to decide which target to shoot at first. She manipulated the FM-12 through a nose-over and then yawed and barrel-rolled around an inbound hovercoaster car. The car screamed by underneath her plane and just missed her wingman. The fighters were jostled harshly by the atmospheric disturbances left in the wake of the rapidly passing enemy vehicle.

"Fox three!" she grunted and squeezed her legs and abdominal muscles against the excessive g-forces of her turn. The mecha-to-mecha missile locked its quantum membrane sensors on the power plant of the hovercoaster and tracked through until it exploded in a white flash, composite parts scattering in all directions. A large chunk of elephant trunk smashed into the cockpit and then bounced harmlessly off the transparent armor. "Shit, there is no telling what the damned techs are gonna paint on my plane after that."

"Jawbone, Jawbone, you got inbound on your three-nine line left," her wingman Lieutenant Junior Grade Carl "Saw" Wilson warned her. "And right, fuck me, and on our seven o'clock!"

"Take it easy, Saw. Just stay frosty now." Jawbone increased the contrast of her QM display so that in any direction she looked, it was as if she were floating in space and looking in full daylight. The computer removed the plane from her field of view, so she had a completely unobstructed viewpoint of the battlespace. Full QMs often were the make-or-break training flight for modern fighter pilots. Anyone suffering from agoraphobia had extreme problems with the full-sphere QM display, especially when they were in midair. Fighting in space was even worse.

There had to be hundreds of hovercoaster cars screaming through the night sky at the marines. Jawbone realized very quickly that they were outnumbered by at least three to one. The armor and weaponry of the mecha and the BY GOD U.S. Marines inside said mecha would just have to make up for the deficit.

"All right, listen up! We are overwhelmed with the numbers game here, marines. We need to go to full scatter. Wingman groups only, no more than twos. Spread out! If you need to mix mecha modes, do it as you see fit," Jawbone ordered the forward group, and then banked just in time to miss incoming. "Guns, guns, guns! What the fuck was that?"

"I think it was a goddamned flying monkey," Saw answered. "Fox three!"

"Affirmative on the flying monkeys. We got an entire squadron of them up here," another voice commented over the tac.

"Fuck, are there falling houses too?" another voice asked over the net.

"Okay, listen up!" Jawbone ordered. "I want all railgun cannons to go to full auto anti-aircraft algorithms. There are enough targets here that the AICs should have a field day, same as us. I want AICs on cannons and marines on DEGs and missiles."

You got that? she thought to her AIC.

Roger that, ma'am, James One Nine One Nine Tango Seven replied. The fighter mode FM-12 housed two forty-millimeter cannons. One sat atop the bird just aft of the cockpit and was best suited for targets behind, beside, and above the fighter in most of the upper-rearward hemisphere. The other sat on the belly of the plane and covered the lower and forward sphere. Almost instantly, James locked multiple red-force tracking algorithms against several blue-force, identify-friend-or-foe codes and started firing away. The sky around the FM-12 filled with forty-millimeter rounds, moving with relativistic energies into enemy targets. The codes were designed to disable the cannons when any civilian casualties or property damage might occur. The AICs had to modify the codes on the fly to enable them to shoot at roller-coaster rides. Spontaneity and improvisation were the two largest arguments for both marines and AICs.

The heavy railgun rounds fired from the mecha of the entire first group ripped through the morning air, leaving behind violet and blue fluorescing trails. Some rounds tracked out of site while others tracked into explosions where the rounds met their target's vital components. Power modules of the hovercars made a beautiful array of reds and oranges when an armored slug of nylon passed through them at two hundred million meters per second.

Whatever AI was controlling the overall attack for the amusement park rides was quick. It learned almost immediately new flight patterns to maximize the potential for collateral damage and adjusted the hovercoaster cars' flight paths accordingly. That mostly consisted of bringing them in lower and closer to the buildings of the amusement park.

The FM-12 pilots responded by flipping through mecha modes and dropping to ground, then shifting modes again and going back to air, and vice versa. Mixing up the modes helped add a confusing mix of convoluted multidimensional combat tactics, which was one of the original reasons for developing mecha in the beginning.

"Ungh! Watch out now!" Jawbone screamed, flexing her thighs and abdominals to their straining point. "Guns, guns, guns." She toggled the mode switch on the HOTAS, flipping the fighter plane upside down as it converted to bot mode. In midair and upside down, she fired the DEG from the hip and swiveled a full circle, like a break dancer spinning on her head.

"I got you covered, Jaw." Saw followed suit going to eagle mode, and then he flew just ahead of her headspin, drawing fire and giving his wing leader the edge of being able to focus on offense for a brief moment. "Fox three!" he cried.

"Great job, Saw!" Jawbone rolled the bot back through the transfiguration to fighter mode, pouring on the afterburners to gain a little bit of altitude following her headlong plummet. "Your turn!"

Saw tripped the HOTAS to bot-mode and fell over like a crazed diver into a wild headfirst spin. This time, the bot spun in the other direction. Jawbone followed the flight pattern and jumped out just in front of his DEG track. The blue-green energy bolts blasted just a few tens of meters behind her into enemy targets; all the while, she drew fire from her wingman. Delilah would have smiled approvingly at the young lieutenant's performance had she not been choking down bile forced into her throat from the high-g corkscrew.

The forward group did its job of distracting and disrupting the strange air force of the no-fly zone. The second group of marines flew like a squadron of giant metal supermen, hell-bent on saving the day.

Captain Elliot grunted with the g-forces pressing him against the pilot's couch as the mecha rolled through a forward flip, dropping the FM-12 from the sky. The two three-clawed feet of the fighter clanged to the ground about twenty meters in front of the amphitheater where the president and his family were holed up. A quick survey of the environment led him to the realization that the president and his security detail were pinned down and surrounded in a small corner with only a short rock wall for cover. He would quickly fix that situation. Various fairy-tale creatures were charging their little redoubt and firing HVARs at them willy-nilly. How in the hell the AI-driven creatures had gotten so armed was a total mystery.

Heehaw marched his mecha between the president and the largest group of attackers, actually squashing under an armored foot an oversized white rabbit with a stopwatch, monocle, and railgun. The pavement and the robot gave way and crunched up under the mecha's feet. The marine captain pulled the directed energy gun in front of him with his giant left mechanized hand like a quick-drawing cowboy shooting from the hip and splashed the blue-green energy bolts over a wave of advancing fairy-tale robots. The burst from the DEG cut through the flimsy AI attackers, leaving them lying on the ground in pieces, sparks flying. He continued kicking and crunching others underfoot.

Several FM-12s landed nearby and converged on the amphitheater. In only a matter of seconds, the First Family was completely surrounded by giant armored bots flashing blue-green directed energy blasts in all different directions at the advancing line. To this point, the flying theme park rides had mostly been consumed by the first FM-12 group, but whatever or whoever was controlling them had shifted their modus operandi, and they started altering their flight patterns toward the mecha surrounding the president.

Heehaw! Red force on collision at eleven o'clock cherubs three, his AIC warned him.

Holy shit! *That can't be good.* Captain Elliot jumped upward, firing his boot thrusters and slightly offsetting his trajectory to the rapidly approaching Pegasus. "Too late for missiles," he grunted.

He shifted his mecha and grabbed at the wings of the attacking robot just as it passed in front of him. The large mechanized hands of the mecha caught the main spar of the right wing of the flying horse. Heehaw then spun two times completely around, converting the momentum of the beast into angular acceleration like an Olympic hammer thrower before letting the thing fly free into the side of the giant dome at Space Mountain. The flying horse collided back first into the dome, and then it shattered into sparks and a million pieces of debris and crushed through the roof of the complex.

"All right second team, give us some air coverage to the exit," Heehaw ordered over the net.

"You got it, boss. Guns, guns, guns," Jawbone replied. Her fighter-mode mecha spiraled and circled overhead and released several DEG bursts. Heehaw could hear secondary explosions in his external mic monitors. "Boss, we've got the strangest damned air force attacking us you've ever seen. And there is a shitload of them converging on you!"

Just then, one of the hovercars finally picked the right vector and impacted directly into one of the fighter-mode FM-12s overhead. The composite triceratops hit the fighter plane's underbelly, where the left-wing spar met the fuselage. The impact did little damage to the heavily armored fighter plane, but the energy transfer forced it into an unstable, three-dimensional spin. The plane continued to spin wildly to the limits of its g-rating, and then it crashed through the Big Thunder Asteroid Mining Colony. The marine never ejected, and there was quite an explosion following the crash on the other side of the park.

"Motherfucker," Heehaw muttered.

Adam, I've got several firing solutions if you want to go to missiles, his AIC alerted him.

We'll stick to ground for now. Let Jawbone handle the fliers. If she starts getting into trouble, you let me know. We've got to keep the First Family covered.

Yes, sir.

"Goddamnit, Thomas! What are these marines trying to do, get us killed? They've attracted more fire than they've avoided." The president kept his head ducked low behind the wall and watched the battle transpire through DTM. They had stopped returning fire since the marine mecha had arrived, hoping to conserve ammo and to avert the enemy's attention to the mecha. It had worked, except for the fact that the enemy had diverted its attention to the mecha protecting them.

"I see that, sir. Don't you think the surge was to be expected?"

"They could do better, Thomas! They could do better!" Moore flinched as something that looked like a giant Pegasus was flung overhead by one of the FM-12s. Then, just beyond that, he could see one of the marine fighters being hit and crashing wildly out of control across the park.

Abigail, where's my backup plan? Moore inquired.

On his way, sir.

"All right, ground team, I want two-on-two coverage, and start sweeping patterns toward the front gate down Main Street, U.S.A. Let's clear a path to get the VIP out of here. If we have to, we'll plow this road under. Shit!" Heehaw's mecha jerked as several railgun rounds zipped into the armor on the torso of the giant bot. "Good thing these things aren't very good shots." He turned his DEG left and returned the fire.

Get me a channel to the security team leader, Heehaw asked his AIC.

Channel is open, sir, and the detachment's client is code-named Bull-dog. It is led by USMC Captain Thomas Washington.

"This is USMC Captain Adam Elliot. Captain Washington, we're here at your disposal to aid in extraction of Bulldog, over?"

"Copy that, Captain Elliot. *Semper fi!*" Thomas responded enthusiastically. "As you can tell, we're pinned down and would appreciate a clear path to the exit, thank you. The damned AI robots are lousy shots, but the hypervelocity rounds have just about chewed away our cover. We've got to make a move soon!"

"Affirmative," Elliott said. "We should make a run for the gate. I understand we have three VIPs?"

"Roger that," Thomas concurred. "Bulldog, Mama Bear, and Ice Cream are present. All three need extraction, immediately."

"Captain Washington, I suggest that three of my crew carry them out. And I suggest we do it now."

"Hold on. I'll get back to you."

Thomas leaned his back against the wall, checking his blaster charge. President Moore sat beside him, reloading his pistol with the last clip he had been given. They were all running out of ammo and were mostly dependent on the mechaheads from here on. It was habit of a good soldier to know exactly how much firepower he had at his disposal at all times. Like someone suffering from obsessive compulsive disorder, he double-checked the charge reading just to make sure.

"Mr. President," Thomas sighed, "I'm afraid we're gonna have to make a run for the door."

"That sounds risky, Thomas. What's to keep the aerial vehicles from crashing into us? That mecha just did stop the Pegasus in time."

"I'd guess that's what the airborne marines are here for, sir. We have to trust they'll do their job. And you have to trust me to do mine." Thomas looked upward briefly at the flashes of DEG fire. "We can't just sit here and wait to be overrun."

"All right then," Moore replied, as he dragged his handkerchief across his face, wiping away sweat that was forming on his forehead. "But I've got a better idea."

Allison, is our backup plan ready? Moore thought to his AIC.

Yes, sir. Approximately one minute, thirty seconds away.

Good. Tell him to come on in as fast as he can.

Yes, sir.

"Thomas, you just tell the marines to stand by and cover our exit. Be prepared to move in one minute and a half on my signal." Moore looked at his watch reflexively. Allison kept perfect time and there was little need for a watch, but it was a habit that he had gotten into over the years.

"Sir?"

"Do it!"

"Yes, Mr. President."

"Heehaw, you've got some serious motion headed your way," Jawbone's voice alerted Adam over the net.

"I see the red dots, Jaw. Can you elaborate a little bit on what it is?" Heehaw replied, and then followed with "Guns, guns, guns." His DEG tracked across the river to a mock-up Nautilus carrying several AI on its hull. The energy bolt burned through a large merman and then continued on into the forward windows of Captain Nemo's submarine. The ship cracked almost into two pieces and started taking on water rapidly. It had almost completely sunk before Jawbone responded to his question.

"Uh, roger that, Heehaw. It looks like there's a giganotosaurus, an allosaurus, a T-rex, a couple of apatosauruses, maybe a titanosaur, a handful of stegosauruses, a brachiosaur or two, and what looks like a pack of velociraptors," Jawbone said flatly.

"You've got to be fucking kidding me," Heehaw replied, almost under his breath.

"Negative, sir. You've got the entire complement of Dinoland coming your way. Shit!" Jawbone reversed the throttle and flipped her mecha in a backward pitch-over to reverse direction, just in time to miss what appeared to be a flock of pteranodons and pterodactyls.

"Holy shit, Jawbone, what the fuck is that?" her wingman cried over the net in a panic.

"Well, Lieutenant Junior Grade Wilson, that one right there . . . Fox three," one of the robotic replicas of the ancient birds burst into a ball of fire. ". . . is a pteranodon. And that one right . . . guns, guns, guns . . . there is a Pterodactyl." Delilah yawed her mecha through the flight path of the flock, firing her DEG and stirring up the winged beasts.

"How the hell do you know that?" Wilson asked.

"Not that it really fucking matters right now . . . uhn," Jawbone grunted and pushed through a high-g turn. The bladders around her legs began squeezing her like a pneumatic vise. "But, pteranodons don't have teeth, and pterodactyls do."

"If you two are quite finished, get down here and clear out Main Street for me!" Heehaw ordered.

"Roger that, sir."

Heehaw searched through the virtual battlescape in his mind for the best escape route. He had just about decided that they were going to pick up the First Family in the hands of the mecha and make a run for it when Captain Washington burst through on the net.

"Captain Elliot, it's Washington."

"Captain?"

"Negative on your moving the package. The package has arranged for other means of transportation and has warned to be ready to run cover in one minute thirty. I repeat, one minute thirty. Over," Thomas alerted him.

"Roger that, Captain. Be advised that aerial recon shows a herd of dinosaurs headed our way, and they'll be here soon. I'm transmitting the ID tags for them now." Heehaw passed along the tagged red dots in the virtual battlescape so that they would be marked as dinosaurs in all the DTM links with the right command codes.

"Acknowledged and understood. I have the data now, thanks. Get ready."

"Ready as we'll ever be."

CHAPTER 8

October 31, 2388 AD
Sol System
Oort Cloud
Saturday, 6:00 AM, Earth Eastern Standard Time

"Quartermaster of the Watch!" Captain Jefferson called through the urgent sounds of the background bridge conversations and the din of the continuous buzzing from the tac-net DTM mindvoices.

"Aye sir!" Quartermaster Senior Chief Patea Vanu snapped away from his viewscreen and looked at the CO sitting in his command chair.

"Chief, I want an eyeballs report every minute to corroborate the sensors. I don't want us getting caught with our pants down like we did during the Exodus." The captain rocked the seat from left to right nervously and looked through the QMSC like he wasn't there. His stare looked right through the main viewport of the bridge and over the deck of the supercarrier out into the deep black space of the Oort Cloud some ten thousand astronomical units from Sol. The *Sienna Madira* was battened down and preparing for a hyperspace jaunt into a battle plan, the likes of which hadn't been seen since the Martian Exodus. Jefferson assimilated data as fast as he could in an attempt to make some sense out of the mountains of premission analyses piling up in the virtual sphere around him.

"Aye, Captain! I've got eyeballs posted about the ship feeding me continuously. I'll let you know if anything sounds out of the ordinary."

"Good." Jefferson turned to his XO. "Larry, are there any last-minute operations lagging?"

"No sir. A group of AEMs decided to ride down the tubes with the Warlords, and they are strapping the last of them in as we speak. We're good to go." XO staffers passed in and out of the bridge carrying out background orders from Colonel Chekov and making certain that the thousands of operational needs of the supercarrier were met. Every department of the ship had issues for the XO, and each of those departments had to function smoothly for an operation. It literally took a massive organization structure and hundreds of assistants to keep the ship functioning properly at all levels. The added layer of the AICs spread about the ship made it even more complicated, while at the same time adding to the capabilities of the mammoth war machine. Besides, it was Uncle Timmy's job to command the AICs.

"AEMs volunteered to ride in the drop tank tubes with the tank-heads?" the CO grinned wryly. "Let me guess, Ramy Roberts' Robots?"

"Yes, sir."

"Goddamned Ramy, you tough SOB." The captain shook his head and continued to smile. "You wonder why his marines love him so much."

"Guess who's riding the first tube out?" the XO remarked. He didn't have to say anything more, as Captain Jefferson knew good and well that the first drop tube out would have Army Colonel Mason "War-lord One" Warboys driving his M3A17-T, and USMC Major Ramy Roberts would be right on top of Warboys' tank in his armored e-suit hanging on for dear life, God, and probably singing the country hymn of the USMC all the way down.

"COB, anything I need to know about my ship and her complement?"

"Well, sir, this reminds me a bit of the Triton mission a few years back."

"I know I'm gonna regret asking this, but how so, Charlie?" the CO asked reluctantly. The COB was renowned for his long-winded tall tales that eventually got around to him being a superhero, along with there being some lesson to be learned or a nugget of wisdom that would be useful in some way or the other.

"The ship is in great shape, the crew is ready to go, and the mission seems all too easy, sir." Chief of the Boat Command Master Chief Charlie Green smirked and sipped at his coffee. "Remember how that turned out, sir?"

"That's it, COB? 'It seems too easy, sir'? Where the hell is the amusing anecdote about some damned space mermaid or a UFO or some such damned thing? That's just no good at all, COB. We need to check with Ensign Rivers about what they're putting in your coffee." Captain Jefferson laughed almost disappointedly.

"That damned Rivers won't make anything but decaf, sir. I've had to hide those colored water packets three times this week," the XO added. "If he does it again, I'm going to put his decaffeinated ass on report."

"At ease, EndRun," the CO replied, using the XO's mecha callsign, which he seldom used unless he was trying to keep the mood light.

"Well, now that you mention it, there was this one time," the COB started, but thought better of it when the captain waved him off with a grin. He paused, almost sulked, and then sipped his real coffee that *he* had made himself. Captain Jefferson, of course, realized all of that. Everybody on the bridge drank the COB's coffee, as nobody could stand that weak-ass stuff that they kept down at the mess hall. And the stuff that Ensign Rivers had insisted on, well, it didn't even qualify as Navy coffee, and an old marine mechajock like the XO sure as Hell couldn't take it. Captain Jefferson had been very pleased once the COB had decided it was his personal duty to make certain that the bridge crew members were supplied with appropriate, thick-as-mud, vile, and extremely stout-beyond-stout java with real caffeine in it.

Uncle Timmy? He sipped from his coffee mug and then snapped the magnetic base back onto his command chair's arm.

Yes, sir. We are packed, stacked, and ready to go, sir.

Hyperspace?

All systems are go and ready for the engagement.

Sound it off, Timmy.

Aye, sir. The ship's head AIC, actually Lieutenant Commander Timmy Uniform November Kilo Lima Three Seven Seven or UNKL377, *the* AIC officer of the U.S.S. *Sienna Madira,* keyed the 1MC intercom and announced the call to start the mission. There were a few short bursts of the bosun's pipe and then Timmy's voice.

"All hands. All hands. Battle stations. All hands prepare for immediate hyperspace transfer to hostile engagement zone and battle deployment. Stand by for hyperspace countdown."

"Well, that's that. Comm, verify that the relay of engagement command to the *Blair* was successful and that mission clock has started," the CO ordered.

"Aye, sir! Message is relayed, and the clock is going. Captain Walker says, 'break a leg' sir," the communications officer Lieutenant Keith Aldridge replied. The young lieutenant held a finger down on his right ear as if he were drowning out ambient noise to listen more closely to his DTM mindvoice.

"Of course she did." Jefferson grinned briefly, recalling that Sharon had indeed broken her leg while commanding the *Thatcher* during the Exodus and practically saving his ass, the *Madira*, and the entire Mons City main dome. It had been a running joke between them since. "Take us in, XO."

"Aye, sir." Colonel Larry "EndRun" Chekov turned to face the viewport and looked sternly over the bow of the *Madira*. "Helm!"

"Roger, XO."

"Commence hyperspace jaunt to predetermined coordinates at your discretion."

"Aye, sir," the helm replied, and turned from the XO to the navigator's station. "Navigation Officer, confirm that hyperspace jaunt coordinates are correct, ma'am?"

"Jaunt coordinates comply, Helm!" Lieutenant Commander Penny Swain verified the jaunt tensors in her DTM and again with her AIC. "We're good to go, Captain Jefferson," Penny added with a nod to the captain. Most officers of the bridge crew historically answered to the CO through the XO, but it was common practice since wooden ships with sails that the navigation officer replied directly to the captain on major course changes.

"Hyperspace is a go, sir. Handing off to Uncle Timmy in five, four, three, two, one, mark," helmsman Lieutenant Junior Grade Macy Marks counted down.

General quarters! General quarters! All hands, all hands man your battle stations immediately! Prepare for short hyperspace jaunt in fifteen seconds. Expect multiple ground targets with incoming surface-to-air defenses and multiple unknown airborne targets. Prepare for evasive! Nine, eight, seven, six, five, four, three, two, one. Hyperspace.

✧   ✧   ✧

"If you don't mind my saying so sir, you sure picked a hell of a day to join the crew." Engineer's mate Petty Officer First Class Vineet Shah made idle conversation as he led Lieutenant Joseph Buckley to the Chief Engineer's staion. The CHENG's station was on the aft side of the hyperspace propulsion unit in the engine room.

"Well, I'd guess today is as good as any," Lieutenant Buckley replied. Joe looked the engine room over as they walked. He was most intrigued by the dancing of the light-pink fluorescence, swirling around the zero point, energy-field-shielding projector. Joe had studied the ship's systems ad nauseam and was knew that the pink light was caused by gamma rays at extremely high energies being generated at the event horizon of the space-time expansion, which was created by the projector. As the extremely high energy gamma rays were ripped right out of space and time itself, they traveled radially—aside from a slight rotation due to the frame dragging of the projector's vortex-like motion—away from the section of space and time that was stretched beyond normal space but were then severely redshifted all the way to the far visible and near infrared. The redshifting was an effect of Einstein's General Relativity, and the extreme gravitational difference at the boundary between the projector and normal space was like trying to escape the pull of a neutron star.

As a main propulsion assistant it would be his job to make certain that the projector functioned properly and continued to generate a focused swirl of expanded space-time in front of the supercarrier. Joe and EM1 Shah walked underneath the giant, swirling tube of pink light. The conduit projector hung just above head height and was more than four meters in diameter. It ran the length of three decks of the ship in both directions.

"Commander Harrison, sir, this is Lieutenant Buckley." EM1 Shah nodded back and forth between the two senior engineering officers.

"Sir." Buckley saluted the chief engineer and then shook his hand.

"You picked a hell of a day to join us, Lieutenant," chief engineer Commander Benson Harrison said with a raised eyebrow. The engineer watched the propulsion control systems closely. The instrument panels spread across the wall, and duty stations around him all were active with digital readouts blinking some piece of information in a myriad of thousands of brilliant flashes that gave Las Vegas a run for its money in artificial illumination.

The instrument panels were complicated enough, but there were also several other layers of information regarding the main propulsion system that could only be transferred DTM; otherwise, there just wouldn't be enough real estate within the ship to physically locate all the sensor readouts. The actual sensors and switches were the minimum systems required to manage an extremely rough jaunt through hyperspace with a several-AU destination-error budget per light-year. The DTM layers and AICs were required to keep the jaunts more accurate.

"That's what EM1 Shah said, sir," Buckley replied.

"Well, Vineet has a good head about him, and you'd be wise to keep him around. Look, we'll be dropping out of the hyperspace conduit in less than a minute. Are you up to speed on this ship's systems enough to take your duty station at Main Prop?" Benson asked.

"Aye, sir."

"Take it easy with that 'aye, sir' stuff, Joe, unless the command crew is around. You can call me Benny otherwise."

"Yes, sir, uh, Benny, sir." Joe just couldn't make himself break the protocols. His last command on board a frigate had a CHENG that was so by-the-book that he had even starched and pressed his coveralls. Buckley was going to have to get used to his new boss's more relaxed style.

"Right. Okay, time to get to work. Melissa, give Joe's AIC full access to all engine room protocols required for position of main propulsion assistant," the CHENG verbalized to his AIC and nodded to his new MPA.

"Yes, Benny," his AIC said over the room's coms.

"Okay, Buckley, she's all yours." The commander slapped him on the back and moved across the room to speak to a young female lieutenant at the damage control assistant's station.

"Yes, si— uh, Benny." Buckley sat down at the MPA's station and typed in his personal password data, then handed the wireless off to his AIC, Debbie.

Debbie, Three November One Uniform Zulu Juliet One logging into MPA station control protocols.

Welcome, Debbie, a subconscious or automated subroutine of Uncle Timmy's replied.

We're good to go, Joe.

Roger that, Debbie. Now DTM me the ZPE field projector status. Joe's mind filled with a virtual sphere of gravitometric tensor calculations and vacuum field probability equations. The intense whirl of space-time in front of the ship was decreasing and about to destabilize in less than a minute as matched perfectly to the flight plan of the ship. "Looks good," he mumbled to himself. However relaxed the CHENG might have been on formalities, his propulsion system control was dead on. Joe assured himself that the CHENG's ship was tight in the best way and was probably why *he* was the CHENG of the nation's fleet flagship.

Captain Jefferson ignored the DTM virtual sphere for a brief moment to look out the viewport of the bridge as the *Sienna Madira* lurched and then phased out of normal space with a reversed cascading shower of violet flashes of light.

"Hyperspace entry looks good, Captain," the ship's navigator said.

"Stay on it, nav."

"Aye, sir."

The *Madira* jaunted through her multidimensional vector and as far as the captain could tell would emerge into normal space just as the battle plan required. It was a short jaunt. The *Madira* and the *Blair* had been prepping for the attack on the Seppy Oort Cloud facility only a few light-minutes away, and so they would be snapping back into normal space very quickly into whatever mess the Seppies might have waiting for them. Of course, Captain Jefferson was fairly sure that the Seppy bastards weren't expecting them at all, but nothing was ever certain when it came to warfare. And the Separatists had proven to be nothing if not clever and full of misdirection and misconception. He tugged his seat belt a little tighter and gripped the arms of his chair nervously.

Uncle Timmy, how're we doing? Captain Jefferson asked his AIC.

All is well, Captain.

Good. Keep on top of it all.

Aye, sir.

"Everything looks right, Captain. Emerging from hyperspace in thirty seconds," the helmsman announced.

"Prepare for incoming. Air boss is a go for sorties," the CO ordered. Violet swirls of hyperspace spiraled rapidly around the supercarrier in a vortex of space-time fabric being warped into submission by the main propulsion system.

The quantum membrane of the universe was expanded beyond its normal flatness in the converging tunnel ahead of the supercarrier, violating the energy conditions of normal space. The exotic matter field generators in the giant field coils underneath the ship projected a focused beam in front of them that interacted with the vacuum energy fluctuations and through negative superposition canceled out a majority of normal space energy bands. This created the vortex region, where less energy existed than even in empty space-time itself. Navy propulsion engineers were often fond of explaining that they would create a region of nothingness that had even more nothing in it than normal.

The CO took one last, brief glance out the stern viewscreen at the twirling, blinking, and flashing light show of super-sized nothing and took a deep breath. He slowly pursed his lips and exhaled while closing his eyes. Taking one last quick assessment of the operations readiness data in his DTM, he tensed and readied himself for what waited on the other side of hyperspace.

"Aye, sir. Go for sorties!" the air boss acknowledged. Without looking up from his screen, he switched channels to the hangar bay. "All hangars, all cats, we are about to reenter normal space. Commence sortie deployment. I repeat, commence sortie deployment."

"XO, forward guns!" Jefferson ordered just as the hyperspace conduit swirled away to infinity and vanished. The *Sienna Madira* phased into normal space with full-forward velocity like the overarmored and overarmed menace from Earth she was.

"Gunnery Officer, begin sensor sweep and lock and commence firing of main DEG batteries at your discretion. Be advised to excise military targets only, and do not hit the teleportation facility as briefed and gamed!" Colonel Chekov tapped at his console, double checking the power levels of the guns.

"Roger that, XO! Multiple targets identified, locked, and firing solutions ready. Firing at will," Lieutenant Rice acknowledged.

"CO, CDC!" the commander of the Combat Direction Center a few decks below the bridge chimed.

"Go CDC."

"We've got multiple sensor pings and are actively jamming on all frequencies. Expect incoming fire, as we are getting lit up like a Christmas tree, sir!"

"Roger that, CDC. Is the jamming buying us anything?"

"It might be confusing their point and track, sir, but they know we're here."

The supercarrier pressed through the active wash of sensor energy from the Seppy facility at maximum normal space velocity. The computers of the ship picked out targets and blasted away at them with mammoth directed energy weapons. The intense blue-green bolts of energy tore through the surface of the Oort object beneath them, blasting away surface materials and manmade structures. Smaller anti-aircraft railguns came online automatically and started searching for enemy flying targets to shoot. Sensor domes and weapons batteries on the planetoid facility exploded into the quiet vacuum of space, scattering debris and chewing up the surface like a behemoth repulsor plow.

Red dots appeared in the captain's DTM sphere, moving toward the supercarrier at extreme velocities. The IFF algorithms not only identified them as foe but also as anti-carrier missiles, hundreds of them.

"CO, CDC! Incoming!"

"We've got it, CDC." The captain turned his chair toward the XO. "Forward SIFs at maximum! XO anti-missile batteries, fire!"

"DEG and railgun Phalanx systems are active, Captain," Chekov replied. "SIFs at maxi . . ." He was interrupted as the first missile detonated against the forward force fields and armored plating. The ship vibrated against the explosion as the debris from the missile washed over the bow and was absorbed by the supercarrier's hull.

"Keep firing. And get me a fix on those launch tubes and start battering the hell out of them!"

"Aye, sir!"

"Good hunting, DeathRay!" The deck chief snapped a salute from the top of the mecha support scaffold and grabbed at the handrail as the ship's inertial dampening systems compensated for a sudden impact against the exterior hull of the supercarrier.

"Roger that!" Jack saluted back, and the chief quickly climbed down and began unhooking the power and com umbilical. He finished by giving the VTF-32 Ares-T fighter one last affectionate pat on the empennage.

Jack pulled his helmet over his head and gave it a twist to lock it in place as he settled into the cockpit. Air rushed into his suit with a faint, hissing sound. He then pulled the hardwire connection from the universal docking port of his fighter and plugged it into the thin rugged composite box on the left side of his helmet, which made a direct electrical connection to his AIC implant via skin-contact sensors in his helmet. The direct connection wasn't necessary as the quantum membrane wireless connectivity was very strong that close to the fighter's computer systems. It had once been thought that enemy jamming of the wireless connection between the AIC and the fighter was almost impossible. The wireless connection was spread spectrum and highly encrypted. But the Seppy attack during the Exodus had shown quite the opposite. The entire fleet had been spoofed, and the wireless systems were told by a Seppy hacker—rumored to have been coded by Ahmi herself—not to see enemy targets with any sensors. Since then, the hardwire was promoted from backup to primary connection, and the wireless was only used in emergencies and in noncombat situations.

"Hardwire UDP is connected and operational. Lieutenant Candis Three Zero Seven Two Four Niner Niner Niner Six ready for duty," Jack's AIC announced over the open com channel. Then directly to Jack, *Let's go get 'em, Commander!*

Roger that, Candis!

Jack saluted the flight deck officer and brought the canopy down. The harness holding the fighter lowered and dropped it the last twenty centimeters to the deck with that ever-so-familiar *squishing* feel from the landing gear suspension. The drop always used to leave him with a lump in his throat and butterflies in his stomach because it meant that he was about to go screaming out the ass end of the supercarrier into a storm of raining and streaking Hell from all directions. Or at least it had meant that up until the Exodus and the few cleanup actions afterward. There had been merely training exercises for the better part of four years now, and Jack preferred that to the horrific sights and sounds of war.

The aftermath of the Exodus was enough to leave serious scars in any soldier's psyche and, indeed, many had resigned from service after it. But Jack was made of sterner stuff, he had told himself. And somebody had to be prepared in the case that America, the Sol System, came under attack again. With the Exodus, he had hoped that war would be a thing he wouldn't have to deal with for a while. He had trained, nevertheless.

Once again, it looked like it was time for war, and all bravado aside, he was good at it. Jack swallowed the lump, calmed the butterflies, and followed the flight deck sequence. He moved his fighter first in line for takeoff. The tricycle wheels of the little fighter squeaked against the deck plate as it rolled into launch position. Jack could feel the supercarrier vibrating from anti-aircraft fire—a deadly feeling that he had almost forgotten.

"This is double zero," Jack called over the tac-net. "This is gonna get hairy, folks, and I want everyone covering their wings and following the plan. Good hunting and good luck." He thought his faceplate down and pulled his mouthpiece closer with his teeth.

"Fighter zero-zero callsign DeathRay, you are cleared for egress. Good hunting, Commander Boland!" the control tower officer radioed. "Handing off to cat control."

"Roger that, tower." Jack went through his ritual. "Y'all just keep the beer cold, and good ol' DeathRay will be back soon enough." Jack taxied to the "at bat" slot and braced himself for the "ball" and chewed at the bite block.

"Fighter double zero, you are at bat and go for cat! Call the ball."

"Roger cat, double zero has the ball," Boland responded as the little gold catapult field alignment sphere blinked on in his DTM view, overlaying the projected launch window circle.

"Good hunting, DeathRay!" the catapult field AI announced. Jack throttled the Ares-T forward and switched to hover as the landing gear cycled and extracted. He bit down harder on the temporomandibular joint mouthpiece and eased the throttle just a little more forward so that the fighter slipped into the catapult field. His tongue worked nervously against the bite block and the roof of his mouth and he began to salivate profusely. Sweat would soon start building, but his suit would evaporate that quickly.

Swallowing hard, Jack worked his hands against the HOTAS grip, feeling the controls. The new bot-mode toggle on his right stick control was beginning to feel completely at home, although this would be the first combat the new transfigurable Ares-T fighters had seen. Jack was and wasn't looking forward to the pending opportunity at the same time. He'd been training in the new mecha for more than two years, and now he'd find out the hard way how good it really was in combat.

"Roger that. Double zero has the cat! WHOOO! HOOO!" Jack screamed as usual through the mouthpiece. The support tube for the bite block started pumping oxygen and stimulants in his face and mouth. The catapult field flung the Ares-T out of the rear lower launch deck, and Jack was thrust hard into his seat at over nine Earth gravities, accelerating the little snub-nosed, fighter-mode mecha to over three hundred kilometers per hour.

The inertial dampening controls of the fighter kept DeathRay's body from being crushed against the pilot's seat and his brain from sloshing around inside his head to the point of fatal trauma. The sleek new fighter-mode Ares-T screamed out of the cat field from zero to four hundred kilometers per hour in one tenth of a second with an acceleration of about eighty-eight Earth gravities. The inertial dampening controls reduced the effect by generating a dampening field around the aircraft that served two purposes: 1) to add structural integrity to the fighter plane as it was thrown into a hail of anti-aircraft fire and 2) to reduce the effect of the g-forces to something that human pilots could possibly withstand—twelve gravities or so. Inertial dampening fields or not, Jack was on one hell of a ride.

"Holy fuck!" Jack breathed rapidly and spat out obscenities almost as proficiently as an enlisted sailor. He grunted as the overwhelming g-forces from the catapult acceleration subsided. He shook his head and squinted the flashing stars and blood from his eyes.

Jack focused on slowing his breathing and scanned the sky and the viewscreens displaying under and behind him. At the same time, his AIC DTMed a full-scale, three-dimensional, immersive, spherical view of the space around him. He could look in any direction and see space outside rather than the interior of the fighter. The view was partially transparent so that he could still monitor other instruments and controls inside the cockpit that were not virtual.

The space around him was littered with explosions and flashes of light above and behind him; beneath him were the icy, bungled-together planetoids and the mangled array of Seppy construction. The DEGs of the supercarrier were digging major gashes out of the facility and slinging debris across the planetoids.

In his virtual mindview, Jack could see the other planes from his squadron being flung from the *Sienna Madira* hangar bays. His young wingman, Lieutenant Karen "Fish" Howser, pulled in beside him on his right. Jack could see Fish scanning around her cockpit virtual view for bogies. Her head whipped around wildly looking for incoming threats. Karen had seen her first combat at the Seppy Exodus and had proven herself a true ace fighter pilot. Jack had originally chosen her for his wingman because she was truly young and raw, and he thought she needed to be looked after. But he kept her as his wing because they had worked very well together and what she lacked in experience, Jack had noted on that day, she more than made up for in guts, determination, and just plain raw talent. And she took to the new mecha like a duck to water. Karen was probably one of the best aviators he'd ever seen, besides himself, of course.

Jack could also see the main gun batteries of the *Madira* firing in rapid succession. Missiles began to spill away from the mammoth warship, along with the DEG bursts through the hail of anti-aircraft fire coming from the Seppy facility. Some of them impacted the Seppy base's exterior hull plating and boiled off large chunks of the armor in brilliant orange and white clouds. The debris spread out in long arcs across the surface of the low-gravity planetoid and spun madly with no atmosphere to drag down its motion.

Jack, I've got Gnats! Candis warned him. The DTM blinked full of red dots.

Roger that, time to go to work! He could tell by the blue dots that the Gods of War had made it out of the ship and through the first barrage of AA fire. Now it was time to face the Seppy fighters.

"Fish, we've got Gomers incoming off our three-nine at angels three." Jack tilted the stick left, diving and spiraling through the anti-aircraft fire into a head-to-head sprint toward the first Separatist Gnat. The two fighters closed on each other with a relative velocity of more than a thousand kilometers per hour. Jack toggled the DEG targeting X in his DTM view and set the missile lock sensors on search. A missile solution dinged in his mindview, and he let a mecha-to-mecha missile loose. "Fox three!" he shouted.

"Roger that, DeathRay! Gomers off our three-nine at angels three. I've got firing solutions. Guns, guns, guns!" Fish reported over the net. Jack only vaguely caught the motion of her fighter yawing and pitching madly into a sideways spin to target an enemy fighter passing beneath them.

Jack's missile twisted and countermaneuvered through DEG fire and hit home on the Seppy Gnat, immediately blasting the left wing from the incoming plane and spinning it catastrophically to pieces. Several of the larger pieces *twanged* against the hull of the VTF-32 as he passed through the spot where the two fighters would have collided. The SIFs and microfiber composite layered armor plating held. Jack tossed the fighter over, giving him a view of the planetoid facility beneath him as well as an eyeball's view of the approaching enemy fighters.

"DeathRay, this is some thick shit! I think we should double back and try to hold closer to the *Madira*," his second-in-command

Lieutenant Commander Damien "Demonchild" Harris said over the tac-net through grunts and bleats of breath.

"Roger that, Demonchild. Gods of War double back in the mix toward the *Madira*. If we can bring these in closer to the ship, it will clear out some of the path for the marines and tankheads. It might spread out the AA some as well." Jack doubled his fighter over one hundred and eighty degrees but left his vector in the same direction. The g-forces pulled roughly at his stomach. He grunted and reversed the propulsion system vector, pushing the left hand component of the HOTAS.

"DeathRay, you got a Gomer on your six firing! Get away, or he's gonna lock you up!" Fish warned him. "Fox three!" The Gnat dodged, while flooding the area in front of the missile with cannon fire, destroying it, and then rolling out of the way, still on Jack's tail.

"Shit! You missed him, Fish." DeathRay spun his head around, trying to get an eyeball on the Gomer that was barreling down on him. He could see it in the DTM but not with visual. "Where the fuck are you?" The range was too close to go to missiles.

"Watch out, DeathRay! Guns, guns, guns." Lieutenant Denise "Crash" Fourier streaked past him, only meters away, firing the cannons as she passed by DeathRay's tail. "Goddamn it, that one is quick."

"Crash missed him, DeathRay. I'm coming."

"I see him, Fish! Just keep your shirt on." The enemy Gnat had slipped in under him and then behind him somehow and had evaded both Fish and Crash so far. For the longest time, he could only find it in his DTM. But he finally managed to yaw his fighter and spin it wildly in order to find the damned thing visually. If he didn't act fast, his situation would deteriorate to shit in a hurry. And Jack didn't like the ramifications of that.

Jack toggled the mode control of his fighter, flipping him upside down and making him gasp and grunt for air; all the while, the g-suit continued to squeeze the devil out his lower extremities. Jack's fighter converted from a fighter plane into an upside-down, armored bipedal robot, wielding a DEG for a head with two forty-millimeter cannons mounted on each forearm. The DEG could swivel more freely in bot mode, and Jack immediately set it to auto-fire mode controlled by his AIC. Candis went about finding targets and blasting the hell out of them. Jack used the cannons on his forearms for spread effect and cover.

His AIC swiveled the DEG around, tracking the Seppy Gnat with green beams dancing all around the enemy fighter. The energy bolts tracked across the plane's trajectory, but it was moving in too close and too fast for the DEGs. Jack rammed the throttle against the stop, accelerating the bot mode Ares-T downward at over a thousand meters per second, nearly causing him to lose his breakfast again. Were it not for the advanced dampeners of the new fighters, that type of maneuver would have killed him, but Jack gave that no thought at the moment.

He choked the bile down and grunted against the nearly overwhelming g-forces and aimed both arm cannons through the DTM virtual sphere. The two yellow targeting Xs in his mind danced around the sphere, trying to lock onto targets as he fired. The railgun rounds hammered out of the guns at the Gnat as it darted in and out of his line of fire. The Gnat loosed two missiles, both of which were radar- and QM-locked on to Jack's plane. It had been on his tail far too long. Far. Too. Long.

Shit, DeathRay, he's locked on! Candis shouted into his mind.

Goddamn, Seppy motherfucker, he thought, stomping the left pedal and throwing a hard spiral into the mecha. Then he slammed the stick backward against the rear joystick stop. He held the HOTAS with a deathgrip that turned his knuckles almost white enough to see through his e-suit gloves.

"Uuuggghh! Fuck you! Fox three!" he screamed against the wild spin. His missile launched from the back of the bot, not locked on to any particular target but flying in the general direction of the incoming missiles. Jack tracked both cannons on the tail of his own mecha-to-mecha missile and fired. The forty-millimeter railgun rounds filled the space, tracking and bouncing around the purple glow from the tail of the missile until several of the rounds hit home. The missile exploded into a flaming debris field just as the two locked-on missiles passed through it, ripping them to shreds from fratricide. The additive effect of the other two missiles exploding slammed Jack's mecha with shrapnel and superheated plasma. The SIFs and armor of his fighter were stressed to the maximum, but they held.

Almost instantaneously, the Seppy Gnat passed through a firing solution of the DEG, and Candis burned him down. Jack followed up on him with a couple rounds from the cannons for good measure, and the enemy fighter burst apart. Jack's mecha still spun wildly with extreme angular acceleration. So, he spread the mecha's arms and legs like a figure skater to reduce the rotation, and then the retro fields kicked in, dampening out the rest. He heaved twice, losing some bile into his helmet, but he managed to keep most of his stomach; then he toggled the fighter-mode control. The bot pulled its arms and legs in and pitched over into a fighter plane again. His suit quickly absorbed the bile on his viewplate.

"Goddamn! What a maneuver, DeathRay!" Fish shouted. "Great fuckin' flying, sir!"

"Right," DeathRay said sluggishly, and swallowed hard at the lump in his throat. He chewed down lightly on the bite block and felt a fresh blast of oxygen and vapor stimulants rush over him. "Stay frosty, Gods of War. What we did three seconds ago won't keep us alive the next ten."

CHAPTER 9

October 31, 2388 AD
Sol System
Oort Cloud
Saturday, 6:05 AM, Earth Eastern Standard Time

"You frosty up there, gyrene?"

"Roger that, Warlord One." Major Roberts dug his jumpboots into the harness and rolled his armored hands around the saddle handles for a tighter grip. The M3A17-Ts were designed with several ports for armored infantry to attach to during drop or maneuvers. Each hover-tank could carry at least four AEMs if needed. But that would be risky. If a tank bought it on the way down, there went four groundpounders with it. If the numbers were sufficient, it was always better to risk the minimum number of lives with each drop.

Since there would be ten Warlords deploying in their mecha, Roberts and Gunnery Sergeant McCandless had decided that they should use a ten AEM recon group—one AEM per dropped tank. Roberts and McCandless had checked on all the marines to make certain that they were saddled in and locked on to the mecha, and then the major had insisted that the gunnery sergeant get locked on. A short discussion followed about how Gunny saw it as her job to make certain that her CO was taken care of. Then Roberts countered with a statement

107

about being the superior officer and that he reserved the right to . . . and so on. The discussion ended with a quick round of Rock, Paper, Scissors, where Major Roberts picked scissors. Gunnery Sergeant Tamara held her tongue, mostly, as she folded her paper and stomped away to her tank.

Roberts had then clanked his jumpboots against the deck and landed straddle just behind the tank's main turret cockpit. The oversized armored suit atop the mechanized hovertank looked like a maniacally twisted combination of knight in shining—camouflage— armor upon his trusty, oversized noble steed. Roberts squirmed his way into the drop position on the tank. The hardpoint connectors of the tank met the suit with superconductor magnetic field coils pulling them into place. The only way the suit would let go of that tank would be to give the software command to shut the coils off or to vaporize either the tank or the suit. After a few systems checks and DTM conversations with his AIC, the launch authority announced that the Gods of War were away and heavily engaged with the enemy. From the pounding the *Madira* was taking, Roberts surmised that "engaged with the enemy" meant fighting tooth and nail for their fucking lives in a very nasty knife fight.

"Hold on, marine, here we go," Warboys warned him as the tank hovered off the deck and approached the drop-tube shroud. The mecha moved almost silently as the quantum vacuum fluctuation power supply fed the repulsor motivator's thirst for power without batting a capacitor.

Warboys piloted the tank into the cylindrical tube and dropped it into place in the adaptor farings with a metal-to-metal scraping *kreee- chunk*. The tube sealed behind them, leaving the mecha and the AEM in complete darkness. There were various vibrations and impulses that rang through the tube and then translated through the mecha to Ramy's suit. Again, it was quite clear that they were "engaged with the enemy."

"Warlord One in the tube and ready for drop!" Colonel Warboys announced.

The composite armored tube jettisoned out the underbelly catapult field like a missile. Roberts could feel AA fire slapping against the exterior hull of the thing and hoped like hell its SIFs would hold. Simultaneously, all ten of the drop tank tubes were thrown from the *Sienna Madira* into the battle at over four thousand kilometers per hour toward the surface of the Separatist teleportation facility. The flight of the drop tubes cut a ballistic trajectory through the AA fire and surrounding dogfights and would take several minutes. Needless to say, those several minutes were dangerous as hell and absolutely hair-raising. The drop was one of the things that made or broke the tankheads. The good tankheads just trusted the tubes and focused on their mission. The really good ones took those last few minutes to nap.

There was nothing they could do, so there was no need to fret about the harrowing environment outside their drop tubes. Hopefully, all the electronic, optical, and quantum membrane countermeasures would mask them. If those active countermeasures didn't help, there were three times as many drop tubes launched as there were tanks. The tubes were simply decoys and sensor-confusing chaff. On top of the CMs and the decoys and the chaff, perhaps the supercarrier blasting the hell out of the surface would help too.

"Okay, marines, sound off with harmony!" Roberts clicked over to the AEM tac-net and could detect all ten blue dots in his DTM. He started the AEMs off, almost on key. "From the halls of Montezuma!"

"To the shores of Tripoli," Lieutenant Johnny Noonez continued.

"We fight our country's battles," Gunnery Sergeant Tamara McCandless belted with vocal affluence as well as volume.

"In the air, land, space, and sea." Sergeant Nicks' blue dot blinked from com input in Roberts' DTM. Roberts continued to feel the drop tube being rattled with cannon fire and forced himself to pay it no attention.

"First to fight for right and freedom," sang Corporal Vinnie Pagoolas.

"And to keep our honor clean." Lance Corporal Tommy Suez's and Privates First Class Danny Bates' and Felicia Kent's blue dots blinked.

"We are proud to claim the title," Privates First Class Sandy Cross and Makera Gray chimed in.

Roberts gritted his teeth against the jar of the tube retrofields firing and the demo blowing apart the tube, leaving them in open space with the ground rushing up at them extremely fast and enemy DEG bolts and railgun rounds zipping about. Roberts gave the command to pop the superconductor magnet free, and he pounded his jump-boots against the hull of the tank, launching him wide and clear of the mecha. He rolled in a forward flip, and then he finished the verse in tempo with the rest of Roberts' Robots, as they all slammed into the ground with their HVARs at ready and spreading out to cover the landing zone.

"Of United States Marines!"

Warboys checked his status as his mecha pounded into the surface of the Oort planetoid, scattering icy dust about as he did. He could see Roberts bounding away in the low gravity through his QMs in the DTM virtual battlesphere. The hoverfield of the tank activated, lifting it upward with a jolt, and the main cannon swiveled forward looking for ground targets. The DTM filled with red and blue dots way overhead, and there was a scattered group of blue dots rapidly approaching the Warlords from space. *The Navy VTF-32s,* he thought.

Roger that, Warlord One. The Demon Dawgs have deployed and are on approach to give us aerial cover, his AIC, Major Brenda Bravo One One One Mike Hotel Two, confirmed.

"Roberts, what's your status?"

"We're free and looking for cover."

"Roger that. Take the predesignated vectors to cover behind the ridge to the south of the teleport pad, and we'll try to poke a hole in the defenses there for you jarheads to push through," Warboys ordered.

"Got it, Warlord One. Thanks for the ride and good hunting, tankheads."

"Warlord One, we've got movement in the forward grid, and I'm getting ATR readings of Orcus! The landing zone is hot! I repeat the LZ is hot!" Major Glenda "Warlord Two" Freeman said over the net.

I've got it, Colonel. Looks like a squad of Orcus, and I've got several Stinger pings!

Roger that, Brenda!

"Warlords, AEMs, and Demon Dawgs on approach, be advised that we've got active sensor hits on Orcus tanks and Stingers. I repeat Orcuses and Stingers!"

"Roger that Warlord One! We'll do what we can to help out with those Stingers!" Lieutenant Commander Wendy "Poser" Hill replied. Her callsign and rank popped up on Warlord One's blue force tracker display in the DTM as she spoke. He had met the pilot a few times on the ship, but he didn't really know her. All he really knew was that she had posed for some men's magazine. That didn't mean a damn thing to his present situation. On the other hand, he did know from general talk around the ship that other pilots trusted and liked her and that the CAG had given her nothing but walk-on-water reports. If Death-Ray liked her—even though he was a flying squid—it was good enough for Warboys.

"Welcome to the neighborhood, Poser," Warboys added. "Let's go to work, Warlords."

The Warlords spread out across the surface of the planetoid in tank mode, going to active ping on the QMs and looking diligently for any sign of a target that they could smash the hell out of. The sensors generated a resonant signal across the local quantum surface and watched for precisely timed and gated return oscillations. Each ping from each tank was then extrapolated back, as so-called multi-path data. The AICs in return built up a three-dimensional map of the battlescape from the data.

The battlescape was full of red dots that were rapidly closing the gap to the M3A17-Ts. Separatist Orcus drop tanks were spreading across the surface of the Oort facility like ants after someone had kicked over the anthill. Warlord One forced the tank at maximum velocity, which was well over three hundred kilometers per hour in that gravity, with every intention of stomping any ant or hill of them he came across.

His mecha bounded over the edge of a steep escarpment and plunged down the side of the jagged surface about forty meters to the bottom of the cliff, tossing ice and rocky debris on the way. Several of his tankheads followed him. He toggled the bot-mode control, flipping the tank in a backward roll into an upright bipedal position. The large forty-millimeter cannon turret rested atop the torso of the bot where a head might be. The barrel of the large cannon looked as if it were an oversized, yet deadly, proboscis protruding from it. He ran the tank fast, pounding the giant armored feet into the planetoid and flinging a rooster tail of ice and dust particles behind each step. Had there been enough sunlight, rainbows might have danced around the debris, but at about one light-year from Sol, the only lighting was coming from artificial sources and weapons fire.

Give me the full battlescape, Brenda.

Yes, sir. The AIC expanded the colonel's virtual sphere, giving him a complete view of the battlescape on the surface and above them in a hemisphere with a two-hundred-kilometer radius. The algorithms running against all of the sensor-system data identified more than two hundred red dots and a little less than half that in blue dots, all within the hemisphere. Of course Warboys knew the battle plan and realized that the number of blue dots was going to increase by nearly one hundred times that in the next pass that the supercarrier made over them. Until then, the tankheads had to move swiftly, knocking out every target they could find along the path to the interior of the teleporter pad.

"All right Warlords, as we move to the line, I want everybody holding off on any long-range shots. They know we're here, but we don't have to let them know how aggressive we are until the last minute." Warlord One continued in a hard run with giant bounds over crevasses, metal framework, rubble, and the general construction of the facility site. He had yet to need to fire but was beginning to warm up to the idea.

"All right Dawgs, just like in the playbook, nice and frosty. Let's spread out and cover the pounders and tankheads. Watch for those Stingers." Poser pushed her VTF-32 Ares-T fighter at top speed toward the incoming red dots. Her wingman, Lieutenant Junior Grade Cory "Skater" Davis, held tight to her starboard wing. The snub-nosed, fighter-mode Navy mecha dropped to less than two hundred meters off the deck of the Separatist facility.

"Poser, this is Punchout. My QMs are showing more than thirty Stingers! This is gonna royally suck!"

"Roger that, Punchout." Poser paused and analyzed the DTM for the Warlords and for the AEMs. They were still ten or twenty seconds from engagement range. If the Dawgs timed it right, they could hit the line of the enemy a few seconds before and confuse the living shit out of the enemy ground forces with some well-placed air-to-surface ordnance. Then the Dawgs would be totally enveloped by the enemy air support. But, hell, that was all part of the plan.

"Hooyah! Fox, Fox Three, Fox One," Poser announced, letting fly a free flier, a QM-locked, and a heat-seeker missile. The three missiles spread out in front of the Dawgs and split off in three different directions. The free flier hit the deck into the line of Orcuses, while the other two detonated into chaff and countermeasures from the Gnats and Stingers approaching head-to-head. "Fire at will, fire at will, fire at will," she added.

The Navy and the Separatist mecha mixed up into a serious furball with the VTF-32s. Several of the Dawgs released missiles or strafing fire into the Orcus line on the ground, giving the groundpounders and the tankheads cover.

"JavaBean, JavaBean, watch your six!"

"I've got it, Tarzan. Guns guns guns."

"All right, Skater, let's take 'em to the deck all the way!" Poser ordered her wingman.

"Roger that!"

Wendy nosed over into a dive into a trajectory that led through the southern boundary of the teleport towers, strafing continuously. Her wingman followed suit. The directed energy bolts and the railgun pellets chewed up the surface of the facility, throwing ice, dust, and metal slag into ballistic trajectories along their path.

"Okay Warlords, there's your path. Good luck. We got you covered up here."

"Hot fuckin' damn, it's thick out here!" First Lietenant Timothy "Goat" Crow shouted over the Saviors' tac-net channel. The catapult field tossed the marine squadron's fighter-mode mecha from the supercarrier right into a hornet's den of Seppy Stingers and AA fire.

"Roger that," Skinny replied, checking her rearview to see that the last of her group had made it out of the ship in one piece. The six mecha, her attack group, scattered around her randomly in a very, very, very loose definition of the word "formation."

Alan, calculate me some options for getting to the deck as close to the southwest apex of the facility as you can, she told her AIC.

Yes, ma'am, Lieutenant Alan Five Five Foxtrot Echo Echo Alpha One Seven replied. He set about wargaming from the QM and lidar sensor data and from the red and blue dots transmitted from the *Madira's* CDC. In a few milliseconds, Alan had calculated several trajectories for the Saviors, and in a millisecond more, he had picked the optimal one and displayed the "ball" in Connie's DTM mindview.

Great, Connie thought. "All right, Saviors, follow me, and let's hit the fuckin' deck. Maximum velocity . . ." She paused for a response.

". . . with maximum ferocity!" the Saviors replied.

Skinny pitched her fighter-mode mecha downward until the Oort object filled her forward field of view and slammed the HOTAS against the forward stop with her left hand. The engines of the mecha whined lightly and spun up to full acceleration. AA tracers passed by her canopy several times, and then tracers from the right side on her three-nine line ripped across the space just in front of her nose.

"Warning, radar lock is being acquired. Warning . . ." her Bitchin' Betty chimed.

"Skinny, we've got three Stingers trying to pounce on us from our three o'clock angels ten!" her wingman, Second Lieutenant "Hound-Dog" Samuels, warned.

"Shit! Bank left, HoundDog!" She pushed the stick hard left into a tight turn, instantly creating an increase in the gravity upon her body and mecha by a factor of nine.

Tracer fire tracked behind the two mecha but couldn't lock them up. Their turn was tighter than the Seppy Stinger pilots seemed to want to manage. The three enemy planes pulled into a slightly wider bank but were still close enough to make very near misses from their guns. Skinny checked her rearview mirror as well as her DTM, and her wingman was right with her. The two of them had trained formation combat tactics for years and were about to put their expertise to the test.

"Ugghh! HoundDog, let's show these Seppy bastards who's boss," Skinny yelled at the top of her voice. She yanked the stick as far left as it would go for a split second and pulled the throttle back a bit. Then she kicked her right lower pedal and slammed the HOTAS back to the right side. The mecha made an even tighter left bank and slowed slightly as it bled off energy. Then it rolled over in a split-S into a tight right turn as the enemy Stingers overshot them. The maneuver put more than eleven times the force of gravity on her, due to the extreme acceleration, but at the same time, it put her staring up the tailpipes of the three enemy planes.

"Guns, guns, guns!" Skinny shouted. Tracers tracked across space into the rear of the enemy fighter formation, hitting home on the rearward Stinger. She held the trigger a second longer, and the mecha exploded.

The fighter on the right wing of the exploding fireball pitched forward and began transfiguring. It was flying backward and sideways in bot mode, going to guns at Skinny. She slammed the left top pedal and killed the throttle, spinning her fighter-mode mecha into a rapid, clockwise yaw. The maneuver changed her flight vector just enough so that the enemy cannon fire missed her. Barely.

"I've got 'im, Skinny!" HoundDog's voice resounded in her helmet. Skinny could see her wingman barrel-rolling over her and kicking his burners, pulling into firing position on the enemy bot. "Guns, guns, guns!"

The bot-mode mecha's left arm exploded free from the torso as HoundDog's tracers tracked across its flight path. The pilot punched out just in time as the mecha exploded. Skinny and HoundDog were moving too fast to do anything but plow right through it and hope that their SIFs and armor plating held. Debris pinged and rattled against their mecha, but they zoomed through the fireball to the other side, taking up the tail of the third enemy fighter. A blue-green DEG blast off of the nine o'clock of the enemy mecha ripped through it, blasting it to pieces, too.

"Splash one for me," First Lietenant Dana "Popstar" Miller confirmed her kill over the net.

"Good shooting, Popstar. Let's keep pushing downward, Saviors." Skinny pitched back over and continued her acceleration to the deck.

CHAPTER 10

October 31, 2388 AD
Sol System
Orlando, Florida
Saturday, 6:05 AM, Earth Eastern Standard Time

"Goddamned if that ain't a sight I'd never thought I'd see in my lifetime," Jawbone commented on her aerial view of the large mechanized spider-thing that had only moments before burst through the line at the entrance gate of Disney World's Magic Kingdom. Dinosaurs, fairies, aliens, scarecrows, wolfmen, and an array of fantasy characters scattered about the spider-thing, attacking it if they could, but mostly running from it.

"Stay frosty, marines, and keep Main Street clean," Heehaw reminded the marines over the net. "Guns, guns, guns." He went to his DEG to burn down a velociraptor that was trying to crawl atop the big, black, mechanical arachnid.

The spider-thing, also known as Bravo India Lima Seven One One Six, or BIL for short, had a body that consisted of two sections. A smaller, rounded head section, which carried the sensors and control systems and looked as if it could carry a couple of passengers, had a forward-looking, armored windscreen and two armored side windows. Its head looked more like the modified control turret of a tank than anything else. The rearward section was more boxy in shape and had no windows. It was also armored to the maximum and looked like a garbage-heap hauler on military steroids. There were mechanisms that ran beneath the spider's rear compartment that suggested that it could dump that compartment over like a dump truck. There was also an armored door on the rear of it that looked as if it could lower like a ramp or open as an iris.

BIL had once been a lost AI garbage hauler in the reclamation facility of Mons City on Mars. Then Senator Moore and his family had stumbled across him and asked him for help in escaping the attack on the city during the Exodus. BIL had proven so useful that day and Deanna had liked him so much that Moore had bought the vehicle. He had it cleaned from top to bottom, and then upgraded and retrofitted it with armor, structural integrity field generators, hoverfield generators, sensors, and a plush interior environment system that rivaled only a space tourist cruise liner's quarters.

In essence, Alexander had tricked BIL out as only a good ol' boy from Jackson, Mississippi, could. Since Moore had been elected president, it had been a common sight to see the First Family cruising in BIL instead of a more conventional presidential limousine—a sight that had caused an enormous number of White House–oriented redneck jokes and a boost in the restoration and tricking out of old, beat-up utility AI vehicles. BIL had even been the guest of the popular vehicle-enthusiast show *Rides of the Stars.*

BIL! We need to get out of here now! Moore thought to his personal transport.

Yes, Mr. President, I am indeed on my way. Although, my progress is being impeded a bit at the moment, BIL responded. Moore could see him raised up on several of his back legs and swatting at velociraptors as they attacked him. BIL was so armored that the AI bots of the theme park were little more than heavy flies to him. They could barely even be considered pests.

Well, quit worrying about those damned things and just bull rush through them. Go back to hover. The marines can deal with the bots.

Yes, sir.

The mechanical spider retracted its legs and levitated on the Meissner hoverfield. BIL accelerated forward, not bothering to dart around the AIs. His overarmored, bulbous head crushed through any of the smaller bots that got in his way. The marine's mecha also bounced around him, giving him cover. Several times flying dinosaurs made kamikaze attempts at BIL but with little effect. They were either burned down by the FM-12s, or BIL extended an appendage and swatted at them.

The gigantosaurus lumbered down the end of Main Street near the castle between the path to BIL and the path to Storytime with Belle, where the First Family were holed up. The gigantic, reptilian beast flung its tail rapidly into the side of BIL and snapped at him with its jaws. The impact of the dino's tail into BIL pushed him over sideways and disoriented the hoverfield generators. Several marine bot-mode mecha dropped in on top of the AI dinosaur, chewing away at it with guns and mechanical hands.

The apatosauruses and the T-rex joined the action and pushed several of the Magic Kingdom architectural sights around the presidential limousine. BIL extended all eight of his legs and skittered up the back of one of the apatosauruses, just as the tyrannosaurus tried to bite at him. With spiderlike agility, BIL sprang out of the way, causing the giant carnivore to bite into the Apatosaurus's back. BIL pierced through the head of the T-rex with two of his rear legs. The laser systems driving the holographic eyes of the robot malfunctioned and erupted with blue flames pouring from the eye sockets of the dinosaur. It rose blindly and on fire with a monstrous roar and then fell over sideways, its internal circuitry fried and dead.

BIL managed to right his hoverfield system through internal diagnostic and self-repairing systems and hovered underneath the gigantosaurus and around several of the stegosauruses to the redoubt at Storytime with Belle. He hovered in front of the Secret Service's line and landed on his legs.

BIL then pitched his rearward section like a dump truck about to dump its load. The rear iris door opened like a dilating pupil.

"Move, move, move!" Alexander grabbed his daughter in a bear hug and made for the rear of the presidential ride. Sehera flanked their daughter while various members of the security detail filled in around them.

They raced into position underneath the open iris, and then BIL dropped the compartment as close to the ground as he could get it, allowing the president and the First Family to scramble up into the seats of the vehicle. Alexander took Deanna by the hand and slung her upward toward a seat to his right, and she caught it with her other hand and dragged herself over the back of the chair and strapped herself in.

By the time he was sure that Dee was belted in, Sehera scrambled up the aisle between the seats beside them and started double-checking the restraints on her daughter.

"I'm in, Mom!"

"Just hold on, baby." Sehera patted her on the head and then plopped into the cushioned synthleather seat beside her, snapping the three-point harness system around her.

"Thomas, are we all in?" Moore scrambled to the seat in front of his daughter that faced a control console and screen. He sat back into the chair and snapped in, while illuminating the screen with sensor data.

"We're in, sir! Go, go!"

"BIL! Close us up!" Moore shouted.

The iris door spun shut, and armor slammed into place around it. The passenger compartment tilted back up and over and locked into its normal position with a loud metal-to-metal reverberation that Alexander felt deep in his bones.

Abigail, expand the DTM for me. I want to see out past the parking lots and all the way to the interstate, Moore thought to his AIC.

Yes, sir. The virtual view in Moore's mind expanded out more than ten kilometers farther than where it had been. He could see the marine mecha overhead, careening about in combat with the flying robots of the park, and could tell that the combat zone ended somewhere just south of the Animal Kingdom and east of Typhoon Lagoon, near Interstate 4.

The Magic Kingdom appeared to be the northern border of the conflict zone. There were red dots on the ground marching north on World Drive by the hundreds. Epcot was one big red blob. Epcot Center Drive, East Buena Vista Drive, and the Osceola Parkway were all solid red. There were blips of red scattered throughout the park's property between the actual theme parks and hotels. In short, they were surrounded and outnumbered and in the middle of some bad karma.

"BIL, go north!"

"Yes, Mr. President." The AI turned toward the castle and began skittering in that direction on eight legs for a few seconds, and then the hoverfield generators kicked in.

The mechanical spider's legs retracted just as the heel of the gigantosaurus crashed down nearly on top of them. BIL barely managed to evade the crushing reptilian foot by turning the vehicle up sideways and banking in a hard turn to the left. Although BIL had missed being crushed underfoot by a mechanical replica of the largest creature that ever walked the Earth, his maneuver flew him directly into the path of a similarly faux, twenty-meter-long, rapidly swinging reptilian tail of an apatosaurus.

"Holy shit! Look out, BIL!" Clay shouted.

The tail of the beast smashed into the armored limousine, rupturing and tearing bioplastic, metal, and synthskin from the AI dinosaur with a shower of sparks and fiber-optic cabling. The tail of the apatosaurus massed over two tons, and the impulse of the impact transferred energy into the mechanical spider like a baseball bat does to a baseball in a grand-slam swing. The limo massed several tons and held a lot of inertia itself to be overcome, but the hoverfields reduced the mass, and the hit sent BIL and his occupants careening across the amusement park, crashing right through the main spire of Cinderella's castle.

The heavily armored presidential limo passed through the façade like a laser scalpel through hot butter, at first leaving an almost cartoon-like hole in the shape of a spider behind. But the castle spire could not withstand the loss of structural integrity. Euler buckling under its own weight began, and the tower collapsed down upon itself into its very own footprint. The failing of the structure generated integrity loss in the rest of the castle façade, and the surrounding spires crashed and toppled like dominoes one after the other around the center. When the dust cleared, the icon of family entertainment that had stood for centuries was nothing more than a pile of rubble.

"Oh my God, BIL!" Dee cried out as the vehicle tumbled through the air out of control. "We're gonna die!"

"Not to worry, Miss Dee. Just hold on."

"You heard him, sweetheart. Hold on!" Alexander reiterated to his daughter, and white-knuckled the armrests of his own seat.

BIL, give me a status DTM, Moore thought to the AI.

Little if no damage, sir. BIL extended his legs to stabilize their trajectory and add lift to the vehicle. The extending legs absorbed some of the angular momentum of the wild spin, the way an ice skater slows down by extending their arms. The hoverfields kicked in at maximum, and he propelled himself as fast horizontally to the ground as he could. As they approached the ground, BIL used his legs as shock absorbers to supplement the hoverfield generators. Their inertia was greater than both combined could overcome, but the impact with the pavement just outside the north wall of the Magic Kingdom was far less than the armor and the SIFs could handle. *Though I cannot fly, sir, I can indeed hover and bounce.*

Good job, BIL. Now get us the hell out of here!

Yes, sir.

"Jawbone, Jawbone! Did you see that! We've got to stay on top of that vehicle and give him cover!" Heehaw ordered. He had just gone to eagle mode and was darting underneath the legs of the gigantosaurus as the presidential limo smashed through the castle. The FM-12 looked most like a fighter plane in eagle mode, but with legs and arms. The legs ended in three-toed claws, while the arms were human-like. The main gun was gripped firmly in the left, and Heehaw was hammering away directed energy blasts at the surrounding fairytale menaces.

"Roger that, Heehaw! I'm on them . . . fox three!" Jawbone responded as she closed in on a pteranodon with a mecha-to-mecha missile. The missile twisted across the morning sky around a flying carpet and hit home between the shoulder blades of the flying dinosaur. "Okay, Saw, pull out on me, and let's stay on top of that mechanical spider!"

"Roger that, Jaw! Guns guns guns," Saw replied.

Jawbone gripped the HOTAS stick with her right hand, diving the fighter-mode mecha through the engagement zone closer to the deck. She pulled back on the HOTAS with her left hand, cutting the power and allowing gravity to pull her through the dive. At the bottom of the gravity well and just before the no-return point, she slammed the HOTAS forward with her left hand and yanked back with her right. The mecha pulled up through the dive at full throttle near maximum speed for the vehicle at over two thousand kilometers per hour. Shock waves formed on her wingtips, tailfins, and nose, leaving four very loud sonic booms behind her. Saw pulled in supersonic formation behind and slightly to her port side. None of the amusement park hovercars could hold that type of velocity and were left far behind, and the mecha closed the gap on the presidential limousine in seconds.

"Okay, Saw, bleed it off!" she told her wingman as she cut the throttle. Then the Bitchin' Betty chimed at her just as the plane slowed and boomed through the sound barrier.

"Warning, warning. Anti-aircraft fire!"

"Oh shit, Jaw!" Saw's plane rocked its wings and then pitched over nose-first and dove.

"Goddamn it, Saw, don't dive into the fucking AA!"

James, burn that AA, wherever the hell it is! she thought to her AIC. *Got it!*

Jawbone yawed and pitched her mecha over and accelerated out in front of her wingman into a wide, corkscrewing dive. The DEGs burned bright green blasts into the swamp surrounding the Bonnet Creek Golf Club and Resort. The back nine of the resort was quickly set ablaze from the energy bolts. Railgun fire continued to pulse upward from several small yachts on Bay Lake, and Jaw could tell that Saw finally went to guns. But it was too late for her rookie wingman. The SIFs of his mecha could no longer take the direct assault line that he was taking and gave in to the impact of the forty-millimeter rail-gun rounds. *Where* whoever owned those yachts managed to get forty-millimeter AA guns was a big question, but to Saw and Jaw-bone, it was a seriously moot fucking question.

The rounds pierced through the nose of the mecha first and then peppered the wings, ripping through the main spar. Several of the rounds passed through Saw's legs, completely separating his left leg at the hip joint and passing into the underside transfigure mechanisms of the mecha. His g-suit sealed off around the wound and immediately began pumping painkillers and adrenaline into his system, as his left leg fell bloody and limp against the pilot's couch. He bit down in pain on his mouthpiece, and the painkillers flooded his body and relieved the searing in his left side enough for him to remain coherent.

"Get out of there, Carl!" Jawbone screamed over the net.

"Aaarhh," Saw screamed to clear his head. Reaching up with his right hand and letting go of the HOTAS, he pulled at the eject handle. "Eject, eject, eject."

The canopy popped, throwing the lieutenant clear from the failing mecha. AA railguns continued to rip away at the craft, tearing through the armor because the structural integrity force fields had been depleted. The wings and the empennage tore free as rest of the mecha was reduced to debris, and then the power plant ruptured into an orange and white fireball. The force from the exploding mecha sent the ejection chair reeling. The autonomous thruster system kicked in and damped the ride, allowing the gliderchute to pop. By this time, the g-loading and the trauma to the young lieutenant junior grade was too much, and he lost consciousness as his chute drifted with the morning Florida winds.

"Goddamn bastards!" Delilah continued to corkscrew toward the lake, burning through two of the yachts to the water beneath them, which was apparent by the puffs of steam spreading out from around the sinking and exploding ship. Several more yachts continued fire, but Jawbone's mecha was too low and fast to get hit by the slow point and track algorithms of the AA cannons.

She tugged the HOTAS back to her stomach with her left hand and toggled the bot mode with her right pinky. The transfiguration at her present speed stalled her, so she kicked down on the right upper foot pedal to add some rudder in order to slip her into the mode change easier. The fighter-mode mecha rolled and then pitched forward into a tumble that left the FM-12 standing upside down in bot mode. The DEGs continued to blast during the entire maneuver.

James, go auto on the cannons, I've got the DEG!

Roger that, ma'am.

The bot flipped upright with the forty-millimeter railgun cannons atop each shoulder of the FM-12 strike mecha, firing in rapid auto while holding the DEG like a rifle at the hip with the left mechanical hand. Blue-green energy bolts danced across the lake as the bot splashed into it. Water and steam spewed around each DEG blast. Just as the plane submersed completely underwater due to the momentum of its falling trajectory, Jawbone could see through the QM sensors that a blast of directed energy had hit home on a third yacht, causing it to explode violently.

Take that, you sorry motherfuckers.

Oorah! her AIC replied.

The mecha finally hit bottom several tens of meters deep and damned near sunk in the muck at the bottom. The bot bumped into an alligator, stirring it and likely scaring it out of its few reptilian wits. The three-and-half-meter-long, green and brown reptile bumped into the cockpit snout-first and stared right at Delilah and then turned and swam in a frightened hurry in the opposite direction from the mecha.

"You better swim away, you motherfucker," she grunted, and then chewed at her mouthpiece for a burst of air.

Jawbone kicked at the yaw pedal and worked the HOTAS until she was swimming, or more accurately, flying under the water. The QM sensors pinged the lake and painted red dots where the boats with AA cannons were located on the surface above her. At full throttle, she pushed her mecha upward through the bottom of one of the yacht's fibercomposite hulls, sweeping the DEG back and forth like a sling blade. She trashed and thrashed through the yacht, somersaulting upward at half throttle and then cutting the power at the peak of her arch, rolling backward, flipping over feet-down, and crashing through another yacht.

A few more seconds of the trash and thrash, and the AA boats were sinking, smoking, piles of wreckage that the EPA would have to clean up. But as far as she could tell, there hadn't been a single human being aboard any of the vehicles. They had all been AI-driven.

James, did Saw make it to ground?

Yes, Jawbone. The SARs have been detached for him. The AIC assured Delilah that the search and rescue (SAR) teams knew about Saw and were on their way.

Good. Now, where is the president?

One mile west, here. A blue dot in her DTM started blinking on and off.

Right. Delilah toggled the bot back to fighter mode and jetted in the direction of the mechanical spider, zigging and zagging through trees and the occasional golf resort condominium.

"Jawbone! Goddamn, girl, you were doing some serious trashing and thrashing down here." Heehaw's voice broke through on the net, as his and several other FM-12s dropped from supersonic above her. The booms crashed against the cockpit, rattling Delilah's bones.

"Yeah, well, tell that to Saw." She pitched up the fighter-mode plane and pushed forward on the HOTAS with her left hand and yanked along the vector to the presidential limo.

"Roger that."

"I've got a vector on the limo. Who's on me?"

"Jaw, take the point. We're with you, Lieutenant Strong."

"Heehaw, DTMs showing incoming on the limo's tail." Delilah checked her QMs for better resolution on the incoming. They appeared to be airplanes. Very old airplanes.

"Roger that, Jawbone. I've got 'em in view," Heehaw replied. "Want to go fishing?"

"I call worm!" Jawbone quickly added.

She slapped the throttle forward and bounced the stick left then right as her mecha dipped below the tree line. The Florida pines stood well over thirty meters tall, giving the presidential limo some cover. She nosed down and rocketed between an opening in several of the trees, finding a driving lane from which to approach the limo. She was fairly sure that the SIFs and the modern armor of the marine mecha could withstand a fly-through of one of the trees at the velocity she was traveling, but Delilah really didn't want to test them. After all, she was only fairly sure. One of the trees ahead of her began to fall toward the limo, and she had to back off of the throttle even more, so as not to hit the tree's top as she vectored in on the attack planes.

"BIL, we've got company!" Alexander shouted. There were several red dots in his DTM careening toward them at a fairly hard clip. The visual sensors showed that they appeared to be ancient, propeller-driven biplanes from World War I. Three of the plastic planes zoomed through the pine trees, hot on BIL's tail on collision trajectories. BIL juked and jinked through the Florida pines, barely keeping the planes off his tail.

Four more of the planes dropped in on them and apparently had railguns, as trees in front of them were being chewed up. One thirty-meter-tall pine's trunk exploded from the cannon fire and started falling toward them. BIL managed to duck under the tree and spring upward through its falling branches, mostly unscathed. But then one of the planes got the angle on the armored garbage truck and peppered the front end of the vehicle with several rounds.

"BIL!" Dee cried out. The ringing of the railgun rounds against his forward hull scared her.

"I'm okay, Dee."

Sir, I cannot evade these things forever.

Don't give up, BIL!

Yes, sir.

"Motorcade One, Motorcade One, bank hard right!" a female voice came over the com-net.

"Do it, BIL!" The president could see the blue dots in his mindview forming rapidly on the red ones. The marines were coming.

Through the visual sensors, Alexander could see one of the marine mecha fighters screaming through the pine trees, going to guns and splattering two of the amusement park airplanes. Then it turned nose-up and accelerated into a transfiguration, flipping over into bot mode, never missing a shot with its directed energy weapon.

Several of the planes took aim on that one marine, who was running and jumping and flipping and firing its weapons in a flash of maneuvers that left many of the enemy attackers in flaming pieces. Three more FM-12s flashed by firing guns at the things. With hindsight, Moore realized that the first marine had been bait to draw the enemy planes onto her, while the other marines formed up on them, taking them out.

At one point, the bot-mode mecha ran directly toward BIL at very high speeds. The bot-mode feet pounded the Florida sand, flinging dust in a rooster tail behind it. Then it leaped forward in a skyward roll over the limo so close that Moore could see the armored helmet of the pilot in the sensors and could read "Lieutenant Delilah 'Jawbone' Strong" painted just under the canopy.

"That marine deserves a promotion," the president said to himself.

CHAPTER 11

October 31, 2388 AD
Sol System
Oort Cloud
Saturday, 6:15 AM, Earth Eastern Standard Time

Separatist drop tanks poured in seemingly infinite supply from the north and both sides. Warboys pressed the Warlords forward, deeper and deeper into the line. The red dots in the colonel's DTM were thick in front of him, but not insurmountably thick. The Demon Dawgs had softened the line all the way north to the first tower of the teleporter complex. Mason was certain that his tankheads could create a corridor in the enemy position and push the AEMs behind the front to wreak havoc as only the AEMs could do.

Brenda, plot the best vector for the Robots in the DTM, he asked his AIC Major Brenda Bravo One One One Mike Hotel Two.

Yes, sir. I'm on it. The AIC began running wargaming scenarios and simulations at blinding computer speeds. A few seconds later, she had several solutions and chose one. The vectors highlighted in green across Warboys' virtual battlescape.

Thanks. I'll pass that along. Maybe they can use it. Warlord One dropped to a knee and took up a firing position with his DEG. Enemy tanks were everywhere, giving him plenty to shoot at.

129

"Two, watch your right flank!" Warboys warned his second, Major Glenda Freeman. An Orcus drop tank pounced from above and to the right part of a squad of bot-mode enemy tanks running down the side of a crater rim. "Shit, guns guns guns!"

"I've got him, Two!" First Lieutenant Sam "Warlord Five" Cortez responded from tank mode, blasting one of the enemy with his DEG. The directed energy beam tore through the enemy mecha at the knee, spinning it off balance and flailing backward in an uncontrolled spin in the low gravity. In response, Warlord Two leaped over Five into a swan dive and tackled the mecha beside it, punching a mechanized fist through the cockpit and tearing out the pilot, tossing him aside like a dead rag doll and making him fall limp in the low gravity against the icy planetoid forty meters away.

Colonel Warboys serpentined through the terrain with his cannon firing auto, his AIC controlling it and using it to spread out the advancing line, forcing them to either duck and cover or turn and run. This gave Mason time to target individual enemy tanks with his DEG. He picked them off like an experienced sniper. The blue-green DEG blasts punched across the desolate Oort Cloud planetoid, punctuating the dust clouds and debris scattering from the battle.

"Move, Warlords! Keep pushing through this line!" They would get the Robots through the line. But Warboys knew that once they did, the Warlords would be on the wrong side of the enemy, with very little support.

"Move, Robots! We have to stay with the Warlords." Major Roberts dove for cover behind what appeared to be the edge of an impact crater that had probably been formed during the joining of the four little planetoids with the Seppy hauler. The crater was fairly new and didn't look anything like an astronomical phenomenon. The marine major spent little time contemplating the issue.

"Major." McCandless slid belly-first up beside Roberts. "This is a hell of a storm, sir." Tanks were going at each other on the ground and taking the occasional shot at mecha in space, and vice versa. The AEMs had yet to see any Seppy ground troops and were glad of it. "QMs got no sign of foot traffic."

"I noticed that, Gunny. Bother you at all?"

"For the moment, no, sir. You think that means that they didn't detect us in the tubes with tanks?"

"I was thinking the same thing." Roberts checked his team vitals and placement in the DTM. All ten of his forward unit were accounted for and in good shape. And as far as he could tell, the Seppies had no idea they were there. Major Roberts liked that element of stealth. After all, they were a forward recon unit, and they didn't need to get in the mix just yet if they could avoid it.

Carol, have you found any other points of entry yet?

Still looking, Major, his AIC, Carol Eight Eight Mike One One Hotel Lima, replied. *Colonel Warboys has sent us some possibilities.*

Keep at it and keep me posted.

Yes, sir.

"Sir," Lieutenant Johnny Noonez buzzed in.

"Go, Johnny."

"The line seems to split around this crater and then over that mooring point at the crater's two o'clock position on the other side of it. The crater is about six hundred meters across, and the southern tower is on the mooring point between the six o'clock and nine o'clock planetoids." Noonez paused for a breath.

"Yeah, so?"

"Well, sir, if we split off from the Warlords at the crater's nine o'clock and then take to the inside rim of the crater, we might be able to slip into or onto the moorings. If we can slip around this crater to that mooring point, we might be able to get into this thing and make our way to the south tower."

"A lot of ifs, Lieutenant, sir," McCandless said.

"Yes it is, Gunny."

"What the fuck, we got no better plans, sir," Gunny replied, shrugging her oversized, armored shoulders.

"I like it," Roberts nodded.

Carol, this sort of matches what Warboys sent. Connect with him and tell him to support us to the nine o'clock on this crater rim.

Yes, sir.

And tell him thanks.

I will, sir.

"Suez, you're up!" Tamara ordered the rookie lance corporal over the net.

"Oorah, Gunny!" Suez bounced over the side of the crater rim, covering a good seventy meters in the low gravity of the planetoid facility. The AEM landed in a belly slide across the surface to absorb his bounce and to take cover. Dust flew behind him, making a slow, falling arc to the ground.

"Bates! Go!" Gunny's voice continued.

Tommy crawled up behind an outcropping of concrete, steel, and other rubble surrounding a giant guy cable. The cable was a stranded material that looked like a cross between steel and some composite and was more than seventy centimeters in diameter and several kilometers long, stretching from one planetoid to the other. There were other smaller cables running from the ground up to the wall of the octagon.

If the phrase "big fucking cable" is in a dictionary somewhere, I'll bet there is a picture of that goddamned thing right beside it, Suez thought.

Agreed, his AIC replied. *If it's not there, somebody should add it. I'll take a picture and add a wiki.*

Good idea.

One of the smaller cables led up into the sky above him and fixed to the southernmost side of the outer octagon of the teleporter that spanned the space between the six o'clock and the nine o'clock planetoids. Tommy increased the magnification of his sensors on the cable and followed it up to where it met the construct. There were no entrances on that side that he could see.

His QMs pinged around him and generated a three-dimensional map in his head of the environment, showing no red groundpounders. For the time being, they were alone and in the clear, more than a kilometer from the center of the fighting. None of the unit had fired a shot yet, and Tommy wasn't sure if he was glad of that or not.

"Got anything, Suez?" Private First Class Danny Bates took a knee beside him. As he dropped his armored knee crunched and shattered a rock beneath him. The dull gray camo of his e-suit blended into the background so well that Tommy had to enhance his vision with the QMs and IRs just to see him.

"We're clean, as best I can tell. Don't see a way in yet, though." Suez turned his armored head toward the private and smiled. "We might just have to blast our way in, Private."

"Would you look at that." PFC Bates whistled. "What the hell kind of cable is that? Look how long that sucker is. It goes damned near out of sight."

"Yeah, it's a BFC," Tommy replied nonchalantly.

"A BFC?"

"Big Fucking Cable. There's a wiki on it. Look it up, Private." Tommy could see the expression on Bates' face. The PFC was obviously having his AIC check it out.

"No shit," Bates mumbled and laughed.

"Pagoolas, take your team!" Gunny's voice buzzed the net again.

Tommy looked back over his shoulder to see Corporal Pagoolas and Private First Class Felicity Kent belly-slide about a hundred meters to their east and slightly up the ridge of the crater, closer to the ten-story-high wall of the octagon. A glint in the sky caught his eye. A small craft crested over another crater rim to the east of them by four or five kilometers and dropped out of sight. Then another one ripped across the deck right after it, firing DEG blasts. The blue-green blast from the pursuing mecha was followed by orange cannon tracers from another plane that must have been the second one's wingman. Tommy zoomed in on the fight and watched as a small detachment of marine FM-12s zigged and zagged over the top of the meteor crater and the facility wall, chasing enemy Stingers. The fighters stormed over the crest of the ridge out of sight, and there was a fireball eruption that followed.

Hmmm, any idea what that was? he thought to his AIC.

I'd say the Saviors have finally joined us.

Then, several low-flying glints caught his eye a little farther south. They were too big and slow for mecha. Tommy watched a little closer and then got a good sensor zoom on one of them. It was the Seppy version of the Starhawk—the Lorda troop lifter. The lifters dropped quickly over the nearest edge of the crater and then vanished out of sight, undetected by any other mecha.

"Gunny, we're clean over here, and there's no way into this thing that I can find," Suez explained. "There is some some enemy air traffic farther to the east."

"Roger that, Suez. You and Bates start making your way along the wall of that thing toward Pagoolas."

"Affirmative." Tommy rose, pulling his HVAR to his right shoulder, and he grinned at Bates, who was still staring at the BFC. "You heard the lady, Danny. Let's get moving."

"Major, the teams are all leapfrogging along the wall, moving eastward," Gunnery Seargent Tamara McCandless informed her boss. Tamara stood back against the facility wall, looking south at the battle that was raging a kilometer or so away on the other side of the impact crater. The line had pretty much stopped any movement forward or backward and was reaching a point of stalemate.

"Good thing we got through when we did, hey Gunny?" Major Roberts replied with a glance southward himself.

"Yes sir. I guess so," she said. "Sergeant Nicks is easternmost, sir. She is probably a good three kilometers ahead of us by now, and we still have no good idea of how to get into this thing. Lance Corporal Suez reported that there is air traffic farther up , and Sergeant Nicks has verified that. Maybe there is something on up worth blowing up."

"Keep moving us east, Gunny. Send the next team twice the distance this time."

"Yes, Major. Suez, you're up again! Double the gap."

"Let's go, Danny." Lance Corporal Suez slapped the PFC on the shoulder. Tommy stood and bounced his jumpboots against the ground, which was mostly metal and concrete now. The bounce tossed him a good fifty meters. At the apex of his bounce, he could see over the ridgeline of the nearest crater and he noticed several other vehicles flying in and out. His trajectory dropped, and he bounced again. After a few minutes of bouncing, he and PFC Bates had leap-frogged Sergeant Nicks' team by more than two kilometers and were quickly approaching the rim of the crater.

"Suez, look!" PFC Bates pointed an armored finger at the edge of the crater where it met up against the ten-story wall of the teleport facility. Below the ridgeline were several hangar doors and Seppy fighters, and support equipment flew in and out.

"Like following honeybees to a hive." Suez smiled. "Gunny, we've got an entry portal up here. Looks like hangars."

"Roger that, Suez. Sit tight, we're on our way."

"Okay, Robots, converge on these coordinates." Major Roberts passed along Suez's position DTM to the unit.

"Well, Danny, looks like we have a couple minutes to kill. Might as well see what we can see, huh?" Suez put his visor on full zoom and started scanning the hangar opening for a good, covert entry point.

CHAPTER 12

October 31, 2388 AD
Tau Ceti Planet Four, Moon Alpha (aka Ares)
Madira Valley Beach Spaceport
Saturday, 6:20 AM, Earth Eastern Standard Time
Saturday, 2:20 AM, Madira Valley Standard Time

On the thirty-minute flight to New Tharsis, Kira and Allison began filtering through the data she had downloaded from the battle cruiser. The biggest issue was that all the data were encrypted using fairly state-of-the-art algorithms. Allison was fairly confident that she could decrypt the files using techniques she had learned from other CIA AICs during her training for this mission.

Allison could easily manage flying the single engine cruiser, the decryption, and DTM the datadump at the same time. The biggest issue was if Kira could stay awake through it. Hopefully, the data would be interesting enough to keep her alert.

It hadn't been just any battle cruiser that Kira had decided to infiltrate. After four years of spying on the Seppies from a fairly influential family, she had come across the fact that the Separatist battle cruiser *Phlegra* was special for some reason. Why it was special and what was just so special about it needed to be uncovered. Kira knew that the ship was different because it had received some very interesting

135

visitors over the four years that it had been commissioned at the Madira Valley Spaceport.

Elle Ahmi herself had made multiple trips to the spaceship and even been aboard during several of the test flights. What would Ahmi care about the test flights of a *common* battle cruiser? Kira would've understood if it had been a supercarrier or hauler, but a simple battle cruiser? There was something *important* about the *Phlegra*, and that is what her trip to the beach had been all for—to uncover the truth about the battle cruiser.

So, start DTMing anything you get unencrypted. Kira leaned back in the pilot's seat and yawned. She looked out the window at the treetops as they flew by underneath just a few meters away. Then she looked up at the night sky filled by a major portion of the limb of the gas giant that Ares orbited. "Breathtaking," she sighed, and tried to relax.

Her arm itched where she had been shot, so she rubbed at it subconsciously. The immunobooster had done its job, and the wound was healed nicely. There was little scarring at all. It still itched. She still rubbed.

Okay, I have several files now complete. Feel free to start in on them, Allison said.

Well, have you read any of it yet?

Not yet. I'm busy flying and decrypting.

Got it.

The first file was fairly mundane, mostly of flight manifests for materials for the different Seppy military ships at the Madira Valley Spaceport.

Here is the battle cruiser's manifest list.

Yes?

Looks like the ship has only skeleton crew and supplies. Shit, the hangar deck was full of people. If that was a skeleton crew, I'd hate to see how crowded that thing gets with a normal one. Kira continued to look through the manifest list.

I've got another one decrypted.

Good. Kira ran her fingers through her hair and continued to read. *Looks like the* Phlegra's *captain hasn't put in any requests for next month's supplies yet. Other ships' lists are here, but not* Phlegra's.

What do you mean?

There are no other supply lists past today's date for the ship. Odd, isn't it?

An interesting piece of data anyway. Maybe the captain is a procrastinator.

Maybe . . . Kira yawned. Supply lists were boring and were not going to keep her awake. It might be interesting to follow the money trail, but it was no immediate smoking gun that she could see. Besides, that type of work was far too tedious for Kira to wrap her head around after such a long day. She would need to sleep before she could think more about it.

The next few files were similar and fairly anticlimactic. There was one very short memorandum from the White House marked "Top Secret" and signed by President Moore three years prior about a field test of a prototype QMT site-to-site test with the U.S.S. *John Tyler*. Kira had no idea what that meant. The fact that somehow a highly classified document from the White House made it to Tau Ceti startled her and told her that there was a highly placed mole somewhere within the U.S. government.

There was a second file marked with the three letters "QMT" that immediately caught her eye. It was large, very large. Kira toggled it open in her mindview, and to her amazement, a report with U.S. Department of Defense markings appeared. The report was again Top Secret. Somehow it had been pilfered from a U.S. classified database.

Aha.

What?

I might be on to something here. Another QMT-related document. Would you give it a quick read and see?

Okay. Hold on. Allison would have to slow her decryption efforts for a moment in order to give the report more processor power, but Kira had a hunch it would be worth it.

Hey, I think you're right, Kira. At first this thing reads like a science research paper, explaining how QMT is possible by transferring energy wavefunctions through any of the multiple dimensions of the space-time membrane outside of normal space.

Uh huh. And?

Well, then you realize that this is a U.S. classified program, and from the dates and markings, it is over forty years old. The interesting part is where it describes applications for large ship teleportations and finally for personnel transport as well. There is a design for a star-to-star QMT bridge.

What do you mean?

This is obviously the basis concept for the transportation mechanism that took us from Sol space to Tau Ceti in such short notice four years ago.

I figured that. So they stole the idea from us. Wonder why we haven't been developing it and using it if this is forty years old? Kira was beginning to realize that there was something bigger than just a rebellion going on with the Separatists. But what she wasn't sure.

Not sure on that one. Could be that we are, but it is classified.

I doubt it, Kira replied. *We haven't sent a lot of help to the colonies because it takes so long to get to them. This technology would make a big difference in the colonization growth.*

Right. Anyway, the final suggestion of this report is that single human transport between stars is possible. There are even some preliminary calculations suggesting that it is possible to do this accurately to within meters.

Sounds out there. Kira rubbed at her arm some more.

So did exporting thirty million people from the Sol System in one day.

Point taken. Anything else?

No, not really.

Okay, get back to decrypting the files.

Right.

Kira flipped through the file, looking at the preliminary design drawings in it. There was one drawing of a proposed facility with concentric octagonal structures. At each vertex of the outer octagon there were towers. In the very center of the octagons was a larger tower that stood at least twice as tall as the others, and it extended in both directions above and below the structure. The caption for the image read "Quantum Membrane Fluctuation Projector." Kira studied the three-dimensional image a while longer and then moved further through the file, looking at other interesting graphics.

Well, we've for certain seen this thing, she thought.

Right. Oort Seven Three Nine Nine Zero One and the one in orbit above New Tharsis here. Been there. Done that.

A smaller version of the large octagonal structure appeared in the personnel transporter section of the report. The design looked more like a pad, though. The octagonal concentric structures were there, but there were no towers at the corners or in the center. However, there *were* small silver circles in their place. "Interesting," she said verbally, hoping that the sound of her voice would help keep her awake. "We haven't seen that. Have we?"

"Not sure."

In order to avoid the eyes-glazing-over effect of reading too technical a report, she closed out the stolen classified technical paper and opened the next file in sequence. This file consisted of flight plans scheduled for the *Phlegra*. The battle cruiser had been conducting flights for more than a year since it was commissioned, and there seemed to be little of interest there until she came to a flight plan labeled with the present day's date on it. There were future flight plans for the ship, but the one for today was intriguing.

"Holy shit," Kira laughed. "We got off that thing just in time. It's scheduled to go back to Sol space today through the QMT bridge."

"Really?" Allison replied over the ship's speakers, realizing that Kira must want—or need—the verbal stimulation.

"Yeah, it just has experimental flight test listed as the reason. It's supposed to depart about two hours from now. One battle cruiser can't be a threat to the system all the way out in the Oort Cloud, could it?" Kira rubbed at her eyes with her palms and then shook her head, flinging her hair loose about her face.

"I don't see how."

"Let's keep this in mind as we filter the rest of the data."

"Makes sense to me."

Several minutes passed, and there was little of immediate use found in the data. Kira yawned and struggled to stay awake as the cruiser approached the outskirts of New Tharsis. Fifteen minutes later, Allison was waking her up telling her that they had landed.

Kira dragged herself to the parking lot of the small suburban airport and crawled in her car. Allison took over again, driving her to the Tangier estates across the county. On the way, she stripped down and tossed her clothes in a bag to drop in an incinerator along the way. She ran a bathwipe over her body and changed her hair back to its normal color. Then she dressed in clothes that she had stored in her car earlier. The clothes reeked of tobacco smoke, spilled cocktails and a mixture of perfumes and colognes.

Five minutes.

Okay.

The gate at the mansion read the wireless ID tag for Kira's car and opened silently. The automatic taxi AI took command of the vehicle and steered the little blue sportscar into Kira's usual garage spot. As far as anybody at the Tangier house was concerned, it had just been another night out on the town for Kira.

"What a long freakin' day," she muttered. Her hovercar came to a halt and dropped to the floor. Kira took a quick glance at herself in the mirror for any telltale signs that she was a spy and assured herself that she was clean. The canopy of the car slid back and the door dropped to the floor, step-ramp style. Kira took a deep breath and shook her head.

"Home sweet home," she said almost sarcastically. She actually hadn't had a real home in decades since she had become an operative for the CIA. Her home was in Virginia, or at least that was where she had grown up. Her father was a Virginian and her mother a Martian. Her natural appearance was a mix of the two. Her hair was straight and dark, and her big brown eyes and her once milky skin gave away that she had Martian heritage. Her parents were still together after more than fifty years of marriage and still lived in Herndon. They had no idea if their daughter was alive or not. The last they had heard from her had been about seven years prior, just after she returned from New Africa and started training for this mission at the CIA "Farm."

The last four years, though, the Tangier estates—there were several of them spread out through the Tau Ceti system—had been her home. People back at the Sol system would be amazed at how vast the Tau Ceti colony was. Nobody on Earth had any idea how much the place had grown. The Separatists had been using their QMT bridge to funnel supplies and equipment back and forth to Tau Ceti for decades and had created a system that nearly rivaled the United States. The economy was similar, supporting work from low to upper class. There were the Sol system equivalents of multibillionaires here, including the Tangier family. The Tangiers had been one of the largest shipping families for the Martian Reservation, and they had levied that power into the Tau Ceti colony.

Kira had luckily stumbled into the family during the Exodus. And she had fit into the billionaire's lifestyle with vigor. Her many trips to the beach properties along Madira Valley had left her tanned and taking on many of the mannerisms of the Separatist locals. She had become one of the second-tier wives in the family so quickly, most likely because, Kira thought, both Elise and two of her husbands enjoyed having her in bed with them on occasion. Any time Kira had the chance, she had gone out of her way to please the Tangiers in any way she could. Any. Way. Her enthusiastic approach toward the Tangier family had enabled her to gain access to business matters of the powerful shipping juggernaut that otherwise might have been unattainable. Kira had learned a long, long time ago to do whatever the mission required. She had fit right in, and her cover had worked perfectly.

Kira clicked the door open with her palm print. The machine didn't actually read her palm and finger prints, but instead it thought that it had and accepted the false one that Allison transmitted to it. She began the process of dragging herself up the two stories and across to the south hall where her apartment was. To fit in with her persona, she stumbled noisily, as if she were inebriated, down the hallway, bumping into a few pieces of furniture here and there until she reached her room. The door opened for her, she stepped through, and it squeaked lightly as it closed behind her.

"Lights," she sighed, half expecting to find one of the Tangiers waiting for her in her bed. She was tired, but would have to keep to her cover and play her part. "Dim."

Kira, look out!

The lights flicked on at a moderate level, just enough for her to see that there were several people in the room with her. Before she could react, a man in military dress and an armored torso step forward and coldcocked her across the bridge of the nose with the butt of a rifle. Kira saw stars briefly and blood poured down her face. Two men wrapped up her arms from the sides, while somebody else grabbed her from behind and sat an airgun against her neck, injecting her with something. The lights tunneled around her and began to close in on her.

Allison, our cover has been blown were her last thoughts as her mind went black and her body limp. *Allison . . .*

Kira! Kira Shavi!

CHAPTER 13

October 31, 2388 AD
Sol System
Oort Cloud
Saturday, 7:14 AM, Earth Eastern Standard Time

"What the hell was *that!*" Captain Jefferson shouted over the reverberating hull. The *Madira* lurched downward with the force of several gravities so abruptly that the captain's teeth rattled. The extreme noise propagating through the supercarrier's hull rapidly approached the danger zone. The CO was certain that standing with his head up the tailpipe of an FM-12 on full burn would be quieter. Jefferson also caught a glimpse of the COB losing his balance and tripping headfirst into the bulkhead. Had it not been so damned loud, he was certain that there would have been some colorful euphemisms to follow the COB's fall as he raised up, rubbing his forehead and sipping from the coffee mug from which he hadn't spilled a drop.

"Not sure, CO," Commander Monte Freeman, the ship's science and technology officer, replied. The STO tapped at his console and reached out for imaginary icons in his virtual mindview but found no answer. The impact or explosion or whatever the hell it was had just appeared to have come from out of nowhere. And whatever it had been had packed one hell of a wallop.

"Captain, we've got damage reports flooding in from everywhere." The XO shook his head to clear the ringing from his ears, just as the ship jerked and lurched a second time. "Fuck me!"

"Goddamnit, I want to know what *that* is!" Jefferson white-knuckled his chair until the ship stopped shaking. Yellow and red warning lights flashed, and klaxons blared across the bridge.

"I'm working on it, CO." The STO continued to work up simulations from the limited data that the ship's sensors had gathered on the impacts, but he was having little luck. The ship's self-diagnostic sensors, on the other hand, were going apeshit. The STO was certain that the CO could see all of this in his DTM, but he might not be paying attention to that particular detail at the moment since there was a battle raging outside and all. "The SIF generators were taxed to ninety percent of maximum and are running hotter than the coolant systems can overcome. From the usage of the SIFs, I should be able to back-calculate the energy of the impact."

"COB, you and Vanu see what you can find out!"

"Aye, sir." Command Master Chief Charlie Green and Senior Chief Patea Vanu started calling in to the watch posts and duty officers of all the decks for reports. All of them had been pounded to hell, but had no idea what had hit them. Nobody had seen a thing.

Uncle Timmy, you got anything? the CO asked his AIC.

Sorry, sir, I've played it back a hundred times already and can't seem to isolate it. Reflectance data from lidar sensors on the hull suggests there is a particulate cloud trailing from the impact region on the ship's hull. But I have yet to isolate what it was. Whatever it was gave us a thrust vector downward along these coordinates. The AIC flashed an image of the ship in the captain's mindview with arrows pointing out the change-in-thrust direction.

Keep at it, Timmy. Make sure the STO has this data.

Aye, sir.

"Nav, get ready for our turn for the second deployment run."

"Aye, sir."

"CO," Commander Michelle Wiggington said, looking up to the command chair.

"Go, Air Boss."

"We need to get the second wave out soon. The numbers game is catching up to us quicker than the sims said they would, sir. Radar and QM tracks are showing about thirty percent more enemy fighters than expected."

"Same on the ground, CO," the ground boss concurred.

"Goddamned intel pukes," the XO muttered under his breath. "They're always off twenty percent here, thirty percent there."

"Understood. Prepare for second run of sorties. XO?"

"Good to go, sir," the marine colonel replied. "The cats are all loaded and ready to fire on your command."

"STO, how about that impact?"

"Still working on it, sir. We need more data."

A few brief moments passed, and then the sound of a massive impact against the upper hull rang like a bell through the ship, again. Impact alerts and fire alarms continued sounding throughout the ship. The CO's DTM for the ship's health had a big bright red spot on the upper level near the aft section of the ship, and it was growing larger, like a viral infection spreading through a computer network. Secondary effects from the impacts were spreading with fires and hull breaches through the aft upper section of the ship. Again, Uncle Timmy flashed an updated vector model of the ship's thrust vector alterations. "Nav, rapid evasives!"

"Aye sir!" Lieutenant Commander Swain punched in an AA evasive-maneuvering algorithm and added a high-speed missile evasion routine on top of it. The ship started to move sluggishly with short jumps and drops, and then it was pounded again.

"I hope *that* is enough data for you, Mr. Freeman," the XO told the STO with a hint of sarcasm. The third-ranking bridge crewman paid the XO little attention. Everyone who was a member of the senior staff was used to, and for the most part fond of, the former marine fighter jock's sardonic wit. "I'm not sure we can survive much more of a study phase."

"I've got it, Captain! It's a mass driver. A *big* f'n mass driver. From my calculations, we're getting pounded with rounds the size of a fighter plane at a quarter the speed of light. There is a faint debris trail, very faint, from the projectile's path." The STO didn't look up from his screens and continued tapping frantically at his controls. His AIC was running mass driver sims in his head, giving him three-dimensional simulations to base his hypothesis against. He compared the thrust vector models of the ship that Uncle Timmy had generated with the dust particle tracks and was working on a launch point of origin.

"Mass driver! Shit. I want all available power converted to the upper level SIFs now!" the CO shouted. "Engine room!"

The goddamned Seppy bastards are adept; I'll say that about them.

Yes sir. Teleporters, mass drivers. What next? Timmy replied.

"Eng here, sir."

"Get me more power to the upper-level SIFs, now!"

"Working it, sir. We've got some loose nuts and bolts rattling around down here. Whatever hit us seems to have been aimed at Engineering. Fireman's Apprentice Ranes, lock that shit down there now! Sorry, sir. We're working it as fast as—"

"Just get me that power to the SIFs." Captain Jefferson cut the channel before the Eng could respond.

"CO, CDC!"

"Go, CDC."

"Sir, we've got a track on the impact. It's coming from the moon planetoid, sir."

"STO concurs with that track, CO!" Freeman agreed. His calculations had just completed and were telling him the same thing. A petty man might have been upset that the CDC had beaten him to the discovery by a millisecond, but Freeman was more concerned with not getting killed. Besides, it was always better to have two separate studies lead to the same conclusion.

"Roger that, CDC." Jefferson expanded his battleview out to the little planetoid above the facility and overlaid the track data sent up from the Combat Direction Center. The bright red line track went in a straight path from the hull of the ship right into the side of a jagged crater in the upper right-hand quadrant of the face of the pale gray planetoid.

"Gunnery Officer Rice! Target that spot and start pouring the DEGs there!"

"Aye sir!"

"Why'd they stop firing again? Anyone?"

"They shot twice, then paused, and then shot twice again," the STO added. "Hmmm . . ."

"Got any other useful analysis there, STO?" the XO said gruffly. "They shot twice, *then* waited, how long? And then they shot twice again."

"Let's see, there was thirty-one seconds almost precisely between shots within each of the two volleys so far," the STO said, answering the XO's challenge.

"Maybe they only have a double barrel, sir," the COB said. "I mean it follows with the STO's assessment."

"If that's the case, let's hope it takes a lot longer goddamned time to reload this go around," the CO replied. "Start a clock, STO. When do we expect the next hit?"

"On it, sir." Commander Freeman tapped away at his console again and conferred with his AIC. "There have been three minutes and fifty-seven seconds between volleys. Precisely, each time, so that implies a recharging, not a reloading process. That is about forty-two seconds frommmmm, now. Mark ticker! Clock is now transmitting to all the senior staff DTMs." His AIC synchronized the clock to the data to within a millisecond.

"Like I didn't have enough in there already." The XO grinned at the STO. A countdown started in the upper right-hand quadrant of his DTM in bright red numbers. The clock overlaid the several layers of DTM data continuously streaming through EndRun's mind. He acknowledged the countdown and went back to his previous display.

"Our casualty rates are getting worse by the second, CO," the air boss said.

"Ground boss still concurs, sir," Army Lieutenant Colonel James Brantley added.

"CO, we've got system failures across the boards." Colonel Chekov scanned through his DTM on the mission status to discern how this new threat was going to impact the second run of troop deployments. "And as the air boss and ground boss have mentioned, the clock says it's time for run two, sir. We better make it while the cats are still functioning."

"Hold a minute, XO. We need to take out that gun first. Gunnery Officer Rice, status?"

"We're pumping energy into the spot, sir, but the data is not that accurate. We might be hitting them, or we might just be hitting an empty crater hundreds of meters away from it," the lieutenant replied. "They're a long way off, sir."

"Keep firing on a standard dither pattern until you hit pay dirt. You see smoke; keep hitting that spot." He thought briefly about missiles, but at that distance, they would be sitting ducks for AA. The missiles only traveled about a tenth of light speed and would likely get shot down long before they got there. DEGs were the only choice for that range, even if they were too precise to take out such an ambiguously located target.

"Aye."

"Okay, XO. Let's set up for the second run. Nav, give me as random a damned path as you can. Let's all pray that goddamned mass drivers can't track on a rapidly moving target."

"All sorties and drop tubes, prepare for a second deployment run through the engagement zone," the air boss ordered over the air wing net.

"AEMs, AAI, and drop tank squads, prepare for ground deployment," the ground boss ordered.

The *Sienna Madira* had passed over the teleporter facility planetoids at a high rate of relative speed, deploying hovertanks, AEMs, and fighter support, while splattering the facility with directed energy blasts and cannon fire. In order for the ship not to be a sitting duck and to pull the AA fire and SAMs with it, the ship continued past the engagement zone and then out of range. Then, according to the battle plan, the supercarrier would make a second pass to deploy an overwhelming number of forces. The first deployment was a smaller portion of the overall blue force number. Using a small force at first was a standard tactic used when intelligence on an enemy force was sketchy at best. The first attack was used to draw out the enemy forces and get a better assessment of what they had. Then the supercarrier would make its second pass, dumping out the full contingent of its fighting force. The tactic had been used for centuries. The CO, being a student of twentieth-century ancient warfare, had taken this play from an ancient battle in the South Pacific over an island known as Iwo Jima.

The waiting was over, and it was time for the second pass. So far, the plans had been going mostly according to the simulations, except for the fact that there were about thirty percent more enemy fighters—and there was the other thing about the enemy's secret weapon. The sims had not accounted for their being a gigantic mass driver on the little moon.

Jesus Christ! A mass driver. How in hell did intel miss that? The clock in his head counted down to ten seconds.

Good question, sir, Uncle Timmy replied, just as perplexed as the CO was.

Sound the warning, Timmy.

Aye, sir.

✧   ✧   ✧

"All hands, all hands! Brace for impact! Multiple hull breaches. Emergency crews standby! Expect two hits thirty-one seconds apart. Repeat, two hits in five, four, three, two, one."

The ship rang and screeched again and shook hard enough that the CO had internal bruising from his seat belt. The inertial dampening fields throughout the ship were taxed to the limit, and in several cases on the middle decks, the fields gave out, leaving hundreds of sailors suspended in microgravity for a few seconds. Jefferson's DTM buzzed massive damage and hull breaches. The *Madira* listed sideways, and the gravity generators wavered slightly, sending a wave of microgravity across the ship. A wave of nausea likely followed right behind the microgravity for most.

"Shit, they've most certainly reloaded. Right on schedule, STO."

"Captain, we've got SIF generator failures on multiple decks. Coolant system is overwhelmed and ruptured on multiple decks. Hull breaches reported," the XO exclaimed. "It *must* be a double barrel, sir! Good work, STO."

Timmy, sound a brace for impact! Captain Jefferson dug his fingernails into the armrests of his chair and watched the seconds tick down in his mindview.

Aye, sir.

"All hands, all hands! Brace for impact! Multiple hull breaches. Emergency crews standby! Second hit imminent in five, four, three, two, one. . . ."

"Rice! Knock that goddamned thing out!"

"This is so gonna suck, sir," the COB slammed his magnetic coffee mug into its holder, gripped his chair, and then pushed his feet against the underside of the station for extra support.

The second shot of the mass driver pounded right on top of the previous spots. The severely sublight evasive maneuvers were of little effect to an object traveling twenty-five percent photon speed. The projectile poked through the nanocarbon composite metal hull, vaporizing two decks before it completely disintegrated with the violence of turning several tons of slag metal to vapor instantaneously. Four decks deeper, the rupture stopped. Unfortunately, that deck was where the all-important space-time dragging sublight propulsion system was.

The power system to the sublight engines exploded like a mininuke, destroying decks all around it in every direction for at least thirty meters. A violent orange fireball swept across the decks, hot enough to turn solid metal to molten lava. Hundreds of sailors were vaporized almost instantly, and hundreds more were dumped into space. Fortunately, the vacuum of space extinguished the fireball almost as rapidly as it formed, leaving a gaping hole in the back of the now listing and propulsionless supercarrier.

"Sublight propulsion system is gone, CO!" Larry shouted. "They knew right where to hit us too! Jaunt drive took serious damage."

"Auxiliary propulsion?" the CO asked.

"Not sure, sir. The flow loops for the power were so disrupted, who knows," the STO shrugged.

"Engine room! When will I get my propulsion back?"

"Working it, sir. We've got massive casualties down here. I need every fire crew you can get me to reroute the systems. The aux prop is out too, for at least thirty minutes, until I can get power to it."

"You have three minutes and fifty-two seconds, Eng!"

"Aye, sir!"

"What about the sorties, sir?" the ground boss asked. "My guys are getting chewed to all hell and gone down there."

"Comm! Get the *Blair* in here now!"

"Yes sir!"

"Air Boss, launch all the sorties now!"

"We're waaay out of range, CO." The air boss did some quick math in his head via the help of his AIC. The fighters were typically rated as having a top speed of two thousand kilometers per hour. That wasn't true, actually. In an appreciable atmosphere that was mostly true, but in space the fighters could accelerate as long as they wanted to and eventually reach an extremely fast velocity. The problem with that was slowing down. In order to slow down, the fighters had to decelerate just as long as they had initially accelerated. And, the inertial dampeners could only handle so many g-forces and the SIFs, and hull plating could only handle so much impact. A micrometeorite at speeds much faster than the max rated safe speed put the pilot and aircraft at much greater risk.

"CO."

"Go, Air Boss."

"The fighters at double the rated safe speed would still put them about ten minutes from the engagement zone. Engineering might have aux prop up by then."

"They might. Deploy all sorties now. Pilots have volunteer's discretion for approach speed." The CO suspected that allowing the jocks to volunteer to push their planes beyond the limits might encourage them to push the performance envelope of their systems. Hell, the air boss was all the time writing up the pilots for violating the speed protocols, and now he was giving them free reins. "Air Boss, make certain to reiterate the suggested safe speeds."

"Aye, sir."

"What about the ground, sir?" the ground boss asked.

"Sorry, James. Unless we get prop of some sort or the other, they're gonna have to do the best they can. Relay that message."

"Air Boss."

"Sir?"

"Pull the Gods of War from high-altitude engagement, and tell DeathRay to help out the ground troops."

"Aye, sir. That might prove difficult, as they are covered up more than three to one right now."

"Pull them down. It might force the Seppy bastards into a more confined engagement zone and shrink the bowl." The "bowl" was what fighter jocks had called the engagement zone for centuries. In space, the engagement zone was a full three-dimensional sphere, or "ball." But over a surface, it was a hemisphere or an upside-down bowl. By pulling the fighters in closer to the ground, the ball became a bowl, and the closer they could pull down, the smaller the bowl got. This made turns tighter and maneuvers harder, giving better pilots and more advanced technology the biggest advantage in the dogfight.

"The goddamned bowl is too big for certain," the XO added. Being a marine mecha jock in his earlier career, EndRun understood the tactics of dogfighting firsthand. The captain was glad that his XO agreed with him.

"Roger that, sir."

"XO, make certain that all power is put on the SIFs. We're sitting ducks out here." The clock had reset after the last mass driver round hit the ship and started counting down again. Two minutes thirty-eight seconds to go. "Rice! Tell me you are going to hit that thing before it hits us again!"

"Firing, sir. The DEGs are dithering the target area, but spectral analysis doesn't show anything other than ice or rock being hit yet, sir. They may be too deep in the ground."

"Keep firing, son."

God help us now.
Agreed, sir.

"Engineer's Mate Shah, hit that motherfucker right there with this BFW until I tell you to stop!" Main Propulsion Assistant Lieutenant Joe Buckley II shouted over the whistling and crackling of the raging fires and hissing flow system leaks as he hefted a really *big fucking wrench* toward the EM1. The meter-long tool clanked against the deck near Shah's feet, and the EM1 grunted as he picked the heavy thing up.

A crackle of electricity broke free from the hyperspace-lensing system and reached out across the gas vapors in the air, finding a path to electrical ground through the lieutenant's coveralls. The high-voltage shock knocked him a good six meters through the foul, vapor-filled air into the bulkhead on the aft side of the Engine Room. The lieutenant landed back first against the metal plating with his arms and legs akimbo. His head hit with a crack, sending a wave of stars across his vision to go along with the white lightning arc still there from his saturated retina.

"Lieutenant!"

"Keep fucking hammering on that stress valve, Shah!" Buckley blinked hard and pulled himself up to his feet, shaking his head. More arcs were jumping free of the projector power grid and had to be brought under control. Buckley ran to the control board for the power system, looking for any visual clues as to which systems could still be used, for anything, *anything* useful and which ones absolutely had to be turned the fuck off.

The power conduits had been fried all over the goddamned ship, and the board was lit up like a Christmas tree. The sublight prop was completely gone. It had been literally smashed to hell and vaporized with several decks of the ship above them. The aux prop was out, too. But the CHENG thought that he could get it back online in a few minutes.

According to the clock that the CO had just put into the entire engineering crew's head, Joe could tell that he had about two minutes and thirty seconds to figure something out. Sitting around and waiting for the Eng to get the aux prop online didn't seem like a good idea to him.

The power couplings between the vacuum fluctuation energy collectors and storage system and the hyperspace projector and fluctuation field shields were intact, and the tube was swirling a perfect pink and purple hue. The problem was that there was no way to get the energy from the storage units to the projector so that it could generate the hyperspace vortex in front of the ship. That took a lot of energy. There was energy stored away in the collector and storage capacitors and there was a hyperspace projector, but there was a gulf between them that might as well have been light-years. Another finger of high voltage leaped across the room into the bulkhead grounding out, and a relay on the board went red as the arc died. There was a faint puff of smoke and some foul, burned-plastic smell coming from within the power-grid couplings.

"Well, that solves the random arcing problem," he said to nobody in particular.

Buckley ran through the standard training for such a situation. The supercarriers were designed so that all the plumbing and power conduits could be interspersed in "worst-case scenarios" according to the training manuals, but there was always a mess to clean up afterward, so the manuals emphasized the worst-case-scenario bit. Buckley considered his situation and decided that imminent death from a relativistic mass driver round qualified as a worst-case scenario, and he also recalled the way his father had rerouted coolant systems for the DEGs on the *Madira* during the battle at the Martian Exodus. He hoped like hell that this wasn't "déjà vu all over again."

"Sir! The valve broke off, and this thing is getting goddamned heavy," EM1 Shah shouted.

"It broke?"

"Yes, sir! Broke off! What do I do now?"

"Nothing, Shah! That's exactly what I wanted. Now get the fuck away from that thing. It's gonna blow ethylene glycol all over the fucking place in about five seconds."

"Shit, sir!" EM1 Shah shagged his ass across the engineering section over debris and to the propulsion station with Buckley.

"Let me see . . ." Buckley rubbed at his chin, smearing soot across it as he did. "Shah, get the biggest fucking power cable you can find and tie it off to the coupler box on the projector power intake."

"You're the boss!"

Debbie, find me an alternate route for the power between the collector bank and here. I'm gonna plug into this tertiary cooling loop.

I'm looking, Joe. That flow goes down two decks, then over seven. There is a DEG system across the hallway there. Then there is a . . . His

AIC explained the route as highlights along the ship's engineering schematic appeared. At each new highlight, Joe authorized a valve, a switch, a relay, or even a door in a few cases to be opened, closed, thrown, or cracked as needs be. In another instance, he sent a fire crew down a deck with a laserwelder to weld a hatch door across a hallway, connecting two separate flow loop conduits. He had emphasized that they needed to fucking hurry.

"Lieutenant Buckley, we've got the hatch door welded across the conduits, sir," the chief of the fire crew reported.

"Good, now get the hell out of there."

"Roger that, sir."

"CO, MPA Buckley!"

"What is it, Mr. Buckley!"

"CO, I need Nav to put in a coordinate location for the jaunt drive now!"

"What's up, Mr. Buckley?"

"I think I can give us one short jaunt, sir."

"Roger that, MPA."

"Air Boss! Hold those fighters!"

"Uh, sir, they're out of the ship," the air boss replied sheepishly.

"Damnit all to fucking hell, will nothing go right today?"

"Ground Boss, get ready for rapid drop."

"Yes, sir."

"Okay, Nav, set jaunt coordinates to . . ."

Ethylene glycol that was heated to about ninety degrees Celsius burst from the smashed valve across the engineering corridor and spewed hot coolant into the room like a rocket nozzle spraying propellant. The coolant spread out quickly and cooled to nearly safe temperatures. Boots, gloves, and coveralls would be enough to keep the engineering crew safe from the heated coolant leak. The system quickly drained and covered the floor on the port and aft side of Engineering about three centimeters deep.

Fifty-three, fifty-two, fifty-one . . .

"Goddamnit, Buckley. What the hell are you doing?" Commander Harrison screamed from two corridors down in the aux prop room. "I just lost all the tertiary coolant pressure to aux power."

"Saving our ass, Benny, uh, sir!" he replied to the CHENG.

"Cable is connected to the input coupler, Lieutenant!" EM1 Shah yelled over the noise to Buckley and shrugged. "What next, sir?"

"Tie the other end of that thing around the pipe you just smashed with the BFW!"

"Huh, oh! I see, sir." The engineer's mate first class tugged at the ten-centimeter-diameter power cable and dragged it across the deck, sloshing through the hot coolant pooled on the floor. The weight of the cable was too much for him to wrap around the conduit by himself, and two other firemen joined in his struggle with the thing.

"Pull, Fireman's Apprentice Cain! Pull, goddamnit!" Shah shouted as the three men struggled against the cable. Shah had both his feet against the pipe and was pulling with both hands at the cable, tug-of-war style.

"As tight as you can get it, Shah!" Buckley glanced over his shoulder at the EM1 and his team working at the cable. "Weld that son of a bitch into place!"

"Yes, sir," Shah held onto the cable with all his might. "You heard the lieutenant, Fireman. Weld that son of a bitch down!"

Buckley frantically rerouted power couplings via the board and through various DTM connections. His AIC was always four or five switches ahead of him, but he had to authorize each throw, unless he were incapacitated for some reason.

Twenty-eight, twenty-seven . . .

"Engineering! Any time now."

"Almost there, Captain!" Buckley replied.

"Lieutenant! Cable is in place, sir!"

"All right, clear out."

The fire crew cleared out, and Shah took Buckley's left flank.

"I'm here if you need me, Lieutenant."

Buckley was too busy to respond at that point. The clock was ticking down, and the board had to be reconfigured just right, or a power breaker could trip and the power would never make it to the jaunt drive. He reached up to the control board and tracked down the relay switch to set the power rerouting into motion. All of the system was going to dump a small star's worth of exotic energy through the various parts of the ship, and hopefully it would reach the projector. And, hopefully, it wasn't going to fry everybody along the way.

"Here goes nothing," he said.

The clock in Joe's head ticked to seven seconds as he finally depressed the relay switch, and lights on the board all turned red in sequence, like a stack of falling dominoes. Several of them physically blew out. Sparks began flying across the switching system, and several fires broke out on the back side of the computer controller rack. Had every alarm and klaxon not already been sounding in the ship, they would've most certainly started blaring then.

"Uh, EM1 Shah, I suggest we get the fuck down!"

"All hands, all hands! Brace for impact! Multiple hull breaches. Emergency crews standby! Second hit imminent in five, four, three, two, one . . ."

"CO, CDC!"
"Go, CDC."
"We've got massive electromagnetic signatures forming above the teleport facility!"
"I'll worry about that in a minute," the CO muttered.

A bolt of electricity stronger than most bolts of lighting jetted out from the busted valve stem of the coolant flow loop through the large power cable and across the gap to the projector power coupling. The cable danced around, at first wildly like a poorly thrown jump rope, and then it was locked still with a *snap* by the extreme electromagnetic bottle created from the field lines of the system. The cable sheathing melted away, and the metal strands glowed bright like the filament of an incandescent light bulb. Then the cable vaporized into a plasma of metal gases, and the electric arc hummed and filled the gap between the conduit and the projector power coupler. The bolt grew white-hot with shades of violet pulsing through it. The projector began to whirl up. It whirled faster and faster as the gamma particles tried to breach the massive gravitational boundary of the event horizon within it. The exotic energy flow pulsed through the space-time bubble created within the field projector.

It's working, Joe!
Yeah, let's hope and pray it does quickly!
Sparks exploded off of several systems as smaller fingers of the electric bolt tried to dance free of the electromagnetic bottle. Each time a bolt would strike a bulkhead, part of the metal would be vaporized, and more nasty gaseous fumes would be added to the room's already nauseous atmosphere. Joe's DTM still displayed the engineering drawing of the makeshift power conduit path that he had created,

and along the path, he could see emergency systems being activated. There were fire alarms, secondary explosion alerts, loss of atmosphere, overpressure, and any other type of alert that was in the safety protocols of the ship's systems. Then there was a rupture along a maintenance corridor six decks down, and the power drained off to ground in the deck plating of the floor for a microsecond before the power supply ground-fault circuit interrupters kicked the breakers. The lightning bolt across Engineering vanished, and the whirling of the projector slowed to idle.

"Maybe that worked." Buckley crawled up to his feet giving the engineer's mate first class a hand.

"We're gonna need a shit load of mops, sir." Shah shook his head at the mess in the Engine Room.

"Actually, Vineet, we need to run as fast as we can to sickbay."

"Why, sir? I feel fine."

"Yep, so do I. But in about five minutes, our bodies are going to realize that we've just been hard-boiled by all the extremely high energy x-rays that we were just exposed to, and we're gonna start dying of extreme radiation dosage." Buckley looked at his hands to see if they were swelling yet. He felt the need to grunt and clear his throat, which was definitely a bad sign.

Start a clock, Debbie.

Already did, Joe. In three minutes, it will be hard for you to keep walking. Now, get moving. Joe?

Yes, Debbie?

The ship is still here. Your father would be proud. Joe noticed that the clock for the mass driver impact was now at plus twenty-eight seconds.

"Let's move it, EM1."

"Jesus, sir. I don't wanna die!"

"Well then, you'd better fucking hurry to sickbay."

CHAPTER 14

October 31, 2388 AD
Sol System
Oort Cloud
Saturday, 7:17 AM, Earth Eastern Standard Time

"Splash another one." Jack stomped the left lower pedal to stop his bot-mode spin and then toggled back to fighter, yanking his HOTAS hard right to pull back into some sort of formation with Fish.

"Bank left, DeathRay! Hard left!" Fish exclaimed over the net. "Fox three!"

"Whoah!" he pulled back left on the stick, adding some throttle and slip and gritted his teeth into his mouthpiece as a mecha-to-mecha, QM-guided missile passed within a meter of his cockpit. "Fish, where the hell are you?" He could see her in his DTM but didn't have a visual on her.

"Splash four!"

"Holy goddamed hell, DeathRay, we're getting hammered!" Lieutenant Dave "Deadstick" Barber cried over the net.

"Just think of it as a target-rich environment, Deadstick," Fish replied.

"Roger that shit, Fish," Hula grunted, obviously working against a high g-load.

"Fish, you with me, girl?" Jack scanned his DTM for more Seppy Gomers and caught a formation of four directly above them, engaged with Demonchild and his wingman, Stinky. He finally caught a visual of his wingman in his rearview mirror, as he toggled over from bot mode into fighter mode and pulled in tight on his right wing.

"Roger that, DeathRay."

"Let's help out upstairs, angels twelve, two o'clock high." He gave Fish a moment to catch the bogies in her DTM and gave a shout-out to Demonchild and Stinky. "Demonchild, Stinky, you've got four Gomers taking up the angle on your seven o'clock trying to gain advantage on you."

"Roger that, DeathRay! Can't seem to shake these motherfuckers!"

"Just hold 'em off for a few more seconds. We're coming." Jack pulled the stick back to his stomach and slammed the throttle forward against the stop. The Ares-T fighter plane rocketed upward, farther away from the planetoid facility into the higher altitudes of the engagement zone and deeper into the blackness of space. The acceleration of the maneuver pushed him against his seat with a steady six gravities. His wingman held tight right beside him.

"What's the plan, DeathRay?" Fish said faintly against the added gravity.

"Okay, Fish, we fly in there, and we kill those motherfuckers," DeathRay grunted.

"Uh, great plan, boss."

Candis, give me some scenarios here, he thought to his AIC.

Roger that, DeathRay. Several flight vector lines started bouncing around in his virtual mindview, giving him flight paths of the Gomers and showing where he and Fish could converge on them. The red and blue lines twisted around each other like stripes on a candy cane— and showed that they could get the drop on the enemy fighters if they did it right.

Pass it along to Fish.

Done.

"Okay, Fish, follow my lead and take a shot if you can get it."

"Roger that, boss!"

Jack kept the hammer down with the throttle full-forward against the hard stop. He jinked and juked through the trajectory that Candis had calculated, adding a touch of his own to it here and there.

"Hurry up, DeathRay! I've been locked up!" Stinky said shakily.

"Pull into the tightest, hardest left bank you can stand, *now*, Stinky!"

"Roger that! Banking left!"

Stinky's mecha pulled tight into a very tight, counterclockwise turn, throwing g-forces on him that pushed him to the brink of blacking out. Demonchild pulled up and across a firing solution for one of the Gomers.

"Damnit, Demonchild, don't pull up! Flatten out!" Fish shouted.

The enemy Gomer fired a streak of cannon tracers into Demonchild's fighter, bouncing it into an uncontrolled roll. Another streak of cannon fire blasted the power plant in just the right spot, causing the fighter to explode violently and too quickly for Demonchild to pull the ejection handle. He was killed instantly in a raging space inferno.

"Fuck!" Jack screamed through his bite block. "Keep it tight, Stinky!"

The three remaining Gnats banked through the turn, with Stinky trying to get a firing solution on him. The enemy fighters appeared hell bent on not letting him get away. As the three Gomers all pulled in tight behind him, their trajectories led them right across Jack and Karen's line of sight. A firing solution tone sounded in Jack's head.

"Hold on, Stinky! Almost . . . Guns, guns, guns!" Jack's railgun cannon tracers cut in across space in front of the lead Seppy Gnat and tracked its trajectory until it flew right through the forty-millimeter cannon rounds. Several of the baseball-sized, high-incendiary, armor-piercing tracer rounds ripped through the empennage of the enemy fighter, scattering debris and gas vapors from it. "Guns, guns, guns!" He continued to fire until the lead Gnat broke up. Its pilot punched out at the last second.

"I've got two. Watch number three!" Fish shouted. "Guns, guns, guns!"

A blue-green DEG beam pulsed across the wing of the second Gnat, vaporizing important structural members there. Welds and composite-to-metal junctions delaminated from the blast. The high-g turn pulled the wing the rest of the way off, spinning it madly out of control. The fighter exploded with no sign of an ejecting pilot.

The third Gnat pulled off of Stinky's tail and banked hard upward, but by that time DeathRay had managed a barrel roll over Fish putting him in behind the third Gomer. Jack brought the Separatist Gnat fighter through a firing solution that blinked on and off between yellow and red.

"Guns, guns, guns," he said, and strafed through with his DEG missing. "Fox three!" He loosed a mecha-to-mecha missile that twisted and spiraled around until it hit home with a white ball of flame engulfing the enemy plane.

"Hot damn! Take that, you Seppy Gomer son of a bitch!" Stinky cheered.

"DeathRay, DeathRay, *Madira!*"

"Go, *Madira!*" DeathRay replied.

"Pull high altitude plan and go for the deck, ASAP. I repeat, all Gods of War are to give coverage on the deck!" the air boss ordered.

"Roger that, *Madira*. Gods of War are hitting the deck!" Jack checked his DTM and visuals and didn't see an immediate threat. That only meant that nothing was shooting at him *right that second*, but his DTM was still filled with more red dots than blue. But their maneuvering upward had pulled them to the top of the "ball." He looked down toward the planetoid more than ten kilometers away. There was a buzz of air-to-air and surface-to-air combat going on between them and the deck.

I guess we just plow through it, he thought.

Only way to get there without getting your ass shot off, Candis replied.

Right.

"Okay, Gods of War, we are taking this fight to the deck. The groundpounders and the Demon Dawgs need some more backup down there. And maybe we can force this ball into a small bowl, if we're lucky." Jack pitched the nose over, pushing the HOTAS forward on both sides. The sleek fighter fell downward like a missile at maximum velocity through the spherical combat zone. As his speed picked up, the planetoid continued to fill more of his field of view until there was nothing left in it but the surface. Flashes of explosions danced around the cockpit as he pushed harder and faster to the surface.

He and Fish tore rapidly by several close calls as enemy and friendly fighters both zoomed past with relative velocity of well over three thousand kilometers per hour. Then several glints strafing a blue line on the ground caught Jack's attention. His DTM quickly identified them and turned them red. Five Seppy Stingers were giving the tankheads a seriously bad day.

"Fish, I've got five Stingers at about cherubs two off to the right. See them?"

"Roger that, DeathRay. Want to teach them not to mess with our guys?"

"Exactly what I was thinking."

"Watch for AA coming off the ridge to the east," Lieutenant Commander Penikea "Hula" Moses warned. "Looks like it's coming just north of the line near the tankheads."

"Roger that, Hula," Fish replied.

"Okay, Fish, get ready to start bleeding off speed!"

The plunge to the deck had accelerated their fighters to nearly twenty-seven-hundred kilometers per hour. There was no way that they could pull out of the dive at that velocity. Jack pulled the throttle all the way back and kicked in reverse thrust. He tracked the Stingers, formed in a V-shaped formation low on the deck, and gently added right slip and stick to veer his trajectory across the Gomer's flight path.

"All right, Fish, let's pull in behind them and start picking them off."

"Roger that, DeathRay."

"Pull out of the dive in four, three, two, one, now!" Jack pulled out of the dive, slamming his body into the couch at over ten and a half gravities. The force load on his body grew from the standard eight hundred and eighty-two newtons to well over nine thousand. In old body weight standards, he would have grown from a hundred and ninety pounds to over nineteen hundred pounds. The plane was actually pulling much heavier g-loading, but the structural integrity and inertial dampening fields protected it and the pilot from them. But maneuvers like this one taxed the living hell out of those systems.

"Uh, uh, whoo," Jack grunted and squeezed his abdomen and leg muscles to fight the gravity and keep the blood in his head. The g-suit constricted on him like a giant anaconda crushing its prey and forcing blood back into his brain. Jack bit down on the bite block, holding on to the edge of consciousness and struggling to breathe as he pulled through the dive. The engines of the little snub-nosed mecha screamed against the turn and then settled back down as it leveled off at over eight hundred kilometers per hour, just two hundred meters off the deck. He looked over his right shoulder, and Fish was right on his wing.

"Whooo! That was a fuckin' thrill a minute," she said.

"Uh huh." Jack was still swallowing his stomach and barely managed the response. Stars raced across his vision as the blackness that was threatening to engulf him faded out of view.

"Gomers in sight just below us, cherubs one."

"Got them on eyeball. Going to missiles. Fox three!" Jack fired. A missile leaped from underneath the fighter and silently zipped across the sky, locking QM sensors onto the tail of the Stinger. The Seppy Gomer would never know what hit him. Jack and Fish had dropped in on them so fast that there was no way they would have time to react.

"Fox three!" Fish shouted. Her missile twisted in only milliseconds behind Jack's at the next-to-last enemy fighter in the formation.

Jack's missile hit home, totally destroying the Stinger. The plane tumbled and spread out, leaving a field of debris along its trajectory that finally crashed into the surface several kilometers away. The fighter's wingman burst into a fireball almost as quickly as Karen's missile tore through it.

"Splash six! Ace plus one for the day," Fish said.

"It could still be a long day, Fish," Jack replied.

"It's already been pretty goddamned long," she added.

The lead two Stingers pulled up from the deck and to the left. Jack and Fish quickly overtook them since they were still flying at a much faster relative speed. The enemy fighter's bank slowed them enough that the two Gods of War flew right by them—almost an amateur mistake. Almost.

The two enemy planes barrel-rolled over each other and banked behind them, accelerating and going to guns. Jack toggled his mecha into bot mode, and the snub-nosed Ares-T fighter pitched over and transfigured quickly. The mechanized bot stood upside down on its head and spun around, facing the enemy Stingers on his tail. With no atmosphere, his bot continued along the same vector at eight hundred kilometers per hour.

Two yellow Xs appeared in DeathRay's mindview, tracking the paths of the Seppy fighters that were bouncing and bobbing in and out of his line of sight. The yellow X on his left attacker blinked red, then back to yellow, then back to red, and finally locked on red.

"Guns, guns, guns," Jack said, firing the forty-millimeter railgun cannon now on his right arm. The tracers tracked into the incoming enemy mecha, blasting it to bits. The second yellow X blinked red and locked on, and he fired the cannon on his left arm. The cannonfire ripped through the Stingers right tail but didn't do enough damage. It kept coming and firing at him.

"Shit," Jack muttered as he kept aiming with the cannons trying to close a firing solution on the enemy plane. It fired at him again, and the tracer rounds zipped past his cockpit. Jack kicked the HOTAS and spun clockwise and head-over-feet into a full flip, trying to evade the enemy.

"Warning. Enemy targeting system has lock. Warning. Enemy targeting system has lock," Jack's Bitchin' Betty repeated.

"Fox three!" Fish said, loosing a missile that blasted out in front of the enemy fighter and exploded just as it was starting to go to guns again. The fighter flew into millions of pieces with a bright orange fireball.

Jack looked over his right shoulder to see Fish's mecha in fighter mode, flying backwards and upside down. Her fighter yawed back and forth as if she were looking for something else behind them, and then it pitched back over to normal flight. He heard her groan and curse from the g-loading.

"Good shot, Fish." Jack toggled back to fighter mode and fell back into lockstep formation with her.

"You owe me one, partner!"

"DeathRay, this is Poser. Glad y'all decided to come down from on high and join the party."

"Roger that, Poser. Looked like there was more action going on down here."

"You got that . . . shit . . . fox three!"

CHAPTER 15

October 31, 2388 AD
Sol System
Tampa, Florida
Saturday, 7:17 AM, Earth Eastern Standard Time

The marines had formed up around the presidential limo and finally led the First Family to safety out of the madness that had ensued at the Magic Kingdom. Something had taken over all of the AIs within the entirety of the Walt Disney World Orlando property as well as several lakes and businesses surrounding it. But the president had made it to safety.

Several bot-mode FM-12s trotted along beside the limo, while others in fighter mode and eagle mode followed above at treetop level. The marine mecha had led the hovercraft down Interstate 4 at over two hundred kilometers per hour until it met up with a Starhawk that picked them up and then flew them the rest of the way into MacDill Air Force Base and the U.S. Special Operations Command headquarters.

Lieutenant General Howard Brown met the First Family personally as they landed on the lifter pad just outside the main HQ in the center of the USSOCOM pentagon. The joint forces of the special ops squads stood guard in FM-12s, along each apex of the

exterior pentagon. The marine squadron of FM-12s that had protected the president stood at attention in bot mode, surrounding
the Starhawk in a circle and looking outward from it.

"Mr. President! It is very good to see you in one piece, sir!" The
three-star general offered President Moore a hand, then likewise to
the First Lady and their daughter. The battered and haggard-looking
Secret Service agents took up positions around them as they walked
down the rear ramp of the troop carrier.

"General," Moore nodded. "What the hell is going on?"

"Let's get you inside, Mr. President."

"The First Lady and your daughter are getting cleaned up, and
we're having a doctor look at Dee's arm. They are just a few doors
down if you need them, sir," Thomas whispered into the president's
ear.

"Thank you, Thomas." Moore nodded. The young marine had
been battered to hell and back, and he was still not faltering and not
budging from the president's side. Thomas blended into the wood-
work and stood at the ready quietly with his back against the wall.
Moore sat back in his leather chair in the general's conference room
and sipped at the coffee that the Army lieutenant colonel had just
brought him. "Mmmm. Needs sugar, and how about some breakfast
in here."

"Yes, sir. Right away, sir."

"General, there is a transmission going out over the news services
that I think we need to see, sir!" A full-bird Air Force colonel rushed
into the conference room and started tapping controls on the projection system.

A wall holoscreen jumped to life with the Earth News Network
logo emblazoned across the bottom with the ticker-tape newslines
running at a speed reader's pace. The scene playing was from somewhere inside the Disney World Magic Kingdom amusement park that
looked like the inside of the White House.

"Been there," Moore said.

"Uh, yes sir. That is the Hall of Presidents at Walt Disney World as
best we can tell. It gets really interesting in just a minute," the Air
Force colonel replied. The general leaned back as he sipped his coffee
and nodded at the colonel approvingly.

Several AI-driven dead presidents walked into the view. Two of
them were dragging a woman kicking and screaming at them the

whole time. George Washington and Theodore Roosevelt took flanks on either side of her. Each of them was holding a railgun pistol. At that point, several other dead presidents filed in behind. Each set of two presidents were holding a human against their will.

Then another figure walked in behind the crowd. Like a sea parting, the dead presidents pulled their hostages aside to allow Sienna Madira, the one hundred and eleventh president of the United States, to walk through. The AI-driven amusement park robot looked just like the former beloved president. The Madira likeness walked deadpan and expressionless up to the woman in front between George Washington and Theodore Roosevelt. With robotic efficiency and coldness, the Sienna Madira bot pulled up a pistol, held it to the young woman's head, and pulled the trigger.

"Oh shit!" Moore said startled. He sat his cup down and leaned forward.

"Yes, sir," the general agreed.

Blood splattered out of the back of the woman's head and onto a screaming man behind her. The dead presidents let go of the body, and it fell limp with a thud to the floor behind Madira as she turned around.

"Greetings infidels," Sienna Madira said. "The United States of America simply decided to ignore the fact that the Martian underclass has suffered for ages since your so-called great leader President Sienna Madira drove us to the Reservation. We left your space four years ago, but *we* have not forgotten what was done to us. We only wish to be left in peace, out of the reach of your evil government and far from the reach of its tyranny.

"We truly believe that the congress and senate and the people of the Sol System wish to leave us alone for the most part. But. But . . ." The Sienna Madira robot shook its head for dramatic effect. "But your executive leadership has continued to threaten and coerce the peace-desiring members of your government toward military buildup. You still continue to build up your supercarriers and your squadrons of mecha and armored vehicles. I ask you this. If there are no longer any of us Martians, true Americans, left in your system, then what are you building up your military might for?" The robot paused for a brief moment.

"I will tell you. Your President Alexander Moore is preparing to attack the Separatist refugees. We fled your system so that we would no longer have to interact with you. But if you continue to allow this criminal of war to track us across the stars and hunt us down like animals, we *will* respond in kind." The robot nodded at Garfield and Carter, who in return dragged another human in front of her. The Madira likeness raised her pistol and blasted the poor man in the side of the head. More screams filled the background as the man's body collapsed to the floor.

"There are over twenty thousand employees of the Disney World complex that we have taken. We will kill one of them every minute until you hand over this war criminal to us. Hand over President Moore, and the shooting will stop. Until then, the body count will continue to rise. We will wait for the criminal, Moore, to be dropped by himself outside the Hall of Presidents. At that point, all hostages will be freed, and we will then take the criminal with us back to be tried by Her Majesty, Elle Ahmi." Again, the robot paused for a brief moment as another human was pulled forward.

"There is one more thing. There is a gluonium bomb right here," the bot pointed at her stomach. "The bomb is large enough to remove the entire Disney World complex from the face of this planet, as well as several of the outlying areas. Do not attempt an attack, or we will detonate the device. Do not attempt to evacuate the surrounding cities and homes, or we will detonate the device. Give us the criminal Moore, and all will be fine." The bot raised its hand and shot a third victim between the eyes and then the transmission was cut.

"Jesus, fucking, Christ, Almighty, God!" Moore spat. *Abigail, start a clock and keep a body tally for me.*

Yes, sir.

See if you can find out any more data on how these damned amusement AI things work.

Absolutely, sir. Good idea.

And don't forget Ahmi's modus operandi, the AI kitties and all that.

Yes, sir. All of her technical history is relevant here.

"Yes, Mr. President, those are my sentiments exactly."

"How the flying fuck did they get all this put in place without anybody knowing about it?"

"I don't know, sir. Perhaps that is a question for the CIA and the DNI." The general nodded again to the Air Force colonel at the end of the table, and she tapped away, bringing up a new scene that showed a classified dossier of a spec ops team in armored e-suits training. "Sir,

I've got JFCOM team three and SEAL team four in place and ready to take action. I can send them in immediately at your order to take those bastards out and commandeer that bomb."

"General, those damned fairy-tale things gave a full squad of FM-12 Marine strike mecha a hell of a hard time with no telling how many casualties. I think that sending in more meat for the grinder would be a bad idea." Moore's face grew grim, and his eyes began to burn with a vengeful rage.

"Any suggestions then, Mr. President?"

Moore slammed his fist down against the table and started laughing maniacally. He stood and paced back and forth, cursing under his breath and kicking a small trash can across the room. He had been fighting and running from that bitch for thirty years it seemed like. That goddamned Elle Ahmi had captured and tortured him almost to death at the Martian Desert campaigns, and had it not been for Sehera springing him, he'd have probably been among the thousands of soldiers that had been tortured to death. He had struggled with all his might to get away from the damned Separatist forces during the Martian Exodus. He had done all that he could to get his family away safely while that crazy bitch tried her damnedest to blow up Mons City. And then today, his family vacation had been turned into a crazy nightmare that would probably scar his adolescent daughter for life. Moore was tired of running. He was tired of the Separatists, and he was, by God, tired of Elle Ahmi! It was about fucking time that *Major Moore* did something about it if *President Moore* couldn't.

"Get Gail Fehrer and Calvin Dean on the line, now. And get me a communications link to that crazy robot, ASAP." Moore picked up his coffee cup, poured sugar from the bowl until it was empty, and then killed the oversweet mixture quickly. The hot, strong flavor burned his throat and sinuses as he forced it down. The last few teaspoons of the coffee oozed from the sugar settled at the bottom of the cup. Moore finished it all. "This isn't strong enough. Make another pot using the full bag of coffee and get me some energy bars, stims, immunoboost, and painkillers. And an AEM suit loaded for goddamned polar bears, fairy-tale creatures, dinosaurs, and crazed fucking robot dead presidents. Now!"

"Mr. President?"

"I'm all the way in Tampa! For the love of God, stop the killing! I'm coming. I will be there in thirty minutes or less!" President Moore pleaded with the crazed AI that was controlling the dead president on live television. News station ENN had pulled the feeds from a video-conferencing system in the general's conference room and was playing the feed live. The video image from the robot was being fed off of a holoscreen.

"I am pleased that you have decided to surrender yourself. And as stated before, we will gladly stop killing the hostages once you have landed, alone." The robot's cold eyes stared through the screen at Moore, and the heartless reply was obviously part of the programming for the damned thing. Moore ground his teeth together, flexing his jaw muscles tensely.

"If you persist in this killing, it will not help your case any with the American people! Stop this madness. I will surrender myself to you, but not alone. America must see this, and I am bringing the noted action reporter Calvin Dean from ENN."

"His life is in your hands," the AI replied. "This madness, as you call it, is yours, not ours. The Separatists have been trying to live free, and you are the one bringing this upon yourselves. The killing will stop once you arrive." Sienna Madira smiled wildly into the viewer.

"Well, note this! I'm coming. Alexander Moore is coming!" Moore slammed his fist down on the Transmit button, killing the feed to the AIs. He turned to look at the camera system in the conference room so that his face would be seen in every living room across the system. "By Section Three of the Twenty-fifth Amendment of the Constitution of the United States of America, I am declaring a temporary incapacity to perform the duties of the office of the president of the United States. Following this verbal declaration, a written letter will be delivered to the speaker of the House of Representatives and to the president pro tempore of the Senate, declaring that the vice president will become Acting President in my incapacity. The vice president will continue to act as president until such time that I am again able to fulfill the office duties. At that time, I will send another letter to the speaker and to the pro tem." Alexander Moore rubbed his eyes and took a deep long breath. There were no tears there, only rage.

"To the families who have already lost someone in this madness, you have my most deepest and heartfelt sympathies, and I will personally visit each and every one of you when I return. I have a wife and daughter that I love dearly and understand how I would feel in your situation. I am truly sorry. For those of you who have loved ones there, don't give up hope! I *will* stop this! God bless you and God bless the Unites States of America."

"But why do you have to go, Daddy?" Deanna cried. Tears rolled down her pink cheeks. Alexander brushed them away with his thumbs and pulled her closer to him.

"People are dying, baby. Every minute I waste, more innocent people die. I have to go and stop that." Moore hugged his daughter to him, kissing her head. Tears welled in his eyes, but he tried not to shake since his little princess didn't need to see fear or sadness from him at this point. He had only a moment to spend with his family while the SOCOM people readied an aircraft and his gear. That moment would cost another life, but there was nothing he could do about it.

There was very little chance that Alexander would be able to walk away from Ahmi this time. He was one man, and there were thousands of AI bots there and one big-assed bomb. But the one thing that would push him through it was in his arms at that moment. Sehera slipped in behind her daughter and stroked her hair. His daughter already stood nearly to Alexander's chin. He leaned his head forward and propped his cheek against top of her head, stifling a sniffle against her.

"Daddy will be back," she said, looking at her husband of thirty years and stroking her daughter's long, straight black hair. Sehera was understandably shaken, and Alexander could see it in her eyes. Not since the Desert Campaigns had the two of them seen such a no-win situation. But they had come out of that hellhole alive, and they had to have hope now.

"You come back, Daddy! You hear me! You come back," Deanna pushed back and pounded him in the chest with her fist and then laid her head back down against it, drying her tears against his shirt.

"You know, you get more and more like your mother every day. I'll see you soon. I love you, princess." He kissed her one last time and then hugged her and Sehera to him in a three-way hug.

"I love you, Daddy."

"I love you, too, Alexander," Sehera whispered in his ear and nuzzled at his cheek.

Alexander stood straight and winked at his daughter and patted her head one last time. He turned, choked his tears down, and stepped through the doorway of the office that Deanna had been using as her room. Once out the door and out of the sight of his family, Alexander propped against the hallway wall, allowing himself to collapse in a torrent of emotions for a brief second. He struggled against tears that now flowed from his eyes. He sniffled and wiped his eyes and then stood straight, turning his emotion to pure rage. Pure. Rage.

Thomas, Clay, and Michael had been standing watch outside the doorway, and the three marines made every attempt to act as if they hadn't seen or heard what had just transpired. They all stood stiff and soundless, but Moore was certain the three soldiers turned Secret Service had seen him in his moment of weakness.

"Thomas, you take care of them."

"You have my word on that, Mr. President," the marine assured him.

"Sir, we need to get you to the Starhawk. We have everything ready for you there."

"Calvin Dean?"

"He is in route to intercept up just outside the park on I-4," Kootie replied.

"I wish I could talk you out of this, sir, but I gave up on talking you out of things nearly four years ago." Thomas looked solemnly at him.

"I have to stop this, Thomas."

"We understand, Mr. President," Clay replied with a nod. Alexander wasn't sure if the big marine NCO looked as if he could cry or bite super-hardened, metal-plated composite nails in two. "Sir, I have a family, you know. And I've always felt that it was the love I have for them that was the reason I kept doing what I do. You know what I mean, sir?" Moore only nodded at the marine, and then he took a deep, calming breath, swelling out his chest.

"All right, let's get on with this. I've got a bunch of crazy fucking Seppy robots to slay!"

"Oorah, sir. Oorah."

"Intel shows only the one gluonium source, sir," General Brown pointed out in the holoprojection of the Disney World complex to Moore.

"Are we sure?"

"Yes, sir. Gluonium is pretty damned hard to hide. We just weren't looking for it at Disney World. We'll have to start looking for it everywhere from now on."

"Yes, you will. Okay. One bomb. That is good."

✧ ✧ ✧

The Starhawk zoomed at six hundred kilometers per hour across the Tampa treetops. Thomas sat at the gunner's seat on the left side of the lifter, while Clay sat on the right side. The two marines scanned for potential threats beneath them that they could pepper with the forty-millimeter cannons. Two FM-12s flanked each side of the lifter in fighter mode. The formation of the Starhawk and the four mecha fighters tore across the Florida morning toward the Disney complex.

Moore dropped his underwear to the deck of the troop carrier, feeling the warm, humid air wash over his body, giving him a slight run of chills up his spine. A marine colonel helped him step into the organogel undergarment for the armored environment suit. The cool pseudo liquid immediately adjusted to his body temperature and lubricated itself so that the garment slipped on like a second layer of skin, forcing the chills to dissipate rapidly. The gel filled in all the space between his body and the outer layer of the bodysuit and was filled with anesthetic and other chemicals that would keep him from itching, burning, chafing, or any other uncomfortable thing that might require a physical adjustment that couldn't be made once inside the suit. The garment was comfortable. In fact, it had been suggested that it was the most comfortable "second skin" garment ever invented by mankind. Moore didn't really give a shit. It was part of the suit. He needed the suit to do what had to be done. Doing what had to be done was the only thing going through his mind at the moment.

"Been a long time," he said to himself. Alexander eyed the little needle-nosed vial in his palm. Then he jammed the injector into his neck and then pulled the zipcord up his back. He placed the sticky-tab tight over his right shoulder and worked his neck from side to side, forcing the air bubbles out from the turtleneck with a *schlurrp*. Then the colonel helped him into the back of the e-suit jumpboots. Alexander could feel the warm sensation of the stims, painkillers, and immunobooster coursing through his veins. With each heartbeat, he felt a surge of invulnerability flood his body.

"Obviously, not your first time in an e-suit, sir," the colonel said with a grin.

"I once spent thirty-seven and a half days in one, Colonel. Worst fucking time of my life," Moore replied. The colonel looked approvingly at him. The young lieutenant on the other side of the suit looked at Moore skeptically. "I highly recommend it if you ever get the chance."

"I thought the record in one of these things was only nine days, sir?" the lieutenant said knowingly, almost calling out the president for lying.

"Nobody ever told *me* there was a record," Moore shrugged and pulled the arms into place. The seam in the back of the armored e-suit sealed itself, and the armor grew hard in place over the seal layer.

"Lieutenant, don't you follow politics?" the colonel asked, snapping the glove layer on with a *slap*. "That is the official witnessed record they teach at suit quals. President Moore here had an AIC-confirmed, thirty-seven and a half days of survival in his suit during the Desert Campaigns."

"No, sir. I'm not very interested in politics. And the Desert Campaigns was before I was born, sir."

"Young man. Lieutenant, uh," Moore looked at the kid's nametags. "Ulrich. Lieutenant Ulrich, just because you aren't interested in politics doesn't mean it isn't interested in you. I suggest you start learning to follow who leads you a little more closely."

"Uh, okay, sir." Lieutenant Ulrich didn't have the slightest idea what Moore was telling him, but he might, one day, if he lived long enough. Moore dropped it and focused on his suit.

Abigail, how's our plan coming?

I think I've got it figured out, sir. But I suspect you'll have very little time, from debilitating the AIs to taking the bomb away. I estimate that you'll have seventeen seconds. Then keeping it away will be the hard part. There is no doubt that once they overcome the jamming, they will detonate the bomb.

Understood.

"Mr. President!" General Brown shouted from the cockpit. The soft whining of the troop carrier's engines nearly drowned out his voice.

"Yes, General?"

"The U.S.S. *Abraham Lincoln* and the U.S.S. *John Tyler* have just come out of hyperspace in a hovering orbit of about three hundred kilometers above Orlando, sir."

"Understood. Have my orders been relayed?"

"Absolutely, Mr. President."

"Colonel, if you please?" Moore took the helmet from the spec ops marine and dropped it in place over his head with a hiss, a swish, and a twist. The brain bucket locked into place, and cool fresh air filled with vapor stimulants flooded Alexander's face.

The colonel knocked three times on Moore's faceplate and held a thumbs-up. Moore relaxed and felt the suit come to life around him and then manipulated his armored hand, giving an armored thumbs-up.

"This is Mobile One, copy?" Moore said. His visor kicked on with a faint red and green glow, and a system readout zipped past his eyes. His DTM battleview flooded his mindview, and the menu icons floated out in front and to the side of him in his peripheral vision.

"Mobile One, copy that. We read you clear on wireless, lidar, and QMs," his AEM handlers at the USSOCOM pentagon Tactical Operations Center replied.

"Mobile One, hold tight for sensor update package."

"Roger that," Moore replied. Then he DTMed the open channel for the aircraft. "General, where are we?" He popped his visor up, causing a slight hissing sound from the overpressure air escaping.

"Sitting down now on I-4. Dean is standing there like an idiot waiting on us."

"Right." Moore brought up the weapons store list in his DTM. The HVAR on his back was fully loaded, and his armory pack was maxed with rounds, grenades, and his special surprise.

Abigail, you finished handshaking with my suit?

I own this suit, sir.

Thought as much. Tell me what I have.

It is state-of-the-art and brand new, as far as I can tell. The jumpboots will take you a little farther than your old one, but you should adjust quickly. If you want lidar or QMs, just tell me or you can do the DTM interface toggles yourself. There's more, but you'll be fine, sir.

Thanks, good girl. You do whatever has to be done if I ain't doin' it. Got it?

Got it, sir.

CHAPTER 16

October 31, 2388 AD
Tau Ceti Planet Four, Moon Alpha (aka Ares)
Near the Tau Ceti QMT Orbital Facility
Saturday, 7:28 AM, Earth Eastern Standard Time
Saturday, 3:28 AM, Madira Valley Standard Time

Kira wiggled her fingers and toes and could feel them still there. The throbbing in her face hadn't stopped since she had regained consciousness a minute or so earlier. She tried to open her eyes, and the light penetrated through them like needles. She squinted several times trying to regain her senses.

Where am I? Kira asked her AIC.

As best I can tell, we are on the Phlegra *battle cruiser again,* Allison answered.

How long have I been out?

About thirty minutes.

That's not enough time for them to bring me back to the Phlegra.

You're right. They didn't. We met it in orbit. We are somewhere in space now. Closer to the star, I think.

Where are we going?

My guess is back to Sol space.

But why?

179

That I don't know.

Any idea what blew my cover?

I'm thinking the bullet wound or some blood on the airplane ejection seat?

But they'd still need a DNA sample that you hadn't fudged with to compare it to.

Perhaps we trusted that Elise Tangier too much. She must have gotten one somehow. Maybe in one of her sexcapades she kept some of your fluids. Who knows?

I was sloppy?

Sounds like it.

Shit. We've got to get out of here.

Therein lies the dilemma.

Kira struggled against her bindings and then moved her head up enough to look at herself. She was naked and zip-tied with her arms out wide and her legs spread over stirrups of a gynecological exam bed with zip ties around each foot and one at each knee. She struggled against them but that only managed to dig them deeper into her skin, making them more uncomfortable.

This can't be good.

No, it's not. You've been examined in every way imaginable. I fear that the worst part has yet to happen.

Any ideas?

I'm scanning for something to hack into that will help, but so far, nothing but a centrifuge in the next room will talk to me. After we left earlier, they reset all the security protocols. I'm still hacking away, but it will take a while.

Keep at it.

"Comfortable, I see," a female voice said, following a hiss of the hatch sliding open. Kira struggled to get a better view. A slender woman in skintight camouflage pants, army boots, and a black, skintight, long-sleeve, armored pullover approached her. The black turtleneck led up into a ski mask of red, white, and blue stars and stripes and a long black ponytail of hair flowed up and out the back of it.

"General Ahmi," Kira said, trying not to look back at the woman in a way that would give away her fear. But Kira was terrified, and there was little way of hiding that.

"They call me Her Majesty now." Elle leaned in over her and slid a synthleather gloved hand down her cheek, to her neck, and then to her breasts. Elle lingered on Kira's nipples a bit and then dragged a finger sensually to her navel. Then instantly changing from sensual to angry, she slapped Kira across the face. The hit reawakened the pain from the rifle butt to the nose she had taken earlier, and her head rang like a bell with pain. She was most certainly lightly concussed, if not worse. Kira fought back at the pain and the stars surrounding her vision.

"Her Majesty, we are coming up on the facility in five minutes," someone out of Kira's field of view said.

"Good, Scotty. That gives us time to figure out what our young friend here was doing on my ship." Elle slapped Kira again and then seemed to lose her temper. As if something had snapped in the terrorist's mind, the slap acted like a final snowflake that triggered an avalanche of violence. Ahmi commenced to beating Kira in the face with her fists and cursing at her. The leather in the maniac's glove cut into Kira's nose, ears, and chin and left her face battered and bloodied. Kira was afraid that she would lose consciousness if the beating lasted much longer.

A few seconds of the crazed frenzy, and Ahmi stopped at the edge of Kira's limitations. The terrorist must have been a pro at torture, for she knew just when to stop before she rendered Kira useless. There was a splatter of blood on Ahmi's leather gloves that she licked away with almost sexual excitement. A doctor, or what Kira assumed was a doctor, entered the room beside Ahmi. He leaned over Kira and checked her vitals with a scanner and then held some sort of wireless sensor over her head.

"She has an AIC," the doctor said.

Allison?

Don't worry, we're good.

Oh God, we are so fucked!

Stay calm. Don't stop thinking. There has to be a way out of this. In the meantime, put your mind somewhere else. Let's keep going through the data we got today. Maybe something there will buy us some time.

Good idea.

Kira did her best to ignore the doctor's pokes and prods and Ahmi's nonstop questioning followed by more violent frenzies. The Scotty fellow stayed quiet mostly and only interjected here and there.

"What were you doing on my ship?" Ahmi asked again, and slapped her across the face another time.

"She's not talking, Scotty. Suggestions?"

"It can't be a coincidence? Can it?" Scotty said. He leaned against the bulkhead and put his hands in his pockets. "We haven't seen a spy in years, and now, on the day of one of our best moves, she shows up."

"She's been here all along according to the Tangier records. Remind me to tax the hell out of Elise when we get back. Somebody should hang for this. Literally." Ahmi pounded her fist against her open palm, causing the leather to slap together loudly.

What about today? Allison?

Well, the Phlegra *is scheduled for a trip back to Sol, right?*

Yes, so? Apparently, ships go back and forth to that Oort Cloud base all the time.

Remember the manifest? Nothing goes to this ship after today.

Hey . . .

"What tho thpecial bout today," Kira managed through swollen busted lips. She licked at them and swallowed blood.

"Ha ha, the nerve," Ahmi turned back to her. "I'm the one asking questions here."

"Since you have to kill her anyway . . ." Scotty shrugged.

"Today, we are going to fix an election." Ahmi stood straight and looked deeper into Kira's swollen eyes. "So that is why you have to tell us what you know and who you have told."

An election?

Presidential election is Tuesday, Allison answered.

Why?

Who knows, she's crazy as a fucking fruit bat.

Wait, how would they fix an election? Kira had studied Ahmi for years now. She never did anything haphazard. This would be a well-managed and thought-out scheme. *How would we fix the presidential election?*

Let me think. It looks tight. President Moore is likely to lose if he doesn't take Florida and Luna City. The Democrat nominee Senator Webb might even win the popular vote, but without the electoral votes from the Moon, she can't win.

So that's it! The Moon is the common factor for both candidates. She's gonna do something to Luna City.

Like what?

I dunno, what is her standard MO?

Well, during the Desert Campaigns, she had kamikaze AI-driven fighters fly into the front lines until the AEMs were toast.

Yes! And during the Exodus, she used the kamikaze ships in several different cases. Kira had a good idea what was going on and how Ahmi planned to do what she was going to do. *But even if they got to Sol space in the Oort Cloud, that is still months at top hyperspace speeds to Earth space.*

Use that. Keep her talking.

Right.

"Ha, ha, ha . . ." Kira broke into laughter as best she could. "You're gonna fix the election? Luna City. You're going to crash this ship into Luna City."

"What?" Scotty laughed and looked surprised. "You're about four hundred thousand kilometers off."

Ahmi looked back and forth between the two of them. Kira noted that there was a hint of surprise from her body language. She wished she could see her face through that damned mask.

"Florida? No way. Its not important enough," Kira managed through her fat lips. "Florida won't win it for either candidate."

"Oh, you just wait and see." Scotty again laughed, a bit too cocksure of himself.

Allison. Could Florida win it for either one?

Well, there is the slimmest chance, but . . .

Ahmi doesn't take chances like that.

That is what I was thinking.

HE DOESN'T KNOW!

You must be right. Use it!

"He doesn't know, does he?" Kira laughed, not breaking her eyes from Ahmi. "Go on, tell him the whole thing. Florida is just a diversion, isn't it?"

"What is she talking about, Elle?" Scotty took his hands from his pockets and walked closer, looking directly at Ahmi with anger in his face. There was obviously some history between the two of them, and this topic must have been a sore one.

"Not now, Scotty." Ahmi waved him off. "So you have figured it out, have you?" Ahmi caressed Kira playfully. Kira was most certain that the general was off her rocker.

"Well, what I can't seem to figure out is how you plan to get this ship from the Oort Cloud to the Moon so quickly." Kira lay still, trying to look calm and trying with all her might not to react to Ahmi's touch. Each one made her skin crawl and not in a good way.

"Ah, so you don't know everything. That is good." Elle turned to the doctor. "Take the AIC."

"Yes, ma'am," the doctor nodded.

"Wait! What do you want to know?" Kira attempted to stall further.

"Nothing more from you. Without access to the QMT, you haven't been able to contact Earth. My guess is that you are completely isolated and have yet to manage a message to home. Good try, though."

The doctor held a glass tube up to the side of Kira's head just behind her right earlobe. The tube sealed off with a vacuum hiss against her skin, drawing blood to the surface it attached so harshly. A spring-loaded metal tube within the glass tube crunched through Kira's skull and extracted the bone. Kira screamed in pain and blood poured red into the tube. A little metallic finger snaked itself into the hole in the side of her head and pulled out a small gray object shaped like a sunflower seed.

"Motherfuckers! I'm gonna kill you!" Kira screamed.

Allison? Allison! Allison! There was no response.

The tube hissed, and the AIC popped out into the doctor's hand. He handed it to Ahmi, who then held it between her gloved thumb and forefinger.

"I know how you can grow attached to these things. I'm so sorry for your loss." She sat the little seed-shaped AI implant on a table in a metal pan and picked up a small hammer lying beside the pan and then smashed the little implant to a thousand pieces.

"What about her?" the doctor asked with an evil grin on his face, reminiscent of a child molester's on a kindergarten playground at recess.

"You can have her," Ahmi said as she turned and walked out of the sickbay. Scotty looked back at her and turned his head as he followed his fearless leader like a lapdog.

"You know, my sister was a security guard on this ship until this morning. I believe you killed her. I think I should get something to ease the pain of my loss."

Kira ignored him. Tears and blood oozed down her neck into her hair. The doctor stepped between her legs and leaned over her. His breath smelled of coffee. He leaned in closer and began to fondle Kira's body clinically. He lowered his face to hers and glared into her eyes but she turned away from him as best she could.

"I am so going to fucking kill you," she whispered.

"Oh, I don't think so. I plan to leave you right here for a long time. Right up until this ship explodes. Believe me. I plan to make you suffer until the last possible minute. My little sister would have wanted it that way." He held an injector in front of her battered face that was filled with a pink fluid.

"What is that?"

"This, my dear, is pain. Pure, liquid, pain. Enjoy it." He stuck the needle into her neck and drained the pink stuff into her.

The injection started burning from the instant the needle touched her skin. At first Kira felt a tingling and burning spreading out through her face and then down her body. Her hearing heightened, and she could hear her own heartbeat begin to race as if it would beat out of her chest. Kira tried to shallow and control her breathing, but the burning grew and grew to the point were her body felt like it was being burned from the inside out. She screamed in pain.

"I am so going to fucking kill you!" Kira did her best to put her mind somewhere else but the pain was too great to ignore.

"You can't just destroy Luna City, Elle!"

"Scotty, I can and I will. That is the only way to be sure that the election goes our way." Ahmi paced back and forth in her cabin. "Now, that's enough of this."

"Elle, millions could die from an event like that. It was different when there were millions being saved on Mars, and we always expected that the U.S. would save them, but this is just murder. It's mass murder on the largest scale known to man. For what, just to sway an election!"

"A means to a better end," Ahmi replied.

"Damnit, Elle—" Scotty was interrupted by the door buzzer.

"Yes?" Elle snapped the door open to face the ship's captain.

"More info on the attack at the facility, General."

"Yes?"

"It appears as if we have overwhelmed them. The supercarrier has taken several direct hits from the mass driver on the moon. The space and ground forces are outnumbered more than three-to-one and are attritting." The captain stood still in the doorway awaiting Ahmi's response.

"Good, Maximillian. And the other mass driver?"

"They are too close to it for any useful firing solutions. The crew has been moved to the moon facility for more efficient use of their abilities."

"The defenses of the base are working as planned. Good." Elle tugged at her ski mask, adjusting her ponytail in the back. "We will drop out of QMT and start the immediate recharge of the projector. The hauler and other battle cruisers will protect us until we teleport again. Once the cruiser is in the Earth-Moon sphere of influence, we will evacuate the ship completely. Got it?"

"Understood ma'am." The captain saluted, and the door closed behind him.

"How long were you going to keep this from me, Elle?" Scotty asked.

"Right up until the last minute. I knew you would get all defiant about it."

"You know I have family there! Why didn't you warn me about it?"

"Would you have swayed one way or the other?"

"I, uh . . ."

"No, you wouldn't have. I know you too well. Now stop it, Scotty. I've got a battle plan to think about." Elle waved him to the door. Scotty shook his head and reluctantly dropped the topic, leaving the general to her work.

Allison? Allison?

Don't worry, I'm still here.

You got really quiet on me.

I didn't want to transmit just in case they knew how to detect it. Looks like our decoy implant worked. How do you feel?

Yes it did, and I feel rough as hell.

The CIA had discovered decades earlier that the Separatists often removed the AIC implants of captured agents and either hacked them or destroyed them. And in many cases, they killed their biological counterparts in the process. Allison was a member of the Top Secret AIC family that had been developed to grow as microfilaments along the human nervous system, rather than to be implanted as a small device in the brain. Allison's components were dispersed and intermingled throughout Kira's body and would likely only be removable if Kira were dead. The implant was just a copy AIC that had been put there years ago to act as a decoy. Most CIA operatives had similar

AICs. The AICs had to volunteer and so did the operatives, as it pretty much made them symbiotic and intertwined for the life of the human.

Any luck getting us out of here?

The troop carrier we rigged this morning hasn't been repaired yet! Allison said excitedly into Kira's mind. That was a glimmer of hope. The lifter that they had commandeered in the hangar bay to fly them up to the mecha that they had ended up stealing for the getaway was still in line to be repaired. The Seppy repair crews had just rolled it aside for later maintenance. And it still had the hacks in place that Kira and Allison had previously applied. And it was still keyed into the ship's networks.

Can you access it? Kira had put her mind so far out into space that she could barely keep her sanity. The internal burning sensation had finally lessened to a tolerable level, but that had been followed with a strange and frightening euphoria that had lasted for several minutes. The doctor had left her to her chemical trip as far as she could tell and was no longer in the room with her. The bastard hadn't even bothered to cover her up.

I've got control of it now.

Can it bust us out? Kira tried blinking her eyes and shaking her head hoping to keep the pain managed. The remnant of the immuno-boost that she had taken hours ago was probably keeping the pain from overwhelming her, but the chemical had pretty much overcome what was left of it. Her head pounded like a repulsor hammer with each beat of her heart.

It couldn't get through the deck plating. But it's a start and a way out if we can get to it.

If we can get to it. Right. How do we do that?

You have to get untied.

I have no idea about that yet.

The door hissed open and Kira braced herself for more torture. It was the doctor again. This time Scotty followed in behind him. The two were arguing about something, but Kira couldn't make out exactly what at first.

"The general sent me back down here to ask more questions. Is she conscious?"

"I can always wake her up if not," the doctor replied.

"Leave us, now." Scotty glared at the doctor. Kira wasn't sure, but she was guessing that Scotty must be a high-ranking member of Ahmi's inner circle, if she had one.

"If you need me, I'll be in my office," the man said, and the door closed behind him. Scotty turned his attention to Kira.

"Here, this will help," he told Kira as she felt a sting in her neck.

A flood of warmth and well-being coursed through her body. A feeling that Kira had felt way too many times that followed stims and immunoboost injections. But that was a good thing. She never wanted to feel the way she had a few minutes ago ever again. She needed the added strength and for some of the pain to go away. Almost immediately, the throbbing in her face subsided. There must have been painkillers in the injection as well.

What the hell?

This could be our chance?

"I'm not privy to the plan to murder on such a mass scale. Everything we had done before was based on creating a new America. One that we lost so many decades ago. You have to stop this madness!" he rambled rather quickly and then slipped a knife underneath the zip tie, cutting her right hand free.

"Why are you doing this?" Kira rose as he cut her left hand free. She rubbed at the scratches on her wrists that were healing in real time. The swelling in her face reduced, and the cuts began to close.

"I told you. I'm not a mass murderer. Elle has stepped over a boundary that I can't." Scotty focused only on cutting Kira's bonds loose.

"You know she is fucking nuts!"

"No, she isn't. She is the most brilliant woman I've ever met. Probably the most brilliant human that ever lived, but with that great intellect, she has become so logical that she has forgotten the emotional aspects of being human on an individual scale. She only thinks in the grand schema nowadays." Scotty looked nervously over his shoulder. "Her big picture is brilliant but is getting too costly. And I have family in Luna. She could have at least warned me."

Aha, it isn't selfless. He has someone he cares about in harm's way, Allison thought.

Typical. But he must actually care for them to risk his neck for us.

"She will have you killed."

"Not if you do this right." He cut her last zip tie and then put the knife in her hand. "Stay put. Dr. Ross will be back any second. Make it look like he let you loose." Scotty turned for the door. "Stop this ship from killing all those people."

"Thank you. I will." Kira rubbed at the healing hole behind her ear and could feel the soft spot where the bone was beginning to fill in. She palmed the open knife in her left hand and squirmed back into place as if she were still tied down. "Now get the hell out of here."

"Good luck," he told her as he left.

Wasn't expecting that.

Hope it isn't a trap.

Me too. But don't look a gift horse in the mouth.

The door slid open, and Kira could hear the doctor's shoes squeaking against the floor. She lay still as if she were catatonic with her eyes open wide and not blinking. With the pain subsiding in her head, she could focus and control herself better now.

Wait . . . wait . . .

The doctor leaned over to check her with a diagnostic tool, and he looked into her pupils with his flashlight. When he did, Kira grabbed the back of his hair with her right hand and jabbed the knife into his temple with the left. The blade slid into his head all the way to the hilt. Kira twisted the blade, scrambling his brains around, withdrew it, and then stabbed him again, repeating the process. She tossed him to the floor and rolled out of the examining stirrups over on top of him. The deck plating was cold against her bare feet.

She quickly pulled his pants and shirt off and slipped them on. They were too big, but she managed to pull the slip fastener at the waist tight enough to hold, and she rolled the bottoms tight around her ankles. The shirt was still loose, so she tied it in a knot at her side. She hefted the knife in her left hand and backed up against the doorjamb, punching the open switch. The door hissed open. She looked around the doorway into an empty hall. It was clear.

Great. Now where to from here?

We need to stop this ship from getting to the Moon.

Engine Room?

Good a place as any to start with.

"All hands, all hands, prepare for QMT jump in ten . . ."

CHAPTER 17

October 31, 2388 AD
Sol System
Oort Cloud
Saturday, 7:31 AM, Earth Eastern Standard Time

"Captain Walker!"

"Go Nav." Sharon watched the purple and white flashes of the hyperspace conduit swirl in front of her ship. The *Blair* was approaching the Oort Cloud Seppy facility, and from the latest communication from the *Madira,* it wouldn't be a second too early.

"Conduit collapsing in twenty seconds, ma'am."

"Roger that, Nav." Sharon tugged at her seatbelt again to make sure it was good and tight. It was. "XO!"

"Aye, Captain?"

"All the forward SIFs at max and prepare for impacts."

"Aye, Captain. Forward SIFs at max." Commander Brasher tapped at her controls, and Sharon caught a glimpse of her XO tugging subconsciously at her own seatbelt.

"Nav. You got that secondary jaunt plan calculated?"

"Aye, CO."

Okay, Marley, sound it off, the captain told her AIC.

Yes, ma'am.

✧   ✧   ✧

"All hands, all hands, prepare for emergence from hyperspace conduit. Man all battlestations and prepare for incoming. Normal space in nine, eight, seven, six, five, four . . ."

The purple and white flashes of Cerenkov radiation swirled away like water in the bottom of a toilet bowl and then scattered off in all directions, vanishing. The U.S.S. *Anthony Blair* materialized in normal space at maximum normal space velocity only a thousand kilometers from the moon planetoid. The giant supercarrier loomed toward the mass driver suspected location as relayed by the STO of the *Madira*. The surface had been scratched up by what appeared to be DEG fire, but there was no sign of any direct hits or of the *Madira* for that matter.

"STO, I want full sensors on those coordinates looking for that mass driver tube," Fullback ordered.

"Roger that, Captain." Lieutenant Commander Zeke Caldwell toggled through mountains of sensor data being DTMed to him from the ship's CDC and from his own systems. There was nothing useful, yet. But as the ship's science and technical officer, it was his job to figure it out.

"Where is the *Madira*?" Commander Brasher asked.

"I've got a hyperspace conduit opening up about ten thousand kilometers away, XO. That is probably them," the STO replied.

"CO *Madira*? This is CO *Blair*. You copy?" Fullback said over the command-net channel.

"CO, CDC!"

"Go, CDC."

"Captain, we've got massive electromagnetic signatures building up over the Seppy facility. I think there's a teleportation occurring."

"STO concurs with those readings, Captain. And the Madira just came out of hyperspace right beneath it!"

"Roger that, CDC. Roger that, STO. *Madira!* Do you copy?"

"CO *Blair*. CO *Madira*. Good of y'all to join us, Fullback. Watch out for the mass driver; it will be recharged in three minutes and twelve seconds. I'm having my STO synch up our clock to you. Be advised that we are dead in the water. Aux prop is at least five to ten minutes out, and we just did our last jaunt for a while, I'm told." Captain Jefferson's voice sounded a bit strained over the net. Sharon needed to give him some good news, but right now that wasn't about to happen.

"Wally, in case you haven't noticed, there is a QMT disturbance forming less than ten kilometers above you. Is there anything we can do to help?"

"Yes. Knock out that damned mass driver, and then get your ass down here."

"Roger that, *Madira*. Good luck, Wally. *Blair*, out."

"Gunnery Officer Blake, do you have a target yet?"

"Nothing specific, Captain."

"Captain! I've got a reading on the power source for the driver. There is signigicant buildup about a kilometer deep in the crust of that thing."

"That's too deep to get at with DEGs, CO," the XO replied.

"Where is the throat?" Sharon leaned back in her chair, watching the battle thousands of kilometers below them raging in her mind-view. And the large disturbance over the teleportation facility continued to grow and grow for a few seconds more, and then there was a large flash of light in the sensors. The next thing she knew, the DTM was pinging new targets and painting the area with big red dots.

"Looking for the throat, ma'am, but until it fires, we probably won't find it," the STO responded.

"Understood."

"CO, CDC."

"I see the bogies below, CDC."

"Aye, ma'am. Just thought you'd want to know that we just had a Seppy hauler, three battle cruisers, and a couple frigates pop into normal space down there."

"Thanks, CDC." Sharon noted that the new red dots in her mind-view had new labels on them, explaining what they were.

"Okay, Nav, jaunt us out into the line of fire of the last mass driver shot at the *Madira* bow-first. That will put us just a few thousand kilometers from the engagement zone. You have the coordinates."

"Ma'am?"

"Well, we ain't gonna find them until they shoot at us."

"Uh, yes ma'am. Prepping jaunt systems."

"As soon as we take the first hit, or before if you can manage it, punch the jaunt drive. Understood?"

"Roger that, ma'am."

"Okay, we've got more than two minutes to kill here. Somebody, find us some targets to shoot at." Captain Walker made a bright, toothy smile at her bridge crew, hoping to spark an idea.

"Well, Captain," the COB started between sips of coffee. "If we ain't got nothing to shoot at up here, why not shoot at something down there?"

"Damned good idea, Bill." She turned her chair slightly toward the gunnery officer. "Ensign Blake, pick any enemy targets below and fire at your discretion."

"Yes, ma'am. It'll be like shooting fish in barrel, whatever the hell that means," the gunnery officer replied.

"Jaunt coordinates ready, Captain."

"Captain Jefferson! We just had a Seppy hauler, three battle cruisers, and a couple frigates materialize in normal space about ten kilometers straight up, sir," the STO reported.

"Roger that, STO. Gunnery Officer Rice, target those bastards with everything we've got." Wallace spun his chair toward the air boss's station. "Air Boss, where are the rest of the fighters now?"

"Well, sir, we let them out just before we jaunted through hyperspace, and even at max speed, they are still about four minutes out."

"Goddamn, what a pickle," the XO grunted. "Sir, I'm getting reports from all over the ship. Whatever the hell Engineering did to give us that last jaunt blew out almost everything but the DEGs."

"Well, then, keep firing them." This was about as grim as Wallace had seen it get. The *Madira* was wounded badly and floating adrift in space with no structural integrity field generators and no propulsion. Fire teams and damage diagnostics showed a hole through the aft section of the supercarrier big enough to build a housing community in and the majority of the air wing was four minutes away in deep space. Oh, and there was the little fact that there had just been a small fleet of enemy ships appear in normal space right on top of them. This was definitely a typical Navy day.

I'm open for ideas. Timmy?

I'm working on it, sir. The CHENG's team and I are rerouting everything we can to get us some sort of propulsion. With the enemy ships above us and the facility below us, on the other hand, it is unlikely that they would fire the mass driver at us, in fear of hitting them.

That was the whole point of taking up this position, Timmy.

Aye, sir.

Keep at it.

Aye.

"CO! The hauler is dumping out Gnats as fast as it can throw them. I've got more than a hundred and counting!" the air boss shouted. "Our guys are gonna be outnumbered by at least one order of magnitude, sir."

"Warn them and tell them to make do."

"Aye, sir." The air boss reluctantly relayed the order to the CAG. What DeathRay said in return was rather foul.

"Captain. We've got nukes," the XO said with a crazy grin on his face.

"You're damned right we do, Larry. Let's send those battle cruisers a few of them."

"Roger that, sir."

"Gunnery Officer Rice!"

"All hands, all hands, prepare for QMT jump in ten, nine, eight, seven, six, five, four, three, two, one, jump!"

The ship had surged with a strange feel of static electricity, and then there was a crackling sound reverberating down the corridor through the structural members. Then everything seemed as normal as before.

We just jumped to Sol?

Apparently so, I'm asking the Lorda troop lifter now.

Kira raced down the corridor toward the engineering section of the *Phlegra*, scanning through drawings and schematics of the ship hoping to find an internal Achilles heel. On several occasions, she was nearly spotted. But to her advantage, the ship was only being manned by a very skeleton crew.

Kira, I'm picking up handshaking pings from U.S. fleet sources!

What! Here?

There are hundreds of them. And it's the Sienna Madira!

Oh my God! They must be attacking the facility. We have to warn them about Luna City!

Who do I contact? Uncle Timmy? Captain Jefferson?

No! Boland! Contact Jack Boland. He'll remember me. Penzington, Nancy Penzington was my name then.

Right, I recall. I'm handshaking with his AIC now for a secure channel.

✧　✧　✧

Jack! I'm getting a message to you from on board one of the enemy vessels that just teleported in, Candis alerted DeathRay.

For me? Who is it?

All I'm getting is code name Bachelor Party!

Holy shit, put it through!

"DeathRay, DeathRay, this is Nancy Penzington, code name Bachelor Party, do you copy?"

"Penzington, is that really you?"

"Watch your six, DeathRay!" Fish cried out over the tac-net. "Fox three!"

"Oh shit!" DeathRay dove hard to the deck, pulling up with only meters to spare before he slammed the surface. He toggled to bot mode and put his feet down, running and jumping over a catwalk that led down a dugout crater rim, taking cover there. The Stinger on his tail shot past him, rolling over into bot mode himself and firing cannons backwards toward Jack's Ares-T fighter. Tracers ripped past, blasting up dust all around him. Jack rolled over onto his back, tracking the yellow Xs in his mind over the path of the Stinger until they both turned red. "Guns, guns, guns."

"Roger that, Boland. It's good to hear you're still alive."

"What can I do for you, Penzington. I'm a little busy right now!" DeathRay toggled back to fighter mode, going full acceleration back up into the fray and away from the exploding enemy mecha behind him.

"This takes priority over all orders you have, Boland. This battle cruiser that I'm on is about to QMT jump to Earth space and kamikaze into Luna City. It must be stopped."

"I need to relay that to the *Madira*." DeathRay toggled a channel in his DTM.

"Roger that, Boland. I'm gonna try and shake things up from the inside. Penzington out."

"CO *Madira*, DeathRay!"

"Go, DeathRay!"

"Sir, I just got a communication from Bachelor Party. She's on board the middle battle cruiser and has warned me that it is about to jump to Earth and crash into Luna City."

"Understood, DeathRay. Can you help her in any way?"

"I could trash and thrash on the ship, sir."

"Go, DeathRay. We are barely holding our own here, and things just got worse. There's not much we can do to help you otherwise."

"Understood, sir."

"Goddamnit! Air Boss!"

"Sir?"

"Pull the Saviors off of the facility to help the Dawgs support the ground forces. Warboys is getting hammered down there."

"Aye, sir."

"Missiles away, Captain!" the XO shouted. The ship shook and sang out from enemy cannon fire and DEGs ablating the hull plating. Without the SIFs operational, the enemy fire continued to chew away at the ship. It was already battered and couldn't take much more. "Detonation in three, two, one."

"Countermeasures got one of them, sir!"

"The other one got through," the CO replied and used his DTM to look at the onslaught of enemy fighters pouring from the Seppy hauler. The flash of one of the nukes detonating within the cloud of fighters was a sight for sore eyes. More than thirty of the enemy mecha were vaporized within the fireball, and tens more were spun out of control and damaged.

"Keep firing missiles on the nearest ship, XO!"

"Aye, sir."

"Captain! The first wave of our displaced fighters are now entering the mix," the air boss announced.

"About fucking time." The *Sienna Madira* shook and rang, and the sound of the hull plating being vaporized and blown into space continued. But if the fighters got into the mix and the *Blair* could get in it too, all wasn't lost just yet.

The ship lurched upward from an explosion on the underbelly armor. Several lower decks blew out, followed by secondary explosions that dominoed upward through the aft section of the ship. The missile hit in just the right location to rip through the supercarrier all the way to the damaged section on the upper decks, leaving a gaping hole more than ten meters in diameter that passed completely through the ship.

"We're taking fire from the deck," the XO said. "Countermeasures!"

"What a typical Navy day," the CO said through tight lips.

✧   ✧   ✧

"All hands, all hands, brace for impact in ten, nine, eight, seven, six, five, four, three, two, one!"

The mass driver round pounded dead on target into the bow of the *Blair,* shaking the ship like a slinky. There were screeches and groans of metal structural members bending against the force of the massive energy from the railgun impact, but the SIFs held.

"Forward SIFs at seventy percent, ma'am!" the XO shouted.

"Nav! Go now!"

"Aye, Captain! Engaging jaunt, now!"

The ship's hyperdrive system spun up, projecting the conduit just abow of the ship, and it slipped safely into a conduit and out of normal space. Seconds later, the ship popped back into normal space, just above the surface of the moon planetoid and too close to it for the mass driver to get line-of-sight with it.

"STO, find it!"

"There! I've got the barrel, ma'am! Transferring coordinates to Ensign Blake now."

"Blake, fire!"

Ensign Blake targeted the barrel of the mass driver and opened up the DEGs full power on it. The massive photonic energy of the directed energy weapons focused to a brilliant sun hot spot on the barrel, vaporizing materials instantly. The hole at the mouth of the mass driver glowed white-hot from light, scattering off the dust and gas particles being thrown up into space from the energy transfer of the beam to the target.

"Captain, probably wouldn't hurt to drop a nuke down their throat," the COB added.

"You heard the COB, XO. Let's nuke the bastards."

"Roger that, ma'am. Best news I've heard all day." The XO tapped a command into her console. "Two missiles away!"

"Nav, get us back down to the fight."

"Yes, ma'am. Preparing to jaunt."

"Air Boss! Have the Killers up first and out as soon as we hit the ball!"

"Aye, Captain."

"Hyperspace in five . . ."

CHAPTER 18

October 31, 2388 AD
Sol System
Oort Cloud
Saturday, 7:35 AM, Earth Eastern Standard Time

"Let's go, Robots!" Major Roberts pounded through the hangar bay, laying down cover fire across the catapult deck. Several enemy Stingers rushed them in bot mode but apparently were reluctant to go to guns inside their own facility. PFC Kent ran up a wall and flipped over a troop lifter to the left of the major, firing into the back of the vehicle's engine cowl. The cowl blew free as he passed overhead. The PFC hit the ground rolling to cover on the far wall. PFC Gray was right behind him, firing into the open-engine port with a grenade launcher. The grenade detonated inside the skin of the lifter, blowing out the walls of it in all four directions.

"Watch your right flank, Major!" Gunnery Sergeant McCandless warned him, and she dove across the cat lane in front of a Lorda that was catting out.

She rolled aross the runway behind a pylon, and a stack of pallets raised up to fire her HVAR at the Stinger that was racing toward the major. Her HVAR rounds *spitapped* into the armor plating of the vehicle at the knee joint until fluid squirted freely in a shower of

199

sparks. The mecha tumbled like an runner tripping on a shoe lace, face-forward onto the deck. The major bounced into a flip, landed on the mecha's back and fired several rounds into it, and then he bounced again, landing beside the sergeant.

"Good shooting, Gunny."

"Yes, sir." Tamara checked her ammo, and Major Roberts took the hint and did the same. "If you don't mind my asking, Major, what the fuck is it that we are doing in here again?"

"Gunny, we are here to make a general goddamned nuisance of ourselves and to gather intel." Roberts stood and let go with a quick burst of cover fire back toward the catapult control booth, where several drop-tank support troops had filed up to hold the marines at bay. There weren't that many of them, and the major was beginning to suspect that the Seppies hadn't planned for a ground assault by AEMs. And that was a bad mistake on their part.

"Johnny? Where the hell are you, Lieutenant?" Roberts asked over the tac-net.

"We are a story up and east of you, about a hundred meters on the far wall of the bay, sir." Roberts could see the blue dot in his DTM but had no visual.

"You got anything interesting over there?"

"Yes sir, I do. Suez has stumbled across what looks like blueprints to a mass driver, sir!"

"Yeah, there's one on the moon of this place, I've been told." Roberts checked his blue force tracker and mapped out where all of his robots were. Suez was deep inside, several stories in beyond the hangar. How the sneaky bastard had managed that, Roberts wasn't quite sure.

"Uh, no sir. This mass driver is here, sir. Only a few hundred meters in."

"What? Is it operational?" Roberts expanded his mindview and downloaded the blueprints and the map data that Lance Corporal Suez had uncovered.

"From what we can tell, it looks like it is, Major. Any orders, sir?"

"You're goddamned right. Robots! Converge on Suez and let's see if we can't commandeer us a big fucking gun!"

Tamara rolled out from behind the pallets and launched several grenades into the booth, sending it crashing down onto the support troops beneath it. The cat field generators must have been connected somehow because one of the boxes at the end of the runway blew out like a volcano. Secondary explosions followed along a conduit around the hangar wall. Several SIF generators blew as well. The deck shook so hard from the explosion that Tamara and Roberts were both tossed backward off their feet. Had there been an atmosphere in the hangar, the shock wave from the explosion would have probably killed them both. But they were in the vacuum of space, and the explosion did its job with no blast wave. It was a lucky-as-hell shot, but luck counted, as far as the marines were concerned.

"Scratch one hangar." The gunnery sergeant grinned a toothy smile that Roberts could see through her faceplate.

"Scratch it? Hell, I think you broke the piss out of it, Gunny."

"Look, Danny, this tunnel to our left is really a construction elevator shaft to the control room of the mass driver. It goes down probably a kilometer." Suez scanned the adit to the underground facility for any sign of enemy-troop movement but found no trace of it. The computer system at the entrance room had been left unmanned and operational. It didn't take long for his recon AIC to hack the login and to start pulling data. He looked back down the shaft of the elevator. There was only a safety bar at waist height across the opening and no lift in place. The readout to the right of the shaft was lit at the bottom, which suggested that the eleveator was all the way down. He pushed the top button and it lit up.

"Why don't they use the thing if it's operational?" PFC Bates asked.

"Maybe it was their day off? How the hell do I know?" Suez smirked. "You want to wait for the major or check it out?"

"I vote we wait."

"Suez, let us the fuck in!" There was a pounding at the air lock door.

"Did you hear that?" PFC Bates slipped his visor hissing back down into place and nervously turned with his HVAR to the ready.

"Take it easy, Danny." Suez checked the blue dots in his DTM and then cycled the lock on the exterior door. The overpressure air blew out into the hall chamber and then equalized. The lock opened, and the lieutenant, Sergeant Nicks, and Corporal Pagoolas clanked in. From trained reflex actions, each of them popped their visors to get a breath of real air. AEMs never knew when they'd get a chance to breathe real air, so they immediately did so every chance they got.

"Lieutenant." Suez nodded his armored head.

"That's the tunnel?" The lieutenant looked down the shaft and whistled.

"Yes, sir."

"Fucker's deep," Corporal Pagoolas added from beside the lieutenant as he leaned over the safety bar, looking down the shaft.

"The major has ordered us to go down the tube and take the control room to this thing. He and the others will hold this position. Let's find out if we can put this thing to some good use."

"Uh, Lieutenant," Danny stuttered. "I was wondering . . ."

"Spit it out, Bates."

"If this thing is operational, why ain't they using it?"

"Maybe it's their day off." Lieutenant Noonez shrugged.

"Why don't we go ask them ourselves, Private?" Sergeant Nicks added.

The elevator was nothing more than a lifter platform that was the exact shape of and slightly smaller than the shaft itself. The safety rail was about waist high around the periphery of the platform, and on opposite sides of the rail, there were two caution lights and one control box with several buttons and a videophone. The elevator descended the kilometer drop in less than a minute with little acceleration noticeable on the platform. Inertial dampening fields regulated the acceleration of the lift to match that of the facility.

"Okay, on the perimeters. We don't know what's waiting at the bottom," Noonez warned. "Nicks, take point."

"Yes, sir. Pagoolas, you and Bates on my left. Tommy, you have my right."

The four of them lined up and knelt in position with their railgun rifles drawn and ready to fire. They held quietly in place as the lift dropped to the bottom. The lights on the control box dinged as each floor passed until it reached the last one, coming to a stop in a room almost identical to the one they had been in up top. It was empty otherwise.

"Go, Sergeant," Noonez ordered.

Karen slowly removed the safety bar over the opening and stepped into the room. She scanned her weapon left and right and then motioned that the room was clear. Pagoolas and Suez filed in on her flanks, and then Bates and Noonez pulled in behind them. There was nobody around.

"Well, that was anticlimactic," Pagoolas said.

"Just the way I like," Bates replied.

The room was no more than seven meters across with a double door on the other side. There was a yellow dotted line leading to doors, suggesting a pallet-lifter vehicle track. Lance Corporal Suez eased around the periphery of the room to a control panel like the one he had seen upstairs, and he let his AIC handshake with it.

The crew has been put on duty at the other driver. I guess that means the one on the moon. This one's abandoned, according to the records.

Right. Good work.

"LT, it's been abandoned for now. The crew has been restationed to the other mass driver, according to the records here." Suez continued to listen to his AIC for another brief moment. "My AIC says that they went there today, but we're not sure when exactly or how."

"Good work, Tommy." The lieutenant thought about what to do for a brief moment. "Okay, then. If there's nobody here, let's make ourselves at home. Nicks, take point again."

"Yes, sir."

Sergeant Nicks slid the double doors open and led the team into a larger room. There was a construct of electronics, power plants, and a very large two-beam track running upward through a hole in the ceiling of the room. A large conveyor with several solid black cubes on it led to the center of the two-beam metal track. The cubes were about two meters on a side and were the texture of crushed metal like that from a recycling plant.

"Those must be the bullets for this thing," Nicks said, pointing an armored hand at the cubes. "They must weight a fuckin' ton."

"LT! Look at this. I think I found the targeting system." Tommy was looking at a station with multiple flat screens and a universal data port hardwire connector for DTM. There was a joystick system and several buttons on the control board. The viewport had yellow crosshairs in it, and the view was from above, on the surface looking upward. The moon facility above could be seen, and only parts of the battlespace were in view.

"Aha," Noonez nodded. "The battlespace is out of the field of view of this gun. That's why they left and went up there. This gun must be to protect that moon, and the moon is there to protect this base."

"Why build a gun all the way up there to protect us down here?" Pagoolas asked.

"These things can only aim over a very small angle," Tommy explained, moving his HVAR barrel back and forth to illustrate. "The farther away your target is, the more likey it will be in your line of fire. Makes sense to have two of them."

"But that's bad for us. It means we can't use this gun to our advantage," Sergeant Nicks said.

"Shit. I'd better call the major."

"Hey Tommy, check this thing out." Bates was staring down at the floor in the corner of the room.

"Now what do you suppose that is?" Pagoolas patted an armored hand on the PFC's shoulder. "Looks like a drawing of this place."

"What d'you mean?" Bates asked.

"Well, look. The outline here is an octagon, and there are several more octagons inside it, but smaller," Tommy noted. "And look here—there are big circles at the corners where the towers are on the big thing up top."

"I see, and here's a big circle in the middle like the biggest tower in the middle." Bates nodded that he understood.

"But what the hell is it used for?" Nicks turned a full circle, looking at the construction on the ground and kneeling to feel it. The drawing was more than just a drawing. "Looks like circuitry."

"Maybe." Tommy knelt beside the sergeant and looked at it also. He had always been infatuated with the engineering of his armored suits, so he had read a lot of technical literature on them and had taught himself a good bit about modern circuitry. But this was different. "LT, you ought to see this."

"What have you got?" Noonez clanked over to them.

"Hey, look here." Pagoolas was studying a control box with two buttons in the middle of it. One button was directly above the other. The bottom one was lit. "Looks like elevator controls." He reached out and depressed the top one.

"No wait!"

CHAPTER 19

October 31, 2388 AD
Sol System
Oort Cloud
Saturday, 7:39 AM, Earth Eastern Standard Time

"Come on Fish, we need to do what we can to stop this battle cruiser." DeathRay bobbed and weaved his fighter-mode Ares-T fighter at top speed across the surface of the enemy ship, firing missiles at anything that his QMs suggested might be a vital system. His only hopes were that they could hit a major power system that would cause secondary explosions, which in turn would hopefully debilitate the ship.

"Two fighters against a battle cruiser sounds a bit epic to me, DeathRay." Fish dropped to bot mode, clanking into the hull of the ship to avoid the AA fire stations on the aft section near the hangar bay. She ran up behind a cannon, tearing the barrel out of its mount, and then she kicked the power supply with her mechanized foot. When that didn't work, she went to her DEG. The box spewed vaporized hull plating and then burned through to the next layer of armor. "DeathRay! Our weapons are too small. We need a nuke."

"Fresh out," Jack replied. He decided that the best way to do damage would have to be from the inside and that they needed to change their approach.

Candis, can you find us a way in?

I'm scanning. Nothing is deploying from this ship, and it seems locked down tight.

Of course it is.

"We need to make a hole, Fish."

The ship shuddered, and out of the corner of his eye, Jack could see an eruption of orange and blue plasma spewing from the starboard side of the ship. Debris spun out from the opening into space, and then the plasma dissipated.

"What was that?" Fish asked.

"Boland, this is Penzington, copy?"

"Roger that, Penzington. What's up?"

"I just flew a Lorda through two bulkheads into the hyperdrive jaunt projector. Did you happen to notice an explosion out there?" Penzington asked.

"Uh, yeah. It blew out of the hull on the starboard side. I thought that might have been you. We're coming in. Where are you now?"

"I'm about four decks below the center of that blast trying to make my way to the aux prop control room."

"Understood. We'll make for the sublight prop power through the doorway you made for us." Jack banked his snub-nosed fighter over a communications dish and throttled toward the blast area.

"You with me, Fish?"

"Got your wing, DeathRay."

"What the hell was that!" Elle Ahmi stormed onto the bridge of the *Phlegra* up to the ship's captain.

"The jaunt drive power plant just blew out, General," the man replied reluctantly.

"Did we take a hit?"

"No, we didn't. We are protected fairly well." The captain seemed flummoxed.

"Captain, I've got a report from the maintence deck."

"Go, XO."

"Seems that one of the Lorda troop lifters went nuts and flew through several bulkheads at max thrust and crashed into the jaunt containment cylinder," the XO explained.

"No!" Ahmi screamed. Then she toggled her DTM communications channel open. "Doctor, this is Ahmi. Where is the prisoner?" There was no response.

"General?"

"I should have killed her myself!" Ahmi had her AIC open the ship's 1MC and then announced, "All hands, this is General Ahmi. There is an intruder aboard, a young-looking female with long, black hair. She is to be killed on sight! Find her, now!"

"Captain! Two marine FM-12s have penetrated into the hull breach."

"No! Goddamnit, no!" Ahmi pounded her leather-gloved fist into her hand.

"Normal space, Captain!" the *Blair's* navigator warned Captain Walker.

"Multiple targets, ma'am."

"Fire at will, Ensign Blake!" Fullback checked her DTM and mapped out a plan. First thing she had to do was to get the ship's mecha unloaded and into the fight. "Air Boss?"

"The Killers are out, Captain. Drop tubes are firing as we speak."

"That ought to help a little. Order the Killers to drop to the line and help out the tanks."

"Aye, ma'am."

"Okay, we need to draw some fire away from the *Madira* and give them time to catch their breath." Sharon studied the red force distribution for a brief moment and decided to go after the heavy hitter first. "All firing solutions focus on the hauler. All missiles, all DEGs, and all cannons fire at will at the hauler."

"Ares squadrons away, Captain!" the air boss notified her.

"Ground Boss?"

"Drop tanks are going. We'll need a few more minutes. Then we can unload the AEMs and the AAIs." The ground combat commander continued tapping controls at his console.

"Okay. Nav, give me a run on the hauler at full forward."

"Aye, ma'am."

The ship screamed from a violent impact and jerked back and forth so fast the inertial fields couldn't dampen out the rapid change in acceleration. A second later, the ship righted itself, but there were warning bells and klaxons sounding.

"What the hell was that?" the XO exclaimed.

"I've got a debris field erupting from the moon planetoid at the railgun sight, Captain," the STO said. Sharon checked the countdown clock in her DTM, and it was right on schedule. She had just assumed that the nukes had done the job.

"What? The nukes didn't do it?" the COB asked.

"Apparently not. The thing was pretty deep. My guess is that we caved the top of the tunnel in and then melted it shut. The Seppies must have just fired the mass driver right through it, clearing out the hole," the STO replied.

"Shit! It's a double barrel! Nav, hyperspace jaunt, now!"

"No can do, ma'am. That hit got us on the aft section and blew out several power junctions. The SIFs were still full front for our attack on the hauler," the STO interrupted. "Sublight is still up."

"Evasive maneuvers! Now! Try to get that hauler between us and the moon."

"*Madira,* we're getting chewed to hell and gone down here!" Colonel Warboys yelled into the net at the ground boss up top. "The air support is so out numbered that they are getting picked off one by one, and the Warlords are completely fucking pinned down!"

Warboys' tank was in bot mode and leaning up against a crater rim, and his big cannon nose peeked over the edge, twisting back and forth looking for targets. There were plenty of them—on all sides. The Warlords had pushed hard through the line to make a hole for Major Roberts' AEM recon team to sneak into the facility. Once they had gotten through, the tankheads had found themselves behind enemy lines and seriously flanked.

The only cover that they had managed to find was what appeared to be a recycling dump, which was effectively a junkyard of scrap materials that the Seppies hadn't found a use for yet. The refuse was scattered about a man-made crater about fifty meters wide and about five meters deep at the bottom. The scattered debris had come in useful for cover. The tankheads had hefted onto the rim several girders, discarded catwalks, crunched-up metal containers, and anything else that they could dig up to give them a little more cover.

They had managed to construct four quick mecha-sized foxholes at the three, six, nine, and twelve o'clock positions around the crater rim.

"Warlord One, we understand your situation and will get help to you as soon as we can. Shit is thick all over, Mason. Do what you can and keep your fucking head down," the ground boss of the *Madira* replied to him.

"Fuck. Warlord Two, I'm getting way too many red dots on your side of the rim."

"There are too many targets, One. Prepare to be overrun! Guns, guns, guns!"

"Dawgs, Saviors, we sure could use a hand!"

"Roger that . . . fuck . . . Warlord One," Poser responded to the tank-heads' leader over the tac-net. A blast from one of the three enemy Gnats on her tail pinged into her nose SIFs, but the armor held. "Saviors, Saviors, do you copy?"

"Go Poser, this is Skinny!" the leader of the marine FM-12 squadron replied.

"The Warlords need immediate assistance on the ground. The Dawgs are gonna go pukin' deathblossom. That should give you enough air cover to hit the surface and give them some relief." Poser had been contemplating ordering the Navy pilots into the maneuver for which their fighters were specifically designed. It was a deadly maneuver for the enemy, but it also rendered the Ares-T pilots spent for several seconds afterward, leaving them vulnerable.

"Shit! Fox three!" Poser cut the power to the engines on the HOTAS and then yanked the stick hard left to give her some space between herself and the Gnats on her tail.

"I got you, boss!" Her wingman, Skater, rolled in an energy-usurping maneuver to draw the fire, giving Wendy time to go to guns.

"Guns, guns, guns."

"Roger that, Poser. The Saviors will hit the deck in bot as soon as you start puking."

Wendy's fighter spun over from her maneuver, forcing blood to her extremities and out of her brain. The g-suit squeezed her, and she grunted and flexed against the crushing weight. It subsided as her trajectory leveled off.

"Whoah, shit!" She shook her head to clear her mind. "That was nothing compared to this," she said to no one in particular. "All Demon Dawgs, listen up. Give yourself space and go to pukin' death-blossom as soon as you can on my mark! Ten, nine, eight, seven, six, five, four, three, two, one, go!"

Lieutenant Commander Wendy "Poser" Hill stomped on her left pedal and yanked the stick, rolling her Ares-T fighter over nose-first toward the surrounded Warlords below. Slamming the HOTAS throttle forward, she initiated a vector correction that pushed her at max velocity and minimum transit time to give them cover. At the same time that her acceleration line pushed her toward the War-lords, she pivoted the little snub-nosed mecha about its center point, scanning and firing on targets to give the Saviors cover.

The maneuver had been referred to as a "pukin' deathblossom" from some ancient pop-culture reference and because the wild spin put constantly changing g-loading on the pilot. The mad, three-dimensional spin would cause the pilot's inner ear to go apeshit crazy, and at the same time, the ship would spin like a whirling dervish, spewing death and hellfire from cannons and DEGs in all directions. The AICs and the direct-mind linkages were required for such a maneuver to prevent blue-on-blue casualties, but it was effective.

The spinning was usually more than the pilots could take and would force them to vomit violently from the inner-ear confusion. But most good Navy pilots could take a little vomit in their e-suit hel-met, and the inner recycle layer of the suits usually absorbed the vomit in seconds. It was the retching being followed by the pressure suit squeezes and the high g-loading that took real presence of mind, fresh air, and vapor stims to overcome. It would take them a few sec-onds on the other side of the maneuver to be worth a damn. But there was usually very little in the way of targets left following the eighteen-second maneuver.

"I'm with you, Poser!" Skater replied, following suit and throwing his mecha at max acceleration past the cover of Wendy's pukin' death-blossom, and then initiated his own spherical cyclone of mad destruction.

"Roger that," came the reply from the six surviving Demon Dawgs, all rolling into the wild, deadly spin maneuver.

The stars spun wildly around Poser as she tried to stay focused on the targets and threats, but at the moment, vomiting was about all she could manage. "Ugh." She licked at her lips and accepted her bite block back in her mouth. She toggled the water icon, and a small cool squirt filled her mouth. She sloshed it for a second and swallowed it down. Her scratched throat burned from it.

"Hope that helped, Warlords."

The eight deathblossoms from the Dawgs spun out, leaving exploding and scattering enemy formations everywhere. The maneu-ver spread the bowl out and gave the Utopian Saviors time to focus on ground work. But the sky was filled with Seppy Gomers. Even though more than ten enemy planes had just been destroyed and another twenty were hit or at least scared, another forty dropped in from the outer edges of the bowl to support them. The Gods of War were up above and mixed in with the Dawgs, but there were too many holes in the dike and not enough fingers to plug them.

"Warning, radar lock. Warning, enemy targeting engaged." Wendy's Bitchin' Betty startled her, bringing some coherence back into her mind.

"Fuck!" She shook her head while throwing the HOTAS full-throttle and yanking the stick to her stomach. The fighter slammed her into her seat as it climbed at maximum acceleration. Orange tracer fire swarmed past her left wing but missed by mere centimeters.

"Poser! Bank hard right!" a voice warned her over the tac-net. Wendy didn't care who it was. It was a friendly who was covering her ass. She banked hard right.

Her fighter cut into the steepest turn she could manage and she was thrown into near blackout conditions. The suit and the stims were doing all they could do to keep her conscious. But the deathblossom had taken a serious physical toll on her body that she had yet to recover from.

Stay alert, Poser! Wendy! Wen . . . her AIC screamed in her mind, but it didn't help.

The stars stopped spinning, and they tunneled in around her into a distant, single point of light way out in front of her. Wendy's mind felt peaceful for a split second, and the distant point of light started to fade out.

A severe pain in her side burned through the blackness like a torch. Stimulants and a short defibrillator shock from her suit restarted her heartbeat. Wendy's mind was sluggish at first, but soon the tunnel opened back up, and the world around came back into view. Her DTM kicked in, spinning madly around her head. Then the spin dampeners in her ejection seat kicked in too, steadying her and leaving her floating freely, facing the planetoid below. The fireball several hundred meters below her quickly dissapaited to nothing, and a few seconds later she realized that that fireball must have been her fighter.

Antonio?

I've notified SARs. They will get to us when they can.

Be positive. They should get to the wounded first.

Yes, ma'am. You should rest and remain calm.

"Oh my God," Wendy cried. The painkillers were working enough now that she finally had the presence of mind to look herself over. There was a large portion of her left side, the size of an e-suit helmet, that was missing, along with her left arm from the shoulder. Her right leg was gone from the knee down. Her suit had sealed off around the wounds and had stopped the massive hemorrhaging that was taking place there. Immunoboost coursed through her, but so much damage had been done to her body that the wonder drug might not be enough. Immunoboost only stopped the bleeding and allowed damaged tissue to heal. It hadn't been designed to regrow missing organs—in fact, it couldn't. She needed serious medical attention soon, very soon. As she looked across the battlescape, the *Madira* and the *Blair* were both venting and rupturing all across their hulls. That was where her medical attention would come from, if it ever did. Tears formed into balls on Wendy's cheeks and floated around her face in the microgravity. As the balls of salty tears drifted around inside her helmet they were trapped and absorbed by the organogel. Wendy stared aimlessly off into space, praying that she would survive long enough for help to arrive. Another one of the Dawgs' blue dots blinked out of her DTM. The link said that it was Lieutenant Junior Grade Barbara "Farmer" Jordan, BreakNeck's wingman.

"Hang in there, Dawgs…"

"On the deck, Saviors!" Major Caroline "Deuce" Leeland grunted over the tac-net. "The Dawgs are making an umbrella for us, so let's take advantage of it!"

Deuce had been evading three Separatist Gnats that had formed up on her and her wingman, Second Lieutenant Nathan "Hawk" Ford. The two marines had maneuvered their mecha over and around each other, cutting into extremely hard corkscrewing turns toward the deck. The two FM-12s in fighter mode corkscrewed around each other, trying to confuse the enemy planes' targeting solutions. Deuce would have instinctively jerked her head from the orange tracers the size of baseballs screaming past her, but the g-load was so heavy that she could barely move her head at all, much less flinch.

A wild shot from one of the Demon Dawgs VFT-32 Ares-T's pukin' deathblossoms cut through the wing of the lead Gnat. The Seppy Gomer reacted abruptly, slinging his fighter into a deadly spin colliding with his right wingman. The impact ripped his wing the rest of the way clean and sent his wingman reeling. The third enemy fighter banked left to avoid getting caught up in the deadly mélange of entangled fighter plane components. Deuce took that gift from above as the opportune moment she needed.

"Break left, Hawk! Dive, dive, dive!" She yanked the HOTAS left and forward and clamped her teeth down on her mouthpiece. The compression layer of her suit crushed against her as her body weight increased by a factor of nine. She spun her mech around with a one-hundred-and-sixty-degree yaw that let her track across the sky at the remaining Gnat. She toggled to her DEGs and shouted, "Guns, guns, guns!"

Her DEGs locked on, and a wash of blue-green directed energy engulfed the tail section of the enemy fighter, ablating away its hull armor until it burned through to the power system. The enemy plane burst open like piñata scattering in pieces along its trajectory. The pilot never had a chance to eject.

"Warning, collision approaching. Warning, collision approaching," her Bitchin' Betty rang through the cockpit.

"Deuce, your dive's getting too hot! Bleed off and pull out!" Hawk warned her.

Deuce's vision spun as she yawed back around into her dive, and then she killed the throttle and yanked the HOTAS to her stomach. That wasn't going to be enough to keep her completely off the deck. She toggled the mecha over to bot mode with her right pinky and gritted her teeth against the mouthpiece, hoping that the stims and fresh oxygen would be enough to keep her from passing out.

"Uh! God-fuckin'-damnit!" she grunted rapidly as her mecha spun upside down into an armored bot. Bile rushed up her esophagus, and she choked at it, trying to force it down. With right pedal and manipulation of the armature controls, she rolled the bot through a handspring against the planetoid and then absorbed more of the shock with her feet as she rolled over. Then she tucked into a judo roll, putting the elbow of the forearm of the mecha down first and then the back, buttocks, legs, forearm, back, buttocks, legs until she had rolled four times, trading most of the fall's energy with the ground. The jerk—standard rate of change of acceleration as a function of change in time—from the rolling impact was so large that the inside of the mecha rumbled like a thunderstorm on Earth and flung dirt up along with it. Deuce held tight on the HOTAS and then kicked the throttle forward with the last roll as her feet hit, springing her upward.

"Warning, enemy targeting system is acquiring lock. Warning..."

Still dizzy from her rolls, Deuce inhaled sharply and closed her eyes. Using just the DTM targeting system, she focused on the vehicle that was targeting her. It was an Orcus drop tank on the surface of the planetoid. She kicked at two of the pedals on her left side and yanked the stick, sending the bot spinning like a figure skater doing a triple axel with the axis of it precessing in a full circle along the axis of travel.

"Come on!" The yellow targeting X of her cannons or her DEGs in her mindview wouldn't lock, and she was way too close for missiles. The cannons might not hit the enemy mecha, but it was close. "Guns, guns, guns!"

Cannon tracers tracked across her empennage just as her tracers threw dust up around the enemy drop tank. The scattered dust and explosions from the high-explosive armor-piercing railgun rounds created enough of a distraction that the tank driver flinched. The enemy targeting system lost lock, and Deuce killed her throttle, bouncing to the surface and running and twisting like a mad ballerina.

"Hold on, Deuce, I'm with you," Hawk shouted over the net, and Deuce caught a faint glimpse of him to her left as she opened her eyes. The world spun around her, but she kept her mind on that damned tank. She slammed forward, holding her left arm out and hooking it around the upper torso of the bot-mode tank like a professional wrestler performing a crooked arm lariat or a clothesline. The two mecha clanged together briefly, but Deuce's forward momentum sent the enemy tank flailing over backward against the surface. In a wall of flying dust, Deuce continued forward and out of the way as Hawk pounced in behind her, tag-teaming on the downed tank.

Hawk's bot-mode feet tore through the torso of the tank as he stomped down on it with full throttle, and then he flipped forward over Deuce's head, firing his cannons into the tank's wingman before it even realized what had happened.

"Now that's how we do it off the top ropes!" he said through the grunts and growls that the g-load had forced him into.

"Great work, Hawk. Now stay frosty!" Deuce shook her head to clear the spins. More radar warnings pinged at her, and she dove for cover behind the edge of a crater rim. She slid facedown as cannon tracers passed over head. She started to rise up, but something held her in place.

"Don't move, marine! I've got your back." Warlord Three knelt beside her mecha, firing its main gun over the ridgeback at the tank line and giving Deuce her much-needed cover and a few seconds' break.

"Thanks, tankhead." Deuce rolled over when the pressure backed off her mecha from the big M3A17-T's hold and searched for her wingman in her DTM. Then she settled down and located the rest of the Saviors as they scattered around the Warlords.

"Anytime, jarhead."

"Saviors, fan out and let's take it to the tanks. Warlords, give us what cover you can!"

"Roger that, Saviors," Warlord One responded over the net. "Get down! Guns, guns, guns."

Three enemy Stingers transfigured from fighter mode to bot mode and came careening over the edge of the crater on the west side. Deuce hit her thrusters, launching upward and into a backflip. As her bot twisted over the other three enemy bots and over the scrambling Warlords, she pointed her DEG from the hip in the general direction of the Stingers. She fired like a trick-shooting cowboy and scorched across the rear torso of one of the enemy mecha but didn't do enough damage to stop it. Hawk streaked in from the east, tackling one of the bots just as Deuce came down behind them.

The third enemy mecha grabbed one of the Warlords and suplexed it backward into the ground, finishing it off by ramming its armored elbow through the cockpit and crushing the Army tankhead.

Autocannons, Bobby! she orderd her AIC.

Got it! The AIC tracked across the enemy bot with the QM sensors and fired two fraction-of-a-second bursts through the leg of the vehicle before it maneuvered away, wounded.

The bot, with which she had managed a strafe with the DEGs, had turned on her and one of the Warlords. The two bounced and juked and leaped over one another in a flurry of mechanized acrobatics, trying to gain the upper hand on the other. The Stinger tried to go to its DEG and shoot from the hip, but the tankhead kicked it away, only to take a knee to the back inturn. The enemy-targeting system pinged onto Deuce, but she moved in too close for it to fire.

I've got a QM lock on a Gnat straffing from above! Bobby alerted her.
Great. Fox three!

"Watch your backside, Deuce," Skinny's voice buzzed.

"Hawk, where in the hell are you!" Deuce spun and ducked and punched and kicked at the enemy Stinger. The Gomer was good and kept her completely occupied. He'd already stomped through the Warlord that had been helping her.

"I'm pinned down, Deuce!" Hawk replied. "Shit, I'm locked up! Goddami—" He never finished the expletive. Hawk's mecha burst at the torso and spewed red and white sparks from the power system. It fell over limp and exploded. There was no way he could have ejected. The enemy mecha that crunched him into the ground then turned toward Deuce. The two of them had her flanked, and the tankheads around her seemed to have their hands full at the moment.

"Get out of there, Deuce!" Goat shouted at her.

Deuce couldn't seem to evade the two Stingers' flurry of punches and kicks, so rather than trying to fight them both, she decided to focus on one of them and take the hits from the other. She rushed toward the bot that had taken out Hawk, swinging her DEG like a war club. The bot ducked her swing but not her right foot. In a capoeira handspring, Deuce put her left hand down and spun her feet around, catching the enemy mecha on the side with a right-spinning kick. This threw the enemy off-balance, giving her a fraction of a second to spin up backward onto her feet. She now faced the other bot, and with her DEG in her right hand, she fired at point blank against the rushing mecha's body. The blue-green plasma vaporized the armor plating and also the pilot within and ruptured out the back of the Stinger with an explosion of its power core. The blast threw Deuce backward to the ground, off-balance. That was enough time for the other enemy bot to get its balance and to come down on her with its feet.

"Oh, fuck!" Deuce could see the mechanical feet slamming down toward her, and time seemed to stop for a brief flash as Warlord One tackled the enemy mecha like a star linebacker sacking a rookie quarterback.

"Get up, Deuce!" Colonel Warboys buzzed at her as he slammed his fist through the cockpit of the enemy bot, crushing the pilot.

"Shit! Thanks, Warlord One." There was no time to relax. Enemy DEGs burned at them from the south across the crater rim, and Deuce could see Skinny running for her life and diving over the rim as a drop tank took up station on her six. Her wingman, HoundDog, bounced right behind her. Fluid was squirting out from under the right arm socket of his mecha. He never made it to the ground, as the enemy DEG caught him across the lower part of the mecha torso. The legs of the bot blew off, and HoundDog crashed to the surface beside Skinny, cockpit up. The cockpit popped free, and the ejection chair spun upward into space, carrying HoundDog away from his mecha. Warboys and Deuce both pulled their DEGs from the hip and blazed away at the Orcus drop tank. Warboys' autocannons went off at the same time, firing at unknown targets behind them.

Skinny rose up into a prone firing position, firing her DEG over Deuce's shoulder, while Warlord One and Deuce continued to fire over Skinny's head. Enemy mecha exploded all around them.

"Goat, Popstar, Volleyball, Romeo, where the hell are you?"

"In the shit, Deuce, in the shit!"

CHAPTER 20

October 31, 2388 AD
Sol System
Oort Cloud
Saturday, 7:43 AM, Earth Eastern Standard Time

Second Lieutenant Michael "HoundDog" Samuels squinted his eyes hard and controlled his breathing. The ejection seat thrusters righted its flight path, removing the spin, and HoundDog opened his eyes and wished that he hadn't. The Warlords and the Saviors were bouncing around the cover of their makeshift redoubt, barely keeping ahead of the flood of enemy Orcus tanks, Stinger mecha, and Gnat straffing runs. The Gods of War were slugging it out above them at about two to five hundred meters off the deck and were overwhelmed by an order of magnitude. And where in the goddamned hell was that backup from the *Blair*?

HoundDog tracked out a long, slow arc from the weak gravity of the planetoid and started running scenarios in his head as to where he might land. His AIC, Second Lieutenant Bambi Mike One Niner Alpha November Zulu, had calculated the precise landing spot for him and had highlighted it white in his mindview three-dimensional terrain map. Unfortunately for him, he was going to land right in the middle of what looked like a line of AEMs fighting it out hand-to-hand with drop tank armored support squads and other Seppy infantry. In other words, he was about to land in a whole world of shit. Not that he hadn't just come from such a place, but then he had a state-of-the-art fighting mecha around him. Now all he had was his armored g-suit and the rail-gun and survival kit mounted in the back of the ejection chair.

Forty-five seconds to impact, HoundDog. Bambi started a count-down clock along with his trajectory path in his mindview.

Shit.

Semper fi.

At least we'll be landing by marines instead of Army Armored Infantry pukes.

"All right, Killers, hard to the deck! The *Madira*'s flight wing and ground contingent are getting chewed to hell and gone down there. Let's show what a group of real Killers can do to help." Colonel John "Burner" Masterson ordered over the tac-net. The squadron of FM-12s flew formation at maximum acceleration in fighter mode toward the planetoid. Burner checked the whereabouts of the tank squads across the line and found the weakest point. He was making a habit of coming to the rescue of Warboys' Warlords.

"Burner, we've got three Gnats pulling in on pursuit vectors, angels fifteen at seven o'clock," Captain Cordova warned his flight commander.

"Roger that, Boulder. I see 'em. Let's make it too fast for them to keep up. We need to land on the deck and help out those tankheads."

Burner held the HOTAS full-forward, ramming blatantly through AA fire and the continuos hell of the dogfight that was all around them. By maximizing their speed, the Marine mecha squadron plowed away from any of the other fighters trying to engage them. That didn't mean that they were immune to lucky shots, AA from the ground, SAMs, or just the random chance of colliding with a passing fighter.

The deck approached rapidly, and Burner was beginning to get a visual on what had happened there. The tankheads were surrounded in a full three-hundred-and-sixty-degree attack. The only thing saving them was that they had managed to take refuge in a man-made crater about fifty meters in diameter and maybe five meters deep at the center. The M3A17-Ts were spread out around the rim of the crater, holding off any ground advances while several Ares-Ts of the Demon Dawgs and FM-12s from the Utopian Saviors were trying to cover their airspace. Several of the FM-12s were bouncing around the enemy Orcus drop tanks in bot mode and were doing what they could to push the flood back to give the Warlords some breathing room.

The problem with the scenario was that the enemy had deployed over a hundred fighters into the airspace, and the Dawgs and Saviors had started out with less than ten each. The Dawgs had been attritted to only four planes, and the Saviors had fared a bit better, with six remaining. The Gods of War had entered the mix and were fighting fiercely, but the numbers game still weighed extremely in the favor of the Seppies. And to top that off, there was an ocean of enemy tanks on either side of the crater, rushing the Warlords at an almost continuous pace. Burner hoped to change that with the Killers. Another twelve FM-12s in the fight would go a long way. Another dozen FM-12s in the hands of marines went further.

"Burner, I've got a lidar glint off several Gnats straight down," Boulder called him.

"Roger, I see them. Let's lock on their six and start attritting them."

"Oorah."

"Okay, better bleed off the energy." Burner pulled full back on the HOTAS with his left hand and toggled his targeting system. Yellow Xs popped up all over the place. His compression layer squeezed in on his body as he started a tight pull up from the dive, and then one of the yellow targets turned red and dinged. "Fox three!"

Three Gnats were in the middle of a straffing run over the Warlords' position. From the blue dots in the bowl, Burner could tell that the ten remaining fighters were all engaged or being engaged at the moment, and the tankheads were just having to hunker down and take it. Burner pulled completely out of his dive while his mecha-to-mecha missile exploded into the wing of an unsuspecting Gnat. The poor Gomer never knew what hit him.

"Splash one." He looked in his rearview and made certain that Boulder was on his wing. The two Marine mecha screamed in behind the three-Gnat formation going for QM lock. The firing solution algorithms tracked vectors in each of their DTMs for them to follow for best possible chance of a kill.

The enemy planes pulled into a tight bank to the right and upward. Burner barrel-rolled to the right, pulling him over Boulder and meeting the lead Gnat as it pulled through its hard bank. Burner climbed toward it, only meters from the enemy plane, and had to back off on the throttle or he would have overshot it. The enemy pilot was skilled, and he backed off on his power at the same time. The two planes were canopy-to-canopy only a few meters apart, barrel-rolling over each other in hopes that one would gain an energy advantage over the other.

The aerial ballet was a mix of throttle and stick with roll and pedal in a continuous fight not to overtake the other plane. The pilot that made the mistake of overshooting the other would be the one that flew through a targeting solution and would be dead. Burner grunted and squinted his eyes against the g-load.

"Burner! The other two are on us pretty hot!" Boulder shouted.

"Bot mode, Boulder! Kill your throttle and cover my ass! Don't let 'em take your six!" Burner replied, still grunting from his constricting g-suit. "Gigi! You and Dundee get down here and watch Boulder's six!"

"Roger that, Boulder, but we're sort of tied up right now!"

"Goddamnit!" he grunted, and ground his molars against the bite block and took fast breaths from the fresh shots of cool air in his face. The vapor stims gave him just the edge he needed to accept even more g-load and widen his roll, giving him room to go to eagle mode. Burner grunted through the maneuver while the arms and feet of the bird of prey spread underneath the vehicle. Burner reached out and punched the cockpit of the Gnat with his right mecha hand. His mechanized armature cracked against the bubble of the enemy plane, startling the pilot for a fraction of a second. That would be the Gomer's last mistake. Burner dropped his throttle, kicked his pedal, slipped in behind the enemy fighter, and went to guns. The tracers tore through the empanage and across the canopy of the plane, shattering pieces of the fighter along its trajectory. Several of the rounds hit home on the pilot, killing him quickly.

"Scratch two. Hold on, Boulder, I'm coming!"

Boulder toggled to bot mode, spinning left then right to avoid the cannon fire from behind him. Burner had pushed on ahead after the lead Gnat, leaving him for the two on their six. Going to bot and then kicking the HOTAS in reverse was enough of a wild negative g-load that Jason regurgitated bile into his helmet. The organogel quickly started absorbing it, and the suit started pumping adrenaline and other stims into his system to compensate.

One of the Gnats passed by his mecha and clipped Boulder's arm with its tail fin. The impact sent the bot-mode mecha spinning even wilder. His already-spinning head and churning stomach were aggravated by the blow. Jason stomped hard on his left upper pedal to slow the spin, and then he jammed the HOTAS against the forward stop, thrusting the mecha in a vector along an axis from toe to head, which happened to be horizontal with the planetoid's surface. He pulled the DEG sights into his mindview and shot from the hip at the two Gnats as they took positions on Burner's tail. The QMs locked on to the fighter that had clipped him, and Boulder squeezed the trigger.

"Guns, guns, guns," he said. The sensors pinged a missile lock on the other, and Boulder was preparing to fire fox three when his Bitchin' Betty started bitching.

"Warning, weapons lock. Warning, radar lock from enemy targeting system."

"Fox three!" He fired only milliseconds before tracer rounds from a formation of Stingers that had been stalking him ripped through the torso of his mecha. "Oh, fuck!"

The rounds continued to cut into his mecha, sending a leg of the bot exploding off into space. Then secondaries exploded from power systems being ruptured. Boulder quickly assessed his plane's health and realized it was a goner.

Eject, eject, Jason! his AIC warned him.

"Eject, eject, eject!" he shouted while pulling the handle. The mecha twisted against the exploding components, giving it a roll. The cockpit shot free from the upper torso of the mecha, and his couch was launched into space, groundward. Boulder grunted against the g-load of the ejection seat and tried to catch his breath. He managed to force his eyes to focus just in time to see the ground rush up at him at over a hundred meters per minute. He hit head first, snapping his spine and crushing his head almost instantly. The numbers game had beaten him. He had beaten the two Gnats that were on his tail, but three Stingers from out of the blue got to him before Burner could get back to help.

HoundDog, prepare for impact in five, four, three, two, one.

"Fuck!" HoundDog tensed his body as the ejection chair slammed across the ice-hard surface of the planetoid. He could feel the chair creaking as it rolled and tumbled to a stop, throwing up dust and ice particles behind him and leaving a wake floating gently in the light gravity, casting odd rainbows with each flash of light coming from the myriad violent blasts all around him.

He quickly began unstrapping himself from his seat and pulling himself out of the multimillion-dollar g-seat. Several rounds of enemy fire stirred up dust and flung showers of splintered rock and metal around him. The splintered debris zinged against his armored g-suit. The g-suits were nowhere near as bulky and protective as an AEM's suit, but they did offer a downed marine some protection from the environment and minimal protection against shrapnel.

"You'd better move your ass, marine!" a voice buzzed in his helmet as his AIC tuned him to the AEM tac-net. The blue dot that was associated with the voice popped in place about ten meters behind him, near a pile of girders and other metallic refuse from the facility's construction. The name with the blue dot said Second Lieutenant Paul James.

HoundDog crawled behind his chair, keeping his body as low to the ground as he could, and then started digging out the HVAR and survival gear. There was an extra ammo case in the kit as well, and he snapped it to his waist harness and turned toward the blue dots nearest him. Out of the corner of his right eye, he caught a glimpse rushing toward him, and his mindview painted several red dots basically on top of him.

Four enemy infantrymen pounced all around him, firing at the AEMs on the other side of the rubble pile. Only one of them was paying him any attention, and the type of attention he was paying, HoundDog didn't really enjoy. Railgun rounds splashed all around him and were tracking right for him. HoundDog rolled to his left over onto his back and then kicked his heels against the surface, tossing him upward into a backward handspring. As he rolled through the handspring, he gripped the HVAR in his left hand, firing freestyle into the enemy soldier. The low-gravity acrobatics had imparted a considerable amount of angular momentum to HoundDog, but he was a mecha pilot and understood the physics of his situation quite easily.

HoundDog rolled himself into a tight ball to increase his spin rate which enabled him to hit the ground on the other side of his handspring, rolling like a ball. He tumbled through a couple of front rolls until he managed to turn upright and spring forward, using his momentum to slam into the back of one of the enemy troops charging the other marines. HoundDog was first to his feet, firing his rifle full-auto into the back of the soldier's head, and then he bounced with all his strength for the cover of the rubble pile.

✧　✧　✧

"*Semper fi*, marine!" Sergeant Flick Aldridge grabbed the downed pilot by the arm and dragged him over the pile of junk they were using for cover. "You injured, sir?"

"No. I'm good." HoundDog rested with his back against the wall of the foxhole, holding on to his rifle with a deathgrip.

"Samuels. Welcome to our little hellhole." Second Lieutenant James offered the pilot his right hand while firing his rifle over the edge of the redoubt with his left. Several other AEMs lined up along the edge of the refuse materials and nodded at HoundDog, but none of the marines took their eyes off the advancing line of enemy troops or their fingers off their triggers.

An RPG hammered against the rim of the foxhole about twenty-five meters down the line, sending two AEMs flying backward across the planetoid's surface in a white and orange ball of expanding vapor. The explosion spread out in a sphere of hot gas but was mostly dissipated by the time it reached HoundDog.

"We can't hold this position for long if we don't get backup," the sergeant shouted. Another wave of enemy troops bounced into the open toward them.

"I'm not armored up like you guys, but I'm an extra gun," Hound-Dog offered. He rose up over the edge and fired several rounds. The targeting system in his rifle transmitted a yellow X in his DTM mindview that overlaid his vision. The X crossed the armored enemy troop several times, and each time, HoundDog let a burst of automatic railgun fire loose at him. After a few tries, the rounds tore through the armor of the soldier's chest plate, ripping out through his back. "Seein's how my mecha was blown all to hell, I've got nothing else to do, Sarge."

"Oorah, sir," Aldridge replied.

CHAPTER 21

October 31, 2388 A.D.
Orlando, Florida
Saturday, 7:39 AM, Earth Eastern Standard Time

The Starhawk pulled over the Hall of Presidents and hovered about twenty meters above the ground. Alexander picked Calvin Dean up in his arms and then jumped out. His jumpboots kicked the ground with a thud. He promptly set the cameraman beside him and drew his railgun. The Starhawk pulled quickly away from the amusement park's airspace.

"You okay, Dean?" Moore asked through his open visor. Old AEM habits died hard.

"Yes. Shit, that was a thrill!"

"Well, start broadcasting and stay alert. If I tell you to take cover, you do it." Moore had not asked the reporter to come along with him. In fact, he had contacted ENN to get a live-feed hookup to his suit. But the crazy action reporter begged Moore to let him come along. Alexander had emphasized the danger, but that didn't seem to matter. And Dean and Gail Fehrer had been really good to Moore, so when the reporter had asked him to consider this "calling in his last favor," Moore had to accept. Well, he didn't have to, but he did anyway.

Several AI presidents met them and led them to the interior of the Disney World exhibit. They were led down the hallway through the theater and into an employees only area behind the White House

227

interior façade. By Abigail's estimate, the body count should be at over thirty by now, but at least now it would stop. Of course, Alexander wasn't really sure that the damned bots were going to let the civilians go once he had surrendered. He had an ace up his sleeve for that, he hoped.

"Okay, Calvin. Stay back and out of the way and keep safe. And put this in your pocket and hold on to it." He handed the cameraman a small device about the size of a wristwatch without the band and then pushed him back away gently with his armored left hand. Presidents Garfield and Truman led them to a backroom past a line of dead bodies, all with what seemed to be head wounds from a railpistol. "Murdering . . ." He bit his tongue, realizing that what he was saying was going out across the country.

"Alexander Moore." The AI Sienna Madira rose from a workbench when they turned into a shop room. The AI looked as much like the former great president as she did herself. The likeness startled Alexander at first.

"Let the civilians go."

"Not just yet." The AI held up a medical diagnostic tool and waved it in front of his face. "Very well. You are indeed Alexander Moore. Your persistence, perseverance, and tenacity are quite impressive."

"I'm not here to impress you. Let the people go."

Abigail, are you ready yet?

Almost have it, sir. Keep her talking.

Hurry the fuck up.

Yes, sir.

"I said, let them go." Moore held the muzzle of the HVAR against the bot's forehead. "Now!"

"Of course. That was our bargain." The AI turned from Moore, paying no attention to the railgun in its face. "The prisoners are free to leave if they wish."

Robot presidents released their grasp on several people who were next in line to be executed. Frightened beyond coherent thought, a handful of them weren't sure what to do. Moore was.

"Run. Go now!" he shouted at them and amplified his voice with the suit's external speakers. That was enough to snap them out of their fear—at least enough for them to run. "Go to the exit on Main Street U.S.A."

"Now you come with me," the AI president said.

"Wait. Not until I know that every last human is clear of the parks."

"There is no need for that, or time."

"What do you mean, no time? I'm not budging until I know you have freed all of the hostages. I have all day." Calvin Dean remained quiet but kept his camera pointed at the two presidents, one an AI likeness and the other an inactive one in a marine armored e-suit.

Abigail reported to Moore, *I have the QM hopping frequencies that the AIs are using to control the bots. I can jam them whenever you are ready. Be advised that the AI will probably send the detonate signal as the jamming goes into place. As soon as they overcome the jamming, the bomb will go.* Abigail had realized from the start that Ahmi must be using similar code as she did on Mars with the AI kitties. The AI used wireless QM-spread spectrum broadcasts to control the robots' control algorithms. There was no hardwire between them. This was a wireless hack, and Abigail had figured out how to jam it by finding the frequencies that the hack was using.

The Tyler?

It's ready when we are, sir.

Good girl.

"Follow me. We have to go."

Now Abigail!

Yes, sir.

Abigail toggled the QM broad-spectrum transmitter in Moore's suit on. The spectrum had been tailored to the spectrum-hopping sequence that the AIs were using, and when it kicked on, the noise floor of the band went through the roof nonlinearly. The signal-to-noise level increased so much that the AIs lost wireless connectivity with the robots. Moore reached into his carry pack and dropped one of the transceivers on the ground, leaving a second one in his pack with him. He grabbed the Sienna Madira bot around the torso and opened a channel to the U.S.S. *John Tyler,* in hover orbit above them.

"Mobile One to CO *Tyler.* Beam us up!"

"CO *Tyler.* Copy that, Mobile One."

"What the . . ." Calvin said as a bright white light snapped and crackled around them, sounding like frying bacon. A split second later, the three of them were standing inside a chamber that looked like the inside of a spaceship. There were AEMs standing with their weapons drawn, and a Navy captain was there just in front of them.

"Welcome to the U.S.S. *John Tyler,* Mr. President." Captain Ronald Westerfield held out his hand. Moore shook it. Dean captured all of it on live feed to ENN.

"Thank you, Captain. We only have a few seconds before this thing regains control of itself and detonates this bomb. I suggest we beam it out into space somewhere."

"Right. Nav," he said, looking to no one in particular.

"Nav here, sir."

"Emergency jaunt to one hundred thousand kilometers."

"Aye, sir."

"Now, if y'all will just move aside from the teleporter pad, we'll take care of this thing," the captain said.

October 31, 2388 AD
Oort Cloud
Saturday, 7:39 AM, Earth Eastern Standard Time

"CO, CDC!"

"Go, CDC," Captain Jefferson said. "What now?"

"Sir, we're getting that same electromagnetic disturbance buildup near the rearward battle cruiser."

"Understood." Jefferson knew there was nothing he could do about it but hoped that DeathRay had a plan, somehow. The *Madira* was dead. The engines had taken such a beating that it was going nowhere for a long time. The CHENG had managed to divert any new power to the forward SIFs and to the DEGs, but that was failing every other minute. And any minute now, that battle cruiser was about to teleport to Earthspace and destroy Luna City.

"Captain, the *Blair* has tossed her load, and our fighters are all now in the mix. It's pretty even fighter-to-fighter, but with the battle cruisers and the hauler for support, that can't last long," the air boss said.

"Ground isn't much better, sir. The line is a stalemate, for now."

"All right, just hang in there people. We're just getting started." Captain Jefferson white-knuckled his chair in anger. There had to be something that could turn the tide.

"Helmsman, keep that damned Seppy rust bucket between us and that mass driver no matter what it takes," Captain Walker ordered. The *Blair* continued to be hammered by the hualer and the battle cruisers. The enemy forces seemed to realize that the *Madira* was down for the count and were focusing on the *Blair* instead.

"Yes, ma'am."

"Captain, the aft SIFs are at ten percent, and the forward deck SIFs are at nineteen percent. And they are dropping." The STO looked out the window at the giant Seppy ship just above them, firing at near point-blank range into the forward hull of the the supercarrier. The SIF fields rippled opalescent blue with each new hit. "I say we divert the DEGs to the SIFs and go to missiles and cannons only."

"Too close for missiles, STO," the XO warned.

"CHENG! Where is my goddamned jaunt drive?"

"Still working it, Captain. There's just too much power drain from the SIFs. We might be able to manage one jump in a minute or two, but that would put us as dead as the *Madira* is."

"Understood. That's better than sitting here getting the shit kicked out of us. Do it!" Fullback slapped her chair arm.

"Captain." Bill took a sip from his coffee mug.

"Yes, COB."

"This reminds me of that time on Mars where we put all the SIFs forward and rammed a hauler. That worked out, sort of."

"I seem to remember some serious casualties from that, Bill. Us included," Sharon replied.

"Yes, ma'am. But that was a hauler. There are other smaller ships around here we could ram."

"That's not a bad idea, COB," Commander Brasher replied from the XO's station. "We could ram through one of the battle cruisers and then jaunt free for a few minutes and make some repairs."

"Shit." Sharon had never wanted to use another supercarrier as a battering ram as long as she lived, but Navy captains didn't always get what they wanted.

The crackle and pop of the white light stopped and Robert's Robots, minus a few including the major, found themselves in an identical room as the one they had been in, which was filled with a giant mass driver system. But this room was full of people scurrying about operating the railgun. Most of them were extremely surprised by the sudden teleportation of a handful of Armored E-suit Marines.

"Shit! Move, Robots!" Noonez shouted. His mask dropped in place about as automatically as his HVAR pulled up and started firing.

"Look out, Pagoolas!" Sergeant Nicks pushed him to the ground behind a pallet lifter and then bounced behind one of the railgun bullets, all the while firing her rifle from the hip.

"Get the fuck down or shoot, Bates!" Tommy stood his ground firing his rifle in full auto. Yellow Xs filled his visor and his mindview, and he swept his HVAR around, *spitapping* rounds at every one of them. The hypervelocity automatic railgun fire streamed across the room, leaving light purple fluorescent tracks in the atmosphere where the superfast pellets ionized air molecules in their paths.

"Cover the exits, Suez!" the lieutenant shouted.

"Got it, sir!" Tommy bounced his jumpboots against the floor, tossing him across the cavernous room to the double doorway on the other side, and landed on a fleeing man in a pair of gray coveralls. He kicked the doors at the center a little too hard, and they burst off their hinges flying across the anteroom into an elevator shaft opening at the other side. There was nobody there, so he turned with his back to the doorway and kept picking targets to take out.

A few tens of seconds later and there were no Separatists kicking or screaming. The AEM unit had taken them all out. The Seppies hadn't expected a ground unit to infiltrate that deep into their facilities. Tommy ignored the carnage and went straight to work, looking over the big gun's instrument panels. Not that he was a rocket scientist. But a gun was a gun. And Tommy knew guns.

"Where are we?" PFC Bates asked.

"My guess would be the moon planetoid. That's where the computer said all the crew for the mass drivers had gone. They must've used that miniature version of the big teleporter like we just did. Wonder why they only have one crew for two guns?"

"Maybe it was the other crew's day off." Bates grinned.

"Pagoolas!" Sergeant Nicks shouted. "How many goddamned fucking times have I told you not to go around fucking with shit that you had no clue about? Who told you to push that goddamned button?"

"Uh, I don't know, Sergeant."

"When we get home, we're gonna have a motherfucking talk!"

"LT. Check it out. This thing is charged and locked on to the *Blair*, but the *Blair* is hiding behind that Seppy hauler." Tommy pointed to the sensor flatscreen above the joystick console. The sensors were zoomed on the supercarrier, but there was no way to get a clear shot at it. The captain of the *Blair* was clever.

"Can you unlock it from the *Blair* and lock on to a different target, Tommy?"

Yes, we can, his AIC responded.

How?

It was in the data we hacked from below. This is basically a user's manual. Here, I'll walk you through it.

"Uh, my AIC says we can, LT."

"Then do it!"

Tommy stood at the console, carefully touching buttons with a single finger as lightly as he possibly could. His armored hand was twice the size of a normal hand and therefore made the task a bit clumsier. A few minutes of tapping buttons and turning keys unlocked the target acquisition system. At that point, his AIC took control and put the targeting display in his DTM and virtual control system.

"Okay, sir. I've got control of it. Target the hauler first?" Tommy stood still in his suit, watching the battlefield through the railgun's sensor system in his mindview. The hauler looked like it was right in front of him, as if he could reach out and touch it.

"Sounds good to me, Lance Corporal Suez. Fire at will."

"Yes, sir. I don't know who Will is, but if he's on that hauler, he's about to have a bad fucking day." Tommy toggled the virtual fire command.

The room whined with the hum of thousands of repulsor fields firing at once. There was a short *whoosh* of air rushing upward, and out of the tunnel, the metal rails tracked up. Almost immediately following, there was a rapid flash of light against the hull of the Seppy hauler.

"These bars here show the charging of the power banks. They're red because we just fired. When they are green, we can fire again. My AIC says that will take about thirty-one seconds." Tommy pointed out the controls to the rest of the AEMs with a smile.

"Yes! Marines with a big fucking gun!" Pagoolas cheered. "Oo-fuckin'-rah!"

The conveyor kicked on, loading another one of the large metal blocks forward and into place at the bottom of the two-beam metal rails. An automated giant lifter pad loaded it from the conveyor upward into the hole in the ceiling.

"The thing seems mostly automated. I wonder what all those damned Seppies were doing," Bates asked.

"Goldbricking," Pagoolas replied.

"Probably maintenance. Big things like this got to need a lot of spit-polish and jiffy-lube," the lieutenant put it plainly. "Tommy, keep at it. Hammer those motherfuckers into oblivion. I'd better call this in to the major."

✧　✧　✧

"Hold it, Tamara. . . . Yes, Johnny?" Major Roberts held a finger up to Gunny to be quiet. They had been sitting patiently watching the control room topside for several minutes. It had been fairly uneventful once they had left they hangar. "You're fucking where? Uh huh. That is fucking outstanding, marine. We better patch this through up top. Hold on."

"They did what?" Captain Jefferson shook his head in surprise.

"Yes, sir. The Seppies fired the mass driver at the hauler. It was a direct hit. It looks like a large section of the forward section was blown completely out." The STO was just as amazed by the outcome as anybody else.

"Well, damned if that wasn't helpful," the XO replied.

"What the hell would they do that for?" the STO asked.

"CO?"

"Go, Ground Boss."

"I've got Lieutenant Johnny Noonez from Roberts' Robots on the horn. He says that he and his recon unit have commandeered the mass driver on the moon and, sir, he's asking if it is okay to keep firing," the ground boss said with a smile.

"Your goddamned right it is! Tell him to immediately target the straggling battle cruiser! Now!" Captain Wallace orderd over the cheers on the bridge.

"How the hell did they get up there?" the COB asked, looking out the viewer at the small planetoid moon more than ten thousand kilometers away.

"Who gives a damn, Charlie? They're up there. Let's use 'em," the XO replied.

"You heard me, Tommy. That battle cruiser right now," the lieutenant ordered, pointing his gray armored finger at the formation-lagging battle cruiser on the flatscreen view.

"Yes, sir." Tommy put the yellow X over the battle cruiser and locked it on. The X turned red. He waited patiently for the yellow bars on the charger graphic to turn green.

"Look! It's about to teleport," Nicks said.

The final bar went green, and Tommy depressed the trigger.

CHAPTER 22

October 31, 2388 AD
Earth space, 100,000 kilometers above Orlando
Saturday, 7:40 AM, Earth Eastern Standard Time

"Goddamn, what was that!" General Ahmi was tired of asking that question. The *Phlegra* rang with secondary explosions, and warning klaxons sounded.

"I think we were hit by the moon's mass driver," the captain answered.

"Damage report?" Elle said impatiently.

"I'm still checking. The teleport is operating as planned." The buzzing and popping from the QMT projection stopped, and the Moon filled the view of the bridge.

"Well, shut those damned alarms off. We're here." Elle sat back at the empty station behind the captain's seat where she had been. She drummed her fingers against the console, waiting for Maximillian's report.

"Sublight engines are down. We are venting like mad from every seal."

"Tell me some good news."

"Uh, yes, General. The auxiliary drive is unharmed, and we can reroute to that one. I'm working it. Propulsion will be up in five, four, three, two . . . there."

"Good. If aux is all that is left, she'll be going there. All personel are to report to that section of the ship and stop that bitch." Elle slammed her fist into the screen of her console, cracking the cover. "Stop her! Is that understood?"

"Yes, ma'am."

"Full forward to Luna City. Ramming vector!" Elle ordered.

"Damnit, Jack, I'm cut off. I don't think I can get around to you. That last blast closed off several sections between us," Nancy warned Boland. The hallway she had been going down was completely destroyed, and air was beginning to vent out of it. She had been lucky that whatever had just hit them hadn't crushed her in the process. So instead of being killed instantly, she was probably going to die slowly of hypothermia or from lack of oxygen.

"Roger that, Penzington. Can you get out of the ship?" Jack pushed his bot-mode Ares-T back up to its feet and looked out of the gaping tear in the ship's hull above him. The Moon loomed overhead, maybe a hundred thousand kilometers or so away. They were running out of time, and Jack had no real, good idea of how to stop the battle cruiser.

"I don't think so. I think I'm trapped in here." Nancy looked in every direction but could see nothing but crunched metal. The ship had collapsed all around her, and it would take hours to cut her out with a laser cutter. There was no way that one mecha was going to dig her out in a few seconds.

"Hold on, we're coming to you. I'll blast you out if I have to."

"Don't, Boland. I'm too deep in the ship. I did my job. I got some good info on the Separatists' plan. I'm downloading it to you now. I haven't even had the chance to read all of it. You read it and then figure out what to do with it. And don't trust anyone that you don't already trust completely, and be wary of them. I mean no one." Nancy sat down in the corridor, listening to the air hissing through the cracks in the wreckage. She had done her job.

"That's defeatist talk," Jack said. "Now get your ass up and find a way out of there."

"Sorry, Jack. I'm stuck here, and my air is running out." She paused for a brief moment in thought. "If you can't stop this ship, you have to get out with the data I just gave you. Now go. That data is more important than I am."

✧   ✧   ✧

"Come on, Jack." Fish pulled her mecha through the gash in the ship to the exterior hull. The Moon continued to loom closer. At their present rate of acceleration, they would hit Luna City in less than a minute. Fish rolled her bot over into fighter mode and throttled toward Earth. Then her blue force system dinged at her. There were two supercarriers not far from their location. "Jack, I've got two supercarriers Earthward."

"I see." Jack thrust his mecha up through the ship and outward into open space, where he toggled his bot back to fighter mode. He paused during the maneuver, only briefly, but long enough to look back at the *Phlegra* solemly. "Godspeed Penzington, or whoever you are."

Jack?

Yes, Candis.

Blue force tracker identifies the nearest ship as the U.S.S. John Tyler. *Perhaps it can stop the battle cruiser.*

Right.

"Captain! We've got a major electromagnetic disturbance Moonward, and a Seppy battle cruiser just appeared out of nowhere!" the CDC officer of the *Tyler* warned the captain over the command net.

"What the hell?" Captain Westerfeld looked confused.

"Sir, we're being hailed by the CAG of the *Sienna Madira.*"

"Can't be. Wally's ship is way out in the Oort somewhere."

"Well, sir, his security codes validate."

"Patch him through."

"CO *Tyler*, this is Commander Jack DeathRay Boland of the U.S.S. *Sienna Madira.*"

"Commander, this is Captain Westerfeld. What can I do for you?"

"Sir, this battle cruiser is on a ramming vector for Luna City, and we can't seem to stop it! I thought you might be able to help us out."

"Captain," Alexander Moore interrupted. "I have an idea." He shoved the AI Sienna Madira onto the teleport pad.

"Agreed," Westerfeld nodded. "Commander Boland. I recommend that you get out of there as quickly as you can. We'll take care of it."

"Trick or treat, bitch!" Moore said to the AI-driven Sienna Madira.

"General, the propulsion system is locked on. Even if it were knocked out, at this point our trajectory will still take us to Luna City," Maximillian said, nodding toward the bright silver and blue dome of the great metropolis in the Sea of Tranquility. The captain of the *Phlegra* tapped a few keys on his chair arm and moved several virtual icons around in his DTM mindview. Then he turned to Ahmi and said, "We should go now, ma'am."

"All right. Very good. Activate the QMT projector snap-back routine," Elle ordered.

"Yes, ma'am. Recalling all personell to original Tau Ceti QMT projection in three, two, one . . ."

Nancy Penzington or Kira Shavi or . . . well, her real first name had been Nancy at least . . . sat with her back against the collapsed bulkhead of the *Phlegra*, hugging her knees and waiting for the end. The air hissed by her, and it was getting very cold in the corridor, and she was shivering uncontrollably. None of that really mattered at this point, since the ship she was trapped on was about to crash and explode in seconds.

Nancy, we did our job, her AIC consoled her.

Yes, we did. And hopefully it will save some lives or do some good.

It will. Boland will figure out what to do with it. Allison had had the time to read the data when she had finally decrypted it. There was some very interesting data in there and some contacts that went all the way up to the White House. The data was more important than Nancy and Allison themselves. *The data was worth the sacrifice.*

I hope it isn't too big for him.

He'll figure it out.

Nancy?

Yes, Allison?

I've really enjoyed being your friend.

Me too, Allison.

The ship started popping and crackling around her, and then white light filled her vision. Through the light, she caught faint glimpses of the ship exploding all around her. She braced herself for the pain of the exploding hot ionizing plasma rushing toward her. And, she braced for death.

"Damn! That's a fireworks show!" Fish shouted. The battle cruiser exploded into a cloud of vapor and orange and white plasma that could have only been generated from a gluonium explosion.

"*Tyler* ATC, this is DeathRay requesting a landing vector, over?"

"Roger that, DeathRay. Vector has been transmitted, and you have the ball."

"Captain." Alexander Moore turned to Westerfeld and smiled. "Drop every AEM and AAI and tankhead and fighting mecha you have on Orlando and clean it up."

"Yes, sir. Uh, you realize that I officially can't take orders from you." Captain Westerfeld raised an eyebrow and grinned back at Moore.

"Well, consider that a recommendation from an advisor."

"I'm not one to ignore good advice." Captain Westerfeld smiled and finished with, "Mr. President. Now, sir, if you don't mind, I've got a cleanup to take care of and you have a letter to write."

October 31, 2388 AD
Oort Cloud
Saturday, 7:57 AM, Earth Eastern Standard Time

"CO, CDC."

"Go, CDC," Captain Walker said. The last shot from the mass driver had taken the hauler completely out, and it ruptured with violent orange plasma from every seam and weld joint. The hauler exploded, sending debris reeling in all directions. The remaining vehicles from the Separatist fleet scattered and fought for their very lives.

"We need to take evasives from the debris field, ma'am. The cloud is gonna be hell on the flight wing."

"Understood, CDC. Air Boss!"

"Yes, Captain?"

"Pull the fighters in under the ship or spread them out from the debris cloud vectors." Sharon looked at the tracks in her mindview battlescape and could see that if the *Blair* didn't take the brunt of the debris cloud it would be bad news for both the *Madira* and a large portion of the fighters. The *Madira* was still without her SIFs and propulsion and had been battered to bits. It couldn't take much more damage. "Nav!"

"Ma'am?"

"Move us upward into the debris vector to cut off as much of it as we can. SIFs full power to upper decks, XO."

"Aye, ma'am."

The battle was winding down, from a large-vessel standpoint. The mass driver had turned the tide. The hauler and all the remaining battle cruisers except for one had been completely destroyed, which seemed to have knocked the wind from the Seppies' sails. The one remaining enemy battle cruiser was taking up station under the *Madira*, using it as cover from the mass driver. It was taking potshots at the wounded supercarrier from underneath but was reluctant to completely take out its umbrella. For some reason, it hadn't jaunted out, so its hyperspace system must have been damaged in the fray.

With the full flight wing of both supercarriers now in the action, the numbers game was turning, too. The *Blair* had been able to vector within the battlespace without fear of being hit by the big guns, which enabled it to dump its full load of mecha and drop tanks onto the surface. That had made a tremendous tide-turning swell on the planetoid. Last word from the tank line was that it was collapsing, and the U.S. forces were pushing through to the teleport facility walls. That was how the plan was supposed to have worked from the beginning.

"Good work, Tommy." Lieutenant Noonez nodded to the marine and then turned away from the viewscreen and took a few steps away to answer a call. "Yes, Major."

"Well, there's one battle cruiser left, Tommy. You didn't get them all." Pagoolas slapped him on the armored buttocks with an armored hand and laughed.

"I'm not so sure about that," Tommy replied. The yellow targeting X zoomed all the way in to the upper decks of the *Madira*. The view was so zoomed that Tommy could see popped rivets on some of the hull plates. "Wow, she's taken a real beating."

"Seppy motherfuckers," Bates whispered.

Tommy worked the targeting system back over the hull of the ship until he found the large blown-out section in aft decks. The hole went all the way through the ship and was several meters in diameter. Tommy looked over at the metal cubes on the conveyor belt, which were only two meters on a side. Then he looked back at the hole in the *Madira*. He panned the view to the center of the hole and could see the Seppy battle cruiser on the other side using the supercarrier as a shield. Tommy zoomed in through the hole onto the hull of the enemy battle cruiser and locked the targeting system on to a hatch on the exterior of the enemy ship.

"I'm not sure that is a good ide . . ." Sergeant Nicks started to say but was interrupted by the *whoosh*ing of the mass driver.

A fraction of a second later, there was a flash of light from the other side of the supercarrier.

"Got you, you Seppy son of a bitch."

"I can't believe you did that," Bates grunted.

"Oh! He shoots, he scores!" Pagoolas added.

"Oh shit." Then Lance Corporal Suez realized what he had just done. What if the pointing system had been off slightly? It hadn't been, but what if. "Uh, maybe we ought to not brag about that shot. In fact, let's not even discuss it any further. Let's just forget it ever happened."

"What the hell?" Lieutenant Noonez turned toward the marines and the viewscreen.

"Captain, the enemy ship just took a mass driver hit!" Colonel Chekov said, surprised.

"From the facility?" Captain Jefferson asked. The view in his mind-view showed the ship beneath them suffering from secondary explosions down the length of it. It was going to blow. "Shit! Brace for impact!"

"Looks like the shot came from the moon's gun, Captain." The STO gripped his console as the supercarrier was jolted from the enemy ship exploding.

"How's that possible, STO?" The XO banged an elbow against the edge of his station. "Goddamnit all to hell."

"The vector I'm getting from the debris ionization trail of the pellet shows it passing right through the hull breach in the aft section of the *Madira,* sir."

"Damage reports?" Jefferson said as he scanned his own DTM inputs. The damage had been minimal exterior hull dings. They were far enough above the exploding enemy ship that the debris field was scattered, and since their relative velocity had been matched, the debris only had the velocity given to it from the explosion. The hull plating of a supercarrier could handle much worse.

"We're good, sir." EndRun consulted with his AIC and tapped at his console for moment and then added with some enthusiasm, "We're a damned sight better now that there ain't a goddamned ship beneath us blasting us with DEGs."

"Good. Air Boss, how're our pilots doing?"

"They've caught up and are now superior numbers, Captain. It's only a matter of time before they've mopped up."

"Ground Boss?"

"Same story, Captain. The Warlords suffered pretty heavy casualties, but Warboys had pushed them all the way to the southwest wall of the facility."

"Have the Angels been deployed?"

"Search and rescue are in theater, Captain. They're staging them here and to the *Blair*," the air boss replied.

"CO, Captain Walker is hailing us," the communications officer announced.

"Sharon? What can I do for you?"

"Well, Wally, that was going to be my question. Your ship looks like it has seen better days. What can we do to help?" Fullback asked.

"CO, we could take casualties and let them focus on the mop-up," the XO commented, rubbing at his elbow.

"Good idea, Larry. Sharon, route your SARs here. We'll be the hospital. You mop up this mess."

"Roger that, Wally."

"Once we've got this station completely under control, then we'll figure out what we need in the way of repairs. Good hunting."

"Aye, Captain." Sharon showed Wallace a white, toothy smile in the DTM videolink and then saluted the Flagship's CO.

"Air Boss, let's get those wounded in here."

CHAPTER 23

November 1, 2388 AD
Washington, D.C.
Sunday, 8:05 AM, Earth Eastern Standard Time

"Yes, Howard-son, but out of nearly two billion people, we only have eight senators and only twenty-two representatives. How is that fair representation, Howard-son?" Congressman Zhi muttered and shrugged his shoulders as he took his seat next to the esteemed gentlelady from Nebraska and fellow Independent Congresswoman Sharon Howard.

"Mark, Mark, that is a century's worth of water under the bridge, just like that faked-up Chinese accent of yours. And after all, your ancestors started the war, not mine. Ancient history." Sharon grinned and elbowed her colleague from the great state of Henan. "Shhh. I think it's starting."

"My accent *is* authentic, mind you. I trained with old movies for years to get it that way. War? Humph, it only lasted three days. Wasn't much of a war."

"Yes, but how many millions died in those three days, huh? Now shush. I want to hear this. That was then. This is now and important." Sharon leaned back in her chair and thought to her *staffer* a few instructions.

Johnny, translate this immediately and run it in American real time for me.

Sure thing, Congresswoman.

And as soon as it is over, I want immediate wide-sample polling data all the way out to Mars. I need to know how I should vote, after all.

Yes, ma'am.

"The chair recognizes the honorable gentlelady from the great state of Nigeria. Mrs. Amaka Chi, you have the podium." The speaker of the House of Representatives of the United States of America banged the gavel and sat down.

Amaka Chi was approaching eighty-nine years old and could remember before Nigeria had been *joined* to the United States, but the last thirty years or so of her life had led her to truly believe that the Great Capitalists could accomplish anything. In fact, in her lifetime, she had seen the eradication of famines and diseases and tribal war that had forced her beautiful homeland to be a third-world slum for ages. But that was no more. As soon as Amaka realized that the Americans would change her country and elevate its economic stature in the world, she had put down her freedom fighter's banner and rifle and picked up a copy of the Great Constitution. Her people from the state of Nigeria would long remember what she had done for them—what she would do for them. There had basically been an end to the underclass in humanity until the Martian Separatist movement. President Madira had put a big stop to it mostly, but decades later, they had resurfaced. More recently, the Separatists had caused major turmoil in the Sol System.

Amaka flipped her long, dark hair over her shoulders and leaned her long, slender, two-meter-tall ebony frame against the podium. She smiled first to the speaker and the vice president and then turned to the floor, facing both houses of the great governing body at once—along with the entire seven billion voters in the solar system.

Okoro, play me the speech in native tongue and translate on all channels in all tongues.

Yes, Your Highness.

"Mr. Speaker, Mr. Vice President, colleagues of both great houses and from all seven hundred and thirty states and territories of our great nation, I thank you for having me speak with you tonight." Amaka smiled and nodded, then cleared her throat lightly and smiled again.

"I rise tonight to talk to you about what I think is certainly one of the gravest issues to face this nation in the twenty-three years that I have had the honor of serving in this body.

"In this great Congress, Mr. Speaker, I have taken much pride in working with members of the other parties on national security issues, and I have been one of the first and few to acknowledge that many of the struggles that we have won in this body were unfortunately against the White House. Issues that the current administration thinks will go unnoticed or that it feels unworthy of attention involving national security were brought to light by due diligence and were won only because we had the support of strong leadership on the Democratic side, the Independent side, and the Republican side as well. I give those comments today, Mr. Speaker, because I want to focus on what is happening with the debate surrounding the investigation we performed via the Tau Ceti Commission, of which I was a member, and the resultant information that has been put forward to the American people about a matter that needs to be thoroughly investigated.

"As you well know, Mr. Speaker, after the unfortunate events and breakdown of diplomacy with the Separatists at the Mars Summit and then the Martian Exodus that took place four years ago, we have been forced to maintain a tight grip on new technologies that could be used for destructive purposes. An example of this is our new quantum membrane transportation system that will allow us to transport supplies and people the vast distances between stars in mere minutes. The details of this technology have been kept out of the public information simply because we fear that if the Separatists already controlled such technology, they might use it for a preemptive strike against American targets. We saw the use of this techonology yesterday on national television for the first time by President Alexander Moore himself. Now the general public knows that this technology exists, and we also realize that the Separatists already have this technology; otherwise, they could not have teleported a battle cruiser into Earth space with the intent of crashing it into Luna City! This is just the beginning. The Separatists could have an army on our doorstep in no time, catching us off-guard and decimating our system's defenses and destroying our great way of life." Amaka pounded her fists against the podium and scanned left to right for all the news camera angles.

"Now, *would* the people in the Tau Ceti System make such a bold move against us on such a massive scale? I say that they would. It has been part of the Separatist culture from its inception before the Martian Desert Campaigns that all others outside their philosophy are a pestilence to their way of life. In other words, there is no room in the universe for any philosophy other than theirs. Other than the tyrant General Elle Ahmi's.

"I bring this up, Mr. Speaker, because the Tau Ceti Commission report was completed almost nine months ago by forty-three of us from both houses of Congress and from all three parties. We took great pride in the fact that we worked in a nonpartisan manner with the sole driving philosophy of understanding the Tau Ceti problem and shoring up America's national security to prevent attacks like the one we had yesterday in Orlando, Florida, and against Luna City. If the quantum membrane transportation technology details were kept Top Secret, how, I ask you, Mr. Speaker, did a Separatist battle cruiser appear in Lunarspace with the intent to detonate dead center of the great Luna City? How did Separatists take control of the AIs of the great American monument that is Walt Disney World? We are fortunate that our great soldiers of the United States military stood in their way and stopped them. Again, how, Mr. Speaker, were the fanatic followers of the Separatist leader Elle Ahmi able to come so close to killing millions of American citizens on the Moon before our defense net even knew there was a ship coming? And how did they manage to place weapons in the hands of the crazed robots at an amusement park and likewise murder more than forty civilians in the process?

"The reason is quite simple, Mr. Speaker. Somehow, the Separatists were given the designs of the transportation technology! Mr. Speaker, I want to call attention to my colleagues here tonight and to the American people listening and watching throughout our great system to this article found in the July 1, 2385, issue of *U.S. News and System Report*, entitled 'Destruction from Outside the Universe,' documenting the annihilation and destruction that would be caused by a terrorist attack from M-space. In this article, Mr. Speaker, is an artist's conception and illustration of the prototype QMT-4 transportation system. Mr. Speaker, in 2385, this technology was classified and is still today. So how did the detailed design information of a Top Secret program appear in a magazine article three years ago?

"Mr. Speaker, there is only one explanation. The White House, in 2385, leaked this document to *U.S. News and System Report*, giving the entire populace of the solar system including the Separatist spies, through this article, access to the design of the QMT-4 transportation technology. How could the executive officer and commander in chief of our Great Republic be so carefree in protecting our security?

"But how deep does the problem go, Mr. Speaker? When this article first appeared, the Department of Defense, the Senate Select Committee on Intelligence, the Defense Appropriations Committee, and the FBI all began internal investigations as to who would have leaked this design of the QMT-4 to this particular magazine. It is only today that we reveal that the article was based on real classified technology. Mr. Speaker, on several occasions, I have been approached by members of these investigations that were told to stop the investigation because they knew where it was going to lead!

"In this hand, I hold a document that will indeed tell us where the investigation was going to lead. This is a manifest of campaign funds for the Republican National Convention for the previous two elections. On page two hundred and thirty-one of the document, we see that there is an allotment of funds that add up to be on the order of a billion dollars to the RNC from more than thirteen different suspected Separatist sympathizer organizations. At the time of the elections, this information would have been little more than information to be spun against the RNC candidate as sympathizing or having a soft spot for the Separatists. But in light of the events on Mars, the Moon, and in Orlando, I say we can no longer follow that line of reasoning.

"Mr. Speaker, I call tonight to the American people for an official authority to impeach the president of the United States of America on the grounds of treason for leaking information to the press that in turn has led to the deaths over forty American citizens and put at risk many more!"

"Hear, hear!" erupted from left side of the house. The DNC-dominated Congress all had a finger they could point and now somewhere to point it besides toward themselves. The White House was the perfect patsy, and the timing two days before the election couldn't have been better. Amaka finished her speech and stood tall and stern at the podium, looking up at the speaker for a motion and welling with pride at the response her speech was getting. Amaka had been thrilled when the DNC had approached her about making this speech. A political move of this caliber would place her in the higher echelon of the DNC and possibly catapult her career even higher.

"Harrumph!" Congresswoman Howard rose, applauding and shouting.

"Order! Order!" The Speaker of the House banged the gavel a few times. "Do I have acknowledgment for the motion on the floor? Mr. Talbot of New Zealand, you are recognized!"

"The great state of New Zealand seconds the motion to vote for impeachment proceedings, Mr. Speaker!" The Democrat politician pumped his fist in the air and then clapped his hands.

"We have a second of the motion. We will all now vote yea or nay to proceed with an impeachment process of the president of the United States." The speaker banged the gavel once again. "Open voting will be allowed for three minutes."

Alexander leaned back in his chair, letting his bathrobe hang loose a moment, and then he picked up his coffe mug. He laughed to himself at the presidential seal on the mug that matched the one on his robe. The coffee was warm and extra harsh with no sugar, and it was barely enough to snap him out of his morning haze, not to mention the hangover from the stimulants he had taken. The doctor had offered him some counteragents for the drugs, but he wanted to feel the remains of the previous day. It made him remember it more vividly, and it would stick in his mind longer, but it would also help him deal with it and put it behind him. The previous day's events had been plenty to keep him awake most of the night. He had had nightmare after nightmare that Sehera and Deanna hadn't made it out safely. His nightmares pissed him off.

After the marines had mopped up in Orlando, he had dropped to the city in his armored e-suit and surveyed the damage. The damned AI bots had caused a serious mess, and it would take billions of dollars to fix the amusement parks. Disney was already pressuring the White House to let them in to start the cleanup and repair so business could get back to usual. Every day, more than half a million people filtered through the Walt Disney World complex and the corporation was losing millions of dollars with each sunset. Moore didn't care. He wanted to make certain that something like that would never happen again, and the parks would have to stay closed until the Secret Service and the FBI had finished their investigations. Besides, he was still having trouble coping with the roller coaster of emotions from the previous day, and now the damned Dems were trying to impeach him. That was a crock of shit. What was the point of trying to impeach him just a couple days before the election? Moore was sure that the Dems had nothing on him, so the impeachment couldn't stick. It was just a piece of very nasty pastisan politics.

Abigail had warned him that there was something brewing on the Hill, but he hadn't expected this after the terrorist attacks at Orlando and Luna City. She was convinced that this was nothing more than a DNC ploy to sway the election and get Alberts back in, but labeling him as a traitor was over the top. Way over the top. He flipped the channel to ENN to see what his old buddy Gail Fehrer had to say about it.

"The Dems and the Indies are having a field day with yesterday's events, and they are claiming that security leaks from the White House were not only careless but intentional." The ENN news anchor woman turned to look into a different camera and made a sour face. "That smells of political posturing and gaming to me. Look at this footage from yesterday. This is ENN exclusive footage purchased from the Disney Corporation. It is conglomerated from several different camera angles." She nodded to roll the video.

Video from inside the Magic Kingdom began. It became quite clear that there was a group of people taking cover behind a small rock wall in a corner by an amphitheater. The video paused, and a circle was drawn around a man and then another around a woman and a child.

"This is President Moore, and this is the First Lady and their daughter, here." The circles had brighter contrast than the rest of the scene for a moment. "Now watch this," Fehrer's voice said. The circle containing the president zoomed in to see his face. It was clear he was cursing angrily, and then dust and debris flew up around his head, only centimeters from his face.

"That, if you've never seen it before, friends, was a hypervelocity railgun bullet vaporizing against the wall only centimeters from President Moore's head. I ask you this, do you seriously believe that Alexander Moore conspired to be fired upon? And look at this."

The video rolled again, and it was clear that Moore was cursing at his bodyguards about something until one of them handed him a pistol. Moore slid the action on the railgun and rose over the wall and started firing away.

"Now we go to Colonel Roger Sauro, U.S. Army, retired, our ENN military analyst. Colonel, you have an analysis of what happened at the park?"

The colonel started breaking down the day's events step by step with the aid of computer simulations mixed with the Disney footage. It was clear that the Moores had been caught by surprise and in the middle of the terrorist attack. They had just been at the wrong place at the wrong time. Then they finished up by showing the footage of President Moore in an armored e-suit holding an HVAR to the forehead of the lead AI bot and telling it to let the hostages go.

"I don't think there are more than a handful of presidents in history that have ever performed above and beyond the call of duty like this. And I can't recall a single time when a president actually took up arms and put his own life at risk, literally like this." The colonel finished his analysis and sounded thoroughly disgusted with the politicians on Capitol Hill and how they were attacking Moore after such a fine display of true heroism.

"Thanks, Colonel Sauro. We have a physicist from Princeton's Wheeler Laboratories here with us next, and we will be discussing this quantum membrane technology. Stay with us here at the only place for real news, Earth's News Network . . ."

CHAPTER 24

November 1, 2388 AD
Washington, D.C.
Sunday, 8:35 AM, Earth Eastern Standard Time

"I tell ya, Thomas, I just don't believe it. I've been the man's body-guard for four years now and have yet to see him do anything that I thought was untoward. I mean, you've seen how he reveres his wife and daughter, right? He's just not that kind of man. And we've both fought side by side with him. This entire thing stinks of goddamned petty politics." Clay Jackson adjusted his personal shield system and then straightened out his tie. Clay holstered his two mini M-blasters behind his back on his belt clips and then slid his coat on, checking the hidden pockets throughout it to make certain that the knives, daggers, throwing stars, stunners, and miniature explosives were all still accounted for.

"Well, that Nigerian congresswoman seems to think she has him dead to rights, Clay. The so-called evidence she has backs up her claims, and all the polls don't seem to be going in his favor, either. I know what you mean, though. To see him being put through this pis-ses me the fuck off. I'd like to have seen how those political twits would have reacted yesterday when they were being fired on with auto railgun fire. Bullshit!" Thomas closed his locker and adjusted his tie. The two men had been fighting together for years now. They had started together as AEMs on Triton, and then they had met Moore and fought with him at the Martian Exodus just outside of Mons City. They knew the man. He was a United States Marine through and through, and to suggest that he was anything less galled the two of them. "I guess you just can't trust politicians, can you?"

"Goddamned politics is gonna kill us all one day. You mark my words. By the way, how's the hand?"

"Aw hell, the immunoboost had it working fine before we even got to SOCOM. But it's a hundred percent today. There might be a little soreness, well, call it stiffness. Don't hurt near as bad as a meter-long chunk of rebar being jammed through your thigh." Thomas flexed his hand. "Ain't modern medicine just amazing?"

"Oh well. Personal thoughts off, professional thoughts on." Clay nodded to his partner that it was time to go to work.

"Roger that, Gunny," the marine captain replied.

You read me, Clay?

Loud and clear, Captain.

Good. I'll check us in. Clay nodded with the slightest gesture to his partner as he slid his sunglasses on and activated the sensors on them. The display panels in the lenses began downloading situational awareness data from the sensors built into the glasses. The data was then broadcast DTM into their mindview, where both the wearer and their AICs could use it. The glasses had short-range lidar system, IR and QM imaging, and various color and polarization filters built in.

HQ one six zero zero Pennsylvania, over, he thought on the wide area net link.

HQ one six zero zero, here.

Clay Jackson, on.

Thomas Washington, on.

Roger that, Clay Jackson and Thomas Washington. I read you on site, lower security locker room. Shift transition is go.

Roger that, HQ.

"Thomas?" Moore turned the television off as the Secret Service agents swapped out. "Clay? I thought I told you two to take a couple days off." He looked at the marines sternly.

"Can't keep us away that easily, sir. I'll bet you don't take a day off." Thomas smiled at the president with a raised eybrow, barely noticeable over his sunglasses frames.

"Sir, how're the First Lady and Dee?" Clay asked.

"They're still in bed, I think. But fine."

"Good, sir." Clay had grown quite attached to Dee, as she would often request him to guard her. Dee often confided in him like the older brother that she didn't have, which was another factor in Clay's anger toward the damned politicians attacking her father.

"Sir," Thomas said sheepishly. "I, uh, apologize for allowing yesterday to happen and us being caught with our pants down so easily."

"Hell, Thomas, the entire nation was caught with their pants down. The DNI has never mentioned anything to me about a potential terrorist threat on Disney World. I mean, what the hell was that all about? Was it all just a ruse to take me hostage? Seems a bit much if you ask me."

"Yes, sir. But . . ." Thomas wasn't sure what else to say. In some way, he felt that he had let the president down.

"It all worked out, marine. Now buck up."

"Sir, we're here if you need us," Thomas said with a sharp single nod, and then stepped back against the wall. "Otherwise, we're not here, sir."

"Hell, marine, when you get off duty, we need to sit down and have a round of beers."

"Yes, sir. It would be an honor, Mr. President."

"Well, you have to believe that the Independents and the Democrats are going to make the most political hay that they can with this impeachment vote. The vote went as expected from a Dem and Indy dominated House and obviously did not bode well for the Republican President. Some say that the most unbelievable thing here is how *little* the president has come out and said in his defense this morning. After nearly four years of fighting with Congress over his failed policies to deal diplomatically with the Separatists and now this, he has had nothing to say. Is it a sign that he's given up?" Walt Mortimer was one of the so-called expert panel members for the Round Table of News and lead White House columnist for the *Washington Post*.

Mortimer had long been considered one of the "graybeards" of reporters on Washington, D.C., and on systemwide politics. He considered that a noble calling and that his job was to give the public the benefit of his years of experience and wisdom so they could make informed decisions about politics and their daily lives. Others might say that he had made a living by feeding shit to the American public.

"Walt, I disagree with you, as usual. Look at the clock for one thing. It's only noon in D.C., and the president had a heck of a day yesterday. If I were him, I'd be sleeping in for a week. I mean, when was the last time you got shot at and then shrugged it off and went back to work?" Alice St. John was quick to comment. "The president shouldn't come out and start blasting back until he's heard what is said today and has time to absorb all of the allegations. And what about the poor families of the terrorist attack yesterday? We should be talking about that. This entire impeachment is a farce, and it is nothing but politics at its worst. There isn't a citizen from Sol to Kuiper Station that doesn't see this phony impeachment as nothing but nasty election hijinks from the DNC. So, yes, the president should sit on his right to remain silent for a little while."

Alice St. John of the *System Review* was the youngest member of the panel and looked it, with her shoulder-length black hair and more modern dress and demeanor. She was often the sole dissenting voice on the panel. After all, Alice never minded showing the tiniest hint of her cleavage or any restraint when calling one of the "elder reporters" on something that she thought was utter bullshit. Fortunately for Alice, she was smart and pretty and kept things lively, and so she was able to keep her job secure. Since Gail Fehrer had taken the lead ENN anchor desk spot, Alice had become more and more popular. It was fairly clear that Fehrer was an Alexander Moore White House supporter. It was had been a shift from business as usual with the media network, but their ratings had sored since.

"Then you believe he's guilty?" Britt Howard, the show's host and previous anchor of ENN until Gail Fehrer had exploded in popularity, put Alice on the spot.

"How did you get that out of what I just said?" Alice was flustered. "That is for the impeachment process to show months from now, but from all the evidence the public has been shown so far, I would say there is maybe a possibility that a leak in the executive branch exists, somewhere, but Moore? No way. So far, and I will keep on repeating this until it sinks in, this looks like typical political shinanigans to sway an election on Tuesday. President Moore has been pushing Capitol Hill with military buildup budget increases for four years now, and the Dems and Indies don't like it. They don't like the fact that when the Separatists left the Sol System, we lost contact with the Tau Ceti colony and likewise lost our major labor force that had been giving the decades Dem-dominated Congress a flourishing economy.

Now that cheap labor is gone, the economy is adjusting, and who's left holding the bag? I don't see the Dems or the Indies taking credit for that. And now we have yet another serious terror attack on American soil! I'd say after yesterday, there is reason for a strong military now more than ever," Alice replied.

"Oh that is rich, Alice," Mortimer retorted. "This sluggish economy and the terrorist attack were brought on by the White House's policies against the Separatists since the Exodus. It could be argued that the attacks yesterday were directly President Moore's fault."

"That is absurd, and I don't even know how to respond to that." Alice was clearly on the edge of losing her temper with the older editorialist. It was this flare to her personality that the viewers seemed to like. Britt stepped in to keep the peace by tossing a question to one of the other panalists.

"There are some saying it's not fair to attack the White House, President Moore specifically, the day after an event such as yesterday. What say you, George?" Britt Howard nodded to an older man with a trim goatee. George Denton was a columnist and editorialist for National Public Radio and *California Free People's Tribune*. He was also considered an elder of the political media industry.

"Well, Britt, all's fair in love and war. And politics is a much rougher game than either of those two. It would be stupid for the Dems not to bring this out right now. With the election looming and the polls so close, they have to do something to counter any boost that President Moore might gain from his, and I say this with suspicion, most opportune heroics that were broadcast live across the system."

"Oh come on, George. You've seen the Disney video. Moore was struggling for his life and trying to protect his family," Alice said with a look of disgust on her face. "Suspicion of what? You think he set all this up himself just to win an election?"

"Perhaps." The news editor shrugged.

"What about the leaked classified memo from the Oval Office?" Mortimer added.

"Just because the president signed and dated a memo doesn't mean he is the one who leaked it," Alice retorted. "This is nonsense."

"That raises the question to all of us here around the table. Do you think that President Moore is guilty or not guilty of leaking this technology to the Separatist terrorists?" Britt nodded as he named his guests. "Walt?"

"Guilty."

"George?"

"Guilty."

"We know Alice's vote is not guilty. And I guess I'm still on the fence. So, the four of us here sort of match the latest polling data. About half of us think he's guilty, and the other half say it's too early to tell. What do you think? We'd like to see your response. So, please go to www.roundtable-news.com/todayspoll and let us know what you think. Now back to the day's headlines as they break in the ENN newsroom with . . ."

November 1, 2388 AD
Tau Ceti Planet Four, Moon Alpha (aka Ares)
New Tharsis Peninsula
Sunday, 1:35 PM, Earth Eastern Standard Time
Sunday, 9:35 AM, Madira Valley Standard Time

Elle sat in her apartment atop the mountain Capitol Building look-ing out the window at the Madira Valley. The small table for two near the eastern wall was set with a standard place setting and was filled with the typical Sunday brunch array that she and Scotty had enjoyed for ages. The view of the Jovian in the moring light of Tau Ceti was casting brilliant violets and reds across the trees below. The view was absolutely breathtaking. Elle welcomed the Sunday brunches where she and Scotty would sit alone and talk freely. There was usually no need for her mask, and she usually left standing orders with her guards that there would be no interruptions while they were spending their Sunday morning together.

"You haven't touched your eggs, Sienna. Is everything okay?" Scotty sipped at some juice and then wiped his mouth with the corner of his napkin. "The pastries are quite delicious this morning." He made an attempt to be humourously pompous. Elle showed him only the slightest hint of amusement. She was preoccupied and mostly annoyed by it.

"I hadn't expected there to be two U.S. supercarriers attacking that Oort facililty. What the hell was that about? And using our own bomb to destroy the *Phlegra* before it hit Luna City was inspired."

"I've said all along we needed to get rid of Moore. A plan of his no doubt," Scotty said around a mouthful of blueberries and cream-filled pastry. "How this will sway the election is hard to calculate. I looked at it briefly last night. Too many coefficients in the model just can't be narrowed down. Especially now with the last word we have of this impeachment vote. I sure didn't see that coming."

"Models are never exactly right. But these are just anomalies that can be dealt with," Elle said. "The last word I have from our troops is that the facility has been completely lost. That gives the U.S. a QMT portal to Tau Ceti if they can figure out how to connect to us and hack our security system. I'd better have extra firewalls put in place." Elle wasn't really talking to Scotty, more just thinking aloud to herself.

"I can take care of that." Scotty nodded.

"No. I'll do it."

"Okay." Elle's voice seemed to take a different tone. A tone she used for emphasis, one she knew that Scotty didn't like. It was a tone she had when she was about to make a tough decision—usually the type of decision where people ended up dying.

"How did she escape, Scotty?" Elle slammed a fist against the table, rattling the dishes. Her rapid mood shift was something that she knew Scotty had seen over the years when it was necessary for her to shift from the cool, calculating genious statesperson to the hard warrior terrorist. Scotty had often warned her of creating a bipolar or even split personality problem, but Elle never took his comments seriously.

"What? Who?"

"You know damned well who. That CIA agent that managed to slip on board the *Phlegra*. The one that had infiltrated the Tangier family since the Exodus. The one that destroyed the jaunt drive of the battle cruiser at the last minute. The one who almost stopped our plans dead in their tracks. She was zip-tied to an examining table for God's sake. How did she escape?!"

Scotty leaned back in his chair and took a long, deep breath and then exhaled through his lips, making a motorboat sound. Elle watched his reaction closely for any signs of a poker face. Scotty had been at the poker-faced lying politician game as long as or longer than she had, so she didn't expect to catch any tells.

"I don't know. You should ask the doctor." He finished the last bite of a croissant.

"Of the sixty-seven crew returned on the snap-back, Dr. Ross was the only one of them that was dead. Had the ship not been on an extreme skeleton crew, the casualties would have been horrendous when she sabotaged the jaunt drive." Elle glared at Scotty a moment longer. "Ross had knife wounds to the head."

"I didn't realize. I went straight to the transport and came here after the teleport."

"Where did she get a knife, Scotty?"

"Again, Sienna, I'm not sure what this is about." Scotty sat cool and calm in his chair. "She was good."

"Not that good. We scanned her and she was completely naked and immobilized. She had help."

"What are you saying, Sienna?"

"Scotty, I love you. And . . ." Tears rolled down her cheeks, and she inhaled to gain her compsure. "I . . . can't believe you could betray me like this. How long we've worked through our plans and how much we've sacrificed together for you to do this."

Elle reached under the table and pulled the railpistol from its hiding place. She thumbed the biometric ID tab, and the ready light turned green. She looked into her longtime lover's eyes as she brought the weapon up slowly. It had to be done.

"Don't do this, Sienna."

"Tell me the truth, Scotty. The truth."

"I, uh." Scotty cleared his throat. "I couldn't let you kill all those people, Sienna. Plan or not. Long-term or not. That would have been mass murder, and I couldn't let you bear the weight of that on your shoulders."

"Scotty." Elle sounded defeated and continued to cry. "I told you when you signed on to this that we had to sell our souls and that we were going to Hell."

"Don't give me that scapegoat religious nonsense. Do you truly think that knowing your soul will burn in Hell forever is justification enough for you to do whatever you want in this life? It's okay, I'll be punished for it in the afterlife," he said mockingly. "I have a son and three grandchildren and seven great-grandchilderen living in Luna City. You didn't think to warn me of your plan, so how are we in this together?"

"I was sparing you the heartache, because you couldn't have warned them if you knew."

"Bullshit. I could have managed it some way or the other. Even still, that doesn't justify it or make you, us, immune from murder on such a massive scale."

"We have all made sacrifices, Scotty."

"You know as well as I do that this plan has required us to live in Hell on Mars and at Kuiper Station and at Triton and even at times on Earth. That was our sacrifice, our Hell, Sienna. There is no need in making it Hell for innocent bystanders. For *millions* of innocent bystanders." Scotty leaned forward and slapped his palms on the table. "It has been Hell enough to live with the hundreds and thousands, tens of thousands of lives we have taken for the long-term betterment of mankind. There wasn't a point in letting that many people die just to sway this election, which I still argue is only a minor part of our plan anyway. I did this for you, Sienna. So if you have to take another life to protect your little Hell, then do it."

"Scotty . . ."

"Sienna, I love you. I did this for you."

"I love you too, Scotty." Elle pulled the trigger. The round entered between his eyes just above the bridge of his nose, splattering the back of Scotty's head across the south wall of her apartment, leaving red and gray matter drooling down the transparent wall. Scotty's gaze never left her as he crumpled sideways to the floor.

Elle sat the pistol on the table and then continued to sob softly into the palms of her hands. Scotty had lied to her and repudiated her plan once now and that meant he would do it again. It had to be done.

CHAPTER 25

November 1, 2388 AD
Washington, D.C.
Sunday, 1:35 PM, Earth Eastern Standard Time

The NSA, the DNI, the chairman of the Joint Chiefs, and the sec def are here, sir. Abigail roused Alexander from his power nap. The president had fallen asleep in his desk chair, and Abigail hadn't had the nerve to wake him up before.

What? Oh, you should have woken me earlier, Abigail.

Yes, Mr. President.

Send them in.

Alexander wiped his eyes with a tissue and then rubbed at them with his thumb and forefinger. He was still having a rough time overcoming his previous day. The constant badgering from the RNC chairwoman to fight back at the impeachment nonsense was also grating on his last nerve. He would get to it in good time. There was still well more than a day before the polls opened. He would think of something before then. Really, he would. In the meantime, he had the cleanup from the Seppy attack to deal with and the daily grind of running a country.

"Frank, Mike, Sylvia, Juan, y'all come in, come in. Have a seat." Moore tried to sound relaxed and eager to see them. After all, he hadn't been fully briefed on the situation in the Oort Cloud yet.

"Mr. President." General Sylvia Patourno smiled and shook his hand. "I can honestly say that I've never been happier to see you alive and well, sir."

"Thanks, Sylvia. Now let's hear about our operation out in the Oort, shall we?"

"Well, sir, I'll brief you and Juan will jump in here whenever." She nodded to the secretary of defense.

"Of course I will. You know me." He smiled as he interrupted.

"Sir, it was pretty grim for a while. In fact, it was so grim that we thought we were going to lose both the *Madira* and the *Blair*. Each of the supercarriers took heavy damage and suffered major crew losses. The attrition of our mecha and ground forces was bad. Of the thousand pilots deployed during the operation, only about four hundred survived. The top flight units of each supercarrier lost senior experienced officers." The general paused briefly to gauge the president's response, but Moore held quiet and expressionless.

"Yes, sir. Things didn't go as planned at all," the sec def added. "It appears that the Seppies had two large mass driver guns in the area that intel had missed. There was also an unexpected teleport into the battle that consisted of a fully loaded hauler and several other smaller ships, including the one that teleported to our space to kamikaze the Moon."

"The two Ares-T pilots that came through with it were part of the *Sienna Madira*'s flight wing," the national security advisor, Frank Duckett, added. "In fact, one of them was the CAG for the supercarrier. He gives a pretty dark description of the battle, Mr. President. He's a very well-spoken young man. You might consider him as a spotlight hero in your next national address, sir." Frank grinned slyly and nodded with a raised eyebrow. Alexander caught the NSA's hint. It sounded like a good idea.

"You said two pilots?"

"Yes, Mr. President. His wingman, a young woman, stayed with him the entire time. Both of them attacked the battle cruiser themselves to try and stop it from making it to Luna City."

"Two fighters against a battle cruiser? Now, *that* is damned heroic." Moore was missing something in this story. "Wait a minute, how did these two know that the battle cruiser was going to Luna City?"

"That is another really interesting part, sir," the sec def said, then turned to the chief spy of the country. "DNI?"

"Uh, yes sir," the director of national intelligence, Michael Lewis joined in. "Operation Bachelor Party was started actually during President Alberts' term, though I can't say he paid much attention to it. I've briefed you on it before."

"Yes, so?"

Abigail?

Yes, sir. Operation Bachelor Party was set about to place an operative inside the Separatist community. The operative was put into position by a navy Ares pilot on the morning before the Martian Exodus. She was last heard from later that day with a warning that the Separatists were leaving to Tau Ceti.

Right, I remember that.

Who was the pilot?

A Lieutenant Commander Jack Boland, callsign DeathRay of the Sienna Madira *squadron Gods of War. Records show that he is now Commander Boland.*

Okay.

"It turns out that," the DNI continued, "when the battle cruiser teleported into the middle of the attack the agent contacted the CAG because he was the same pilot that had dropped her into the Reservation on Mars years earlier."

"You're shitting me now, right?" Moore looked back and forth at the faces of his senior defense and intelligence staff. They were serious as far as he could tell.

"No sir, it was a lucky coincidence," the NSA added.

"Well, how about that. These two get a medal. No, wait. We blew the hell out of that battle cruiser. I was there," Moore said. "Where is this CIA agent now?"

"The last communication she had with the pilots was that she was trapped on the ship, and they believe she was killed when the ship was destroyed, sir."

"Damn. She deserved better," Moore replied.

"I agree, sir." The DNI nodded.

"All right, all right. It went bad at first. So, then what?" Moore leaned back in his chair and propped his chin on his fist.

"Marines, sir. Armored E-suit Marines," Marine General Patourno said proudly. "A small recon team known as Roberts' Robots fought their way into the facility, found a teleporter, teleported themselves to the big gun on the moon planetoid, and took it."

"Ooh-fuckin'-rah," Moore said as he sat up straight.

"*Semper fi*, sir. Then our boys figured out how to use the big gun against the Seppy bastards and blasted the hell out of them."

"Hot damn, that's what I wanted to hear! Now, those marines definetly get medals and promotions." Moore stood excitedly. "And now?"

"The facility is ours, Mr. President," the sec def said.

"Goddamn. That is great news, Juan. General, that is out-fucking-standing!" Moore stood up and shook their hands, congratulating them.

"Yes, sir."

"Uh, sir," the sec def interrupted Alexander's jubilation. "They have a lot of wounded and damage that they have to deal with out there, and at best, the U.S.S. *Thomas Jefferson* is still a week away. Recall, it's a three-month trip at max hyperspace. We need more presence there also in case the Seppies try to pop through the teleporter."

"Yes, yes, of course, Juan. Send three supercarriers loaded to the gills out there and bring our troops that fought this one home. And every damned one of them gets a promotion, you hear me? And I want medals splashed around liberally."

"Yes, Mr. President."

"And send a damned QMT-4 team out there to set us up a teleporter between Earth and there."

"Yes, sir," the sec def said, and then had a blank stare on his face for a brief moment as if he was talking with his AIC.

"Has anybody figured out how the Separatists managed to teleport a battle cruiser from that facility in the Oort Cloud all the way to the Moon?" Moore sat back down.

"No, sir," the NSA replied.

"We have teams working on it, Mr. President," General Patourno added.

"Tell them to work harder. Give them more money or whatever else they need. I'm still president for at least two more months no matter what happens Tuesday. We need to learn as much about that technology as we possibly can and as quickly as we can."

"Yes, sir."

"You two get with Abigail." He pointed to the chairman of the Joint Chiefs and the sec def. "I want to get some of this in a speech for an address to the nation sometime tomorrow. I'm going to declassify the existence of this threat now that we took it from the Separatists. And I want to meet these two pilots. And those AEMs when they get back."

Moore had the beginnings of a plan for winning the election, and this was a major part of it. "In fact, I want those two pilots with me when I give the speech."

"Yes, Mr. President."

"Okay, Frank, Mike, I'm sure you two want to talk about yesterday in Orlando. So talk."

"We found a teleport pad in the bowels of one of the Disney engineering centers," Director Lewis said. "It was a closed-down section of the park that hadn't been used in years. Somehow, the Separatists built that thing right under our noses. DHS and the FBI are still working out how they managed that. We dismantled it and sent it out to NRL to be studied and retrofitted for other use. I hear it looks like a copy of the QMT-4 from the *Tyler*. That brings us to the leak, sir."

"Leak? You mean you think there really is a leak out of the White House?" Moore asked. "Come on. That has to be just a ploy by the DNC. Although, it is interesting that the article in that magazine had a drawing that looks like it was lifted right out of one of our Top Secret documents. But look, the Seppies have managed a technology that we haven't by teleporting this battle cruiser the way they did. Maybe they didn't need a leak. Or maybe there was a leak, who the hell knows?"

"Yes, sir. Too much of a coincidence perhaps, perhaps not, but we are looking into it. Right now I would say that nobody has any more information on it than I do," the DNI replied.

"Well, then. Mike, let's keep it that way."

"Yes, sir."

"But there has to be a leak somewhere. Any idea where it really is? I mean, the Separatists don't have the resources to build all this and to generate the QMT-4s and a facility like that out in the Oort. Could they have done that without having stolen some knowledge of this concept? If they didn't get it from us, then where did they get it?"

"We don't know."

"I need something here people, anything. Work with me on this. We need to find the leak if it is real or to find out who their smart guys are and stop them, steal them, or whatever else is necessary." The public now believed there was a leak, somewhere. Congress had pointed its collective legislative finger at Moore and blamed him. They would be demanding to know where the security leak was now that yesterday's events had transpired, and today's call from Amaka Chi for impeachment was fuel to the fire. He had to give the public a spy before the polls opened on Tuesday.

✧   ✧   ✧

"Senate Majority Leader Hardin Madira, Dem from Wyoming, is here with us tonight to give his take on the impeachment of President Alexander Moore." Gail Fehrer looked evenly into the camera, showing her unbiased news anchor face. "Senator Madira, as you may or may not recall, is also the great-grandnephew of the one hundred and eleventh president, Sienna Madira. Senator?"

"Thanks for having me, Gail." Senator Madira smiled for the camera, trying to look as comfortable and congenial as possible. "This is a dire time for our country. We see that the unchecked executive order spending of the Moore administration has led us to further terrorist attacks from the Separatist Union and has driven the wedge even deeper between the Sol System and the Tau Ceti colony. To my knowledge, all contact with the colony on Ares has been lost now since the president took office."

"Now, hold on a minute, Senator," Gail interrupted him. "Doesn't the record show that the Separatist Laborers Guild had strong ties to that colony, and isn't it likely that that is where the Exodus took them? So isn't it safe to assume that the Ares colony was just another extension of the Separatist terrorist organization?"

"I'm not completely certain where you're getting this information, Gail, but it is mostly speculation. It is just as likely that this administration has alienated them with the tariffs required to fund this little military buildup of Moore's. And now we see that not only has the White House been spending left and right basically unchecked, but now there are these security leaks of highly classified military technologies."

"That still hasn't been proven yet," Gail replied, not quite completely disgusted with the DNC carreer politician.

"Well, Gail, what we really are uncovering, thanks to the great work done by Congresswoman Amaka Chi and her staff and the tripartisan investigation into the Tau Ceti hiatus and the Martian Exodus, is that President Moore must have known about these security breaches that led to the terrorist attacks on Saturday. To develop the capabilities that the Separatists exhibited Saturday they must have had serious help from within our top research organizations. All of which were funded on executive orders." Senator Madira made a sour face and shook his head to display his disgust.

"So, what is your opinion on what should be done, Senator?" Fehrer asked.

"We're doing it. Moore's regime should be brought to an end, and he should be brought forward as a criminal to the state. The investigation will go forward whether he wins the election or not. I feel as strongly about this as I have about any issue in my thirty years of public service."

President Moore sat quietly, looking out the window of the Oval Office. He had enjoyed meeting the two Navy mecha pilots. The three of them chatted about mecha and discussed the situation in the Oort Cloud at length. It had been a good diversion from the political nightmare surrounding him like a black fog. The fog kept him from seeing through to who was behind all of the false nonsense that could cost him the election.

Although there was a political fog surrounding him, there hadn't been a clearer day in the city in weeks. He watched bluebirds play on the lawn outside the White House as he thought about his situation. The view had pretty much been kept the same for centuries. There were actually laws in place that kept architecture to heights below the peak of the Washington Monument, and there were other regulations that maintained the Capitol City's aging charm intact. The Capitol Mall had been protected by legislation for centuries now, and the Memorials Act of 2117 had made certain that America's historical monuments of the Beltway were maintained in pristine form.

It's a great city, Alexander thought.

Yes, sir, it is, Abigail added.

But his mind was elsewhere. What was happening to him? The election was only a day away and according to the polls was slipping out of his grasp. He had come this far and had taken major steps to prepare the country for what he feared were tough times ahead, but to lose the election before it happened based on bogus charges the way DNC would have it, he couldn't allow. Alexander was certain that this entire security leak mess was a setup. He knew what Top Secret programs he had interest in and which ones he had dealt in detail with. He had paid close attention to the quantum membrane teleportation technology because he feared how it might be used in the near future. The QMT-4 used in the wrong way could be devasting to a system's defenses.

There was no doubt in his mind that he was being set up, but by whom? Sure, there had been donations from the Separatists PACs and corporations, and it was a damned proven fact that all three candidates had received similar donations. The rigors and expense of campaigns required that a serious candidate accept pretty much any donation he got. Moore knew that he had been no different than any other candidate in that regard. Receiving campaign funds from Seppy sympathizers wasn't illegal, and it was nonsensical and circumstantial evidence that would go nowhere. But if they could falsely tie that in with the leaked classified documents it might be enough to impeach him. No, what was really enough to impeach him was the fact that the House and Senate were a large majority Dem and Indy, and they wanted the White House back. That, the politics, truly was the end of the story there. But Alexander knew that he had not leaked those documents or ordered them leaked. It just didn't make sense to him. Hell, if he were going to do something like hand over the system to Elle Ahmi and her fanatical Separatists, there seemed to be better ways than just leaking documents to the press. No, he was being setup—framed—and he was going to, by God, put a stop to it.

Who has the most to gain?

Follow the money, sir. Who funded Amaka Chi's campaigns? Digging there might be a good place to start.

Congresswoman Amaka Chi sure was getting a lot of face time with the public now that she had come out with the smoking gun against Moore. She had gained the most as far as he could surmise.

Could it be that simple? the president thought. *Is this just a bunch of smoke and mirrors to create a windfall of publicity for a practically unknown congresswoman?* The president considered the possibility as he stared out the window at the south lawn. It had only been luck as far as he could tell that Chi had gotten onto the Tau Ceti Commission. In fact, she was the most junior member of the commission, yet she somehow managed to end up as the spokeswoman. *Maybe, she was sent to call me out because of the very fact that she is the junior member and has nothing to lose. If things turned bad for her attack, the DNC could just shrug it off as an attack by a junior member that didn't know better. Hmmm.*

Occam's razor might lead one to think that, Mr. President. But, it also might lead to election posturing. The money trail should help make this clearer. Are Mrs. Chi's strings being pulled by anybody else?

Get to work on that, Abigail. Moore scratched his chin, unsure of what exactly to do next. He needed to take action. But what action?

He would get to the bottom of the situation. After all, he was still the president of the United States of America, and he had called in some favors. An investigation into the complete membership of the Tau Ceti Commission was being conducted—an investigation that nobody in the public knew about—and soon he would have some answers.

Mr. President, Captain Adam "HeeHaw" Elliot and Lieutenant Delilah "Jawbone" Strong are here for your five o'clock. They are the two Marine mecha pilots from Orlando, sir.

Right, send them in, Abigail.

CHAPTER 26

November 1, 2388 AD
Oort Cloud
Sunday, 1:35 PM, Earth Eastern Standard Time

"We've got nine more!" Lieutenant Junior Grade Seri "Vulcan" Cobbs shouted as the ramp to her SH-102 Starhawk dropped to the deck of the hangar. The search and rescue pilot waved at the hangar deck medics as they rushed up the ramp to transport the wounded. "Move it, two of them are critical."

Seri turned back into the transport, grabbing the end of a gurney rack and popping the switch to release it from the electromagnetic gripper. The gurney gripper light went from red to green and snapped open, dropping gently to the deck and extending the wheels as it hit. Seri tapped the console monitor at the head of the thing to make certain that it was still working correctly under its own power. The very weak vitals of the wounded pilot continued to graph across the screen in reds, yellows, and greens. Only a few of them were in the green.

"I've got this one, ma'am," the Navy corpsman nodded and grabbed the handles of the gurney and ran with it down the ramp and to the triage area at the end of the *Madira*'s largest hangar deck.

Three of the wounded pilots were missing arms and were able to walk themselves down the ramp with some help from deck crew. They were led to the staging area for the noncritical casualties. The remaining four were stable but couldn't walk either because their legs were gone or broken, or they were paralyzed or unconscious. Seri pulled the other critical patient from the rack. She popped the gripper, and the gurney slid down from the rack release. She tried not to grimace at the sight of the mangled pilot. Her left arm was missing, including the shoulder. There was a gaping hole in her left side, and she was missng most of her right leg. There were other tears throughout her g-suit that had sealed off. There was no telling how much damage the poor pilot had sustained. And it had taken the SARs more than a day to get to her. Seri had been flying for thirty hours straight, collecting wounded from the most critical to the least in the order prioritized by the SAR logistics AICs. It was just nothing short of a miracle that this woman was still alive. A miracle.

"Poser? You still with me, girl?" She shined a flashlight at the pilot's face.

"I'm here, Vulcan," Poser replied so faintly that she could barely hear her.

Seri checked the "goodie bag" sitting on Poser's chest and noted that the pilot had already absorbed more than half a liter of the trauma cocktail in her IV. Poser had been as near death as a human could get when Vulcan had found her floating almost lifelessly in space; the trauma cocktail was beginning to improve her vitals. But from the scanners, Seri could tell that Poser's liver was damaged, and she was missing her kidneys, most of a lung, and some of her digestive tract. The bones and muscle tissue could be easily repaired if the doctors could fix the missing vital parts. She would have been given up for dead just a few decades prior, but medical technology continued to improve, and apparently Poser had a will to live, because her heart kept on beating.

Had it not been for the immunoboost that her suit had administered, she would have first bled to death, then she would be in serious trouble from septic issues. But her suit organogel and the drugs had done their jobs as well as could be expected. Her abdomen had been flooded with the psuedogel from the organogel layer until it filled the wounds from the massive trauma of the enemy cannon rounds, sealing off the arteries. Her wound was right on the edge of being too large for the seal layer to compensate for, but it had.

"You hold on, Wendy. The docs will fix you up." She pushed her along the deck, waving away another corpsman who offered to take her. Vulcan knew Wendy as a friend and wanted to make sure some emergency room waiting error didn't cost her friend's life.

She pushed the gurney through the sea of wounded until she reached the sealed-off triage room at the forward section of the hangar bay. Seri buzzed the door several times until a nurse covered in blood from head to toe opened the hatch.

"This one is marked as first priority critical," Seri said haggardly.

"Right. Most of them are." The nurse looked down at the mangled body of the pilot and then at the DTM wireless data transmitted to her about the patient. "I've got three more just like her, but you got here first. I'll take her from here."

"Thanks."

"Are there many more out there?" The nurse meant still to be recovered and brought in.

"This is hopefully the last run of criticals. But there are still wounded spread across the battlescape."

"Captain Jefferson, sublight and hyperspace systems are back online," the CHENG said. "Though, if we can wait a while about firing them up, I'd like to get some of our structural damage repaired and reinforced. We're still a good twelve hours from having all the SIFs back online."

"So I have propulsion, but you don't want me to use it, Benny?"

"Uh, yes sir. But you can in a pinch."

"Don't really need it right now anyway," Captain Jefferson said. "How about that big gaping hole in my ship?" He had been down to see it once, and the three-dimensional views of it just didn't do it justice. The hole was huge. It was so big that he was certain you could navigate a Starhawk through it and have room for a fighter escort. It had been plenty big enough for that mass driver sabot to go through to take out the Seppy battle cruiser hiding beneath them.

"Well, sir. There just isn't a lot we can do in the short term. We can seal it off and repair some of the damage with onboard resources, and maybe we can scavenge some materials from the facility below, but I'd rather wait and let the teams on the Lunar Far Side shipyards do it right. For now, I recommend that we find enough plating to cover the holes on the above and below hulls and leave it be. A wounded AEM told me that he saw mountains of girders just lying around in scrap heaps down there. Maybe we could get a couple Starhawks and a team to go down and load some of them up?"

"Make a list of what you could use and do it. I'll notify the air boss to get you a couple lifters and pilots."

"Good, sir."

"We may have to set up temporary shelters in the hangar decks for any displaced troops." Jefferson rubbed at the day-old growth on his face. He was tired and needed to shave. Five decks that housed soldiers had been obliterated by that damned Seppy railgun, and the *Madira* was a three-month ride from Earth at top hyperspace jaunt speed. It would be a long, uncomfortable ride home. "Get somebody working on that."

"Aye, sir."

"And CHENG, how's Buckley?" Benny's mention of the wounded AEMs suggested to the CO that he had been down to see his MPA in sickbay.

"Not good, sir. The swelling in his limbs was so bad that it was easier to amputate them. All of them. Same for EM1 Shah. The doc says that they have a good chance of surviving if they can manage the swelling in their brains without causing too much gray matter damage. It would mean a lot to them if you saw them, sir." Benny cursed abruptly at somebody in the background. "Uh, sir, if that's all?"

"Yes, CHENG, get back to work."

"Aye, sir."

Captain Jefferson stretched his neck by rolling his head a full clockwise circle. He stood and then stretched the kinks from his back as well. A quick survey of the bridge crew assured him that things were in good hands and that jobs were getting done. His crew needed some morale boosting from the senior staff.

Uncle Timmy, I need a break from the mindview. Shut it down for a bit. For more than thirty hours, he had been in DTM mindview active mode, and the massive sensory input was overloading his ability to think rationally. He needed to shut it off and just see things normally for a while—at least for a few minutes.

Aye, sir. It probably would help for you to get some rest too, sir.

Later, Timmy. Later. He inhaled a long, deep breath and let it out with a slow sigh through pursed lips.

Aye, sir.

"Larry." Jefferson turned to his trusted XO, who looked just as tired and frazzled as him, though the marine colonel wouldn't dare admit it. "Why don't we take a stroll down to the triage hangar and then by sickbay? Charlie, you want to join us?"

"Absolutely, sir," the COB replied. He, on the other hand, had finished off several pots of hot and very strong coffee and was wired wide awake. "I was thinking that there was probably some bored sailors down there that wouldn't mind hearing a story or two."

"Air Boss."

"Sir?"

"Stay on top of the casualty retrieval. Let me know when we get them all in."

"Aye, sir."

"And spin up two SH-102s for the CHENG to recover materials from the planetoid."

"Aye."

Captain Walker's ship had come out of the scuffle a little less battered than the *Madira*. The U.S.S. *Anthony Blair* had only taken a couple of direct hits from the mass driver before the marines had taken it from the Seppies. The jaunt drive systems had been down for a brief time during the battle, but all her major systems were functioning to some extent, and it was her job to keep the vigil over the system in case more enemy ships teleported in from nowhere. She had also sent a team of her own AEMs along with some engineers and techs to both mass driver sights to relieve the Robots and to maintain them. The mass drivers would have to play a major role in protecting the facility until more Navy Fleet vessels could arrive. And that could be more than a week.

"Bill, how's my crew doing?" She leaned back in her office chair and wiped at her tired eyes with a moist towelette. She had left the bridge hours before to grab a bite to eat and to think through her next few days. The senior staff worked as a well-oiled Navy machine, and now that the major threat of combat was over, she needed to let them do their jobs for a while so that she could think about their predicament from a more strategic and long-term perspective.

"The wounded are still pouring in, and a lot of our wounded were taken to the *Madira*." CMC PO Bill Edwards sat opposite the captain when she nodded for him to sit. Sharon had ordered the COB to do a walk around the supercarrier and then report on morale to her. "Once things calm down and all wounded have been accounted for, I'd suggest swapping out crew. Our wounded will recover better in familiar surroundings. Not that Captain Jefferson doesn't have a fine ship, but home is home, ma'am."

"Okay, that makes sense. You and, uh . . ." She couldn't recall the *Madira's* COB's name, so her AIC quickly told her, but not before Bill did.

"Charlie, ma'am."

"Right, Charlie. You two get together and see if there is an easy way to make that move." Sharon covered her mouth and tried to stifle a yawn but wasn't very successful.

"If you don't mind my saying so, ma'am . . ."

"I do, Bill. I'll take some stims. Drop it."

"Okay, then. We're in pretty good shape. Our guys feel like we whupped up on the Seppies even though we took quite a beating. Morale is good. I'd say it's a little worse over on the *Madira*. They could use some hull plating also. We need to get our CHENG hooked up with their CHENG, ma'am."

"All right, I'll tell the XO." Fullback leaned back and shut her eyes for a few seconds and didn't make a sound. She considered taking a short nap, but what message would that give the crew? No, she needed to be seen for now, and there were still hundreds, maybe thousands, of tasks that she needed to watch over closely to make sure they would be prepared for the days ahead. "Anything else, Bill?"

"Not really, Captain. Just, this was a hell of a fight, and we've got a big-assed mess to clean up. I guess we do need to start figuring out where we're gonna keep the Seppy wounded and captured. Most of them fought to the end, but there are still a couple hundred that didn't. We don't have room in the ship for them."

"You know, I hadn't really thought about that. Better get with the XO and figure out if there is someplace in the facility that we can set up as a temporary holding location."

"Yes, ma'am."

"Anything else?"

"Not really. But, there is one more thing to consider. We need to figure out how all these wounded are going to get to vote on Tuesday." The COB smirked a little at that, but he knew it was a logistics issue that would have to be thought about.

"Shit. Okay, I'm officially not asking 'anything else' again. Because every time I do, Bill, you say 'Not really, but . . .,' so I'm not asking you again." Sharon showed him a very short and thin smile.

"Good idea, ma'am."

CHAPTER 27

November 1, 2388 AD
Washington, D.C.
Sunday, 5:35 PM, Earth Eastern Standard Time

Alexander sat calmly waiting for something to happen. Anything. Another wild accusation from the media or Congress would be better than nothing at all, but sometimes waiting was all that could be done. There was one day left before the election, and he had nothing yet that would allow him to turn the tables on the DNC's impeachment tactic. But he had put out a few calls for help. He just had to wait and see if anyone would answer his call.

Mr. President, your wife is here to see you, Abigail interrupted his solemn moment.

Oh? Great. Send her in.

Sehera sauntered through the door like a tall leggy runway model. Her height was a product of good genes and growing up on Mars, where the gravity was a little less than on Earth. That and the long dark hair and the milky white skin gave her an exotic attractiveness that camouflaged her steely, relentless resolve. She had grown up during some really bad times on the red planet and had developed a toughness and an edge that only hard times could create. But, by God, she was beautiful. Moore watched her slim figure swaying back and forth at the hips as her heels click-clacked one in front of the other across the tile of his office.

"Alexander, you've been hiding all day." She smiled playfully and sat in his lap, kissing him.

"If it ain't one thing it's another. What with running the country, fighting off terrorists, and getting impeached and all." He started to grin, but she punched him on the shoulder before he could. "Ouch."

"You need to spend some time with your daughter tonight. She is still shaken up from all this." She leaned in to nibble at Alexander's ear.

"I will as soon as I finish here. I'm waiting on an important call." He wasn't even sure he was going to get that call, but he was too antsy to think about anything else.

"I know, Mr. President," she said playfully again and then nibbled at his ear again. This time she whispered in it. "You need to go for a run and feed the ducks down at King Street."

"Huh?" Moore was startled by the message and a bit unnerved that it had come through Sehera. Why had she been the courier? It didn't matter. He had the message and knew what he had to do.

"I think a long run would ease your mind, Alexander." Sehera smiled at him and kissed him again. "Be discreet."

She smiled at him, and then as coolly as she had entered the room, she slinked out of it. Once the door latched behind her, he thought about what she had said.

Hell, a long run would make me feel better. Maybe I'll sweat all the rest of the damned stims out of my system.

Yes, sir, Abigail agreed.

Get Thomas and Clay in here.

Yes, Mr. President.

It had taken some subterfuge to keep the press off his back. Alexander had ordered Thomas to send the double out in the limo and take it for a ride. To help out with the ruse, Sehera and Deanna rode with the double. That wouldn't bother either of his girls because Alexander knew that it took a hell of a lot more to bother Sehera, and Dee loved any chance she got to play with BIL.

Once the press was thrown off his scent, he dressed in plain civilian workout sweats, a Redskins sweat-wicking toboggan, cap and his running shoes. Nobody would have recognized him from more than a few meters away. He also had Thomas and Clay dress incognito as well. Thomas met him in the gym in similar gear but had armor on underneath his sweatshirt. The sergeant was wearing shorts and a Marine Corps T-shirt.

"Clay, don't reckon you'll get cool, do you? It'll be fifty degrees out there tonight," Alexander asked the marine.

"Marines don't get cold, sir, they just get angry at Mother Nature for being so damned hard to kill, sir."

"We need to get moving, boys. The limo is going to pick us up in Alexandria, right?" Moore looked at his watch.

"Yes, sir."

"I really don't like you going out on these types of excursions, Mr. President," Thomas told him.

"I understand, Thomas. But under the circumstances, I have no choice."

The three of them slipped out of the White House using various passageways that the Secret Service had kept out of the public eye for centuries. Once they were outside the grounds, they jogged Constitution Avenue westward to Twenty-third Street. From there, they jogged south around the Lincoln Memorial and then turned back west, crossing the Potomac on the Arlington Memorial Bridge. On the Virginia side of the river, they wound through Lady Bird Johnson Memorial Park until they could hook up with the Mount Vernon Trail.

The trail was full of joggers, walkers, and cyclists going in either direction. Alexander led them south past the airport at an even nine-minute-mile pace. They had already covered more than two miles, and Alexandria was still a couple to go.

Abigail, how about some running music?

What mood are you in, sir?

Whatever you think. Just none of that stuff that Dee listens to.

Yes, Mr. President. A modern version of a classic Martian fusion rock song played in his head. Moore hummed along to it, keeping his head down, and focused on his running pace. Thomas was beside him, in the middle of the lane, and Clay was right behind him with each step.

Thirty minutes or so more of the running brought them far enough south that they were approaching King Street. Moore stopped at the docks outside the seafood restaurant and noticed the ducks swimming around in the river.

"Clay, why don't you step inside the food court and get us some sports drinks?"

"Sir, I'd really feel nervous letting you out of my sight," the big marine growled.

"Yes, sir. Clay and I need to stay close to you. This isn't really a good idea," Thomas added. "Mr. President, sir, I am not comfortable at all with this. We really shouldn't be here without backup and prescreening the area," Thomas cautioned as his eyes continually scanned the park to their north and the alleyways on either side of them that led up to the dock and pier at the end of King Street. Alexander could see how nervous the two bodyguards were.

"Relax, boys. Nobody knows we're here or recognizes us, and besides, this is Old Town Alexandria, so we'll be fine. If the terrorists wanted me dead, I'd be dead already. That damned bot Sienna Madira could have blown me up as soon as I got into range of her. And it didn't. Think about it." President Moore leaned against aging-wood safety rails along the pier to watch the ducks swimming in the Potomac. The ducks quacked at each other and swam up underneath him, hoping that he would toss them some breadcrumbs.

"Yes, sir. Never really thought about it that way, with all the shootin' and others getting killed and stuff, sir." Thomas gave a look to Moore that was boardering on being too familiar for a bodyguard's address to the president.

"Sorry, fellas, I've got nothing for you." Alexander laughed at the ducks and wiped at the sweat on his brow. "Now, Clay, go get us some drinks; I'm dehydrated."

Moore kept his back to the two marines-turned-Secret Service and waited. The ducks were entertaining for a few minutes and to some degree even comical. He wished that Dee were there with him to see them. One mallard seemed to be the alpha of the group. Whenever he bullied his green head through the others, they spread out and let him pass.

"There's one in every bunch," he muttered to himself.

"Sir, your drink." Clay held out the bottle.

"Thanks." He took it and twisted the cap off. The cool, green, thick drink went down easily, revitalizing him. He finished off the drink and then tossed it at a black metal mesh garbage can a few meters away. The bottle bounced off the rim of the can and fell to the ground. "Shit."

"Sir, somebody is coming." Thomas nodded his head upriver placing a hand behind his back to his blaster.

"Take it easy, Thomas," the president said calmly.

A man dressed in a rather average-looking suit and tie approached them cautiously. The lighting on the pier was a bit low for the two Secret Service agents to figure out who he was at first.

"Mr. President, I hate that this is the way we have to meet, but we most definitely didn't need any press." The man looked around in a full circle as if looking for cameras. "I almost didn't recognize you. That is a good cover, sir."

"You think so? Hmmm. I dunno, Senator, everybody knows I'm a Skins fan," President Moore replied with a sly grin. "Now let's have it. What is this all about, Hardin?" He held out his hand and shook Senator Hardin Madira's hand familiarly.

"All you need to know is on this patch," Hardin said, handing Alexander a small, flexible memory tab about the size of a dime. Moore took the patch and stuck it behind his left ear.

Abigail, download and store all information from this patch.

Yes, Mr. President.

And go through it all. Get me a summary quickly.

Already working it, sir.

"So what is this going to cost me, Hardin?" President Moore asked.

"My district in Wyoming needs some economic revitalization. With the Martians gone, somebody needs to do the terraforming systems manufacturing. I want it. I'm earmarking seventy billion for it, and I don't want it cut in a line-item veto."

"You think you can get an earmark that size through both houses?"

"I can if you can convince a couple of your brethren from Mississippi to vote with me."

"I can put in a few good words. Maybe twist some arms. Yeah," Moore said.

I've got the summary for you, sir.

Let me see it.

Here it is. Moore started to scan through the summary that Abigail had developed from the data.

"You're giving me the election, Hardin."

"Well, that's politics. You're giving me a reelection in return." There were always several meanings to every political move. Moore would have to watch himself closely around the senator. Who knows what else he might want in the future. But for now, this was good enough. It would take one phone call to Amaka Chi to put a stop to the entire affair.

"Good enough, Hardin," he said, nodding approvingly. "Good enough."

November 2, 2388 AD
Washington, D.C.
Monday, 9:35 PM, Earth Eastern Standard Time

"In surprise to everyone from Sol to the Oort Cloud today, the impeachment hearings of President Moore were brought to an abrupt halt. The attorney general today released evidence that indeed the blueprints for the QMT-4 teleportation technology were leaked to the press, but not by the White House. It turns out that the blueprints were altered and then leaked to the press by the FBI as part of a sting operation to uncover a double agent in the Department of Energy laboratories at Los Alamos. The sting operation was ongoing and classified in a compartment that the Tau Ceti Commission was not privy to. So, they reached the conclusion that real information had been leaked. Apparently none had been. The interesting question that was left lingering was if the leaked information was false, how did the Separatists develop the quantum membrane teleportation technology? The attorney general replied that just because the Separatists are fanatics does not mean that they don't have smart scientists working for *them* also.

"This news and the replay of footage from the president's speech this morning, where he introduced heroes from the terrorist attacks and from the now unclassified raid on the terrorist facility in the Oort Cloud, has flipped the polls completely. All of the polls now have President Moore taking both Orlando and Luna City, giving him more than enough votes for reelection. It seems now that all that is left to do is vote."

"She wants to see you, Alexander." Sehera sat down beside her husband on the couch in the media room. He was watching the news on every channel at once and was grinning, as he would say, like an opossum.

"What about?" Dee hadn't been in a very talkative mood the night before when he kissed her forehead and told her good night. The last couple of days had been a lot to handle. Maybe now she had reached the point where she was ready to talk about it. Alexander didn't know, but at least she wanted to talk about something.

"I'm not sure, but she wants you." Sehera took the remote from her husband and started flipping the side screens off, leaving just the one larger screen in the middle projecting. Then she started scanning the guide for programming that she fancied. "Well, go."

"All right." Moore sighed and rose slowly to his feet. He was a little sore from his long run the day before. He had been running but hadn't run that far that fast in a few weeks. He stretched his ankles and flexed his toes and then limped slightly to the doorway. By the time he reached the door, the soreness had loosened up enough for him to walk normally. "Shit, I'm getting old."

Down the hall and to the right was Dee's room. She had lived there for four years now, and Alexander had watched her grow from a child to the terror she was today. He tapped lightly at her door a few times.

"Princess, can I come in?"

"Come in, Dad," she said. Dee was ready for bed and sitting up against the headboard, reading. Moore looked at the book with some interest. The cover of it had popular science drawings of modern military mecha and weapons.

"Some light reading, baby?"

"Uh, no. I'm just educating myself on all the mecha that I've seen." Deanna set the book down and looked up at her father. "Dad?"

"What, baby?"

"I'm not a baby, Dad."

"I know, princess. But you'll always be my baby." Moore smiled.

"Uh, Dad." Dee frowned at him the way kids do when they reach that age where they don't want to be called a baby.

"What do you need? Are you okay?

"Oh, sure. I wanted to ask you about the future. Do you think you will win the election?"

"It looks like it. Is that what's bothering you?"

"No. I was just wanting to tell you that I want to be like you when I grow up." Dee looked up at him seriously.

"Oh? You think you want to be president of the United States?" he asked her proudly.

"No, Dad. Yuck, politics is gross." Dee made a sour face.

"Then I don't understand what you mean." Alexander shrugged his shoulders, holding his hands palms-up.

"I want to be a marine."

"Well, what do you expect?" Sehera looked at Alexander. "She has watched you running around in e-suits fighting off tanks with your bare hands since she was really little. You're her hero."

"Yeah?" Alexander's chest swelled a bit.

"Yeah. And mine too." Sehera leaned against him and the two of them sank into the couch under the weight of their lives. "You never did tell me what Hardin gave you."

"Oh that," Moore laughed. "You'll never believe this, but our clever Mrs. Amaka Chi was making deals with some DOE scientists to leak information to the public in a way that she could use to set me up. She thought of it all by herself, too."

"Really?"

"Of course not. Several of the DNC and the Indies were in on it, and the Tau Ceti Commission was nothing but a bunch of witch hunters, bound and determined to find a witch. And when they didn't find one, well, they manufactured one."

"How did Hardin know this?" Sehera raised an eyebrow, more interested in the story now.

"He was part of it," Alexander replied.

"Why'd he help out, then?"

"He says it's for a trade on some earmarks in his district, big earmarks. But you know that can't be all." Moore frowned and hugged his wife to him closer.

"Yeah. He's a puppet. He's working some greater plan angle that he has no idea about. It's his master that has the agenda."

"Which reminds me, I have a meeting in the Oval Office in thirty minutes." Those meetings in the Oval Office in the middle of the night were the ones he never liked.

"Good luck." Sehera kissed him slowly while hugging him tight to her. "Watch your back."

"Right." Moore sighed and sat quietly holding his wife for the next few minutes and trying not to think about anything in particular. That was hard to do.

Alexander closed the door behind him and then toggled the switch to lower the blinds on the other side of the office. He locked the door's manual bolt and then keyed the electronic lock.

Abigail, sweep the room for transmitters.

We're clean, sir.

Set up the jamming fields.

They're on. Nobody will be eavesdropping on you.

Good. Unlock my desk.

Yes, sir. Abigail transmitted the encrypted symbol sequence to unlock the president's desk. A faint click and turning of a mechanism could be heard, and then the middle drawer of his desk slid open about a centimeter.

Alexander sat down at his desk, plopping tiredly into his chair. The legs of the chair barked against the floor, as his weight pushed it backward. He reached to the lower right-hand drawer of his desk and slid it open. He pulled out two glasses and a bottle of Maker's Mark that he kept there for certain stressful occasions. This was one of those. He filled one of the tumblers about three fingers deep and then swigged hard at the liquor.

Then he reached back into the drawer and pulled out a small lock-box. Abigail cycled the lock on it, and the top opened like a jewelery box. Inside it was only one small, oval object with a green button on the underside of it. He set the object on the floor and then depressed the green button.

Moore swiveled his chair around to relax and stare out of the one-way blinds over the window of the Oval Office for a second or two. He filled both glasses this time and continued to stare out the window, but his moment of relaxation was interrupted by a faint, crackling *hiss* sound that was coming from behind him, followed by a short burst of white light. Without turning to see the cause, President Moore sighed again and then put on a fake smile—*an M-space teleportation, directly to the Oval Office.*

"You shouldn't be *here*, Elle; someone could be watching." He scanned around the office nervously. Abigail was good and had assured him that they were safe, but someday, some group of AICs would marry and build an even smarter one than she was. He couldn't be too careful.

"Relax, Alexander, you've got the dampening field on. Nobody will see or hear a thing. If they do, I'll take care of it." Ahmi was wearing her mask as usual. She slipped it over her face and then set it down on Moore's desk. Without asking, she picked up the drink and began taking long draws from it. "I like what you've done with my office."

"Right."

"I see you managed to escape an election disaster," the Separatist leader said, and plopped down onto the president's sofa.

"Yes, I did. It was just an overzealous congresswoman from Nigeria trying to make a name for herself. We all have skeletons, you know, and the lovely Mrs. Amaka Chi didn't want hers to go public. Especially since it would have ruined the Dems for years."

"So I suppose Hardin gave you the information you needed?" Again Ahmi drank from her tumbler, this time emptying it.

"I knew it was you behind that." Moore despised the murdering terrorist even if she had been Sienna Madira. In his mind, she couldn't still be that great person. But he had discovered thirty years before that her plan was too embedded to buck with a frontal assault. He had to play along and bide his time. "What was the deal with Luna City and Disney World for Christ's sake?" Moore asked.

"I had an election to win. If the people of the system saw their beloved Magic Kingdom, the place they grew up fantasizing about, threatened by crazed terrorists, they would turn their attention from their daily pop culture long enough to watch a stalwart hero bounce in and save the day. I knew I could count on my marine. But I hadn't counted on you blowing up my ship before it hit Luna. That was clever. And I don't recall any plans to attack my Oort Cloud facility."

"I had an election to win," Moore said, dryly.

"My way would have assured us that Luna City didn't vote against you."

"My way did assure that Luna City would vote for me." Moore offered her another drink, but she declined. He topped his tumbler off again.

"Tell my daughter that her father is dead," Ahmi said out of the blue. There appeared to be a twinge of sadness to her voice. But Moore couldn't be certain.

"What happened?"

"He betrayed me. So, I shot him between the eyes with a railpistol."

"Sehera will be sad to hear that." Alexander gulped. She had said it so nonchalantly.

"It was the only logical solution. How is my granddaughter?"

Safe, no thanks to you, you crazy bitch, he thought.

Amen.

"She wants to be a marine."

"Ha. The apple didn't fall far, did it, son?"

"No," he said. *I'm not your fucking son,* he thought.

"Well, kiss her for me. Maybe one day I'll get to meet her."

Not if I have anything to say about it.

Me either. Too bad you can't just kill her now.

We've talked about that, Abigail.

I know, sir. It would destabilize the Separatists' union beyond recovery. I'm the one who did the simulations. I recall.

Patience. Her day will come.

"So, our plans for Tau Ceti haven't been compromised?" President Moore said, hoping to hurry this meeting along.

"No, darling." Elle stood and patted Alexander on the head like an elder family member would a child.

"Sehera's gonna want to know what you did with her father's body." Moore had met Sehera's father once while he was in the POW camp during the Martian Desert Campaigns, but that didn't count as meeting him as much as it did wanting to rip his fucking throat out. But he was his wife's father, nonetheless.

"I spread his ashes over Madira Valley on the planet Ares. Poor Scotty, I'll miss him dearly." She picked her mask up from the president's desk and slid it over her head, pulling her long, black hair up through the hole in the back of it, tying it into a ponytail.

"I'll let her know."

"Be prepared, Alexander. You got away with your heroics this time. And you can keep the base in the Oort. I have other means of getting here now."

"Yes, about that. How did you teleport a ship forward without a quantum connected platform on this end?"

"We all have our secrets, Alexander. You have yours. I have mine. Heroics are good and will win elections, but . . ." She paused and poked Alexander in the chest with her finger. "You be careful how you interact with my plans. The last person to *fuck* with my plans just had his ashes spread over a rain forest. Family connections will only get you so far." She smiled and retracted her gloved finger and then depressed a sequence of buttons on her wristband, activating the QMT projector snap-back algorithm. Then the Separatist tyrant and once-great president vanished with a crackling *hiss* and a flash of light.

"Goddamn, that bitch is crazy." He snatched up the oval device and shut off the quantum membrane beacon and then stowed it away with his Maker's Mark, but not before he took another swig from the bottle.

Abigail? Moore wiped his mouth with the back of his hand and sat down.

Yes, Mr. President?

Don't ever let me get that fucking crazy.

Not a chance, Mr. President. Somebody has to stop her.

You're goddamned right we do.

EPILOGUE

"In the largest unprecedented landslide election since the third term of President Sienna Madira, we can now project as of nine twenty-three PM Eastern Standard Time on November 3, 2388, that Alexander Moore has maintained his grip. . . ."